The Spy House

The Spy House

A Spycatcher Novel

Matthew Dunn

HARPER LUXE

An Imprint of HarperCollins*Publishers*

THE SPY HOUSE. Copyright © 2015 by Matthew Dunn. All rights reserved. Printed in the United States of America. No part of this book may be used or reproduced in any manner whatsoever without written permission except in the case of brief quotations embodied in critical articles and reviews. For information address HarperCollins Publishers, 195 Broadway, New York, NY 10007.

HarperCollins books may be purchased for educational, business, or sales promotional use. For information please e-mail the Special Markets Department at SPsales@harpercollins.com.

FIRST HARPERLUXE EDITION

HarperLuxe™ is a trademark of HarperCollins Publishers

Library of Congress Cataloging-in-Publication Data is available upon request.

ISBN: 978-0-06-241673-5

15 ID/RRD 10 9 8 7 6 5 4 3 2 1

To my children

The Spy House

PART I

One

Place des Vosges, Paris

Israel's ambassador to France was due to retire in three months, but that wasn't going to happen because in six minutes he'd be dead.

He had no inkling of his imminent demise, given that he was a healthy fifty-nine-year-old who'd recently undergone a full medical checkup and had been told by his doctor that he wasn't going to die anytime soon. In fairness, his doctor could not have been expected to anticipate that his patient's heart might be targeted by a sniper.

The ambassador was not alone as he walked through Paris's oldest square. Tourists were ambling nearby, taking photos of the striking identical seventeenth-century red-brick houses that surrounded the square. Children were playing tag, running through the vaulted arcades. Lovers were strolling arm in arm, admiring the manicured lawns that partly covered the interior of the square and the rows of trees that had turned an autumnal russet.

Walking forty yards behind the ambassador were three men who had pistols secreted under their suit jackets.

The ambassador took a walk through the square every lunchtime, and on each occasion his bodyguards wished they could be closer to their charge. But the ambassador was stubborn and insisted they keep their distance so that he could have space to unclutter his mind from the hundreds of tasks and problems sent his way during the course of the morning.

Today, he was deep in thought on one issue: indications that American and European support for Israel was on the wane.

He reached the fountain in the center of the square and stopped. He'd been here so many times that his eyes barely registered his surroundings, nor his ears the sound of running water. His bodyguard detail also stopped, silently wishing the ambassador wouldn't do things like this that made him an easy target. Their hands were close to their weapons, ready to pull them

out and shoot anyone who ran toward the senior diplomat carrying a knife, bomb, or gun.

The ambassador moved on.

His protectors kept pace with him.

They were good bodyguards—ex–Special Forces
who'd been given subsequent training in surveillance,
close protection, evasive driving, and rapid takedown
of hostile attackers. But the Place des Vosges was a
nightmare environment for such men. It was too big,
with too many buildings, windows, people, entrances
and exits, and open spaces. They couldn't be blamed
for not spotting the sniper behind one of the top-floor
windows of a house seventy yards away. That window
was one of hundreds that looked onto the square. And
the sniper had chosen it because at this time of day the
sun reflected off it and made it impossible to see anyone
behind the glass.

There was no noise when the bullet left his silenced
rifle, penetrated the window, traveled across the square,
and entered the ambassador's heart. But when the
diplomat collapsed to the ground, the square became
chaotic and loud. Some people were running toward
the dead man shouting. Others screamed, held hands
to their mouths, and pointed at the body. The bodyguards raced to the ambassador with guns in hand,
yelling at everyone to get out of their way, the sight of

the handguns now introducing fear and panic into the square.

Many believed the armed men must have shot the ambassador. Some fled the scene; others threw themselves to the ground; mothers grabbed their children and held them close, their expressions filled with horror. The bodyguards ignored them all.

When they reached the body, they rolled it onto its back. They cursed in Hebrew as they saw the bullet entry point in the ambassador's chest. One of them checked for a pulse, though it was obvious the diplomat was dead. The others scoured the surroundings for a man with a rifle.

They saw no one like that.

The sniper had vanished.

Two

The Palestinian boy Safa was thirteen years old, though he had the mind of an older teenager because he'd grown up too fast in Jabalia, a city in the northern part of the Gaza Strip. His maturity had come from Israeli artillery shells, the poverty in which everyone he knew lived, the constant stench of decay in Jabalia, and the fact of having spent all of his life worrying about where the next morsel of food or drop of drink might come from. But underneath his smooth golden skin, black hair, and blue eyes, he was still a child; one who was encouraged by his parents to read nineteenth-century adventure stories, had a penchant for making model Jewish soldiers and Arab freedom fighters out of bits of broken wood from shacks and scraps of cloth taken from the dead, and drew paintings that most

often contained an imaginary mighty blue river coursing through the center of Gaza, with people drinking
from it and bathing and smiling at each other because
it was a God-given source of life and hope. Though he
was wiser than his years, he was, other Jabalia residents
lamented, a dreamer. They worried about him.

Especially those who resided in the large refugee
camp where he survived alongside his dying mom
and dad, a place that was crammed with the hope-
less, forgotten by everyone except Western do-gooders
and Israeli undercover soldiers. Here were tents that
were torn and laced with bacteria; decrepit huts that
afforded no protection from wind and rats; once fine-
looking buildings that were now bombed-out shells;
and oil barrels that were torn in half and littered along
dusty tracks, some containing burning rags, others
brewing insipid broth that was stirred by women and
watched over with eager anticipation by lines of starving people.

Approximately one hundred thousand refugees lived
in the camp. Most of them rarely smiled. But some did.
There was humor to be found in the camp, and Safa
witnessed it as he ran along an alley toward his home.

"Hey, Safa!" called out Jasem, a thirty-nine-year-old
seller of anything, a career he'd taken up after realizing
his previous vocation of creating tunnels into Israel was

unsustainable due to his claustrophobia. "What you running for? Nobody here has anything to run to."

Safa grinned. "I'm keeping fit."

"Me, too." Jasem started doing squats, his expression mimicking the exertions of an Olympic weight lifter. "I'm on a high-protein diet. It feeds the muscles."

Safa ran on, his skinny limbs hurting from malnutrition, his hand clutching a white piece of paper.

"Go, Safa. Go, Safa," chanted two young Arab girls, clapping in time with each word. They were smiling, though some of their teeth were missing.

One of them asked, "Are you playing Pretend the Israeli Soldier's Chasing Me?"

"I have a piece of paper," Safa replied, racing onward.

Safa reached his home—a room in a crumbling building that had decades ago been the residence of a benign judge and his wealthy family. People like Safa's parents. All of the building's other rooms were three-sided, thanks to Israeli shells that had destroyed their outer walls; only this room was intact. But it was a small room and smelled bad. These days, his father spent most of his life on the rotting mattress in the corner of the room. His mother tried her best to wash their sheets as regularly as she could, but water was scant and her strength was failing. Safa's bed was a pile of blankets in another corner of the room. They were crawling with bugs and exuded a scent of over-ripe cheese. And in the center of the room was a clay pot that cooked everything they ate. Meals, when they could be had, were taken sitting on the floor. To do so hurt his mother's increasingly skin-and-bone physique, but she insisted on the ritual for the sake of Safa. He had to know good manners, she had told him many times, and learn that a meal eaten properly is a meal well deserved. His father, however, could now only be spoon-fed by his mom while he was lying on his back. It broke her heart to see him like this.

"Mama," Safa said, breathing deeply to catch his breath, "I have a piece of paper!"

"Good." His mother tried to smile, though she was exhausted. "The Israelis are starving Gaza to death, yet you have a piece of paper. Today is a good day."

She was by her husband, mopping his brow with a rag. His eyes were closed, and he moaned quietly.

"It could be a good day." Safa thrust the paper at arm's length in front of him. "A man from the United Nations says he can help me. He said the UN can get me to France, where I can be given food, an education, and maybe even asylum."

Safa's mom got awkwardly to her feet, wincing as she did so. She took the paper and read it. The words were in French, but that didn't matter because everyone in her family spoke and read French like natives of the tongue. "A consent form?"

"Yes, Mama. It needs your signature."

"Where did you meet this man?"

"At school. He'd brought books and stationery to my teacher. He asked her which of her pupils showed most academic promise." Safa's face beamed. "She told him, me."

"And how would he get you out of here, to France?"

"My teacher asked him the same question. She told me to wait on the other side of the classroom while she spoke to the man. They were speaking for a long time. Me and my friends couldn't hear what they were saying. Then my teacher called me over. She put her arms on me, said that this was a great opportunity to have a new life."

Had this conversation been held two years before, his mother might have had the strength to shed a tear and be utterly conflicted as to what to do. But the death of Safa's younger sister from an undiagnosed disease, and her and her husband's rapid decline in health, made her emotions numb and her decision inevitable. She knew Safa's father would pass away at any time. His eyes were jaundiced, his skin ashen. Almost certainly he had lung disease, and if that didn't kill him then his inability to absorb nutrients would. She, too, was not long for this world. The once beautiful woman had caught a glimpse of her image in a broken glass window the other day. She was horrified to see how she now looked. So thin, her face etched and drawn, no longer anything like the pretty girl who'd daily brushed her long, shiny hair in front of a vanity mirror. She tried to do everything she could for Safa. But even if she'd been fully fit, she was out of options. There was nothing left in Gaza. It was a country that was being strangled to death.

She sighed as she reread the paper. "The United Nations man must be breaking rules."

"That's what my teacher told me. She said I wasn't to care, and should have no fear. She said he was a good man. Would find me a good home. Would give me a new life."

His mother went to her son and hugged him. "My Safa. Is this what you want?"

Safa looked at his mother's face, and tears ran down his own. "I don't know, Mama. I *am* scared."

This was her final act of strength. The last opportunity for her to save at least one member of her family. She pointed north. "Over the border are people whose grandparents faced these kinds of situations when they were your age. They came from Russia, Germany, France, other places. They didn't know what lay ahead.

But they knew what lay behind. They had no choice." She didn't add that as a result their sons and grandsons should have known better than to do what they were doing to this small strip of land and its population. "But it worked out well for them. They became scholars, businessmen, soldiers, had families, and now they have smiles on their faces and bellies that are full. You must go."

Safa's voice was wavering as he asked, "What if he's a bad man?"

His mother stroked a frail finger against her son's hair. "My experience of people in the United Nations is that they can be naive but never bad. But if this man turns out to be bad, you run. And even that won't be so bad, because you'll be running in a land of fat bellies." She managed to smile. "When everything else is stripped away, it all comes down to food and water. But only you can decide what to do."

Safa went to his father's side. "Papa, Papa, what should I do? Must I leave you?"

His father looked at him, resignation and illness so evident. "We must leave *you*, my dear boy."

"But, Papa . . ."

"You have no choice."

Safa placed his head on his father's chest. "How could they do this to you, to us, to everyone here?"

His father stroked his son's hair. "Most of what they've done is nothing, not something. There is a difference."

"It still makes them bad."

His father's voice was soothing as he replied, "No, no. If that were true then we would all be bad. Charities we ignore, famines elsewhere in the world, disasters, wars, abuse—we can't solve them all. Does that make us murderers? I think not."

Safa wept. "The Israelis starve us."

"And some of us hurt them back. Evil lurks on both sides of the border, but it isn't and cannot be pervasive."

His voice descended to a whisper, and after a moment a slight tremor seemed to pass over his face. Safa held his hand. It was limp and felt wrong. "Mama—Papa isn't moving."

His mother nodded, resignation flowing over her, a feeling that death had exited one body and was drifting across the room to devour her. She had no need to move to her son's side. This moment had been coming for so long. It was inevitable. There was no heartache; that had happened ages ago. Since then, she had just been managing the situation and anticipating the logistics, including disposing of the body in a way that wouldn't spread more disease into the already befouled air of the Jabalia refugee camp. Burning corpses was usually the only way. Even then, one couldn't be sure that airborne bacteria and viruses wouldn't flee charred flesh and attack any nearby mourners.

"He has told you what you should do" was all she could say. She grabbed a pencil and put her signature on the bottom of the paper. "When do you go?"

"Tomorrow. I must meet him at the school. My teacher also needs to sign some forms. He will then take me to a boat. He told me to pack light."

"Pack? You have nothing to pack."

Safa went back to his mother and cuddled her. "Mama, please cook me stewed beef and garbanzo beans tonight."

His mother didn't have any food at all. "We can pretend, okay?"

"Sure, Mama." He held her. "That will be delicious." His tears were unstoppable. "Delicious, Mama."

Three

Soil clung to the CIA officer's perspiring skin after he inadvertently rubbed the back of his aching hand against his forehead. Roger Koenig's sweat made some of the grime enter his eyes, and he had to blink fast to clear them. He grabbed his pickax, swung it over his head, and slammed it into the ground. Three other men were close to him, all natives of Iran's southwestern city of Shiraz, whose outskirts were ten miles north of their current location. They too were using shovels and pickaxes to dig, lanterns around the hole being the sole source of light in the pitch-dark night. Their grunts and the noise of their tools striking earth were the only sounds they could hear in the featureless and deserted rural location. Suddenly one blow resulted in a louder, metallic sound.

Reza, the twenty-nine-year-old son of a watchmaker, was by Roger's side. He said, "I've hit something."

Roger lay flat on his stomach and placed his hand in the hole, which was seven feet long, four feet wide, and three feet deep. The CIA officer had to stretch to touch the bottom. There was no doubt Reza was right. They'd reached something that was metal. Thank God. Roger had previously shuddered at the idea they might find rotting mahogany that would reveal what was inside if they tried to remove the item. He didn't want that image in his head. It would be wrong.

Roger got to his feet and looked at the watchmaker. "Masoud. Very carefully."

Masoud nodded and placed a hand on his other son's shoulder. "Firouz will clear the surface. We'll excavate around the box."

They got back to work, this time digging more delicately so as not to inadvertently damage the box. It took them nearly an hour to completely uncover it. One man at each corner, they slowly lifted the heavy box, which was as long as Roger, and placed it next to the hole.

Breathing fast, Roger grabbed a rag and wiped his face and hands. "Okay. Let's move. Box in the truck first. Then all equipment."

Masoud asked, "Do we refill the hole?"

"No time for that."

They drove nearly 360 miles through the night, Reza at the wheel and where possible his foot to the floor because they were all desperate to reach the southern port of Bandar 'Abbas before daybreak. They made it with one hour to spare. Reza avoided the main roads as he expertly navigated his way through the medium-sized city until they reached the shores of the Persian Gulf. Boats of all shapes and sizes were moored alongside jetties and harbor walls. Most of them were cargo vessels; some were powerful speedboats. All of them were the type of craft that would have got them away from Iran and its naval patrols quickly. But they were too obvious. Instead, Roger had decided they needed to escape in something that no fugitives in their right minds would use.

That vessel was now in front of them. A traditional dhow that had one big white sail, but no motor.

Reza parked the truck. "Fast, fast." He stayed in the vehicle as the other men ran to the back, lifted the metal box, and carried it along a jetty and onto the boat. Reza was driving away as they lowered the box onto the deck. He was headed straight back to Shiraz, where he'd put the truck in a secure garage and leave it locked in there until he was sure that it wasn't being looked for by Iranian police or the country's more insidious security agencies.

Roger was a former member of SEAL Team 6 who had proficiency with most types of seafaring vessels. That experience enabled him to help Masoud and Firouz prepare the dhow to sail. It took them only two minutes to get the vessel moving. Roger scoured their surroundings as his Iranian assets steered the vessel and made adjustments to its rigging. For one hour the dhow crossed the Strait of Hormuz, and even as they exited Iranian waters unchallenged, he continued his vigil as they approached the United Arab Emirates and followed its shores until they entered Dubai's creek.

The CIA officer only let himself relax when they reached the inner part of the creek where the majority of boats docked and unloaded their cargos.

The early morning sun and balmy air soothed his weary face; there were noises of birds and men and vessels, but they were quiet, as if the creatures were half asleep and respectful that others nearby were still in deep slumber. Roger wondered when he'd next sleep himself. Not for a while.

He placed a hand on the metal box. It had taken him three years to identify its location, and he'd done so using his own money, during downtime when he wasn't deployed by the CIA and sometimes during vacation time when he should have been with his family. He'd sacrificed a lot to locate and extract the container by tasking his Iranian sources, bribing officials, analyzing old CIA reports, talking to former Iranian intelligence officers turned CIA assets, and putting his boots on Iranian ground to make his own inquiries. Many times he had risked capture, and he would have been killed if anyone had established his objective. And if that had happened, the CIA would have rightly disavowed him, because no one at the Agency had any idea what he was doing.

His biggest fear now was that the thing in the box was not what he thought it was. After he took it to the American consulate in Dubai and it was flown back to the States, he'd find out if his efforts now and during the preceding years had been worth the sacrifice.

He dearly hoped so.

Because the box was his gift to a British MI6 officer who'd saved his life countless times.

A man who deserved some peace of mind in his otherwise mangled life.

A comrade.

A true friend named Will Cochrane.

Four

For the past few months, MI6 and its American equivalent, the CIA, believed that I'd been sitting at home doing nothing. MI6 occasionally checked up on me, but it had always given me advance notice of its visits, meaning I could make sure I was at my South London pad when the service's welfare department came knocking. Tonight, the agencies probably thought I was going out for a few beers to drown my sorrows. After all, tomorrow was officially my last day as an employed field operative of Western intelligence, because during my last mission a malevolent U.S. senator revealed my identity to the world's media, I tore apart Washington, D.C., to get answers, and the joint U.S.-U.K. task force I worked for was shut down.

My employers told me I'd become a loose cannon without portfolio, and added that I should be grateful that they were giving me four months on full pay to allow me to idle and decompress after fourteen years of near constant deployment. And I was told to use that time to learn how to integrate into normal society. Trouble is, I don't do decompression or integration well, and though I've enough sorrows to fill up a hundred lives, I rarely feel the need to drown them.

Instead, they are prone to drowning me if I stay still for too long.

So, I'd been busy. Secretly busy.

Traveling to different parts of the world; obtaining weapons, and other equipment, and secreting them in dead-letter boxes in the major cities; meeting my foreign assets and telling them that one day I might still have a use for them; and tying up loose ends. Only two people knew what I'd been up to: my former bosses, Alistair McCulloch and Patrick Bolte, from MI6 and the CIA, respectively. They'd helped me where they could with cash and information, and covered my ass when needed. But even they didn't know that tonight I wasn't propping up a bar in London. I was in Hong Kong, walking through the Temple Street Night Market.

It was a tying-up-loose-ends evening.

I was observing a Chinese woman, a highly prized intelligence operative who'd spent her entire career combating the West. I was behind her, disguised as a seaman on shore for a night out after twelve months on a tanker. She was unaware of me and the threat I posed. Around us were hundreds of tourists and locals, haggling with the multitude of vendors who'd crammed central Kowloon's most popular bazaar with stalls selling counterfeit goods, clothes, noodles, and still-twitching bottom-feeding sea life. People were shouting, opera was being sung by troupes busking for a few dollars outside stinking public toilets, and junkies were arguing with old men as they faced each other over games of Chinese chess. Few people would hear a woman scream in pain if someone killed her on the street, and no one would care. There was too much sensory overload to notice anything odd in this bustling and bruising place: people banging into each other; a heavy rain descending from the late summer sky; vast banners with Cantonese characters overhanging the street and flapping loudly in the wind; glowing Chinese lanterns suspended in the air; the smell of crustaceans, soy sauce, and burning incense; and swaths of dazzling neon light around each stall.

But there were also big chunks of darkness in the street, and that was where most people moved, their eyes transfixed by the areas of brilliant glow, like flies attracted to illuminated and electrified death traps.

Street-canny prostitutes chose to work the low-rise tenements behind the stalls. This was a place where they could do their business without being noticed.

It was also an excellent place to ply death on unwitting victims.

I increased speed as the woman picked up her pace, then stopped as my target perused a stall containing fake silks made out of rayon and powdered rhino horn that was actually a lethal combination of ground stone, fiberglass, and bamboo root. I watched the target to see if this was a deliberate stop to catch sight of me.

The target moved; I moved.

I had a knife on me. It was the best weapon for tonight. My target would be taking no chances and would almost certainly be carrying a silenced pistol or blade.

We were getting close to my kill zone.

The woman checked her watch, made a physical gesture of annoyance, and turned toward me.

Shit!

I was a mere ten feet away from her, alongside lots of men, women, and kids. I willed her not to notice me. I had a job to do, and it was one that would take the woman completely by surprise.

But she didn't spot me amid the throngs of people. She was clearly preoccupied, pulling out her cell phone and making a call. I was close enough to hear her end of the conversation. She was instructing her partner to get his car started and pick her up in five minutes or she'd stick something sharp in his gullet.

That wasn't going to happen.

Not if another man had his way.

For he wanted to stick his knife into her gullet.

And I was here to stop him dead.

My target walked fast toward the woman, his blade exposed. I rushed at the large Chinese man, grabbed his chin from behind, and plunged my blade into his throat. As he slumped to the ground, the Chinese woman's shock was amplified when she saw my face.

I walked past her, muttering, "Your cover's blown. Get out of China. Time to retire to somewhere safe."

The Chinese intelligence officer knew me well. Years ago, I'd turned her into an MI6 asset so that she could spy on her countrymen. Recently, I'd learned that her colleagues had discovered her treachery and tonight were deploying one of their best assassins to punish her. No way was I going to let that happen to such a courageous woman.

She opened her mouth to speak to me.

I didn't stop and within seconds had vanished into the night.

And in ninety minutes I'd use an alias passport to fly back to London.

No one would know that tonight an English killer had been in China and that his real name was Will Cochrane.

Five

The reason Admiral Tobias Mason no longer wore a naval uniform was that five years ago he'd reached a stage in his career where he'd felt embarrassed by how he looked. He'd spent thirty-four years on water, half of them captaining U.S. warships, and frequently being the ultimate power in several thousand square miles of ocean. The problem was that this gave him too many medals on his uniform. While inspecting his massed naval ranks on a sunny parade ground five years ago, the medals had made him think he looked like a throwback military dictator.

Mason hated the idea of looking like a dictator because he was by nature a nonconformist who didn't like uniforms. In many ways he was the antithesis of a military man; the only reason he'd run away to sea as an adolescent was because he craved adventure. Nevertheless, his superiors in the navy quickly recognized his superb intellect and passion for unconventional tactics. They promoted him, and kept telling him that one day he'd be an admiral. Mason didn't like the flattery because he could never jettison his nonconformist mind-set, nor did he wish to. His idol was the nineteenth-century British admiral Lord Thomas Cochrane, who'd been a maverick throughout his career, improvising naval strategies that were brilliant. Cochrane tore the rulebook up and won. But he was still made to dress like a clown.

Shortly after his revelation about the uniform, the navy had asked Mason if he'd like a job on dry land that didn't require him to wear a uniform.

As he took a seat at the long rectangular boardroom table in the subterranean White House Situation Room, the diminutive silver-haired admiral wondered, not for the first time, whether he'd made the right decision to leave the sea. Dry land sometimes felt like it had too many captains trying to sail the same ship. It seemed that way now as America's political elite took seats around the table. They all knew Mason, though none of them really understood what he did for a living. Since he was by nature a private man, it pleased him that they didn't know he'd been singled out for a very discreet role that required him to be the president's confidant and to think through solutions that were beyond the intellectual capabilities of the president's other advisers. It was a role that on paper didn't exist.

The president walked into the room and sat at the head of the table. His chief of staff was close behind him and turned on three wall-mounted TV monitors with video links to the premiers of Britain, France, and Israel.

After formal introductions and greetings were exchanged, the Israeli prime minister dominated the first fifteen minutes of the meeting. He told everyone that a week ago a senior Hamas official had been killed by an Israeli missile strike in Gaza. Nobody in the room seemed particularly interested because Israel had announced the kill hours after it had happened. But as the Israeli premier moved on to the reason why this meeting had been summoned at such short notice, he made no attempt to hide his anger. His voice shook as he spoke about yesterday's assassination of Israel's ambassador to France. He spoke about how they'd gone to school together, served in the army together as young men, attended each other's weddings, and on more than one occasion shared a drink while watching the sun go down over Tel Aviv.

Mason wasn't watching him. Instead he was

observing his American colleagues and the premiers of France and Britain. Did any of them know why they were here? Even the U.S. president hadn't been given a clear agenda for the meeting by the Israeli premier, except that it was to discuss what happened in Paris. But Mason was sure he knew where this was headed.

He checked his watch and estimated the Israeli would drop that bombshell in three minutes. In fact, he was fifteen seconds wide of the mark. And that's when the room became a chaotic cacophony of people trying to talk over each other, some with insincere smiles on their faces, others looking hostile and slapping their hands on the table. During the following hour, the chief of staff had to call for order seven times. The room seemed evenly split between those who were supportive of Israel's bombshell and those who were against. Mason was the only person who was silent throughout this unproductive period of too many generals and chiefs and secretaries of this and that all trying to take control of the ship and drive it in the wrong direction. He wanted to sigh, but maintained his composed and professional demeanor while his mind raced.

The chief of staff called for order again, this time with the look of a man who'd rip anyone's head off if they didn't comply.

The president began asking people individually not

only for their calm assessment but also whether there was a solution to this problem. All of them gave their views, and none of them had the slightest idea what to do about them. The president turned to the head of the CIA, the one man who technically would have some answers. He did, but the answers were unsubstantial and certainly not enough to placate the Israeli premier.

Finally, the U.S. president locked his gaze on Mason at the other end of the table. He asked the admiral if he had a solution.

All eyes were on Mason.

He didn't yet speak.

Didn't need to.

Instead he gave the tiniest of nods.

Admiral Mason was chauffeured in a bulletproof vehicle from the White House to the Pentagon. The car stopped in the secure underground parking lot; Secret Service men escorted him through the vast labyrinth of corridors to his office and returned to their vehicles. Mason entered the large oak-paneled room that he'd furnished like the captain's quarters of an eighteenth-century man-of-war and pressed a button on his desk's speakerphone. "I'm back. In here now. Both of you."

Mae Bäcklund and Rob Tanner entered without

knocking and sat in leather armchairs facing their boss.

Tanner was in his early twenties and had the ready charm and confidence of a man who didn't have a care in the world. Courtesy of the Michael Anthony Salon at 661 C Street, his auburn hair was cut in a medium-length ruffle that looked asymmetrical yet was strand perfect and fashioned to exude playboy nonchalance. His suits, hand-tailored by Michael Andrews, hung gracefully on an athletic physique that carried no surplus fat because it was toned by a personal trainer. And his teeth and eyes shone, because they were fixed that way. On the surface, Tanner was a fraud. He was, after all, a trust fund baby, though unlike the majority of those who shared his financial ease in life, he had a Harvard-sharpened barrel-load of intellect. It wasn't enough. Tanner wanted to position himself to one day have power. And real power, he understood, rested in Capitol Hill and the Pentagon. That was why he was in Mason's shitty office, sucking up rules and regulations and pocketing a government salary that barely made a dent in the bill for a bottle of Krug Clos d'Ambonnay fizz.

Tanner needed Mason to set him on a path where riches and cleverness would pale into insignificance compared to what could be achieved by a click of his fingers. The admiral knew that, and Tanner didn't care, because if Mason didn't employ him he'd have to employ someone just like him. Mason mentored Tanner, knowing that one day Tanner might try to stab him in the back. The trouble for Tanner was that nobody had ever successfully outwitted the admiral.

Mason needed his employees to have independent wealth. Those he'd previously employed had lacked that financial freedom and had quickly left to work in high-salary positions in investment banks and law firms. It had been a major irritation, because Mason required subordinates who would see out the duration of the tasks at hand. But that requirement came at a cost, and in the case of Tanner it was having to endure the young Harvard grad's inflated ego and flippancy.

Mason had trawled Ivy League universities to find someone with Tanner's attributes. None of them suited him, and it was only by good fortune that the young man's résumé had landed on Mason's desk with a Post-it note on page one stating that the guy wanted a job in government.

Bäcklund was different. She'd worked for Mason for half a decade, and had seen other employees come and go. Only she remained, because she was loyal, self-less, and adored Mason. It helped her work considerably that she was also calm, cerebral, and courageous

in thought and conviction. Bäcklund was fully cognizant of the fact that Mason viewed her as the perfect
counterbalance to the Machiavellian exuberance of the
young bucks whom he'd handpicked to assist him. Her
usefulness in countering Tanner's excesses was no different. But that wasn't the sole reason why Mason had
hired her. Mason had been a dear friend of her father's,
so much so that her dad had asked him to be his only
child's godfather. Fourteen years ago, Mason was a
ship's captain when her dad had asked him, "Do I walk
from this?"

"Admiral, you're on your deathbed," Mason had
replied.

"I expect better precision from you, Captain."

"Yes, sir," Mason had said. "I'll walk out of the hospital room. You'll float."

"I want angels and trumpets. Can you organize that
for me?"

"I'll try my best, my friend."

"Want you to try harder on something—my daughter, Mae. With Patty gone, she's all that's left."

"I don't have much money, but it will always be
enough to look after her."

The admiral coughed, choked; nurses came; he
waved them away with his liver-spotted hands. Then
he fixed his eyes on Mason, who had dark hair back

then and a reassuring demeanor. "Mae's got money. Made sure of that. Man to man, I need . . ."

"I'll look after her."

"She'll tell you no man should be tasked to look after her."

"Then I'll tell her I need her to look after me. It's not far from the truth." Mason bowed his head and held the admiral's hand as it grew cold. "I can't promise you angels."

Since her father's death, Bäcklund had considered Admiral Mason to be an uncle of sorts. Five years ago, she was twenty-seven, didn't need to work, and had just completed a Ph.D. at Stanford. Mason took her out for a celebratory dinner during which he asked her if she'd come to work as his assistant in a land-based Pentagon job he'd just been assigned to. At first she declined, but Mason was canny and knew that she had aspirations one day to get into politics. He gave her sage counsel that before that day came, she could learn the ropes from the inside. He would teach her the ways of politics until such time as she was ready to withstand the ugliest realities of government and run for office.

And teach he did. She respected the fact that he gave her no special dispensation because of who she was. On the contrary, Mason could be as withering in his comments to her as he was to Tanner. Only when they were alone would he soften and speak to her with a light touch and a paternal combination of admiration and concern for her well-being. Maybe Mason's role in her life would recede if she got hitched to a guy. Right now that wasn't in the cards. On the rare occasions that men fleetingly entered her private life, she had felt sorrowful and unfulfilled. Finding the right guy was tough when you were an independent woman with a job that frequently shunted your brain into overdrive.

Bäcklund and Tanner were silent. Mason sat on the edge of his desk and said, "Interesting meeting."

"President, Secretaries of Stuff, you." Tanner's smile broadened. "Who else was there?"

"Britain, France, and Israel." Mason patted his short silver hair. "Their premiers, anyway, via video link."

Bäcklund was motionless. "France equals pedantic legal jurisdiction. Britain equals meddling has-been. Israel equals rabid dog on a leash."

Mason eyed her with the look of a professor addressing a gifted but overly forthright student. "Perhaps I've been too long at sea to realize that the psyches of three countries can be distilled down to one sentence each."

It was Tanner who responded. "Perhaps you have, *sir.*" He was careful because Mason would crucify him for too much sarcasm. "Israel wants blood."

"Yes. Why?" Mason was very still, watching them

like a killer who would turn on his captives if one of them gave the wrong answer.

Bäcklund put a cigarette in her mouth and left it unlit. "Israel kills a Hamas official last week; yesterday someone kills Israel's ambassador to Paris. Has to be Hamas; ergo two egos need to have a head-to-head in the locker room. Should we care?" She glanced at Tanner, wondering whether the man-boy seven years her junior would take her bait and make a crass remark. "Boys with dicks and toys. Right?"

"Yeah, right." Tanner tried to decide whether tonight he should finish writing his monograph on God and physics or instead play Texas Hold'em poker with his pals. "Last time I checked, shit happens a lot in the desert. We shouldn't care."

Mason ran a finger along the crease in his trousers. "But we do care, don't we?"

"Not me." Tanner smiled.

Mason did not. "Then I'm in the company of a fool. *Think*."

Bäcklund withdrew the unlit cigarette from her lips and looked at its sodden butt. "Escalation."

Tanner added, "Not just a few missiles lobbed into Gaza."

They took it in turns to articulate their thoughts at rifle-shot pace.

"It's an excuse."

"One Israel's been waiting for."

"Take revenge against Hamas."

"Big style."

"Invade Gaza . . ."

"The West Bank . . ."

"And . . ."

Mason nodded expectantly.

Bäcklund concluded, "Lebanon. Shit, this is a whole different story."

The admiral was pleased with his assistants because they'd nailed what the Israeli prime minister had said in the meeting. Israel believed the assassination of its ambassador gave it legitimacy to obliterate Hamas once and for all. And it had no problem invading two territories and one country to do so. "What do you think is the position of France and Britain?"

"You know the answer to that. You were at the meeting."

Mason said, "If I hadn't been there, I'd still know the answer."

Bäcklund placed the unlit cigarette in her jacket pocket, her craving momentarily over. "They'll have made the obvious point that Israel has no concrete evidence that Hamas killed the ambassador, and in turn they'll say Israel doesn't yet have any legitimate cause in international law to start a ground offensive."

"Correct. Going to war on a hunch." Mason loosened the knot on his tie. "And what is our beloved president's stance?" This was to Tanner.

The young man was silent for three seconds. "He'll be urging Israel to be restrained. But he'll also be worried that if he can't persuade Israel to hold fire, he's going to be in a political quagmire, because if he doesn't show public support for Israeli actions he's going to suffer big time at the domestic ballot box."

"U.S. voters are not the only issue, though I concede it is a relevant one." Mason looked out of the window at the manicured grounds beside his office and wondered if he'd be able to sneak in some Japanese *Salix integra* "Hakuro-nishiki" miniature trees for one of the flowerbeds. "The only solution for the president is to prove to U.S. voters that his decision to back or not back Israel is undeniably the correct one." Mason returned his attention to his employees.

Tanner asked, "You got an idea?"

"I do."

"You gonna share it with the president?"

Mason smiled. "I already have." His smile vanished. "And to everyone else present at the meeting. It's bought time. Israel's given me two months to make the idea work. If it doesn't, international law be damned as far as Israel's concerned. It will go to war with or without our blessing. People will have *opinions* about whether going to war is the right or wrong thing to do, but no one will know for a *fact* whether it's the correct course of action because no one knows for a fact that Hamas killed the ambassador."

"And the Middle East will tear itself apart before looking west." Bäcklund shook her head. "Anarchy. Bearded crazies foaming at the mouth and turning on us."

"Yes." There was a tinge of sadness in Mason's otherwise piercing cold blue eyes. "If my idea fails, the world should be wishing that I'd been a smarter man."

Tanner asked, "What is your idea?"

"We must get undeniable proof that Hamas did or did not conduct the Paris assassination." The admiral added, "My solution's being enacted right now. It's called Gray Site."

Six

Mosques were calling people to pray in Beirut, the amplified sounds nearly drowned out by the noise of traffic on the streets, the buzz of people going about their early morning business, construction workers building and repairing buildings, and cargo vessels in the Mediterranean sounding their horns to warn other vessels that they were cruising slowly into and out of port amid a mist that still hadn't been burned off by the sun.

A tall man named Laith Dia—though that wasn't the name he'd used to enter Lebanon two days ago—ate a freshly baked za'atar croissant while standing in a doorway and watching not only a large derelict house, underneath which a newly constructed intelligence station had been established, but everything around the building. He was a paramilitary CIA officer. One of the men in the nearby subterranean complex was a colleague; the three other officers were respectively British MI6, French DGSE, and Israeli Mossad. Right now they were testing the newly installed electronic surveillance and intercept equipment. Laith was here to watch their backs for twenty-four hours, trying to establish if there were any indications that people knew they were here. It was his last job for the CIA, because a week ago he'd resigned from the Agency.

Though he was a big man with a striking visage, Laith blended in just fine. He looked like he was Lebanese or North African, and he was wearing clothes befitting an entrepreneur who was grabbing a bite to eat before heading off to his car dealership or dockland import-export business. It was a great time of day to do surveillance, because the people moving past him were bleary eyed from drinking wine and smoking hookahs last night, oblivious to everything beyond getting to work and forcing their minds into gear. It would be easy to spot professional threats to the Western intelligence complex.

Laith sauntered along the street, taking another bite out of his breakfast while casually taking in his surroundings. The street was on the outskirts of Beirut, lined with a mix of residential and commercial buildings and bustling with traffic and pedestrians. It had looked very different the previous night. Then, it had been almost deserted, though the sounds of the city had been evident throughout Laith's all-night vigil.

He saw an SUV stop. Two men got out and began walking, one on either side of the street. Clearly, they were looking for something. They didn't look bleary eyed. And though the young men looked similar to many of the pedestrians around them, they moved with vigor and purpose, showing no signs of having just dragged themselves out of bed after an evening of over-indulging. After years of serving in the CIA, and prior to that in Delta Force, Laith knew the type. Still, they could just be innocents rather than Hamas terrorists who were looking for hostile intelligence officers spying on their activities.

Laith quietly spoke into his radio throat mic while watching the men. "May have something. Two men on foot. Just got out of an SUV. About one hundred yards from you. They're walking the street."

The MI6 officer in the underground office responded in Laith's earpiece. "Suspicious?"

"Hard to tell at this point."

The men were stopping people in the street, speaking briefly to them before moving on. Maybe they were asking directions. Or maybe they were inquiring as to whether the local residents had noticed any strangers recently arriving and positioning themselves in their community. Perhaps these men were Hamas but their intentions were benign. Though it was a terrorist organization, Hamas spent more time acting like the Mafia—trying to get a grip on the streets of Beirut, policing it, doing business with locals, punishing them sometimes.

The men stopped outside the derelict house containing the intelligence complex.

Laith placed a hand over his concealed handgun, ready to run to the men if they went inside. "They're right outside your building. At stop."

"Shit!" The MI6 officer made no effort to conceal his unease. "But just two of them, right?"

"On foot, yeah." Laith glanced at the vehicle they'd earlier disembarked from. "But there's another three in the SUV. And the SUV's following them at their pace, about fifty yards behind them."

Five potential terrorists versus five Western intelligence officers. But that wasn't the sum of it—what worried Laith and his colleagues was that a firefight would not only compromise the new intelligence station; it would also mean that he and his colleagues would somehow need to escape Lebanon alive. And there was every probability that if the men he was watching were Hamas, they'd have reinforcements nearby.

"What are they doing?" The British officer sounded professional, yet tense.

"Just standing outside your building, looking around."

"Can you get to them if they enter?"

"Not sure, because I'd have to take out the vehicle first."

Laith looked in the opposite direction. He saw another SUV at the end of the street. Again, the occupants didn't look like the locals. "Damn it. Another vehicle. Five more men."

"Coincidence?"

Laith answered, "I'm thinking not. But that doesn't mean they know you're here, or are looking for you."

The MI6 officer—a man called Edward whom Laith had briefly met and who'd seemed as cool as a cucumber—said, "We're trapped in here! One route in and out. We won't stand a chance."

"Steady your nerves."

Laith saw the two men on foot get back into their SUV. It drove off at speed. The second SUV turned off the street into another road.

Laith said, "Never mind. They've left."

Rob Tanner walked across the vast parking lot and got into his car, looking back at the Pentagon. It was midafternoon; all the cars around him belonged to people who were still ensconced in the Pentagon, hard at work and wishing it was closer to 6 P.M. He unlocked the glove compartment and took out a cell phone that only one other man knew about. He turned it on and typed in the number that he'd memorized because the phone had no contacts list or any other compromising information in it. While it was ringing, he recalled the man who'd placed the phone in his hand saying, "This is your first test. I hope I'm not making a mistake."

The man answered on the fourth ring, but didn't speak.

Spots of rain hit the windshield. "I have news."

The man was silent.

"He's set up something called Gray Site. We need to meet."

Seven

The previous evening, Safa had watched a movie before getting into his new bed, whose sheets felt like an angel's hand enfolding him and gently rocking him to sleep. The movie was made by Hollywood, and for most of the film there was only one actor—a man he'd never heard of. Because Safa's English was limited, his guardian had put on French subtitles. The American character was a courier whose flight across the Pacific Ocean had crashed into the sea. He'd had to survive alone on a desert island for five years, his only companion a football on which he'd painted a face. To avoid death or the loss of his sanity, the American had finally decided to throw his life to fate and ventured away from the island on a raft. By pure luck, he was spotted and picked up by a cargo ship. Later, after receiving medical treatment and having his hair and beard cut so that he resembled the man he once was, he was flown back to the States. During that flight, he was given a glass of Coca-Cola with cubes of ice. The American could barely remember ice; it seemed remarkable and otherworldly to him.

Safa knew exactly how that felt.

He'd been on a desert island of sorts for all of his young life. Of course, he'd had glimpses of the outside world and had knowledge of what it contained. But it is not until you gaze upon these things in person, smell them, feel them, drink and eat them, that you truly understand their wonder.

Since he'd arrived in France, there'd been so much to wonder at, almost to the point that everything around him was overwhelming. His guardian—the United Nations official who'd rescued him from Gaza—was aware of this and careful with Safa's integration into the West. "Little by little," he'd told him over the preceding weeks. "We don't want your delicate mind overloaded."

Safa was educated by the UN man and lived in his home. It was a palace as far as the Palestinian boy was concerned. The house was tastefully furnished, had open fireplaces, books and oil paintings everywhere, wooden beams, ornate candles that were more often the source of light than electric bulbs, and an overall ambience of love, academia, warmth, and passion for locally sourced and well-cooked food. It was the home of a *seigneur*, a term that Safa had never heard before but one that was explained to him by the guardian. In Napoleonic times, a seigneur was a privileged gentleman, but also a true leader who had compassion for all those who needed him. Seigneurs were not nobles; on the contrary, they desired to destroy the elitism of undeserved royal ascendency. They were rebels, but supremely powerful ones.

Safa had to be careful, the UN officer had told him upon arriving in France. Somehow, his guardian had managed to secure false papers for his charge, including medical history. They were all in the name of Safa, though with a different surname. But they were not enough to protect the boy, because it was technically illegal for Safa to be in France. He needed a cover, his guardian had told him. If anyone asked, Safa's parents lived in Marseille, were French citizens, and had recently died. His guardian had legally adopted him. The UN official had given Safa many more details about his false background and current circumstances, and had made Safa memorize and recite these details over and over again until he could do it faultlessly.

Safa was in his bedroom when the UN man called, in French, from downstairs, "Safa, I need to speak to you."

Safa entered the open-plan kitchen–cum–living room, his favorite part of the house, and sat at the dining room table. The UN officer brought him a cup of cocoa. The smell of roasting chicken and rosemary wafted across the room from the large oven. Today was special. Since Safa had arrived in France, his guardian had taken him back and forth to private doctors, who had placed him on a strict diet that allowed his body to slowly recover from malnutrition but didn't cause it to crash. He'd only been permitted small portions of meat and fish. But today, all bets were off. The doctors had given the boy the all-clear to eat as much as his slim belly could cope with. And roast chicken was his meal of choice.

He sipped his cocoa, yet another addition to the repertoire of foods he was now permitted. Blessed God, it tasted so good.

His guardian sat opposite him and gently placed his hand on Safa's arm. "I've just received a call from one of my colleagues in Gaza. I'm so sorry, son. Your mother has passed away."

"Passed away?"

"Died."

Safa was unable to think clearly. He thought he should be crying, shaking, calling out to his beloved mama. But the news came as no shock to him. Did this make him a bad boy, one with no heart? It all seemed so confusing, because he thought he had a huge heart.

His guardian must have sensed the conflict within him. "Listen carefully. I've traveled the world, seen more suffering than any man should. When people are surrounded by death, it has a different meaning. It's almost as if it's part of . . ."

"Life."

"Yes."

Safa took another sip of his cocoa. It didn't taste so good now. "How did she die?"

"The phrase 'passed away' is apt. Because that's how she went. Peacefully. In her sleep. No pain."

"Is she with God now?"

"Yes, and your father is by her side." The UN official removed his hand from Safa's arm. "You have no one now. You must face up to that reality."

"I have you, sir."

"I am not family. Nor can I be."

"You look after me."

"I do, and I will do everything in my power to make sure you're not sent back to that place." The guardian's face showed concern. "Don't worry, Safa. I have connections. I know what I'm doing. And I will always look after you. But"—he adopted a stern tone, though his expression was now one of true warmth—"I am a man of rules and principles, and it is a rule and principle that my household always eats a good meal, no matter whether we are elated or full of sorrow."

The meal was unlike any that Safa had eaten. His tummy was swollen afterward, though he didn't care. He'd consumed chicken with crispy skin, steamed fresh vegetables that were lightly glazed in butter, roasted parsnips, and stuffing, all covered with a homemade gravy. It was food fit for kings, and that was exactly how Safa felt—or maybe he felt like a prince who dwelled with a good king.

They retired to the guardian's study. This was their evening ritual. Safa would always have a glass of water; the UN official would allow himself a small glass of port.

The guardian picked up a book from the many on his shelves. It was red and looked old. "Charles Dickens was a very skilled English author. This book is written by him and is called *Hard Times*. I want you to close your eyes and relax. Don't worry that you can't understand the English words. Tonight, that's not what's important. Instead, I want you to listen to the rhythm of my voice, feel the musical flow of each sentence, and where possible remember how I pronounce some of the words. You are fortunate to speak French and Arabic. In sound, at least, the English tongue falls somewhere between those two languages."

He read for thirty minutes, regularly glancing at Safa in case he opened his eyes or betrayed signs of not listening. But the boy looked entranced. In a calm and soothing voice, the guardian said, "Now we must turn our attention to your required medication and our daily reflection."

This was the part that the boy least enjoyed about his days in France, though the guardian said he was under strict orders from Safa's doctors to administer their prescriptions every evening. In truth, each day was getting easier, and tonight the warm roast chicken in his tummy distracted him from his fear.

The guardian opened a plastic box and withdrew from it a bottle of pills, a tourniquet, and three syringes. Safa knew what to do. He swallowed two pills with some water, rolled up his sleeve, and held out his arm.

"That's my lad," said the guardian as he wrapped the tourniquet around Safa's biceps. He swabbed disinfectant over a prominent vein inside Safa's elbow, and eased the needle of the first syringe into Safa. "The first one's always the more painful one, isn't it?"

Safa nodded, his teeth gritted together.

"Just two more. Smaller needles; almost no pain."

The medicine was administered. Many times Safa had asked what was in the pills and syringes; always his guardian had answered, but the names he used to describe the medicines were in Latin and so long that Safa could never remember them. Still, all that mattered was that his doctors and guardian could.

As always, he felt an almost instant tiredness overwhelm him, but also a sense that he was looking at himself from the other side of the study.

"It's the outside-in effect," the UN official frequently told him after his evening administrations of Safa's medicines. "It's the drugs' way of letting your mind watch your body get stronger each day. And in turn, they make your brain stronger because they give it reassurance that it's no longer in a weak vessel."

Safa rolled down his sleeve after Band-Aids were applied over the puncture wounds and the tourniquet was removed.

The guardian positioned four mirrors alongside each other on his study's desk. "Remember the drill?"

Safa swiveled in his chair to face the mirrors. "Yes. Though why so many mirrors this time?"

"We shall explore your question together." The guardian turned off the light so the room was in pitch darkness and stood behind Safa's back. He shone a flashlight at the mirror on the left. "Look at the reflection of light, while we consider what we have learned and what we must still learn."

Safa nodded, his eyes transfixed, his body feeling as if it were floating.

"Today, we have a new tragedy to add to the others, do we not?"

"We do, sir."

"What is that tragedy?"

"The death of my mother."

"Correct." The guardian turned off the flashlight. "Is she gone?"

Darkness.

"Yes."

"Has the tragedy gone?"

"No."

The guardian illuminated the second mirror. "That's right. The tragedy does not want to die. Look at the light, Safa. What does it say to you?"

"Burning. Things burning in eternity."

"Hell?"

"Like hell, but on earth."

The guardian rested the flashlight on a shelf so that its beam remained focused on the second mirror. He picked up another flashlight. "The mirror on the left has no light and holds the lives that have been unnecessarily extinguished. Your sister, mother, and father belong there. No light. Their deaths were avoidable."

"Avoidable." Safa knew that with certainty. "Avoidable."

"And the light that you can see reflected by the second mirror is the tragedy that we must allow to singe us with its flames. It must never be forgotten. But maybe one day it can be extinguished. Repeat that for me, please."

"It must never be forgotten. But maybe one day it can be extinguished."

"Good. I want you to look at the third mirror while allowing the tragic light to continue to wash over you. Can you do this?"

Safa looked at the barely visible third mirror. "Is it bad? I don't know if I want it to be bad."

"Oh, no. This is the most wonderful thing in the world. It is a thing that forges a path into the future while correcting the past. The light I will shine on it will be bright and virtuous. But if you're not ready to see it then we can do this during one of our subsequent daily sessions."

"I want to see it."

The guardian illuminated the third mirror. "Do you know what this is?"

Safa shook his head.

"It is you."

"Me?"

"The brightest light. Look at the mirror. It holds a reflection of you."

Safa stared at the mirror. Its light would normally hurt his eyes and cause him to blink, but the drugs inside him dulled his nerves and made him calm, at peace. He felt different, though he always did after receiving his medication. And every morning after, he felt his mind was developing greater fortitude and clarity. He was evolving. "Me?" he repeated.

"You." The guardian's session was nearly at a close. There was so much more work to be done. Safa was nowhere near ready. But each daily session had to contain cautious little steps. Just as Safa's body had to be coaxed carefully, step by step, back to normal nutritional balance, so, too, his mind had to be gently manipulated to the place where it would never be the same again. The guardian owed that to the boy in his care, a child who could otherwise be traumatized by the horrors of his young life. "The mirror on the left with no light is beyond the control of you or anyone else. What has happened can never be undone. The mirror next to it burns with unbridled indignation and sorrow because it captures and holds tragedy. Only you can extinguish it, and only when matters have been put to rest. The third mirror is you. The brightest and purest light." He paused, wondering if he should stop now.

Safa asked, "The fourth mirror. Why does it have no light?"

"It does have light. But it is an evil one. I'm not sure you're ready to see what the mirror reflects."

"It reflects the bad in me?"

"There is no bad in you. The fourth mirror is the key to everything—the death of your family, the terrible circumstances of your childhood, the unnecessary deaths of so many others."

"What is it?"

"Gluttony, power, murder." The guardian hesitated. "We've never given that light a name, have we?"

"Never."

"Do you think it's time to do so?"

Safa was silent for a moment. Tonight his caring guardian had taken him to a whole new level of well-being. Thank goodness the man had singled Safa out for a better life where he could recuperate in the West. A child, still, but one receiving a very good education on what it took to be a balanced adult. "Yes, it's time."

The guardian turned off all flashlights. Then he illuminated the fourth mirror. "Don't be scared. But do be very cautious. Look at it."

The light was more intense than the others. Safa didn't like it. He felt angry, wanted to smash the mirror, though he wasn't sure why.

The guardian crouched next to Safa, his mouth close to the boy's ear, his eyes following his gaze toward the mirror. "It is a painful thing, is it not?"

Safa felt uneasy. "Gluttony, power, murder?"

The guardian whispered, "The embodiment of those nasty things in grown-ups who slaughter children."

"Where do those grown-ups live?"

"You must look to the two mirrors on the left. They can answer your question. It would be wrong for me to do so."

Safa thought about his dying parents; the way his younger sister had grabbed his arm while shrieking in pain, her expression terrified as she vomited blood onto his raggedy shirt; the wails from Arab mothers in Gaza who served as belated air raid sirens as they ran down streets and alleys, their sons and daughters killed; and worst of all, the starvation of his country. That was the insufferable horror, a rot that was surgically injected into a landmass; the life of people evaporating over months and years, rather than seconds and days. "I have a word for the fourth mirror."

Safa's guardian placed his hand over the boy's shoulder. "But we must not run before we can walk. Our lesson is at a close. It is your bedtime now."

The guardian watched his care walk as if drunk toward his bed. In a few minutes he'd check up on him, make sure he had water next to his bed, was warm enough, and when he was asleep he would gently pinch his flesh to check its growth. He would never let the boy be without the tools to navigate his way through this world with success. The guardian owed him that. It was the duty of a man who called himself Thales.

Eight

Beirut, Six Weeks Later

The CIA officer bade his three colleagues good night, watched them ascend the stairs toward the abandoned large house above, and shut the bomb-proof steel door. The air's musky scent caused him to pinch his nostrils with one hand while using the other to slam seven titanium bolts into place and turn keys in additional locks. He walked along the long, wide corridor that led back to the four rooms in the underground complex, while thinking it sucked to work the night shift alone in a place that resembled Hitler's Berlin bunker. The officer had operated in many hell-holes and had done so with exceptional composure and bravery. But this place gave him the jitters. Everything about it felt, looked, and smelled wrong. Particularly at night.

The bunker contained the most sophisticated communications intercept equipment in the world, but the CIA technical guys who'd outfitted and reinforced the house's big wine cellar had evidently not been overly concerned with ensuring there were enough lights in the complex. Day and night, the bunker was too shadowy because no natural light could get in, and the air was rank because air vents weren't allowed in the hermetically sealed fortress. It wasn't intended to be a permanent station.

The steel door was the only portal to the outside world.

It was impossible to enter or exit the station by any other means.

And now that it was locked, the officer felt the weight of the slimy concrete walls, ceiling, and floor closing in on him. Above him was a city that he and his English, French, and Israeli partners spied on. Elements within the city would happily behead him and his MI6, DGSE, and Mossad colleagues if the complex were discovered. But on nights like this the American operative often wondered if it would be preferable to take his chances in the city, rather than sit, cornered, in a basement. His three foreign colleagues always felt the same way when it was their turn to be night duty officer. Tonight they'd be relieved they were heading back to their hotel rooms, rather than sitting alone on the cruddy furniture they'd bought at short notice from a local purveyor of cheap, flammable shit.

Five weeks they'd been in here, one officer per room, for the most part with earphones on while listening to intercepts of Hamas cell phones and landlines, as well as more traditional bugs in situ. So far, all of it was giving the Agency nothing bar insight on God's peace, Real Madrid's soccer scores, and the best way to debone and grill a goat. The officer sneezed as he walked along the corridor containing tall metal filing cabinets and an oil-powered electricity generator. He entered his room. All it needed was an oil lamp to make it look like the nighttime communications post of a lieutenant on the front line of the Somme. Tiny flies emerged from a hole in the acrylic armchair the officer slumped in as he attached his earpieces.

An hour into his shift, one of the communications units' lights flashed, meaning a call was being made to a Hamas target. The officer flicked a switch so he could listen in. He heard code name Stravinsky talk in Arabic to code name Stradivarius on their cell phones. The two senior Hamas leaders were on this occasion not discussing mundane matters. Instead, their tones were wary and urgent, and their words made the CIA officer's heart beat fast.

When the call ended, the officer dashed to the computer terminal he used to send encrypted telegrams to the CIA headquarters in Langley, Virginia.

Using two fingers, he typed fast.

STRAVINSKY HAS JUST CALLED STRADIVARIUS. THEY AND OTHER HIGH RANKING HAMAS LEADERS WILL BE MEETING FOUR P.M. LOCAL TIME TOMORROW TO DISCUSS THE "PARIS SHOPPING TRIP." I HAVE COMPLETE ELECTRONIC COVERAGE OF THE LOCATION OF THE MEETING AND WILL ACTIVATE INTERCEPTION THIRTY MINUTES BEFORE THE MEETING. STRAVINSKY SAID THAT "THALES" HAD CONTACTED HIM AND TOLD HIM TO BE VERY CAREFUL BECAUSE THE AMERICANS MAY BE WATCHING HIM. I HAVE NO IDEA WHO THALES IS. ANY INSIGHT?

Langley responded in less than a minute.

EXCELLENT. REPEAT, EXCELLENT. THIS IS GOLD DUST. WE WILL IMMEDIATELY INFORM MI6, MOSSAD, AND DGSE. THE MEETING WILL GIVE US THE EVIDENCE WE'VE BEEN LOOKING FOR. THALES HAS NO MEANING TO US.

The officer breathed out slowly and felt his shoulder muscles relax. Admiral Mason's initiative six weeks ago to establish the bespoke intelligence station in Beirut had been the right call, although everyone involved in his initiative had always realized it was a long shot. And so much was at stake if the station couldn't deliver. But it looked like the initiative had paid off. Tomorrow's meeting would prove whether Hamas had killed the Israeli ambassador to France or not. But that wasn't the only reason the officer felt relieved. He and his three colleagues had been going mad cooped up in the station. They were desperate to leave the complex for good.

An intelligence complex that carried the name Gray Site.

The American withdrew his handgun and stripped it down to its working parts. After he cleaned each part, he reassembled the weapon and placed a fresh clip of bullets into the pistol. He waited for his colleagues to arrive in the morning.

Nine

Tucked behind a side street off London's bustling Strand is the tiny Savoy Chapel. It was originally built in the Middle Ages and dedicated to St. John the Baptist, and throughout its rich history the religious site has been owned by royalty, who've used it for centuries as a discreet place of worship. It is also the last surviving building of the Savoy Hospital, once a hospital for the homeless. Very few residents of London and even fewer tourists know about the chapel. They're missing out on something special, because though the exterior of the chapel is unremarkable, the inside is gorgeous. Its current owner is Her Majesty the Queen. Sometimes she comes here.

And sometimes so do I.

Not to pray, because I have no views on religion beyond thinking it can be a nuisance when idiots grab its principles and do bad things in its name. My American father and English mother rarely attended the church close to their home in Virginia. The schools I went to favored science and reason over more ethereal, other-worldly concepts. And I've spent my entire adult life dealing with the harsh and all-too-immediate realities of humanity. I've had no time to contemplate anything other than the sometimes chaotic hell that life on earth can be.

I come to this spiritual site for two reasons. The first is that it is a quiet place and allows me time to think in peace.

The second is that, despite my father being very much like me when it came to the topic of religion, according to my mother he, too, would often come here during his CIA posting to London in the 1970s. I can barely remember him—he was captured by revolutionaries in Iran when I was five years old, and subsequently murdered in Tehran's Evin Prison—but my mother spoke a lot about him. She told me that he would come here to complete the *Times* crossword and stare at the ornate altar and the gold and blue mosaic on the ceiling.

During my visits to the chapel, I imagine him sitting next to me on a wooden pew, wearing a nice suit, man and his boy looking near identical aside from age, both of us contented and silent. I like to think that part of his soul lingers in this place, that he watches me when I sit where he may have sat, attempting to complete my crossword, wishing he could help me solve the clues.

Today was the first time I didn't think of my father as I sat in the empty chapel. I wondered why and joked to myself that perhaps I'd come here to pay my respects to Her Majesty and tell her that I was no longer wanted by her Secret Service. I smiled at the notion of her and me being the sole occupants of the chapel and our speaking about such matters. The smile felt forced, and I realized it was because there was some foundation of truth in my frivolous image. I was here to say farewell to the British Establishment after fourteen years of serving it well and being in its inner circle of trust. And though I'd never been able to abide the pomp and ritual within the ranks of Britain's elite, I did feel that my country gave me some purpose and prevented me doing something that would land me in an English prison.

I opened my copy of the *Times* onto the page containing today's crossword, withdrew a bullet-gray fountain pen that had once belonged to my dad and bore an inscription of his name, left both on the pew, and walked out of the church.

I decided I'd never return.

The angle of the glaring midafternoon sun was all wrong as I walked toward Millbank, adjacent to the north side of the Thames. Though there are few high-rises in the capital, there are plenty of midrises, and their windows reflected the sun's beams to produce painful flashes of light that were sometimes so blinding one could easily bump into the surly road workers who perpetually commandeer London's streets. I hated London when it was like this—overexposed with light, soulless, loud, air thick with the saccharine smell of sugar-coated nuts roasted by cash-in-quick hawkers; everyone except tourists pissed off because the city had become a sweaty see-the-sites tart. It affected my mood, which was already bad enough. The capital was rubbing salt into my wounds as I walked with the Houses of Parliament behind me, past MI5 headquarters in Thames House, and toward the Babylonian headquarters of MI6. The government institutions were places that I could no longer enter. And I felt that they were turning their noses up at me.

I walked over a bridge to the South Bank, and kept walking until I reached Southwark's West Square. The small, beautiful area contains a cluster of Edwardian houses, all of which have been converted into apartments. My home is one of them, an antiquity-strewn bachelor pad on the top floor, above the three apartments containing a champagne-swilling thirty-something art dealer called Phoebe, a middle-aged divorced mortician called David, and a seventy-something retired Coldstream Guards officer called Dickie. Even by London standards, we are the oddest collection of cohabiters. Yet, thanks to the malevolent U.S. senator who outed me, they have recently discovered what I do for a living and don't care. Because we are friends.

Sort of.

Dickie Mountjoy was outside in front of our terraced house, cursing his arthritis as he was painting the frame of one of his windows. Despite his task in hand, he was, as ever, wearing pristine clothes fit for an off-duty major partaking of a glass of port in the officer's mess. I wondered why he bothered, given that he was a widower and had been out of the army for decades.

"Good afternoon, Major."

Dickie replied in the well-spoken but clipped, angry-sounding tone favored by British army officers. "Ah, Mr. Cochrane. Good afternoon to you too, young man." His eyes narrowed. "What yer wearing a suit for? Been for a job interview?" Dickie, Phoebe, and David knew about my change in circumstances.

"No. Church."

The major huffed. "Bit late in the day for you to ask His forgiveness for all the stuff you've done."

I examined the window frame. "You've missed a bit."

Dickie looked affronted. "I haven't finished the job yet, plus guardsmen never miss anything. We know precision too well because—"

"Yes, yes. You've lectured me on this before." I smiled.

Dickie painted over the bare spot I'd referred to, and his expression momentarily softened. "Fancy joining me for a tea break? This'll need at least thirty minutes before I can apply a second coat."

Dickie and I both knew he'd struggle with the three flights of stairs to my pad, so we headed straight into his ground-floor apartment. As he was filling up the kettle, he asked, "What you going to do?"

"For work?"

"No, your bleedin' lack of love life. Of course, work."

"I've one or two ideas."

"Hope they don't involve some poor chap having you as his employee, 'cause you're unemployable. Too many antisocial traits. Not a team player. Ill disciplined."

"Not when I'm working." I sat on the sofa in the living room adjacent to the open-plan kitchen; to have sat in Dickie's favorite armchair would have made him apoplectic.

"When you work, you spy on people or kill them. I doubt there are any positions in the local Job Centre requiring those skills."

I joked, "I suppose I could join the Coldstream Guards."

"Age forty-one?" He walked in, carrying two mugs of tea in one hand and a plate of biscuits in the other. "You're not cut out for the army. Too—"

"Ill disciplined." I nodded while wondering how Dickie would react if I told him something about myself that he didn't know: At age seventeen I'd killed my mother's four murderers with a kitchen knife and fled to France to join the Foreign Legion. I'd spent five harsh years in the Legion, initially in the elite 2e Régiment Étranger de Parachutistes, before successfully completing selection into Groupement des Commandos Parachutistes (GCP), a Special Forces unit of the 11th Parachute Brigade of the French army. And during my time in GCP, I'd been frequently requisitioned by France's intelligence services to conduct assassinations.

I knew all about army discipline in its most extreme form, though I didn't tell Dickie about my history because it would have made us too alike. The army meant the world to Dickie, and it gave him purpose to tell civilians like me that we could learn a few things from him. I wasn't going to take that away from the old man.

I looked at the ceiling as a rhythmic banging noise

came from David's apartment above us. "Jesus, what's that?"

Dickie sat opposite me in his armchair and followed my gaze toward his ceiling. "Er . . . that'll be David and Phoebe."

"Ah." The two neighbors had recently become boyfriend and girlfriend. Clearly Phoebe had gone to David's apartment for some intimate time. "We . . ." I'd no idea what I was about to say.

The banging continued. Dickie looked as uncomfortable as I felt. We lowered our eyes in unison as he pushed the plate of biscuits toward me. "Home baked. Try one."

"Thanks." I wasn't particularly hungry but was grateful for the distraction. "How long will the banging last?"

"Usually not more than ten minutes."

We both gave up trying to make small talk. The thumps got faster. Every second felt like a minute. Eventually the noise stopped.

Dickie shook his head. "I'm counting down the days until Phoebe and David reach the jaded phase of the relationship."

That made me laugh. "What are you up to this evening?"

Dickie shrugged. "My club's temporarily shut for

refurbishment, so I guess I'll stay in and watch a bit of telly."

Since Mrs. Mountjoy had passed away two years ago, Dickie spent most weekday evenings at Pall Mall's Army & Navy Club. In his finest attire, and with a rolled-up umbrella no matter what the weather, he'd march from his home to the club at precisely 7 P.M., ignoring the pain of his arthritis. There he'd have one drink with fellow former guardsmen—never ex–naval officers, heaven forbid—eat his meal at the club, and return home in time for the ten o'clock news. It was a ritual that gave him purpose and prevented him from dwelling on the absence of the love of his life.

But tonight that was taken away from him because a few carpets needed replacing. That worried me. "I'm also at a loose end. Why don't I cook us a beef and ale pie with some fresh veg and bring it down here; maybe a game of chess?"

Dickie gave me a stern look. "Meals on Wheels charity for the lonely causes?"

"A couple of bottles of Châteauneuf-du-Pape? Help numb the pain of being in my company."

"Sir." The major's back was ramrod straight. "Men of my generation do not sit opposite another man with a bottle of wine between us unless we are queer, theatrical types, or French."

"Calvados?"

"No!"

Oh Lord. That left the inevitable. I lied, while thinking I'd need to go to a liquor store. "I've got a lovely vintage port, plus a bottle of thirty-year single malt, both getting dusty and thirsty."

Dickie's eyes twinkled. "That's better talk, Mr. Cochrane. Seven o'clock sharp. And make sure the beef is tender."

I finished my mug of tea and was about to leave.

But Dickie leaned forward and grabbed my forearm for the first time ever. "I asked you in here because I did need a break. But . . . but I also wanted to ask you . . ." His voice was trembling; I knew he'd loathe that. "Wanted to ask you if you'll be okay. Rent? You got enough money to tide you over? Hate to see you . . . have to leave 'cause you don't have the funds."

I placed a hand over Dickie's. "I've got a bit of cash. Enough for a while."

Dickie blurted, "After everything you've done for me, I was thinking I could help you out. Some of my pension. Just make sure you can keep paying the rent until you get a job on a checkout at a local supermarket."

"I haven't done much for you."

"You took me to the doctors when I thought I had lung cancer."

"Someone had to."

Dickie leaned back, warmth evaporated.

He was glad.

So was I.

"Why would you give me your money?" I asked a man who was as belligerent as I imagined I'd be at his age.

"You hate beef and ale pie" was his answer.

This was true. But I knew it was Dickie's meal of choice. "I promise you, I'll come to you if I need cash."

"Promise? No bank managers and crippling loans?"

"For sure."

The major nodded. "Very well. Now, if you don't mind, I need to get back to painting." He winced as he pushed himself to his feet. "It's not just money I worry about. The normal world isn't the place for you. You need work, and not the regular kind. But I just can't see where you'll find it."

The CIA analyst ran when no one was around her and walked when she passed other officers on the third floor of the Agency's headquarters in Langley, Virginia. She knew her change of pace made no sense, and even when walking she was aware that people were looking at her clammy face. Perhaps they thought she was ill and needed to get to a restroom.

More likely they understood her mind was deeply troubled. It was, but she didn't want anyone to know that. Not yet.

She needn't have worried. People in the building run a lot, usually when something really bad has happened. Witnesses get used to it, because many of them have done the same—dashing to someone who just might know what to do, like a child who's fallen over and needs his mom or dad.

In a normal organization, a colleague would likely ask a runner, "What's wrong?"

Within the secret cell-like structure of the Agency, such a question would be answered, "You're not cleared to know."

But the analyst was young and had only worked for the CIA for seven months. She didn't know that it was a common occurrence for officers to go into headless chicken mode. She banged on a door, breathless, clutching her heaving chest.

"The door's shut for a reason!" a woman barked from inside the room.

The analyst's stomach cramped. Her boss had had an exemplary fifteen-year career as a field officer before being promoted away from her overseas missions into management. The boss had been pissed off ever since, and for the most part the juniors on her team bore the brunt of her frequent fury. The analyst raised her fist to the door, hesitated, and banged again.

"God damn it! I'm busy."

The analyst felt teary and confused. No, she couldn't be confused. She had to go into the room. She did so.

And immediately wished she hadn't.

Her boss wasn't the only one glaring at her; so too was the head of the Agency, the director of intelligence, and the director of the National Clandestine Service. Part of her wanted to turn around and run. But instead she stood before them, shaking, her petrified eyes darting from one person to the next.

"What is it?" her boss asked with an expression that suggested she was going to sack her junior.

"It's . . . it's . . ."

"Spit it out!"

Screw this, the analyst thought while deciding she couldn't hack this job. It gave her momentary strength. But her voice still shook as she said, "It's Gray Site, ma'am. It's gone silent. Telegrams, calls, I've tried everything for hours. The station's manned twenty-four seven. But I can't get hold of them. Haven't heard a peep from them since Gray Site's night-duty officer sent us a telegram yesterday evening. The one I showed you about the Hamas meeting today." She felt light-headed. "Gray Site's gone dead."

Ten

That night, six CIA men were silent as they disgorged from the stationary SUV and ran off a street into a derelict house in Beirut's urban suburbs. The three technical officers in the team had been here weeks before. The other three were paramilitary officers, men who'd told the techies moments ago to move fast, watch angles, and drop to the ground if ordered by them to do so. The shooters were former Delta and SEALs, the techies were former Microsoft and builders of U.S. fighter jets.

The techies felt sweaty and breathless as they lugged their equipment—gas canisters, pipes, bags containing other equipment. Though their immediate surroundings were dark, the specialists felt exposed and ill at ease because they didn't like being on foreign soil.

Especially soil where American government employees are prime kidnap bait. Mosques were calling the faithful to prayer; the salty smell of the humid Mediterranean air was mixed with the aromas of fried okra and grilled beef shawarma; distant cars were honking; and someone was playing bongos while women sang. Good people were socializing too close to the team's entry point, and all intelligence operatives—whether field trained or not—always assume that bad lurks amid good.

The team ran through the empty shell of the huge house, which had been partially destroyed during Israel's siege of Beirut in the 1982 Lebanon War. They moved downstairs to the basement and confronted the bombproof steel door. Locked, of course. The techies had put it there. And they'd made sure the cellar that had once contained thousands of bottles of Château Musar was impenetrable. Wine cellars didn't need such protection. Intelligence units did.

The techies put on visors and ignited blowtorches. The fire burned through the metal; the techies knew what they were doing. The shooters felt useless as they stood guard and wondered if armed men were going to come for them from ahead or behind. There were twenty-two steps back up to the house, and a sealed door in front of them. The shooters gestured the techies to hurry. The stressed techies flipped them the finger.

The men were different, and yet all of them would suffer the same fate if caught. The blowtorches moved around the edge of the door. Sparks, blue light, and smoke caused the men to wince; and an acrid stench filled their nostrils. For forty minutes they continued their breach, burning what they'd installed with pride.

Most of the door fell to the ground. The impatient shooters rushed through the hole. One of them shouted "Fire!" because sparks from the blowtorches had ignited a nearby sofa. "Black smoke," he said. "Number six: reposition." Five of the team moved along the spy house's corridor, using their flashlights to guide their way in the pitch dark; the sixth moved away from his predetermined position of standing guard at the door and started putting out the fire while coughing.

The team headed farther into the complex. The corridor was broad; its floors, ceiling, and walls were thick stone; on one side were metal filing cabinets that the techies and the station intelligence officers had placed there after purchasing them from a nearby school that was closing. Dust on the floor was displaced by the men's boots, its specks looking like agitated fireflies in their flashlight beams. They moved forward; ahead of them they couldn't see anything save glimpses of the subterranean structure. But they could smell must and decay, a scent that grew stronger with each tentative step they made. They reached the end of the corridor, which ended in four rooms of identical size. The techies knew the rooms well because they'd installed all the equipment the Gray Site officers needed inside them. One of the CIA shooters gestured that they check the first room on the left first. They did so, then two more of the rooms. The windowless rooms were empty except for old furniture, desks, and state-of-the-art CIA surveillance equipment that had been systematically smashed to pieces. Even the hardened shooters were uneasy as they moved to the last room, their handguns held high. The techies trailed them, scared beyond belief, thinking that this wasn't what they'd signed up for. The shooters rushed the room. Within seconds, the techies outside the room heard them shout.

"Clear!"

"Clear."

"Clear."

The technical specialists entered the room. One of them immediately vomited; another exclaimed, "Oh dear God, no!"; the third held his hand to his mouth. The men who'd manned Gray Site were in the room—one CIA officer and his three colleagues from MI6, DGSE, and Mossad.

They'd been killed by gunfire.

The CIA analyst had inadvertently summed up what had actually happened.

Gray Site was indeed dead.

Eleven

Four P.M. in Washington, D.C., equaled 11 P.M. in Lebanon. It was also the time that Admiral Mason had wanted to head home, because lately he'd been working fourteen-hour days and he needed a night off. He lived alone in a one-bedroom apartment on the outskirts of D.C., ever since his wife had passed away and he'd subsequently sold their beautiful sea-facing home in Norfolk, Virginia. His two grown-up girls had long ago left home, so he'd felt there was no point staying in a six-bedroom residence with so many good memories that were now tinged with sadness. Nevertheless, he liked his tiny apartment. It was far bigger than the quarters where he'd slept on ships. And he was looking forward to being there this evening, cooking a pheasant breast and rosemary mashed potato, and watching his DVD of *Das Boot*.

But that wasn't going to happen yet.

Because he'd been summoned to the White House by the president's chief of staff.

He wasn't the only one. Alongside the chief of staff, there were a former U.S. ambassador to Israel who was now an adviser to the president, the heads of the NSA and the CIA, and another middle-aged CIA officer who Mason didn't know. Though the president himself wasn't here, they were meeting in the Oval Office, a room Mason always felt uncomfortable in because its curved walls seemed unbalanced with the angular shapes of the room's furnishings. And it was an odd choice of meeting location because it didn't have a boardroom table. But it was the only room free, because the White House was abuzz with numerous crisis meetings. So the six men had to sit where they could: some on the two small sofas, others in corner chairs, the chief of staff in an armchair that made the burly man look like he was squeezed into a child's seat. It was all a bit too higgledy-piggledy for the tastes of an admiral who liked things to be shipshape.

For once, Mason didn't know why he was here. The CIA had called this meeting.

The Agency boss twisted awkwardly on the sofa. "You've all read the encrypted message sent by Gray Site's CIA officer regarding the Hamas meeting today.

After it was sent, we heard nothing from the station— tried to reach out to it in the usual ways, informed MI6, DGSE, and Mossad, who tried to do the same. When that didn't work, all of us broke security protocols and called our respective officers on their cell phones. Nothing. It's fair to say we got the almighty jitters. So two hours ago I deployed an Agency team to check Gray Site. Our guys had to cut their way in. Place was trashed. Data lost." The intelligence leader met the eyes of each person in the room, one by one, before continuing. "There'd been a gunfight."

Mason closed his eyes.

The Agency head concluded, "All four officers dead."

The chief of staff asked him, "Coverage of the Hamas meeting?"

"None. That was Gray Site's task. Only its officers had the capability to do that job. Looks like they died hours before the meeting."

"What's Hamas doing now?" This was to the head of NSA.

He replied, "We're getting the usual chicken shit from lower-level Hamas guys and girls. Nothing about Paris."

"You can spy on Americans, but you can't tell us what the top loony tunes are doing?"

The NSA head wasn't afraid of the chief of staff. "Fuck you."

"Not tonight, Josephine." The chief of staff puffed his chest out, aware that he must have looked ridiculous in the chair. "We gave you the Hamas cell numbers and other stuff that Gray Site was listening in on. Can't you access those numbers remotely?"

Mason opened his eyes.

The NSA head responded, "We can access the cells, but we can't access the bugs. Only Gray Site could do that because it had to be within range of their signals. But even the cell phones aren't of any use. The Hamas leaders your guys were listening in on change their cells once a week at minimum. We've tried. The numbers they used to set up today's meeting are no longer functional. That's why Gray Site was key—be on the ground, grab cell phone numbers, be ready in an instant to be all over those numbers when they're active, grab new numbers when old ones are discarded, put bugs in place and keep doing so if they're discovered." He looked at Mason. "It *was* an excellent idea."

The head of the CIA said, "We could set up another Gray Site. Start over."

The chief of staff barked, "We don't have time! Israel will be ready to mobilize in two weeks. In any case, the Israelis have told us in pretty blunt terms that they did what we asked and waited for evidence, but our plan failed. All they're concerned with now is getting their troops battle ready." He perused the room, like a bloated vulture that had eaten enough flesh but was lusting for more. He grinned at the former American ambassador to Israel. "You must feel like crap."

"Why?" asked the man with dyed hair who spoke three Arabic dialects fluently.

"Because your whole career hasn't made a blind bit of difference to the Middle East." The chief of staff's menace was palpable. "What happens next?"

The former diplomat looked like a posturing academic as he tossed back his head and unnecessarily delayed the length of time it took him to come up with an answer. "We cannot obtain evidence. We should therefore choose sides, based on our principles. We must decide whether to back Israel or not."

The chief of staff looked at Mason.

Mason was motionless, his mind thinking on multiple levels. "The ambassador's analysis is correct, though *principles* shouldn't drive our decision making."

The ambassador tried to interject, his expression affronted.

But Mason quietly continued. "There is a vast swath of global opinion that is currently sitting on the fence when it comes to the subject of Israel. And it is probable they will get off the fence, to one side or the other, when Israel goes to war. No doubt the president understands that whatever decision he takes will affect his political survival. But far more important, he should be aware that this isn't about politics; it's about interstate allegiances. The world will be watching America to see which way it jumps; and when it does jump we will lose friends and win friends. The question for you to ponder is which friends do we want to gain, and which friends are we prepared to lose. The answer to that will inform the president's decision."

The chief of staff said, "Arab nations versus non-Arab?"

"Were it only as simple as that."

"We could just sit this one out. Stay neutral."

"We'll lose more than we gain that way." The admiral was deep in thought, and for a moment was oblivious to the others in the room. "I dearly hoped Gray Site would ascertain that Hamas did not kill the Israeli ambassador."

"I'm sorry your plan didn't work, Mason." The chief of staff's tone with the admiral was respectful. "You're right. This is now about deciding who we want as new friends. What are your thoughts on that?"

Mason had many. But instead he said, "Sir, I am a mere cog in your machine. I can't answer you with any meaningful authority." He turned toward the head of the CIA. "What happened in Gray Site?"

The intelligence officer responded, "*Why* it happened is beyond us. Israel, Britain, and France are also clueless. But *what* happened is clear. One of the four Gray Site personnel turned on the others. His bullets were found in their bodies. But they retaliated before they died, because their bullets were found in the body of the officer who turned on them. We've removed the corpses and weapons, conducted a forensic analysis on them, and sanitized Gray Site."

Mason asked, "You are convinced no third parties entered Gray Site?"

"Certain. There's absolutely no way for anyone to get into the site by any other means aside from the door. And the door had seven bolts and other locks that were in place on the inside when my team forced entry. Plus my guys searched every inch of the station. No tunnels, other signs of forced entry, or forced entries that were subsequently covered up. Zilch."

The chief of staff shook his head in disbelief. "How could the officer have done this to his colleagues?"

The Agency head replied, "Britain, France, and Israel keep asking . . . *demanding* to know the answer to that, because . . ."

"The man who went rogue was our CIA officer. The individual who sent us the telegram about the Hamas meeting today."

Mason looked at the other CIA officer in the Oval Office. who had just spoken for the first time. "Who are you?"

The tall, silver-haired officer replied, "Patrick Bolte."

"And why are you here?"

"Perhaps because, like you, I enjoy wasting my time." He spoke with a warm Texas drawl.

Mason smiled. Patrick? Who was he? Mason was sure Patrick had seen death and had probably dealt it. Moreover, he looked like a man who didn't give a damn about protocol. Mason's lightning mind grabbed other accurate assessments about the man.

Powerful. Razor-sharp brain. Incorruptible. Untouchable.

This assessment made him like Patrick. "We are dealing with the question: What happened in Gray Site that would prompt a CIA officer to murder his colleagues? You, Patrick, are here because you think that question has far broader relevance. Perhaps you have a hypothesis that—"

Patrick interrupted, "Maybe the Mossad officer feared the Hamas meeting would prove that Hamas wasn't behind the assassination. He tried to interfere with coverage of the Hamas meeting. The CIA officer found out. Gunfight ensues. MI6 and DGSE officers don't know what's happening and run to help the Mossad guy, thinking CIA man's gone crazy."

Mason nodded. "And the Mossad officer was either doing this through his own volition, or he had the authority to do so from the State of Israel because it's never wanted evidence that would undermine its reasons to finally obliterate Hamas."

Patrick nodded. "That's my take."

The chief of staff looked unsettled. "Backing a country that's going to war on a hunch is one thing; supporting an outright lie is another."

Mason resisted the urge to tell everyone that there were precedents for going to war on a lie, most recently the invasion of Iraq. "I agree. We have a two-week window to find out what happened inside Gray Site."

The head of the NSA was exasperated. "You heard what the chief of staff said. Israel's going to war regardless. There's nothing we can do."

Mason replied, "If we can find out what happened in Gray Site, we might be able to uncover the truth about the Paris assassination."

The NSA officer retorted, "You're just desperate to make up for the fact that your initiative ended with dead men."

"Desperate!" Though fully in control of his emotions, the admiral deliberately looked angry. "Have you been to war? I have. Only three things keep men fighting in a conflict: orders, fear, and the hope they're doing the right thing. I don't know about you, but I'm keen to find out if this impending war is the *right thing*. And I say that as much for the sake of Israeli lives as I do for everyone else who'll be involved."

The chief of staff stepped in. "Admiral. My colleague's right. There's no point chasing after a fool's errand that can't change the inevitable."

Mason's voice became quiet again. "I wonder what Israel would do if we could prove that Hamas didn't kill its ambassador in Paris, and demonstrate that Israel tried to hide that fact. I suspect it would back down from war. In fact, I know it would."

"Demonstrate?"

"Go public."

"And what if learning about what happened in Gray Site shows Hamas *did* do the kill?"

Mason shrugged. "Then we return to my point about interstate allegiances and choices."

The room was silent for a minute.

Patrick broke the silence, his gaze fixed on Mason. "You and I need to talk."

"Yes, we do. Do you have someone who's up for the task? Someone totally deniable?"

Patrick nodded.

Mason said to the chief of staff, "I could ask your permission to task an investigation into what happened at Gray Site, or I could simply go to the president. You choose."

The chief of staff drummed his fingers on his leg. Finally, he replied, "Okay. You got it." He said to Patrick, "We can't have the Israelis or anyone else getting a whiff of this. Has to be completely under the radar. He works alone, okay? And if he's caught, we'll let him be strung up by his balls. Who do you have in mind?"

Patrick seemed hesitant. Then he answered, "His name's Will Cochrane."

On sunnier days, the Georgetown Waterfront Park usually contained walkers, cyclists, skaters, and people picnicking while taking in views of the adjacent Potomac River. But today a fine rain had driven most people away from the site, leaving only a small number of solitary individuals, most of whom were using the park as a shortcut to access central D.C. Only one person here had no intention of moving through the park as quickly as possible.

Rob Tanner pulled up the collar on his raincoat, thrust his hands into his pockets, and sat on a bench next to a footpath, in front of trees and overlooking the river.

The young man felt exhilarated to be here, sensing that he was operating within the epicenter of power and was doing so without anyone knowing his true role. He was a chameleon, he told himself, duping the fools around him and snatching their secrets. It made him feel armor plated, contemptuous of those who lacked his courage, and that he had a higher calling. It particularly pleased him that he'd managed to fool Admiral Mason.

A man sat next to him. He was middle aged, wearing a suit and light beige coat that was peppered with raindrops. He fixed his gaze on the river. "I could smell your fancy cologne a mile off."

"You paid for it." Tanner grinned. "Together with everything else about me."

"You liking your new lifestyle?"

"Think I am."

"Don't get used to it. Next time I might send you to the third world, just to give you some humility."

"I don't do poverty or humility. That's why you chose me."

"I'm prone to making mistakes, but key to my

success is that I'm not averse to correcting them." The man clasped his scarred hands. "Talk."

Tanner watched a slow-moving pleasure cruiser pass by; miserable-looking tourists were huddled underneath the vessel's canopy. "Mason spoke to me couple of hours ago. This morning he was at Capitol Hill. He knows Gray Site's dead and wants what happened in there investigated. And he's only got two weeks to do so before Israel goes to war."

The man huffed. "He won't find anything. Who's he using to do the investigation?"

"Some guy called Will Cochrane. You know him?"

The man was silent for a few seconds, his expression now tense. "I know *of* him." He looked directly at Tanner. "The priority now is that Cochrane can't move without you knowing it. Got it?"

Tanner nodded. "Got it."

Twelve

The River Findhorn was up to my chest, waders keeping me dry, as I fished for salmon in a place that for me was heaven on earth. The isolated white stone cottage I'd rented for the week was in the distance, nestled in a glen in the Scottish Highlands. The mountains on both sides of the valley were covered in heather, looking craggy yet majestically ancient. On one mountainside, the local farmer's adult son was using a seasoned sheepdog to help train a younger one. They were not having much luck; I could hear the farmhand bellowing instructions at the young dog, then cursing as the pup scattered sheep in all directions and flushed red grouse out of the brush. An otter a ways off was eyeing me curiously from the bank. Like me, he was here to fish. There were no other noises save from the fast rush of water hitting boulders, a cool autumn air coursing through clusters of pine, and Rory.

I come here every year and always fish this beat: a three-mile stretch twelve miles south of Inverness that belongs to the local estate. Rory was my guide, a ghillie who knew every inch of the stretch he was paid to preserve, a proud individual who wore modern clothes that were fashioned old and were made to brave the elements all year round. He loved his surroundings because every day the flora and fauna gave him new surprises that he embraced with the intelligent wonderment of a man who had no sense of what it meant to be jaded. Tall, seventy-one years old, an offshore engineer pre-retirement, Rory was a gentleman Highlander who spoke softly and with precision and had a permanent glint in his eye. We'd known each other for years. He liked me, he'd told me several times. I suspect it was because I worked this beat hard, preferring to fish it on foot no matter that it required me to clamber over rocks to reach new pools to cast my line. A day's fishing the Findhorn was arduous and Rory knew that, hence his fitness and relatively youthful appearance. I also suspect he compared me favorably to the champagne-swilling rich knobs from London who came here for a jolly and required Rory to drive them to each new pool, where they would drink on the banks far longer than they'd fish.

"Your arms are getting too low again, Mr. Cochrane," he said while sitting on the grassy bank and pouring us both a cup of sweet coffee from his flask. "Arms high, fly line high."

I pulled back my fifteen-foot salmon rod and cast my fly line so that it hit a patch of the river forty-five degrees to the left of me.

"Better."

I watched the floating line drift fast toward the center of the river; once there, the chance of a salmon was gone and I'd have to move a few feet farther downriver and recast. Working the pool, it was called. "Hey, Rory?"

"Yes?"

"Read something interesting recently." Nothing yanked on the three-hook fly that was on a long tippet at the head of the fly line. I started walking through the river, careful with my footing because the current was fast and the stones on the riverbed were slimy. "DNA analysis has proved that there are more Celts living in the southeast of England than there are in Scotland, Ireland, and Wales combined."

Rory often proclaimed he was a devout separatist because of his Celtic identity. His Scottish wife told him he was just playacting the part, and I suspected she was right.

"Aye." Rory crossed his legs and smiled at the blue sky. "That'll be because you lot raped and pillaged us in the thirteenth and fourteenth centuries, before buggering off back home with our womenfolk."

"Us lot?" I recast my line.

"The English. Actually, not *you lot* because you're not English; you're Scottish."

"No, I'm not. My surname is."

"You're a Scot." Rory chuckled. "It's in your blood."

My fly line tightened quickly; the reel screamed as line shot out. Salmon on. Big one.

Rory leaped to his feet. "Ten pounder! At least. Let him do his thing. Only bring him in when he gets tired."

I let the line run off the reel. The fish leapt. My heart leapt with it, and I could hear my estranged sister's voice when I was a lad.

What is it about boys and fishing? Why don't you find it boring?

This was why. I started winding in the reel, desperate to land my catch. The magnificent sport fish leapt again and snapped my line because I hadn't followed my ghillie's instructions. Too impatient. Shit!

Rory looked genuinely bothered as he paced up and down the bank. "He was a beauty! You lost him, son."

My expression must have said it all.

Rory smiled sympathetically. "Come for a brew, Mr. Cochrane." He held his arm out and grabbed my hand. "Easy, now. Steady with your footing. And don't break my rod!"

He hauled me out of the river. I placed his rod against a steep incline. "I'm sorry," I said, because I was. I'd lost a fish that mattered to him. Ghillies are God's shepherds. They love their creatures, braving hypothermia to feed red deer in winter when they come down from the foodless mountains, placing eggs in rivers so salmon can spawn, and culling their beloved when it's time.

Many don't understand this way of life.

I did. "Is he going to be okay?"

"Aye." Rory sat down on the bank and handed me a coffee. "He'll be okay," he whispered while looking at his river.

It was early evening. We finished our coffee and I walked with Rory back to my cottage. His jeep was parked there, crammed with everything a ghillie needed to do his job. We entered the kitchen and I lit the log-burning stove. "Beer?"

"No. My wife's expecting me. What you cooking tonight?"

"Venison stew."

Rory beamed. "That's lovely to hear. Good effort."

The comment touched me. "I genuinely like the local food."

"You fancy another day on the beat tomorrow?"

"Absolutely."

"I'll be here seven o'clock." Rory's cell phone rang. He frowned and asked the caller, "Did you tell them?" After ending the call, he looked at me. "Two men. In Tomatin."

Tomatin was the nearest village, five miles away.

"They're asking about you. Trying to find the location of your cottage." He pointed at his cell phone. "That was the village store. The owner told them nothing."

"What do they look like?"

"Younger than me, and older than you. The man who spoke to the store owner was English. They're wearing suits. Nobody around here wears suits aside from weddings, funerals, and court hearings."

I pushed the beer I was about to pour myself to one side. "Have you told anyone I'm here?"

"No. Only me and the estate owner know. And we wouldn't say a word . . ."

"Of course. Why did the store owner call you?"

Rory answered, "Because long ago I put the word out in the village. The estate owner and I don't like people inquiring after our guests. Especially guests like you."

"They'll find the cottage, whether someone talks or not."

"What are you going to do?"

I shrugged. "Cook while I wait for them."

Sometime when I was a boy—maybe when I was fourteen or fifteen years old, can't be sure—my mother bought me an old French cookbook. I don't remember its title or author but I do recall its scratched leather cover and the fact that when opened and laid on a surface, the pages would remain flat. I think every recipe in the thick book had been made over and over again, and the binding had become loose. All cookbooks should have their bindings loosened before sale, I remember thinking at the time. It makes them so much easier to use.

I studied cooking at school and enjoyed it. I was the only boy in the class, and while the other boys in my year group thought metal and woodwork were the ways to young ladies' hearts, I knew different. My friends taunted me. But I didn't mind because at the end of the day they took home useless bits of wood; by contrast, I gave my mother and sister something to eat.

The book elevated me to a whole new level of capability, to the extent that my cooking teacher suggested

I enter the profession by training to be a chef. I seriously considered it for a while, until good grades in other subjects, a full scholarship to do an undergraduate degree at Cambridge University, and killing my mother's murderers put aside such aspirations.

Today I didn't need the book as I pan-fried cubes of venison and added cracked pepper, red wine, chopped tomatoes, a dollop of French mustard, and herbs. Over the years, cooking had become almost instinctual for me—I lived alone; it had to be.

The meal was simmering nicely when I heard the unmistakable sound of a vehicle driving over the cattle grid on the track leading to the cottage. I placed my hands behind my back and walked outside.

A Mercedes was stationary on the small fenced garden. Sheep that were not supposed to be in the garden ran to the enclosure's wire fence, calling to their flock on the other side. Two men, in their fifties and looking like they'd be more at home in the City of London, got out of the vehicle and cursed as their expensive shoes encountered fresh animal droppings. Their car was a rental—the transparent No Smoking sticker in the window gave that away, plus the fact that it had local plates; most likely a pickup from Inverness Airport.

One was blond, the other had silver hair. Otherwise they looked similar—tall, slender. They'd brought with them the whiff of the metropolis and I resented that, though was aware that I was unshaven, in jeans and wet socks and a stained vest, and smelled of the river. They picked their way to me with care, avoiding more dung, and stood before me. I let them.

"This week, you are a fisherman," said the blond Englishman.

"I am," I replied.

"And next week, who are you?" he added.

"Don't do that."

The other man asked with a Texan drawl, "Why is your phone off?"

I responded with honesty. "I hate the things. They're attention seeking. I've divorced my cell phone."

"It would've saved us a journey if you hadn't."

I looked at the horizon high above me. Something moved. Maybe an eagle. "Your journey and convenience is irrelevant to me."

"Can we come in?" the American asked.

I relaxed my arms by my sides, my hand gripping a large kitchen knife. I whistled three times and watched Rory saunter down from the mountain, slinging his hunting rifle over his shoulder.

He reached us. "Mr. Cochrane?"

"It's okay, Rory. I know these men. I don't need to kill them. Nor do you."

I smiled at Alistair, the Englishman who'd been my MI6 controller, and Patrick, the CIA officer who'd run Task Force S alongside Alistair and had deployed me for fourteen years. "Both of you have been too long out of the field. My friend had you in his sights. He's an excellent shot."

Rory looked at me with concern as he placed his hunting rifle in his jeep. "I guess I'll have a lie-in tomorrow?"

I nodded.

"Shame, eh?"

"Yes, it is a shame. I wanted to catch that fish." I also wanted another day of being who I truly was. As Rory drove off, I said to Alistair and Patrick, "All right. Come in the house." I poured them both a glass of whiskey that had been made in the local distillery in Tomatin, and ignored them bickering about who should drive back to the airport. They sat at the circular kitchen table, two of the West's most powerful intelligence officers looking immaculate and out of place in my holiday home. Leaning against a bench with my arms folded, I asked, "A job? Or have you uncovered one of my secrets and are here to say farewell before I go to prison?"

Alistair replied, "A job."

"On the terms and conditions we discussed?"

One-third payment up front, the balance upon successful completion of the job. Cash that came from a slush fund under Alistair's control. Alistair and Patrick had previously made it clear that if they tasked me under this new freelance arrangement, they would stand in a court of law and deny any involvement with me if things went wrong.

"As we discussed," Patrick replied.

To prepare for a moment like this, I'd spent weeks setting up my network and secreting equipment around the world. The fictional Sherlock Holmes had declared in the nineteenth century that he was the first consulting detective. It worked for him, on paper. I drew inspiration from that to position myself as a real-life consulting spy. This was my new job, details of which I'd withheld from Major Dickie Mountjoy because beneath the old man's gruff exterior he genuinely worried about me.

As well as financials, and my deniable role, the third aspect of the deal was that only Alistair and Patrick could be my clients. All work had to go through them. This suited me because I trusted them wholeheartedly; that trust had been gained not only during my operational career, but more importantly because my father sacrificed himself to save them in Iran in '79, and they repaid the debt by secretly financially supporting my mother, my sister, and me. They were no doubt tough

minded and on occasion told me I was an obstinate liability, but their moral compass was always pointing in
the right direction.

I poured my beer. "I'm listening."

Patrick spoke for thirty minutes. The assassination
in Paris; Israel's response; Admiral Mason's initiative
to establish Gray Site; the CIA's officer's telegram about
the Hamas meeting; the reference in the telegram that
an individual code-named Thales had warned one of
the senior Hamas officials that they needed to be careful because America might be watching them; what
happened in Gray Site after the telegram was sent; and
Mason's further initiative to investigate why the CIA
officer in the complex could do such a thing.

"And that's where you come in." Patrick took a sip
of his whiskey. "Damn, this is good."

My mind working overtime, I muttered, "It's
blended. Most Scots are right to prefer blends to
single malt. More nuanced." I looked directly at the
men. "Why me? Why not a cadre officer from your
agencies?"

Patrick replied, "Because Israel can't know anything
about this. For that matter, most people in Europe and
the States need to be kept in the dark. If an Agency
or Six operative gets involved and someone finds out,
chances are Israel will put two and two together and
realize he's one of ours. If you get spotted, you—"

"—could be a private investigator acting on behalf of a grieving widow of one of the men who died in Gray Site."

"Yes."

I smiled. "Plus, I'm very good at what I do."

"Actually, we came to you because you're unemployed and available."

Alistair tapped a finger against the table. "Admiral Mason, Patrick, and I know this is a long shot."

"Long shot?" I couldn't stop myself from laughing. "The men who can give us answers are dead. The crime scene is in a hostile location and has been sanitized. The people who might have some idea what happened in there are the Israelis, but I can't go knocking on their door. And I've got less than two weeks to not only establish why the CIA officer turned on his colleagues, but also extrapolate from that concrete evidence that can link or not link Hamas to the murder of the Israeli ambassador."

Patrick's expression turned to what I termed his rattlesnake look. Poised, ready to strike. "You don't want the job?"

I needed the money—no doubt about that—and the nonrefundable third up front was thirty thousand pounds. That bought me fifteen months of rent for my home; or thirteen months and one week here in

Scotland. I could take the job, knowing I'd fail, and still be financially buoyant for the near future. But it wasn't just about money. I took pride in my work and didn't want to let Alistair and Patrick down. And who else could do this task if I didn't? I didn't know. Spies hate mixing with other spies. It puts us on duty and forces us to be people who sometimes we just don't want to be. That's why I was in Scotland—to get away from myself.

Alistair stared at me, his brilliant intellect weakened by the fact that he wore it on his sleeve. "You've always achieved."

"Over seventy operations." I thought about another sip of my beer, but the desire wasn't there. "You've told me they were all successful."

"But you think not?"

"Yes."

"Because of casualties along the way?"

I was silent.

"William, if the time has come for you"—Alistair gestured to the surroundings—"to be at peace, then Patrick and I will not stand in your way."

I looked out the window at the mountains, my beloved mountains. More to myself, I said, "I cross the border, head north, arrive here. But there's not much more *north* than this."

"To escape to?"

I returned my attention to my former bosses. "I'm fully aware I'm shrinking my world. I've seen too much of the real deal. It hurts."

"That's life."

"Not your life." I locked my gaze on Patrick, silently daring him to strike. "Not recently, anyway."

Patrick repeated, "You don't want the job?"

Perhaps one day I'll be like my former mentors: putting my faith in youth. Maybe not. Espionage ages individuals dramatically, first the mind, then the body. I know I'm wise beyond my years. Too wise. When I am older, I'm sure I'll recognize the same trait in younger men who have to do what I did. I couldn't be like my mentors and lie to them. "The job is impossible."

"Even for you?" Patrick's hand was still, his glass of whiskey motionless in midair as he stared at me with eyes that had many times looked at my father.

"Yes. For me, and for fucking everyone." I lowered my head. "I'm not that man anymore. Perhaps, never was. Others had a wrong view of me."

Alistair stood and pressed a finger against my chest. It wasn't aggressive, rather it was his way of thinking he could transfer strength into me. "You can solve this Beirut problem."

I moved away from him while washing my hands and saying, "I can't. I'd need to understand the CIA officer's mind at the time he killed the English, French, and Israeli men. I could get an interpretation of that via investigation, but it would be convenient and false. I don't *know* him."

"You do."

I stared at them, my gut instinct telling me I was about to be sucker punched.

Patrick said, "You know him better than most. The dead CIA officer who killed his three foreign colleagues was Roger Koenig."

"What?" I felt myself getting light-headed. Alistair gripped my arm as my feet grew unsteady. Patrick rushed to my side, knocking over his whiskey as he did so. I shouted, "Roger? That can't—"

"It can. It was." Patrick held my other arm. It must have taken both men all their strength to keep my big frame upright, as my legs began to buckle.

"My friend" was all I could mutter as I was guided to a chair.

My former bosses sat in silence for five minutes. They looked sad and didn't know what to say.

"How could this happen?" My head was in my hands.

"We don't know," replied Alistair. "Do you want to know?"

I stared at them. "Yes," I said. "I *have* to know."

Thirteen

The toddler had just learned to walk and did so while tossing his head back and laughing with glee and pride. Uncle Laith sat on a swing chair on the porch of a suburban house in the town of Wolf Trap, close to Langley, Virginia. While sipping a beer, he was watching the boy playing on the front lawn. Laith Dia wasn't the boy's uncle or any relative whatsoever, but he was family of sorts to the child's mother, Suzy Parks, because they'd both served together in Task Force S—the highly secretive joint CIA-MI6 unit used by the West to combat the most complex and toughest threats. The section was now closed down. Its co-heads, Alistair from MI6 and Patrick from the CIA, were redeployed; Laith's paramilitary colleague Roger Koenig was dead; the unit's prime field operative, Will Cochrane, was out of a job; Suzy had chosen to leave the Agency and devote time to her child and husband; and Laith had resigned from the Agency and signed up for the National Guard, where he got shouted at and treated like some dumb cannon fodder because no one in the Guard knew he was a former Airborne Ranger, Delta Force soldier, and incredibly capable CIA paramilitary operative. He'd wanted to become invisible. Retire into a pale shadow of his previous life. The National Guard gave him that.

Alistair, Patrick, Will, Suzy, Roger, and Laith were the only people who'd permanently comprised Task Force S. Aside from Cochrane, all had been handpicked due to their expertise and experience. Cochrane was different. He'd had to endure MI6's twelve-month-long Spartan Program before he was permitted to be the section's top agent. No one understood how he hadn't died on the program, because it was designed to destroy body and mind, and had done so to numerous previous applicants to the course. Even though he'd graduated from Ranger and Delta training, Laith knew he'd never have been able to complete Spartan. Still, though he had the biggest heart, Laith was a very tough man. As boring and perfunctory as the National Guard was, it kept him moving. And he believed that overt and covert soldiering was all there was to him.

That wasn't strictly correct. Will Cochrane had often described Laith as a man who was, in mind and body, like Othello: a noble man, deep voiced, his huge frame coated by a marble-smooth ebony skin. It was an apt comparison, because at school Laith had eschewed the numerous opportunities to be a football quarterback in favor of acting in the drama class—something that in later years came in very handy for his intelligence work.

Laith was a heavy smoker, yet could run marathons in respectable times. And he could bench-press weights that would make a bodybuilder blush with envy. But he was a modest man, with a southern drawl, a razor-sharp mind, and a wicked sense of humor.

"Little man," he said while cracking open another can of beer, "your legs will give you freedom. But this isn't where it ends. One day your dick will get bigger, and for a while you'll think it's a mighty fine thing. It isn't. Trust me—I've had three marriages, all failed. Women take your dick and at first think it's a good thing. Then they blame it for everything. My advice to you is, keep it in your pants."

"That's enough, Laith." Suzy sat on the chair next to him and handed him a homemade muffin.

Laith took a bite from it. "Jeez, woman. You cook this in a furnace?" It was rock hard.

"Andrew does most of the cooking at home." She shrugged. "He's a rocket scientist. He understands the science behind baking and stuff. I'm not good like that."

But when she'd worked at the CIA, she was the Agency's best analyst. Her ability to remember and process vast amounts of data was coupled with an ability to stay awake for days. "Andrew's given me a cookbook. I'm trying to learn, but I guess I need to apply myself better."

"If you want to."

"That's the trouble." She grabbed Laith's can of beer and took a swig, then handed it back. "How are your kids?"

"Good. As far as I can tell."

"Your ex still being a bitch?"

Laith sighed. "I don't like to think of her that way. She has her reasons, I guess—new guy in the house and all. But they're my girls as well. I just want to be there for them. Teach them stuff. Wish she'd let me see them more often." Laith glanced at Suzy. "Do yourself a favor. Don't get divorced. It sucks when kids are in the equation."

Suzy looked at her only child. She was lucky to have him at the age of forty. "You're great with kids. Hang on in there. Camp on your daughters' doorstep if necessary. Ignore the bitch and her latest boyfriend."

Laith laughed; it was almost a bellow. "I thought you girls never broke ranks and spoke ill of each other."

"Then you don't know women. In any case, I'm a parent now. Gives you a different perspective."

Quietly, Laith responded, "I hear you on that."

"Are you going to Roger's funeral?"

"Damn right." Laith drained his beer.

Suzy asked, "Will you be wearing one of your army uniforms? I . . . don't know much about army stuff." Suzy was hesitant to mention Roger's death because Laith had worked so closely with him and they'd often faced death together.

Laith placed the empty beer can by his feet. "I hadn't thought about uniforms. But . . . I don't think so. I never knew Roger when he was in the military. When we worked together, most times we were wearing jeans, boots, and jackets. Sometimes suits."

"Then wear a suit. You can't turn up to a funeral in jeans. His wife would . . ."

"Yeah, I get it." Laith was silent for a few seconds. "What the hell was Roger thinking in Beirut? Turning his gun on the others? Just doesn't make sense. I . . ." He stopped talking because his voice was starting to waver.

Suzy placed her hand over his. "Whatever the reason, he's gone. We can't change the past."

Emotion and anger welled inside Laith, though it was not directed at Suzy. "Roger hauled me out of more shit storms than I can remember."

"And you did the same for him." Suzy rubbed his hand. "You going to be okay?"

Laith cleared his throat. "I want my friend back. But I know I ain't going to get that. So, I want the way I knew him back. Don't want him to be a murderer, or some guy who turned crazy. That's not the guy I knew. That *wasn't* Roger, full stop."

Suzy got to her feet. "Wanna stay for dinner? Andrew's going to be back any time now. And he can cook."

Laith breathed in deeply to compose himself. "Nah, but thanks. Just wanted to see you're okay."

"Out of the section?"

"Yeah, out of the section. And, you know, since Roger's death."

Suzy picked up her son and said to him, "That's enough walking for today, my adventurer. Say good-bye to Uncle Laith."

Laith made the boy giggle by holding out his hand and then withdrawing it and making a funny face. "Stay safe, wanderer, and remember what I said about your dick."

Suzy looked sternly at her former colleague. Her expression softened. "I worry about Will. They made him into something on the Spartan Program. How's he going to survive on the outside?"

Fourteen

When I first met Roger Koenig, I probably appeared aloof to him. Then again, he came across that way to me. Some people disparagingly and crudely describe such encounters between men as pissing contests. I don't think of them that way, certainly not in my line of work. Instead, they have real purpose: establish whether the man before you is a weak link; ascertain whether he has the strength of character to do the job under tremendous stress; forget what he says he is on paper and decide whether one day he is likely to make a mistake and you will die as a result.

But most men who work at the sharp end tend to yearn for more than that from their colleagues. Once the box has been ticked that they can do the job, we want what everyone else wants: friendship, banter, laughter, emotion, and companionship. Roger and I were no exception. We worked hard together, no doubt. He was the senior paramilitary officer in the joint CIA-MI6 task force I worked for before the unit was shut down. While I was running around the world being a spy, he'd watch over me; many times he'd stepped in and got me on my feet after someone or many persons had knocked me over. In that way, I thought of him as my big brother. A quiet type who'd nod at me as I dusted myself off, with an expression in his eyes that said he'd been where I was and the only way to learn from the experience was to keep going.

But in time there was more to our relationship than work. We often shared a drink together; he invited me to his home in Virginia, where his wife would tell me to pretend to be a zombie and chase after their twin sons in the yard while she cooked us dinner—an experience she knew I was uncomfortable with at first, but one that made her and Roger laugh; and sometimes he would make me a cup of Assam tea and sit next to me in silence.

He was a very decent man, the only man I'd worked with whom I could call friend. And Alistair had told me in Scotland that Roger had recently been to Iran and done something incredibly special for me. I couldn't understand how someone like that could murder three foreign allies. But I had to find out. I owed him that and so much more.

The issues I faced were significant. Every case I've worked as an intelligence officer has started with at least one piece of information that I've been able to use as a hook. These hooks have ranged from the obvious, such as a man wishing to defect and spill the beans, to tiny scraps of information that have given me a chink of hope from which I created a cavern of opportunity. I've targeted and successfully recruited an Iranian colonel based on the hook that his teenage daughter had taken to wearing tight tops; identified and caught a traitor because he'd started smoking again; got a London-based Russian diplomat to work for me after I learned that his credit card had been declined at a clothing store; and thwarted an assassination attempt against the pope because the would-be assassin was ashamed of his addiction to porn. Like men working abattoirs, a spy's day at work involves putting hooks into people.

But I had no hooks in this case.

Only questions and the need for key data.

My train car was empty save for a young woman who was sitting opposite me. Earlier the car had been full, but nearly everyone had alighted at the last stop. I wondered if the woman wanted to move to one of the numerous empty seats so that she could have extra space. Perhaps she was conflicted, because to move would appear rude. Either way, she'd have to make a decision, because the next stop was London and that was two hours away.

With every mile we traveled farther south, the outside countryside became tamer and less contoured. I decided I couldn't look at it anymore, grabbed my newspaper off the table in front of me, and immediately tossed it back down because I'd read it cover to cover twice.

"We should have flown," the Englishwoman on the other side of the table said. Her tone was educated.

I looked at her and smiled. It was nice of her to speak to me; no doubt she was also seeking any distraction she could get. She was a brunette, in her late twenties, with striking sapphire-colored eyes, and was wearing jeans and a sweater. "We most certainly should."

Normally I did fly, but I'd been watching my pennies and had secured a supersaver return train ticket at a fraction of the price it would have cost me to purchase a plane ticket. It was now ironic that I was traveling so cheaply, given that I was now carrying a brown envelope stuffed with Alistair's cash.

"After London, do you have farther to travel?"

I sighed. "Regrettably not. London's my home."

"Regrettably?"

"I think I'm getting too old for the city." I thought about the nineteenth-century American novelist Herman Melville's observation that there are two places in the world where men can most effectively disappear: the city of London and the South Seas. Melville was right, and that was why I still lived in the capital.

"You don't look that old." Her pure white skin blushed ever so slightly.

"Well, give it time." I didn't want her to be embarrassed. "I'm desperate for a coffee. Fancy one? On me."

When I returned five minutes later with two coffees I'd purchased from the buffet car, she was once again composed. I sat down while saying, "My name's Will."

"Mary." She offered her hand to shake. Her fingers were bare.

I shook it. "What about you? Live in London?"

"I live *and* work in London. I tried commuting in for a year once, but hated the commute more than living in the city. So I moved back. It's the only reason anyone lives in London."

Not for retired Major Mountjoy, I thought. He lives in London so he can be close to the queen, because the former guardsman still thinks he needs to protect her. "Been north of the border?"

She blew over the surface of her coffee. "Edinburgh. My boss sent me there last night. Some paperwork needed sorting."

"I hope your boss is grateful. That's a long round trip. He *should* have put you on a plane."

Mary laughed, glanced at me while taking a sip of her coffee, then quickly averted her gaze.

I said, "If you like, maybe we could meet for a drink sometime. I mean . . . if you're single."

She looked momentarily confused and didn't respond.

I was disappointed. Because though spies don't like mixing with other spies, the most highly attuned of us can spot another from a mile off. And that's why I'd just asked Mary out on a date. She hadn't expected that. But I'd expected her nonverbal response. "He sent you."

She frowned, but I could see she knew all was lost.

"Patrick. Or Alistair. But I'm betting Patrick."

"What are you talking . . ." She drummed her fingers on the table and looked away. "It would have been nice."

"To go for a drink?"

She nodded and I saw a trace of emotion on her face. "When did you know?"

"I'm afraid to say, straight away."

"Really?"

"Really."

Mary, or whatever her real name was, said, "It was Patrick." She reached into her handbag and withdrew an A4 envelope. "The data you need." She handed it to me. "Patrick said you wanted it urgently."

"When I next see Patrick, I'll tell him that it came as a great surprise to me."

"Please don't patronize. You saw through me." Her voice was trembling. She walked to another car.

I felt low as I opened the envelope and began reading the contents inside.

There wasn't much to read: a few details about Roger Koenig, statements from all of the Agency officers who'd had to force entry into Gray Site, and a grid reference giving the precise location of the complex. My heart sank. This scant data was all Patrick could get his hands on. The chances of its being helpful to me were zero.

Dickie had stories to tell—standing next to his broken-down tank in the Middle East while an Iraqi soldier tried to kill him; previously serving in the SAS and countering communist insurgents in Oman; growing long hair and a handlebar mustache to be an undercover state-sponsored hit man in 1970s IRA-ridden Ireland; and single-handedly storming an Argentinian machine gun post in the Falkland Islands. His stories were headline-grabbing tales.

But I was equally intrigued by the tales my two other neighbors had told me about themselves. Among those tales, David the mortician had once started using a scalpel to try to make a dead man's face look better, but had stopped when the man screamed. Phoebe had once made a skimpy dress out of candy to officiate over the pretentious opening of her London art gallery's latest show, only for the confectionery to melt under the heat of the gallery's spot lamps and for her to be rushed to the hospital with minor burns and major embarrassment.

They'd only been dating for the last few months, and made for the most unlikely couple. David liked jazz and cooking, had a flabby physique, and wore scruffy clothes. Phoebe was into provocative fashion, any alcoholic drink with bubbles, and Chinese takeout, and her ideal night out was ringside at a middleweight boxing match. But somehow they worked. David calmed Phoebe's excesses; Phoebe showed David that there's more to life than death.

Today they were in my apartment. They often popped up to see me after I returned from my travels. On this occasion David wanted to know whether I'd brought him back a salmon to poach, and Phoebe wanted to know if I'd met a nice Scottish lass who could move in with me and she could be best friends with. They were nonchalant when I disappointed them on both fronts, because I'd told them that not all was bad news. I'd secured temporary work overseas, political advisory work for an NGO charity, I lied. I added the truth that I'd be leaving tonight.

David took this as a signal to go to my kitchen and start preparing me sandwiches and other snacks for my journey. I swear, in another life David must have been a farmer's wife and mother of six children who spent most of her waking hours ensuring her family was well fed.

His girlfriend remained with me in my living room. Though she's not my type, I love Phoebe—she is the epitome of a good-time girl who doesn't give a hoot about anything remotely serious. And heavens above, she's all woman and shows it. Sometimes I don't know where to put my eyes when in her presence. Today was such an occasion. She was wearing the tiniest red figure-hugging dress and platforms, and her long black hair flowed down her naked back. All tits and ass, Dickie Mountjoy often inappropriately said of her, though, like me, he had a genuine soft spot for her because she had a heart of gold and could stand her ground against anyone.

"Darling." Her eyes were penetrating and she struck a sexy pose. "While you're away, I want you to put some serious thought into how you're going to find a wife. When you get back, I'm expecting you to put those plans into action."

"How?" I asked, feeling cornered. All Phoebe needed was a riding crop to finish off the image of a dominatrix.

"You're a spy, for God's sake. Identify someone you like, target her, make her do things she doesn't want to do."

"Like marry me?"

"Yes."

"That doesn't sound terribly romantic."

Phoebe leaned forward in her low-cut dress and rested her elbows on my sofa. I wished she hadn't. "Take her out to dinner and—"

"Just be myself?"

Phoebe pretended to look shocked. "Don't be ridiculous. You'll never find a wife if you do that."

"You're not helping, Phoebe." I wanted David back in here.

Phoebe winked at me. "You've had female acquaintances in the past."

"Most of them were killed."

"Next time, be nicer."

"I don't mean killed by me!"

"I know, naughty boy." She stood; I was relieved. Then she placed one leg forward, revealing the top of her stocking, and all relief abated. "Perhaps you're a lost cause."

Long ago, I'd come to the same conclusion.

She grabbed my hand, her expression now earnest. "Where are you really going?"

I said nothing for five seconds. "You'll keep an eye on the major? His club's being refurbished, so . . ."

"We'll look after Dickie." She squeezed my fingers. "Who's going to look after you?"

"I can take care of myself."

"When you're working, yes. But when you're not?"

I shrugged. "I can take care of myself then, as well."

"I know. And that's your problem."

Thirty-six hundred miles away, Admiral Tobias Mason summoned Mae Bäcklund and Rob Tanner into his oak-paneled office in the Pentagon. As they walked in, Tanner was twirling his pen around his fingers as if he were a majorette. The admiral, sitting behind his large, leather-topped wooden desk, had allowed himself the informality of working without his suit jacket, but otherwise he was dressed sharp: crisp white French-cuffed shirt, silk tie fixed in place with a Windsor knot, immaculately pressed navy blue suit trousers, and black shoes that were polished to the standards of parade grounds.

His employees sat in armchairs. As ever, Mae Bäcklund looked respectful of her boss. Rob Tanner did not.

The admiral stated, "This evening, I will be dining with the First Lady."

"She has the hots for you?" asked Tanner.

"She does not. The First Lady has invited me to dinner with six other ladies, all of whom have transcended glass ceilings to become corporate CEOs, captains of industry, political power players."

Bäcklund frowned. "Why did she ask you to come?"

"Perhaps to show them that an old dog can learn new tricks. I'm there to impart the navy's latest strategy to attract more female talent into its ranks." Mason checked his watch. "The point of mentioning the aforementioned appointment is that I don't have much time right now. So, bullet points, please." The admiral looked at Bäcklund. "What have your sources in the Agency told you about Patrick and Cochrane?"

Twenty-four hours ago he'd tasked Tanner and Bäcklund to find out if Cochrane and Patrick were up for the job.

Bäcklund replied, "Patrick joined the CIA after a short service commission in the infantry. Prior to that, he graduated from MIT. Thirty-six years in the Agency. Overseas postings to Tehran, Beijing, Moscow, Damascus, London, and Paris."

"Plum postings," Mason mused. "He's on the fast track."

"Well, yeah. Sort of. He's a director, though that's kept quiet; not many in the Agency know what he does or his rank."

"They've given him seniority, but he won't reach the top?"

"Exactly. No doubt he's an excellent operator, but he doesn't tolerate fools. Playing politics—internally or externally—isn't his thing. That said, the Agency knows his strengths. A few years back, it gave him control over a joint U.S.-U.K. task force." Bäcklund looked momentarily annoyed. "My sources couldn't give me any details about the force, beyond that it was recently shut down, and Cochrane was its lead field operative."

Mason decided the CIA officer was a rule breaker, someone who'd do whatever it took to get the job done, even if in doing so he forestalled any chance of further promotion. This increased Mason's respect for the man. He turned his attention to Tanner. "Cochrane?"

Tanner stopped spinning his pen. "Grew up in the States. Father was American and worked for the CIA; mother was English. Both are dead. One sister who's a couple of years older than him. She's a lawyer, doesn't have much contact with her brother. He joined the French Foreign Legion when he was seventeen and served in its parachute regiment before being selected for Special Forces. When he left, he went to England. Four years at Cambridge University. Graduated with a double first-class degree. Was talent-spotted by one of his professors who put him forward for selection into MI6."

"And?"

Tanner shrugged. "Aside from knowing that he worked for the joint task force, that's pretty much all I could get on him. Although, there's a rumor that on joining Six, he was handpicked to go on a twelve-month program. Only him. Others before him had failed. The course was designed to push his mind and body to their limits and way beyond. He passed." Tanner held a hand up. "But I stress that's only a rumor. I know you like hard facts."

That wasn't strictly true. Admiral Mason also reveled in possibilities. "What's his status in MI6 now?"

"There isn't one. He was told to leave four months ago."

"Interesting." Mason stood and grabbed his jacket. "I can't afford to be complacent. Almost certainly, the first thing Cochrane is going to do is travel to the States to speak with the dead CIA officer's wife. He may even be this side of the pond by now. I want one of you to liaise with Patrick's office and tell him that when Cochrane's in town, I need to meet with him."

Fifteen

The farmhouse, in a rural area of southern Lebanon near Rmaich, was being observed by eight Israelis who'd crossed the border in the dead of night. Two of them were highly trained Mossad officers, the remainder Special Forces. They'd parachuted into Lebanon and walked fifteen miles, wearing head scarves and Bedouin clothes, underneath which they wore military uniforms and had assault rifles strapped to their bodies.

They'd been in position for three hours, their Arab disguises discarded until needed for their return journey, spread out and lying on the ground in places that gave them sight of the isolated property from all angles. All of them had night-vision binoculars and were using them to watch the place. Two vehicles were parked outside the house; six men were inside. Beyond the farmstead was rolling countryside that contained Roman ruins and not much else. The warm air was filled with the sounds of insects, the volume intensifying as the night wore on.

The senior of the two Mossad officers was in charge tonight, because this was an intelligence-led operation and he had to be certain they were observing the right men. It was his idea to come here in person, rather than using a heavy-handed long-distance strike wherein they wouldn't know for sure if they'd neutralized the correct target. But, as a result, the risks to him and his men were obvious.

He checked his watch. Three hours until sunrise. They were running out of time because they needed to extract themselves under cover of darkness and reach a stealth helicopter that would whisk them back over the border into Israel. Glancing at some of the soldiers nearest to him, he knew there was nothing more he could do now than trust them to do their job. He hated that reality, because his whole career had required him to trust no one else to get things right. Spies, he'd long ago decided, were borderline obsessive-compulsive-disorder types. They had to be. Getting the tiniest detail wrong could result in your death. Whether it was OCD or meticulous attention to detail, a spy survived not by his wits, but by assuming others would mess up if the task in hand was delegated to them. Now, the Mossad officer had to watch others go to work and finish what he'd initiated.

He spoke into his radio. "One more minute of watching the place. Providing all remains quiet, after that we move." He stared through his binoculars, the night-vision equipment giving his surroundings the look of the rudimentary 1980s computer games he'd played as a kid. Nothing suggested that the occupants of the farmstead were aware of being watched. But he kept looking for anything that suggested they were agitated. It was vital that he knew their state of mind, because they were experienced murderers. "Everyone good to go?"

His team members responded in the affirmative.

"Remember, no head shots. Okay. On my command: three, two, one. Go!"

The men leapt to their feet and ran silently toward the farmhouse from all sides of the property, their rifles held high and ready to fire. There were two doors into the building. Four men moved in a crouch position alongside a wall toward one of the entrances; on the other side of the building, the others did the same.

In a whisper, the Mossad officer said, "Breach."

Two Special Forces soldiers used breaching hammers to force open the two doors. Behind them other men tossed in stun grenades. All then rushed into the building. What followed happened too fast for the occupants to do anything in response. Four of them were staggering on their feet, their hands clasping their ringing ears, and they were immediately shot in the chest. The remaining two were sitting at a table, still disoriented as they tried to reach their pistols. They were knocked off their chairs as bullets slammed into their upper bodies.

The two Mossad officers stayed with the dead bodies as the rest of the team searched the house. They relayed their location and findings in turn.

"Stairs clear."

"Room one clear."

"Corridor clear."

"Kitchen clear."

"Room two clear."

"Room three clear."

"House clear."

The Special Forces team immediately went back outside and set up a protective perimeter.

The senior Mossad officer took out photos that had been shot three months ago from a distance by covert Israeli cameras. He crouched by the two dead men at the table and examined their faces, comparing them to the photos. He glanced at his Mossad colleague, who nodded. Standing, the senior officer placed the photos in his jacket pocket and withdrew his cell phone.

He called his boss in Tel Aviv. "No doubt about it: correct targets neutralized."

The dead men at the table were two high-ranking Hamas leaders. Code-named Stradivarius and Stravinsky, they were the men the Gray Site team had intended to eavesdrop on to find out what happened in Paris. The sole purpose of today's Israeli assault had been to neutralize two very dangerous men who Israel was convinced had ordered the assassination of its ambassador. But, in successfully conducting the assault, Israel had killed two men who would not only have been able to provide evidence about the assassination, but also information about Thales.

Sixteen

Experienced spies are furtive and fearful travelers. But less experienced secret agents are emboldened by their initial experiences of first-or business-class air travel. They drink free champagne with panache; strike up conversations with nearby strangers because they want to flex their superior minds; and revel at traveling in the guise of someone else, as if they're attending a classy masquerade party.

It is not until you get dragged into an interrogation room upon landing in Beijing Airport that you realize you're not James Bond. If you're en route to Bangkok and your plane makes an unplanned emergency landing in Tehran, you have no panache when Revolutionary Guards inflict a mock execution on you. Fear and sometimes tears emerge when a gun is pointed at your head and you realize your life may end in Damascus, or Moscow, or Pyongyang.

If a spy survives all that, he becomes a nervous traveler, constantly aware of real danger. The passport he carries could be his death sentence, because it's not in his real name. It belongs to a false life that he must know backward—the schools he went to, the names of his teachers and friends, the jobs he's had, the places he's lived, the false reasons why this false man is entering a country he wants to spy on, and the minutiae such as the name of his hometown's church and the beers on draft in his local pub.

The immigration and security desks of transportation hubs are the places spies fear the most. Will the official behind the desk remember that the man pretending to be a businessman traveled here six months ago but with a different name? Did he go to the same school that the spy allegedly went to? Worse, did he once live on the same street that the spy claims to live on? These things happen.

I once got questioned by an official as I entered Luanda. The name on my passport was Paul Jones. When asked what I did for a living, I told him that I was an academic from the University of East Anglia's School of Development Studies. I added that I was traveling to his country to study the results of aid agencies' work to enhance the yields of farmers' crops. The official was a young native of Angola, and he beamed as he responded that last year he'd undertaken a Master of Arts at my school. Naturally, he started barraging me with questions about lecturers at the school and students who were still studying there. Through a combination of prior preparation and quick-thinking bullshit, I managed to get through the immigration desk without raising his suspicions.

But it could easily have gone the other way.

Despite entering what was technically a nonhostile country, as I approached one of the immigration desks in Washington, D.C.'s Dulles airport my stomach muscles tightened as they always did in these situations. I was traveling under the name Richard Oaks. I'd had to return all of my other alias passports to MI6, and the only reason I'd managed to keep this one was that Alistair had covered up that it was still in my possession.

An angry-looking official stared at me as I handed him my passport and the immigration questionnaire containing questions such as "Have you ever been a Nazi war criminal?" and "Have you ever been engaged in espionage activities?"

"What's the purpose of your visit?" He kept his eyes on mine.

I rubbed my face, as if I was tired after the overnight flight. "Research. I'm writing a book about political capitals around the world."

"You're a published author?"

"Not yet."

"What's your day job?"

"I'm a teacher."

The official handed me back my passport. "Okay." He looked at the next person in the queue, no longer interested in me.

After collecting my luggage and clearing customs, I entered the arrivals hall. Numerous men were lined up, holding placards marked with the names of passengers. Written on one of the placards was my false name. I introduced myself to the driver. Without saying a word, he led me to the parking lot nearest to the terminal. He placed my bag in the trunk of a black sedan, opened the rear passenger door, and gestured for me to get in. Patrick was sitting in the back.

The driver engaged gears and drove the car out of the lot.

Patrick was wearing a suit. "Good flight?"

"It was crap." I was wearing jeans, a hiking jacket, and mountain boots. "Cattle class."

Patrick laughed. "You better get used to it. Ninety-nine point nine percent of normal civilians travel that way."

"And abnormal civilians?"

"Same statistic, if they're no longer getting fancy travel on government or corporate expenses."

"Where are we going?" All Patrick had told me was that he'd meet me when I arrived.

"The fucking Pentagon" was his response. He said nothing else for the duration of the journey.

I've been to the Pentagon twice, and on both occasions I felt that its vast pentagonal shape resembled a 1960s NASA installation. Inside it is an endless series of offices, conference rooms, operations centers, smaller arterial routes, and around its circumference a vast corridor.

It was close to 9 A.M. when we stopped in one of the Pentagon's parking lots. I could see legions of men and women exiting their cars and heading toward the building. I thought of them as worker bees, all homogenized into the singular purpose of protecting a queen bee who wasn't here but instead lived in the White House.

Patrick said, "Come with me."

We joined the worker bees on foot, me looking out of place in my casual attire, the bees all wearing coats to protect them from a fine rain. We approached the reception desk.

Patrick gave one of the guards his name, pointed at me, and said, "He's got an appointment with Admiral Tobias Mason."

Ah, that's why I'm here, I thought. The admiral wanted to check me out, see if I was up to the task of investigating Gray Site and giving America just cause to prevent or support war in the Middle East.

The guard told me to hand over all my ID and my cell phone. I gave him my false documents. Together with my cell, they were sealed in a plastic bag. I was told to collect them when I left the building.

Patrick gestured to the bag. "Good to see you're carrying your phone again. I want you to be contactable day and night. I've got another driver who's going to take me to Langley. My driver will wait for you, take you wherever you're staying in D.C." He held out his hand.

"You're not coming with me?"

He shook his head. "Mason wants to see you alone." We shook hands as Patrick added, "And I won't see you again until you've finished your job. Good luck." He walked out of the building.

Another guard guided me through the labyrinth for twenty minutes before stopping by a door. He said, "This is you. I'll come back and get you when you're done."

I knocked on the door and entered.

A man, quite small, immaculately dressed in a suit, in his mid-fifties, I estimated, rose from behind a large wooden desk and walked quickly to me. "Mr. Cochrane. Admiral Mason." He shook hands and gestured for me to sit in a part of the oak-paneled room that contained comfortable chairs and a coffee table. After pressing a button on an intercom and saying, "He's here. Make sure we're not disturbed," he sat opposite me and rested one ankle on his thigh. His shoes were military-gloss standard. "When did you arrive?"

"I came here straight from the airport."

"Where are you staying?"

"The Mandarin Oriental hotel." I wanted Mason to cut the pleasantries.

He stared at me for a while before saying, "Cochrane's a good name."

"It's not the name I used to enter this building."

"I do hope not." His eyes were fixed on me, and they were flickering. No doubt, he was thinking fast. "Are you related to him?"

Him? I had to identify who he was referring to, otherwise I would fall at the first hurdle. Mason was a military man through and through. Navy, though. Patrick had told me that he'd had an excellent career at sea and had been singled out by the president to be his close and trusted adviser. Patrick hadn't told me much else about him. Within the space of two seconds, thoughts raced through my mind. Gray Site was Mason's idea. Clever. Creative initiative. Adviser? One the president would turn to when no one else had a clue what to do? The president had plenty of military experts around him. He didn't need another. Mason was therefore different. He was an independent thinker. A creative man. And that meant he was unconventional. But he loved the navy—his appearance, his demeanor, and the décor of the room showed that. He'd be fascinated with naval history. The combination of both traits meant he was referring to the nonconformist nineteenth-century British admiral Lord Thomas Cochrane.

I said, "My father was American, not Scottish."

Mason smiled. "So you've guessed who I'm talking about. And your ancestors?"

I shrugged. "I once tried to find out whether I was related to the admiral. But my family history is vague."

Mason interlinked his fingers, keeping his gaze on me. "Do you know much about Thomas Cochrane?"

I told Mason that I knew Cochrane was probably the first person to use other countries' flags to dupe French and Spanish men-of-war, and that he consistently defeated far larger and more heavily gunned vessels, such as the skirmish in which his small frigate famously encountered the Spanish destroyer *El Gamo.* He had once attended a fancy dress ball in Malta dressed as a common sailor, whereupon he'd got in an argument with a French officer and they'd ended up in a duel. Cochrane wounded the officer and later corresponded with the man, apologizing for the incident.

Mason looked satisfied. "You forgot to mention that he was dismissed from the Royal Navy."

"Years later, he was pardoned and reinstated with the rank of rear admiral."

"Correct." Mason's fingers were now together, their tips against his nose. "Do you hope to be reinstated into MI6 at some point?"

I hadn't anticipated the question. "No."

"Why?"

"Because I'm a liability."

"That's what they've told you?"

"That's what I am."

"You lack confidence in your abilities?"

"No. I'm liable to do things that make my former employer nervous. Ergo, I'm a liability."

"Ergo, you're like your forefather."

"If indeed Admiral Cochrane *was* my forefather."

Mason poured a glass of water. "The possibility of a family connection is irrelevant; the comparison of personalities is not." He pushed the glass across the table toward me. "Do you expect me to ask you questions about how you will investigate Gray Site?"

"I don't know. But if you do ask, I won't answer."

"Why?"

"You task me. I set to work. But my methods must be my own business. I gain nothing from sharing my investigation with you."

"You gain everything from doing so. You must report your findings to Patrick and me on a daily basis. SMS's, calls from your cell or pay phones—we don't care. But we must be regularly apprised of your progress. Or failings . . ."

"I trust Patrick."

"And he trusts you, otherwise you wouldn't be here today." Mason's expression was cold. "But you don't know whether to trust me?"

"I don't know you."

"Then what better way for us to get fully acquainted than by working together. Only Patrick and me. Don't share anything you find with anyone else. There are too many unknown variables in certain quarters to take the risk of broadening the number of people who have access to your work."

I studied him. Did I trust Mason? It was difficult to know. Clearly, he held his cards close to his chest. But the key element here was Patrick. So many times, I'd trusted Patrick with my life and he'd never let me down. Plus, he was one of the canniest senior spies I knew. If Patrick got one whiff that Mason was playing a game, he'd be all over the admiral like a rash. "Okay. I agree. I'll make contact with Patrick at least once a day; even if I've nothing to report."

"Good," Mason said. "It is quite possible the Israelis, or at least elements within Mossad, may kill you if they find out what you're doing. They want this war."

"And you? What do you want?"

The admiral's expression changed. Quietly he replied, "I want the truth." His voice strengthened when he said, "You *set to work*. And you don't tell anyone, apart from Patrick and me, what you're doing until it's over. Is that understood?"

"That's fine by me." It was. "I do have one question for you. The reference to Thales, in the CIA officer's Gray Site telegram. Does the code name mean anything to you?"

The admiral shook his head. "I've pursued that line of inquiry with the Agency, NSA, and a number of non-U.S. allies. So has Patrick. It means nothing to any of us."

"Can we get to the Hamas leaders Stravinsky and Stradivarius? Maybe extract them for enhanced interrogation? Anything they can tell us about Thales will help me."

Mason momentarily closed his eyes. "The Israelis have advised us that Stravinsky and Stradivarius will never trouble the world again. An Israeli team killed them last night."

"What?!"

Mason opened his eyes and shrugged. "Look at it from their perspective. They're convinced the men were involved in the death of a highly respected Israeli diplomat."

"Or they killed them so they could kill the truth."

Mason withdrew a leather-bound notepad, placed reading glasses on, and studied notes he'd earlier written. "You were in the French Foreign Legion. An unusual choice of military unit for a man who should have known that the Legion has never been a romantic escape."

"Who said I was a romantic?"

"Why did you join?"

Because I killed four criminals with a kitchen knife and needed to get out of the States fast. "I craved adventure. Much like you did when you ran away to sea." I smiled.

"You know my background?"

"Yes."

Mason carried on reading. "GCP Special Forces; seconded to DGSE black ops units. I'd have understood if you'd sought your *adventure* within a British or American unit, given your dual citizenship of those countries." He looked at me, his expression somewhat superior. "And yet you seemed to have no problem doing another country's dirty work."

I shrugged. "The French haven't been our enemy since your beloved Thomas Cochrane was at war. Times have changed, Admiral."

"The principal of loyalty hasn't." He tapped his notepad. "After the Legion, how did you settle in to life at Cambridge University?"

The truth was I'd struggled. It was hard being around normal people after five tough years in the military. "Just fine."

"Really?"

I could see Mason wasn't buying my answer. "I enjoyed the chance to sleep until late morning."

"And then MI6. Why do you think British intelligence singled you out for special training?"

"*Special* training? Who told you I received that?"

"It's just a rumor I heard about you. Is it true?"

I shrugged.

"Let me put it this way—if such a training program existed, why would they choose you to go on it?"

"Maybe they'd do so because they wanted to kill me."

"Your flippancy is not appropriate, Mr. Cochrane."

"Neither is your assumption that it is perfectly reasonable to address me as if I were one of your junior lieutenants on board your ship." My expression and tone were now serious, my eyes locked on his. "If you want a foot soldier, then find one. I'm not that man."

Mason stared back at me, appearing to weigh his response. "Good. I don't need a foot soldier. I want someone who can operate under extreme duress. Alone. Your background says you can."

"You know much about what I've done in MI6?"

"Probably only five percent. The rest is barred to me. But that five percent is enough." He put his notepad away. "My question to you is, can this be done? Find out what made a man turn on his colleagues in Gray Site? Establish whether Hamas killed the Israeli ambassador?"

I hesitated. "It is . . ." I was searching for the right words.

"Yes?"

Involuntarily, I rubbed my chin, silently cursing the action because it betrayed doubt or the possibility that I was lying. I breathed in deeply and told him exactly what I thought. "I won't stop. You have my word on that. But this investigation is incredibly challenging. I've virtually nothing to go on."

Mason studied me silently for a while. "Roger

Koenig was more to you than just a former colleague, I've been told. He was a friend."

"Correct."

"Don't let his death cloud your judgment. I need you to be clearheaded."

"And I need *you* not to tell me how to think or act."

Mason held his ground. "I'm fully aware of the challenges. And whether you're prepared to take my advice or not, do understand that I'm putting my faith in you."

He deserved a better response from me this time, given that his intentions were sincere. "Roger had become a dear friend. I'm shocked by his death. But that won't stop me doing my job properly."

He stood. Our meeting was clearly over. "Keep the wind in your sails, but don't forget to look over your shoulder."

I shook his hand. "Did I pass?"

Mason looked solemn. "In less than two weeks, Israel will go to war. What you do between now and then will enable me to answer your question."

Tanner got into his car in the Pentagon parking lot, unlocked the glove compartment, and used his secret cell phone to call his contact. "The investigator's just met Mason and has left. I'll find out what I can from the admiral."

Seventeen

The drugs seemed stronger tonight. Safa felt like most of his brain had been put to sleep, but the small part of his mind still working was doing so at an optimal level.

His guardian explained to him it was like taking the boy's brain to the gym. One day we focus on the arms, the next the legs, the day after the abdomen and back. It was piecemeal reconstruction of the most important organ in the body. And when all parts of the mind were put back together again, the result would be not only full mental health, but also an acuteness of thought that was as accurate as a precision tool. The guardian had elaborated that it was about setting some neurons to work while allowing others to recuperate. Safa didn't understand what any of this meant but didn't care, because all that mattered was that his guardian was caring for him under expert medical advice.

His guardian had never worked for the United Nations, though when he was last in Gaza he had carried impeccable credentials that said he did. Nor was he receiving medical advice. The drugs he administered Safa were stolen; his techniques had been honed in situations that would make most people gag if they knew about them. But they didn't know. Nor did they know that the man in the dark study room called himself the code name Thales.

The guardian whispered, "Safa, can you feel the black?"

"The black?"

"The pitch darkness. No light."

Safa outstretched his hand. "It feels . . . empty."

"A void, perhaps? Endless nothing?"

"Yes, like space without planets and stars."

"A pointless space."

Safa frowned. "It just seems so silly. Something that shouldn't really exist, but is real and doesn't have anything in it."

"Ah, now you take us into the realms of quantum physics, mathematics, and philosophy."

"What do those words mean?"

"One day, maybe I will teach you their meaning."
The guardian placed his hand on Safa's shoulder. "Can you feel the weight of my hand?"

"Yes."

"How does it make you feel?"

"It makes me feel like . . . something has changed. Something is here."

"Excellent. The weight has meaning. Maybe it is telling you that even in voids things can exist."

"How can that be possible?"

"You've been in a void, a chasm between one place and another. Life and death, even. Yet, here you are." He lifted his hand. "You are thinking clearly for the first time in your life, are you not?"

"Yes, sir."

"You see things differently?"

"You've helped me with that."

"I have." The guardian picked up a flashlight. "Four mirrors. One is death that cannot be undone; it will never hold light. The second is angry tragedy, its light shines too strong and erratically; one day you will ease its pain and allow it to sleep forever. The third is you, a beacon of hope, a mighty good thing. And the fourth . . ."

"Gluttony, power, murder."

The guardian turned on the flashlight, shining its beam directly at the last mirror. "It is time to put a name to the fourth mirror."

The memory of the boy who'd run through the alleys of Jabalia holding a white piece of paper seemed comical as Safa reflected on it. He wished he'd met his guardian and received his help earlier. The man had empowered him, given him hope and courage and clarity of thinking. Perhaps Safa would have grown up to be ruler of Gaza, made wise decisions that put food and water on the table of every Palestinian family, invented disease-free toilet systems, constructed houses, made rivers gush through the land. These were the thoughts of a boy. A dreamer, some had once said. But he wasn't dreaming now. At least, he didn't think so. It was hard to tell.

He imagined himself in his homeland now. His father was by his side, pointing north and talking about Israeli grandparents and where they'd come from. He seemed distant, and his words were barely audible. Safa looked at his finger and followed its direction. "The fourth mirror is Israel. Gluttony, power, murder. Israel."

The guardian smiled.

Later that evening, when the boy was sleeping, the guardian's cell phone rang. A long-distance call.

"Do you have what I asked for?" The guardian spoke in his native English, his voice posh and precise.

"Yes." The caller talked for three minutes.

The guardian wrote notes on a piece of paper. "And the Israeli? Close colleagues? Family or friends of interest?"

The caller gave him details.

"Very interesting. Call with any further news. Don't let me down. I will take over from here."

He looked at his piece of paper. On it were details about an Israeli man, together with his address. Below those details, the guardian had written Will Cochrane's name, his alias of Richard Oaks, and the precise details of Oaks's passport and credit card.

He called one of his U.S.-based assets. After briefing him, he concluded, "I want four of you to take care of this. Don't let me down."

Eighteen

It was midevening as I left the Mandarin Oriental hotel to take a walk through D.C. I was wearing a suit in case I got hungry and wanted to eat in a better restaurant. But that wasn't the reason I was getting some air. I needed to clear my head.

I walked east across the city, with no particular destination in mind. My mind tried to extrapolate possibilities from the scant data I had on Gray Site. Trouble was, there was so little to go on that the task seemed futile. Getting to Beirut was a priority, but I needed more data before making that trip, and I was hoping to get that from three individuals who lived in the States. One of them might slap me, the second would be desperate to call the cops when I stood before him, and the third would be severely tempted to kill me on sight.

I crossed the Anacostia River and turned north—I had the loose idea that I'd do a circular walk and find another bridge to cross back over the river so I could return to the center of the city and my hotel. The area around me was built up, a mix of residential and commercial buildings. They barely registered as I continued walking, my hands in my pockets and my head low as thoughts whirled through my brain. I hated feeling this devoid of ideas and information. It was like being given a blank piece of paper and being told to identify an invisible image that had been drawn on it. No doubt police detectives felt the same when confronted by a murder scene that had no witnesses, no evident motive, no weapon, no suspects, and zero traces of the murderer's DNA. My task was harder than anything I'd done as an MI6 operative.

Despite the time of day and the fact that it was getting dark, people were still on the streets, laughing, and calling to each other. Cars were driving alongside me on Minnesota Avenue SE. I unfairly resented the presence of others; I just wanted to be alone. It seemed to me I'd stumbled upon an oasis when I spotted the Fort Dupont Park. I'd never been here before; didn't know it existed. But the wooded park looked quiet and inviting. Plus, a sign welcoming visitors to the 376-acre park said nothing about restrictive opening hours. I followed a footpath leading through wooded areas interspersed with open spaces of grassland and picnic areas.

The ambience was now calm, and I couldn't see anyone else in the park. But it didn't make one bit of difference to my state of mind and frustrations. In MI6, I could fail and still have the safety net of a job. Now my reputation and ability to secure future work rested solely on my success or otherwise in this job. In all probability, this would be my first *and* last freelance job. I feared that Mason, Patrick, and Alistair had placed their faith in a man who always thought he thrived working alone, whereas in truth he needed the option of institutional resources even if he rarely drew upon them. That thought changed the way I perceived myself. Perhaps understanding my fallibilities was an indication that I was becoming wiser. That didn't help me right now.

I was about to turn around and head back to my hotel when I heard a woman or girl scream.

I ran toward the sound, wondering if instead I'd heard the screech of an urban fox. It was much darker now, and the darkness was exaggerated by the density of the trees. I stopped when I saw a woman on the ground, lashing out with her arms and legs. A man was above her, trying to either rape her or steal something. I shouted, "Hey!" and ran straight toward the pair.

The assailant glanced at me, grabbed the woman's handbag, and sprinted away, off the footpath and into the woods.

I reached the woman. "Are you hurt?"

She shook her head, her demeanor disturbed but also displaying an element of defiance. "Damn mugger," she said as she got to her feet. "Hate them."

"Call the cops. Get out of the park and wait by the entrance, where people can see you." I ran after the thief, following his route into the trees and emerging into another picnic area clearing. That's where I saw them—three men coming at me fast. The man in the center looked like the thief. Was this a gang of thieves who worked the park? I had no idea. The men were wearing hoodies, but weren't kids. They were about thirty yards away. All were holding knives.

From behind, someone grabbed my arms and held me firm. I jerked my head back, connecting with his face. The man yelped and loosened his grip on me, sufficient for me to spin around and punch him in the throat. As he fell to the ground, I turned back to face the other three men and ran fast to the man on the left, who was ahead of the others. There was just enough light to see that he looked surprised as I got close enough for him to slash his knife toward my gut. I dodged the strike, grabbed his knife-wielding arm, and twisted it so that it was in a lock that would be excruciating for him, twisted it some more until he dropped the knife, got behind him, and placed my free arm around his throat.

The other two men stopped, five yards away from me.

I held the man right against my body while partially strangling him; his legs were thrashing against the ground as I slowly walked him backward. "I'll snap his neck if you come closer."

They were silent, both of them big men in their thirties who didn't look the part of desperate muggers. I glanced at the man who'd earlier grabbed me. He was lying on his back, trying to suck in air while clutching his throat. Maybe he'd live. I didn't know and didn't particularly care right now.

"I *will* kill him." I squeezed harder on my captive's throat. "Then I'll kill both of you." It was bluster, because I'd no idea if I could take on all the men. Plus, when knives are involved in a fight, rarely do things go according to plan. "Your friend needs medical attention. Urgent attention. I'm going to leave here. You don't follow me and no one gets hurt. You follow me—at least one of you will die. Probably more. Do we have a deal?"

The man who I'd seen attacking the woman glanced at his friend, then looked back at me. He nodded.

I jabbed my knee into the small of my captive's back, releasing my grip on him at the same time. He fell to the ground, writhing in agony. I turned and ran, listening for signs that I was being pursued by the robbers. But I heard nothing as I sped through the park, reached the footpath I'd taken earlier, and followed it to the entrance.

Minnesota Avenue SE was lit up with streetlamps, people were still on the streets, cars' headlights added further illumination. Breathing fast, I looked around to see if I'd been followed by the attackers and to try to spot the woman who'd been assaulted. Nothing. I wondered if she'd called the police and they'd taken her to safety. But if that were the case, other police would have entered the park. Or maybe she didn't want police involved because she had some connection to the robbers, they'd fallen out and a fight had ensued, and I turned up. But her attacker had grabbed her bag before he ran. Perhaps she wasn't thinking clearly and just wanted to go home. It would take a callous person to do that and leave me to my fate. This didn't make sense.

The paranoid spy in me did have one idea that made sense. I'd been followed from my hotel. That was the only way anyone could pin me down to the location of the park. The woman was part of the team who followed me. She posed as bait, her colleague and her enacting a fake crime, and he deliberately fled, hoping I would follow him into a trap.

That would mean the group weren't robbers. They had another agenda. The knives were there to kill me, but also to make my death look like the result of a robbery.

Maybe this *was* just me being paranoid. I walked back to central D.C.—this time conducting anti-surveillance drills in case I was being followed. My mind was now more confused than ever. But I was certain about one thing: when I got back to the Mandarin Oriental, I'd immediately gather my things, check out of the hotel, grab a cab, and ask the driver to take me to a motel outside central D.C. Somewhere no one could find me.

Nineteen

His location and convenience allowing, at seven o'clock most Saturday mornings a well-groomed English gentleman in his early sixties would take a constitutional through parts of Brittany's university city of Rennes. His route would be via the old quarter's cobbled streets and regal eighteenth-century half-timbered architecture that surrounded the weekly market sprawling with food, flowers, and vegetables. People who worked the Marché des Lices knew him well. He was Monsieur William de Guise, a Francophile due to heritage that he'd traced back to courtiers-turned-generals who'd followed their Norman king into battle against the Anglo-Saxons almost a thousand years ago.

Monsieur de Guise was neither tall nor short. He carried no excess fat, but neither was he skin and bones. He wore a ready smile and spoke softly, with the charming tone of someone who was concerned about his interlocutor's well-being. Sometimes he walked with a maple cane whose handle was polished smooth from years of use. His bespectacled eyes were of different colors—one blue, the other green—but that was the only unusual feature of a refined individual who was worthy in all respects to walk amid the civility and history that oozed from the walls of Rennes.

The fishmongers knew de Guise had a discerning palate. Tonight he'd be preparing soupe de poisson, his favorite seafood dish. The fishmongers marveled at his culinary sophistication, and after he left them, carrying his white plastic bag of newly purchased seafood, they argued with each other as to whether Monsieur de Guise should use fennel or turmeric or aniseed in his latest reinvention of a traditional French dish.

"Monsieur de Guise, mon beau!" the gushing flower seller, who had once stabbed her husband in the eye, called to de Guise as he walked away from the fish market.

De Guise approached her stall, which displayed the best sunflowers. He always responded in fluent French whenever anyone spoke to him during his walk. Depending upon who he was addressing, his accent would be guttural or smooth, provincial or Parisian. With the man-killing flower seller who had been acquitted due to a technicality, he used the voice of a kind gentleman of the provinces. "My lady. As ever, beauty stands behind beauty."

She placed one hand over her breasts and fluttered her eyelashes. Cynics might call it a cheap gesture. Monsieur de Guise was no cynic. He purchased some flowers and moved on.

The farmers' wives who hawked gnarled but tasty carrots and artichokes appreciated Monsieur de Guise's pennies though they were unreceptive to his charm, condemned as they were to a tiresome life of servitude to the soil alongside their impoverished husbands, who slept no more than four hours per night. As he purchased asparagus and root vegetables from them, he switched his character to one of bluntness and precision, because the wives lived their lives in weights and measures. But after his purchase, he still got a slight and involuntary smile from them as he lifted a melon to his nose and smelled it to see if it was ripe. He looked at them as he did so, a trace of humor and appreciation on his face. They looked back, proud, momentarily feminine.

Men and their wives sold live and dead flesh in the covered area of the market. The women were big, the men small but wiry. They nudged each other as de Guise approached their stalls, carrying his fish and flowers. This morning de Guise wore a cravat. Forever, he was a man who wore clothes befitting a scholar—expensive, rich in color and texture, classy and apt for his age. The sellers wore immaculate whites, because that's what good butchers do. If one speck of blood shows up, it proves a butcher to be clumsy and unclean.

De Guise stood before the killers who transformed chicken, sheep, and cattle into poultry, lamb, and beef. Now, they gave him a live and tethered cockerel to take home, slaughter, and boil. He put the cockerel in a bag alongside the other, which contained a huge spider crab that was barely alive but still moving and had the ability to snap a finger with its pincers. Two unlikely companions who faced death. De Guise walked with them to his home, wearing an easy smile.

Students recognized him on the cobbled street that was lined with ethnic cafés and restaurants. This quarter of Rennes was full of university students. Some were taught by Monsieur de Guise. They all knew he had a brilliant mind and was a man of taste who appreciated art but distilled it into numbers. Paintings and music, he would tell them in lectures, are mathematics. That was a callous stance, some of the more emboldened would retort. "No," the professor would conclude while smiling at them warmly. "Mathematics is the beat of our hearts. Even Mozart couldn't decipher the brilliance of his notes. So that is a task left to me."

His young scholars pointed at him while loitering outside a *bar-tabac,* some of them smoking in front of ruddy-faced adult men who laced their breakfast tea with rum before working for twelve hours. They whispered to each other, speculating what might be in their professor's twitching white bags. Monsieur de Guise smiled at them and continued onward.

He passed the grand entrance to the Jardin Botanique and entered the Thabor area of the city, a place that housed Rennes's most well-heeled and urbane people. Alongside colonnades, Thabor's rich classical buildings had cream facades, wooden exterior beams, and huge walled gardens. Monsieur de Guise's home was one of them.

Entering the house, he placed the trussed chicken on the center of his dining room table and the other items in his kitchen. De Guise had always lived alone in the three-story house because he had long ago realized that he'd never find love comparable to that which he had for his mathematics. It also enabled him to furnish his home as he wished. The walls were crammed with art from all over Europe, each room contained Greek and

Roman antiquities, and bookshelves supported obscure
journals, academic papers, and leather-bound volumes
about history and magic.

Magic was his secret passion.

He placed a big pan of water on the stove to boil,
picked up a cleaver, and approached the motionless
chicken. It was standing, bug eyed, its feet and wings
lashed in twine.

His cell phone rang. A U.S. number showed on its
screen. De Guise accepted the call and listened to a
man telling him that they'd failed to kill Will Cochrane
in Fort Dupont Park. He displayed no emotion when
he said, "How very disappointing. You and your
people are of no use to me now. I will use more expert
resources to complete the task."

De Guise grabbed the chicken by the neck, walked
back into the kitchen, and chopped its head off. The
water in the pan was boiling. He dropped the spider
crab into the bubbling liquid and ripped the feathers
off the chicken.

After washing blood off his hands, he entered his
study, sat at his writing desk, and withdrew expensive
stationery from a drawer. He also took out his notes
from the international call he'd received yesterday—
notes about Will Cochrane's identity and alias, and
details about an Israeli man and his address in Israel.

Using a fountain pen, he wrote on an envelope. Then he began writing on a sheet of paper.

Mr. Stein

We don't know each other, but we are in a momentary situation of overlapping mutual interest.

No doubt you must still be grieving the loss of your brother in Beirut. My condolences. For reasons unknown, he was murdered by the CIA officer serving alongside your brother. Not knowing why he was killed must make your grief all the more unbearable.

You should know that there are certain people in America who wish to besmirch your good brother's name. They wish to plant blame on him by falsely proving that your brother attempted to prevent coverage of a Hamas meeting at which the terrorists were to be discussing the prior assassination of your ambassador to France. They wish to cast doubt that Israel has legitimacy to take revenge against Hamas by engaging in total war with the organization. In the process, your brother's honor will be sacrificed.

They have deployed an individual to investigate what happened in the intelligence complex in Beirut. His real name is Will Cochrane, though he is traveling under the name Richard Oaks. His passport number and credit card details are written on the reverse of this letter.

Like your brother, I understand that you are a Mossad combatant. I imagine that you must be a resourceful man. I suspect you have the ability to track Mr. Cochrane and stop him from ruining your family name.

I too have reasons of my own to stop Mr. Cochrane conducting his task. I have a man at my disposal and am deploying him to hunt Cochrane down and neutralize him. He will be traveling from the west. You have the ability to travel from the east. Whoever reaches him first should have no hesitation in doing what must be done.

Yours sincerely
Thales

The guardian called out, "Safa. Dinner will be ready in one hour."

PART II

Twenty

Until it went badly wrong, fall in Virginia was a time of joy and freedom in my childhood. Every fall, my friends and I would lash ropes to oak trees and swing through their russet leaves to emerge over rivers, our bare feet skimming water; make rudimentary bows and arrows and run through forests of beach and hickory while pretending to be Cherokee Native Americans; fish for trout using corks as floats and bent pins as hooks; and camp under the stars. We could spend hours, days when we were teenagers, in the tree-covered hills and mountains, time frozen and without meaning, with a feeling that life would last forever. The light was always good, better than in summer, and especially so as the sun started to set and sent lashes of golden light over the ground, the aromas around us loamy and fresh, the screech of a red fox reaching our ears from over a mile away because the air was still and untainted.

I was sixteen when my mother told me she'd been too trusting to let me and my friends pursue our adventures in the nearby wilderness. Between sobs, she said that I was never to go back to the woods again. The other moms were in agreement, and one in particular could no longer bear to think about the outstanding natural beauty that surrounded her rural home. Her son—my best friend, Johnny Caine—had snapped his neck when he fell from one of our tree houses deep in the forest. My three other friends and I had been with him in the tree house when it happened, daring him to crawl along a high branch and collect the prize of a bag of cookies that I'd positioned at the end of the limb. When Johnny fell, it was as if God had gripped us with his enormous hand so that all we could do was watch. It seemed like minutes before Johnny hit the ground headfirst, but it was probably closer to four seconds.

When God released me, time sped up and tears ran down my face as I clambered to the ground. Johnny was dead, I knew that; his neck was at the wrong angle and his frozen expression was one of surprise. My friends and I panicked because this was something that belonged to the grown-up world, not our world.

I cried the whole time as I carried him in my arms for two miles. My arms throbbed. I was scared, we were all scared, and Johnny's head kept hitting my shoulder.

My arms were about to give up when we reached his parents' home. I laid him on the porch and wanted the world to end as I rang the doorbell. His dad opened the door, a decent man who ran the local library but had recently seen his fair share of death in the first Gulf War. He was silent as he looked at his son, then us. He shut the door behind him, almost certainly because Johnny's mom was inside, and walked to us. I expected him to strike me down. Instead, he placed a hand on my shoulder and whispered, "I need to know details, son. But I also need you to know that you did a good thing bringing him home. I'll take over now." He staggered a bit, muttered to himself, "God damn it, not yet," and lifted his boy. His grief lasted his lifetime, but at that moment he was in battle-torn Kuwait, holding a dead comrade, keeping it together, or at least trying to, under enemy fire.

Now, once again I was in the Virginia countryside, driving my rental car along a road that wound around a mountainside covered with poplar. I drove another mile before recognizing the driveway that I'd driven down before and the name of my destination.

The Traveler's Rest.

Previously, seeing the name of the property had always put a smile on my face because the woman of the house had chosen the name. It was her heartfelt message to her husband when he returned from overseas. But seeing the sign today made me want to vomit.

At the end of the driveway was an isolated house. I parked in front of it, making no effort to be quiet as I got out of the vehicle. I was in a suit: neat, formal, neutral, chosen with care. I rang the bell and it reminded me of when I'd done the same after bringing broken Johnny to his home. This place was similar—no other houses for miles, forest and undulating hills all around. The difference being, the home was in the midst of being repainted.

A woman answered. She was in her late forties, but looked older than when I'd last seen her because no doubt she'd been crying a lot of late. Her face was drawn, and I could tell she hadn't been eating properly. She was wearing track pants and sneakers; probably she was trying to kid herself she was healthy when in truth she was anything but.

Roger Koenig's wife let out an involuntary gasp, ran to me, burst into tears, and gripped me tight as she sobbed on my shoulder. Katy said, "It's so good to see you, Will. I didn't know if you'd be able to come."

"I had to."

We held each other for a few minutes before she led me into her living room.

It was just as I remembered it from my last visit. Walls were crammed with family photos, pictures of Roger smiling in his full-dress naval uniform while standing next to Katy in her wedding dress, other various shots of Roger in SEAL combat attire alongside gun-toting colleagues, framed school certificates belonging to their twin boys, a big old map of the world that took pride of place over the fireplace, and next to it a much smaller silk map that on one side had a detailed image of Iraq and on the reverse a message in Arabic saying that if anyone helped the owner of the map they would be rewarded in gold. Roger had worn that map under his vest while behind enemy lines.

The tastefully furnished room was usually immaculate, with only a few telltale signs that two eight-year-old boys lived in the house. But today it was cluttered, with used plates and cups on side tables.

Katy was clearly embarrassed. "If I'd known you were coming I'd have cleaned up."

"And if you'd done so I'd have been offended." I meant what I said. "This is your family home. You can make as much mess as you like. Where are the boys?"

"Playing in the backyard."

Looking out of a window, I could now see the twins. They weren't playing. Instead, they were staring at nothing while sitting side by side on swings. "How are they doing?"

"They're very quiet during the day. When they're in bed, I hear them talking to each other for a while. Then their tears start. I go to them each time it happens. Breaks my heart. Every night they ask me different questions. Was Daddy a hero? Why did the men from his job come here and search the house? Why did they look angry? Why did Daddy go away when he knew it was our birthdays next month?" Katy slumped into a chair. "Last night they asked me if their daddy had done something very bad."

I turned to her. "Where is he?"

"I buried him. Our nearest town." She pulled up one leg of her jogging pants to reveal her calf, which showed patches of stress-induced exzema. She scratched an area that was already raw. "We had a service. Family, of course. Some of Roger's, from Germany. That was so kind of them to come this far. They haven't got much cash. And some of his colleagues from the team and the Agency." She stopped scratching as she saw that I was looking at her. "It all happened so fast. I couldn't get hold of you."

Because I was fishing in Scotland and had turned my phone off. I felt like shit.

"You want a cup of tea?" she asked as she walked to the kitchen.

"That would be kind." I wondered if it would be rude of me to collect the dirty plates that had clearly been left in here after a family meal the night before, probably because Katy had broken her rule to eat at the table in order to distract the boys in front of a movie. Afterward, she didn't have the energy to clear up. To hell with it, I thought, and gathered up the plates.

I entered the kitchen, placed the stack of china onto a surface, ran a sink of hot water, and, without asking her permission, started washing the dishes. "The Agency's branding Roger as an officer who went rogue. Actually, it's saying he lost his mind. I don't like that assessment. I want to believe that Roger had another reason for killing his colleagues."

"Why . . ." Katy was trying not to cry again. "Why does everyone assume he shot the English, French, and Israeli guys first? Maybe they shot him. He retaliated in defense."

I hated what next came out of my mouth, even though it was the truth. "Your husband opened fire first."

Katy was visibly angry as she slammed a mug next to the kettle. "The other people who came here didn't give me details about the gunfight. Maybe they don't know for sure that Roger opened fire first."

I hesitated, wondering if I should tell her what I knew. She had to know, I decided. "Roger was shot in the head. Only the head. The three other men were shot in the chest and abdomen."

"Why are you telling me this?"

"The others were mortally wounded but stayed alive long enough to fire their guns at your husband. Roger died instantly. It would have been impossible for Roger to return fire after he'd been hit."

"Maybe they fired first and missed. Roger fired back and hit them. They returned fire and killed him."

I felt truly sorry for her as I said, "There were four men in a tiny room. All of them were highly trained marksmen. A blind man who'd never fired a gun before couldn't have missed hitting Roger somewhere on his body. These are the facts. They're not in dispute and can't be."

"But he called me from Beirut the day before he died!" Her hand was shaking as she sprinkled loose tea into a pot. "He said it was a little weird working with three other nationalities, but bizarrely they all jelled. Got along. Laughed together. Talked of inviting us wives to a barbecue once their job was over."

"Men who get along can still turn on each other if the need arises. Did he tell you what he was doing there? Beirut?"

"Oh, come on, Will."

Of course, she didn't know. Wasn't allowed to. But I wasn't bound by those rules anymore. "He was listening in on terrorists. Hamas. His work in Lebanon was vital."

"Enough to get him killed!" She put her head in her hands. "I just don't get it. How could he do this?"

"It's not the how but rather the why that we need to establish."

As she poured tea, she said, "What difference does it make? He's gone."

I stacked the last dish in the draining rack. "Ascertaining Roger's motive will explain everything."

She tried to lift a mug but had to put it back on the counter, for fear of spilling its contents. "We'll never know."

I placed my hand on hers. "I've been tasked to find out."

She stared at me, her expression quizzical. "But you're out of the task force."

"And that's why they want to use me to investigate what happened. I'm totally deniable."

Was there a momentary expression of hope on her face? It appeared so. But no doubt that was quickly replaced by hostility. "And what happens if you find out Roger went insane? Or worse, that he was corrupt?"

I embraced the woman who'd been so dear to me, whose heart was now torn to pieces. I whispered in her ear, "If I find out anything negative about Roger—*anything*—I will bury it. I promise."

I took the mugs of tea into the living room and we drank in silence, images of Roger watching over us. When I finished my tea, I said, "I'd like to speak to the twins. I've brought them something."

Katy nodded.

I walked into the backyard.

The boys were still on their swings, motionless and silent. Like their father, they had jet-black hair and cute dimples. Today, their eyes were bloodshot. "Hello, sir," they said in near unison. Their voices were grave and meek.

I got on my knees, my suit trousers quickly sodden from the dew on the grass, and held their hands. Quietly, I said, "No need to call me sir. Did you have breakfast?"

"Yes," said Billy.

"Mommy made us waffles," added Tom.

"And what did you have for dinner last night?" I asked.

"Mommy made us gravy, fries, vegetables, and steak."

I smiled. "In that order?"

They nodded, no smiles.

"That was a good meal. Your mommy loves you very much."

"Yes," they replied.

"And she will always love you. But she needs your help." I carefully squeezed their hands.

"How?" asked Tom.

My smile was still on my face. I dearly hoped it looked warm and reassuring to the boys. "Keep your rooms tidy. Help Mommy wash the dishes each evening. Do your homework. Remind her that you need a bath every two days. Tell her all the time that you love her."

Billy kicked his legs involuntarily. They hit my chest. "We love Mommy. We miss Daddy. We don't know what to do."

"I know." I shuffled closer to them and put my hands on their shoulders. "Your daddy was the bravest and kindest man on earth. He was sometimes scared, like you. But he overcame his fear every day. And that was his greatest strength."

I withdrew two things Roger had given me and I'd brought from my apartment in London. I placed one

186 · MATTHEW DUNN

of them in Billy's hands. "Your great-grandfather was given this for extreme bravery in battle. It is the Iron Cross, the best medal a German can get. Your daddy gave it to me after I saved his life."

Billy weighed the medal in his hand. "What battle did my great-grandfather fight in?"

"He was a paratrooper in the Second World War. He got this for his actions in the Battle of the Bulge."

"But Germans were bad then."

I pointed at the medal. "Not ones who got that. They were the best of us all. And now it's yours."

In Tom's hand, I placed another medal, this one the CIA's coveted and rare Intelligence Star, awarded to Roger after he single-handedly rescued an asset who was in severe danger of being executed in Tripoli. I'd acquired it after Roger and I got drunk in Berlin and he'd bet me the medal in exchange for me running naked down Kurfürstendamm, the city's famous shopping street, at 2 A.M. He handed me his medal at the end of the street and then ran with me, laughing because I was being pursued by cops. Roger never gave a damn about medals. Nor did I, for that matter—not that MI6 ever gave its officers medals; instead it liked to give peerages, and the queen was never going to give me one of them. But now I thought Roger's family medals had some poignancy.

I said to Tom, "Men who get those put their lives at risk to save America." As soon as the words exited my mouth, I silently cursed what I'd said.

But Tom held the medal high, watching it sparkle in the sunlight. "A piece of metal."

That was the sort of thing his dad would have said.

I replied, "It's not what it is. It's what it means. It's priceless and can't be bought in any shop in the world. It means your daddy was a hero." I stood. "These are your medals now. They require you to be brave."

They both started crying.

Billy said, shaking and red faced, "Medals are for grown-ups."

I stepped forward and pulled them to me. I'd been stupid. Bloody medals. What was I thinking? I decided I'd ask Katy if I could stay the night in her spare bedroom, cook her family a nice meal, and help her with getting the boys to bed.

Two days before he'd died at the Somme, the English poet and soldier W. N. Hodgson had written a poem containing the line "Make me a man, O Lord."

Perhaps I'd just tried to do that with the twins.

Dumb.

A catastrophe was soon to be unleashed in the Middle East, but right now I just had to make two boys remember they were only children.

Twenty-One

The seawalls in Israel's northwestern coastal city of Acre had been built by the Roman Catholic Church's Crusaders in the twelfth century and were subsequently reinforced between 1750 and 1799 by the Arab rulers of Acre—well enough to survive Napoleon's siege. On the walkway on top of the wall stood a handsome man of above-average height with the physique of an athlete. The man's blond hair was long enough to cover part of his face as the balmy Mediterranean wind caught its strands and blew them out of place. He was leaning against the wall, looking at the azure waters of the sea, wearing a shirt and slacks. Female passersby gave the man, who looked twenty-five but was ten years older, admiring glances. He ignored them and pushed his hands against the wall, feeling the solidity of the fortification, absorbing its nine-hundred-year history defending the old city against army after army of invaders. It felt impenetrable; there were no signs of it having weakened since his numerous trips here as a child to learn about his homeland's history, nor since he'd visited as an adult to conduct covert meetings.

Behind him, alfresco restaurants' waiters were preparing for lunch by laying tables; glasses clinked as they were set in place; chicken and freshly caught fish were being grilled in kitchens; and steaming rice was being infused with saffron, chili, and cardamom. Seagulls hovered nearby, squawking at each other while poised to dive and pick up any food scraps that might soon become available. The sea air felt fresh against the man's smooth, lightly tanned face. His blue eyes watched fishermen haul nets onto their boats while shouting at Jet Skiers to stay away from their vessels and get a life.

The man tried to gain a moment of solace away from his pain as he took in the sights, sounds, and smells of his favorite city. But this desire seemed a betrayal to the memory of his younger brother. As kids, they'd been best friends. As adults they had done everything together. Both went to Tel Aviv University, served three years in the Israeli Defense Forces, and—much to their father's disgust, because he wanted them to return to civilian lives and become academics—both subsequently joined Israel's top Special Forces unit, Sayeret Matkal, a unit that was directly modeled on Britain's SAS. They'd spent six years in Matkal until they both refused to call in an air strike while behind enemy lines in Gaza, because the intended strike was too close to a children's hospital. After they were court-martialed and thrown out of the unit, Mossad had snapped them up. The older brother remembered his younger sibling's delight that they were once again going to work together. And he remembered his brother's disappointment when he realized that serving in Mossad meant they might as well be working on different sides of the world.

The younger brother was put into the mainstream intelligence cadre, which meant the majority of his career would be spent operating out of overseas Israeli embassies. The older brother was singled out for something special. He was given extensive and unusual training in all aspects of espionage and paramilitary activities, made a full-time member of Mossad's assassination unit Kidon, and deployed deep cover to different hostile locations around the world. He and his brother barely saw each other.

It was only recently that the assassin found out his younger brother had been sent on an urgent short posting to Beirut. And only a few days ago that he learned of his death.

Michael Stein checked his watch. Because of the nature of his cover, he wasn't permitted to enter the Mossad headquarters in Tel Aviv. When he was in Israel, Michael and his Mossad handler would meet in places like this. And they'd always be places of Michael's choosing.

A man, one foot shorter than Michael and twenty years his senior, stood by his side. He was plump, bespectacled, and wearing an ill-fitting black suit. "Have your injuries healed from that thing you were doing in Mandalay?"

Michael nodded while keeping his eyes on the sea.

"I wasn't due to redeploy you for another three weeks. I thought you could do with the time off. Why the need for this meeting?"

The assassin gave his handler the letter he'd received in his apartment that morning. "Read it carefully, then give it back to me." Two minutes later, the single sheet was returned to his hand. "I don't know who Thales is, have never heard of Cochrane, and have no idea how Thales established where I live."

His handler replied, "The names mean nothing to me. But we'll have them checked."

With no warning, Michael started walking. His handler stayed by his side.

Both men were silent as Michael led them away from the seawall to an area that once contained the Templar fortress. They walked down steps to an entrance that had plaques outside proclaiming they were about to enter the Templar Tunnel. The tunnel had been discovered in 1994, and excavated so that it could be opened to the public. Over 350 yards long, carved in stone, the tunnel was used by the Knights Templar as a means to connect their fortress to the west and the port to the east. During the Crusades, men wearing chain mail and white tunics with red crosses would have walked along the tunnel using flames to light their route. Now, tourists used the tunnel, and it was tastefully illuminated by ground-level golden spot lamps.

But right now Michael and his handler were the only people in the tunnel. Nevertheless, they spoke in a near whisper as they walked along.

Michael said, "I want to find Cochrane."

His handler stopped, then had to resume walking because Michael didn't stop. "I can't allow you to!"

"I can't allow my brother to be made into a scapegoat because of what happened in Gray Site." Michael's voice remained calm as he added, "Whether this man Cochrane is on official or unofficial business, it appears to me that he's trying to cover the ass of the CIA officer who shot my brother. That's not going to happen."

"It is, if I tell you to!"

"Really?"

His handler looked unsettled; either the heat in the tunnel or being in Michael's presence was making him perspire. "You don't know Thales or what his game is. You could be walking into a trap."

"I don't think so. Thales has no reason to bring me in on this other than to neutralize Cochrane. And Cochrane has no reason to be investigating Gray Site unless he's trying to shift blame away from the CIA officer. I don't care or need to know who Thales is or his agenda. He may well want Cochrane dead for another reason. So what?" They were now in a part of the tunnel covered with a barrel dome. Michael imagined knights running along this stretch, torches in one hand, unsheathed swords in the other as they rushed to confront Saladin's encroaching forces. "All that matters to me is protecting my brother's name."

The handler gripped Michael's arm, and this time the action was sufficient to make Michael pause in his stride. "Suppose your brother *did* try to disrupt coverage of the Hamas meeting. Suppose the CIA officer was right to open fire on him. How will you feel if that turns out to be the case? If Cochrane finds evidence that your brother acted inappropriately?"

"Inappropriately?" Michael smiled, another vain attempt to make his sorrow thaw, and removed his colleague's hand. "I know my brother. He always acted appropriately."

The handler was imploring as he said, "Maybe your brother thought he was acting in our country's interests. He had doubt as to whether Hamas killed our ambassador. But he believed in our cause and desire to obliterate Hamas once and for all."

With contempt, Michael replied, "Is that what your pals in the Knesset think? My brother did his job as he saw fit and the truth be damned?"

"They're not my pals."

Michael continued walking. "I don't care about your politics. Or your war. I just want to kill any friends of my brother's murderer."

Michael's handler struggled to keep pace with his assassin's longer and more youthful limbs. "I need to deploy you soon back into the field."

"But not yet."

Exasperated, his handler asked, "What do you want from me?"

When they reached the end of the tunnel, Michael looked back down the barely illuminated channel. When it was built, the fortress had once been the last stand against the West's perception of what embodied savagery and sacrilegious union. Since that building had fallen, nothing much had changed, thought Michael. In conflict, the brave, ignorant, and fearful stand shoulder to shoulder to survive. There is no righteousness when confronting death, only an overriding desire to put the knife in the enemy before he puts the sword in you. Michael's brother might have fucked up. But at the end it didn't matter. He was fighting.

Michael looked at his handler. "We have Cochrane's false passport and credit card details. They can be tracked when he uses them. Have someone in headquarters do that for me and call or SMS me whenever Cochrane moves. I will take care of everything else."

His handler responded, "You killed too many people last time."

"I killed exactly enough."

"You must stop. It is not good for you."

"That's rich coming from the man who doesn't let me stop."

His handler momentarily lowered his gaze. "As ever—clean. No trail back to us."

Michael nodded. "No trail. But I promise you there'll be no *clean*. Cochrane will suffer."

Twenty-Two

Citizens of Rennes were correct to believe that William de Guise was a professor in one of their city's universities. And their conclusions were right that the Englishman was refined, with good manners and a breadth of knowledge that could captivate an audience. But they had no inkling that he was a criminal, nor that he'd previously served eighteen years in MI6 and had been tipped to one day be the organization's chief until unproven suspicion fell on him that he'd betrayed his country for a considerable sum of money.

That money was real, as it turned out, and had not only enabled him to purchase art and antiquities way beyond the budget of an academic, but had also given him the ability to set up a global network of assets.

Only a handful of his most trusted employees knew he used the name William de Guise. None of them knew it was false.

As de Guise sipped a coffee in a café in Mayenne, one of those trusted assets entered the premises and sat opposite him.

He was a rangy Englishman, forty-five years old, with brown hair, red sideburns, and a sinewy body. He looked stiff, yet he could go without sleep for days while covering hundreds of miles on foot. The man was a hunter, formerly a colonel in Her Majesty's Royal Dragoon Guards, and during his army career he had broken the world record for the longest confirmed sniper kill. He left the army after shooting one of his own men because the soldier owed him an unpaid gambling debt of five pounds and thirty-four pence.

De Guise dabbed his mouth with a napkin. "I want you to kill a man."

"You always do." Colonel Rowe had jaw muscles that tensed as he spoke, an authoritarian demeanor, and cold eyes that were unflinching and stoic. "Does he have abilities?"

"No man is bulletproof."

"Wounded animals can be painfully aggressive."

"Then don't wound him." De Guise stirred his coffee. "His name is Will Cochrane." He gave him the alias Cochrane was using. "Via his passport and credit card usage, I will help you know his movements. He's currently in America."

"Complications?"

De Guise smiled because Rowe's question was indicative of his focus and intellect. "Michael Stein. An Israeli assassin. I've triggered him to go after Cochrane."

"You doubt my abilities?"

De Guise tapped his spoon against his cup, his eyes fixed on his employee. "No. Stein will push Cochrane to you. I've done you a favor."

Colonel Rowe asked, "Is this related to the Israeli project?"

"It is, but that's all you need to know."

"I helped you get the boy out of Gaza. I thought that was all that needed to be done."

"Alongside what we did in Paris, it remains the key strategy, and I'm throwing all of my efforts into that. But killing Cochrane is insurance. Also, there's something else I want you to do. It will require you to travel to the States." The man who called himself Thales told Rowe what he had in mind. "You might think of it as bloodying Cochrane's nose before you track him down and kill him."

"Understood." Rowe repeated, "Cochrane's abilities?"

"My source says his abilities are superb. That must end."

"It will end. You know that."

William de Guise drained the last of his coffee. "I *do* know. Otherwise you wouldn't be sitting opposite me now."

Colonel Rowe nodded. Thales paid his employees handsomely if they did what he ordered. But Thales always judged them on their last task. Thankfully, Rowe's last mission had been successful. His bullet had struck the center of the heart of the Israeli ambassador in Paris.

Twenty-Three

Mae Bäcklund entered Admiral Mason's office. "You wanted to see me, sir."

Mason looked up from the piles of reports he was wading through. "I wanted to see both of you. Where's Tanner?"

Bäcklund checked her watch. "It's lunchtime, so I guess he's taking his run along the Potomac."

Mason made no effort to hide his irritation. "We don't have time to take breaks." He was silent for a moment before gesturing at the chair on the other side of his desk. "Still, it matters not."

"Is everything okay, Tobias?" Bäcklund blushed and darted a look at the door as she took her seat. "I'm sorry. *Admiral.*"

Mason reached across the desk and patted her hand. Quietly, he said, "In here we must stick to the rules."

Bäcklund understood that, but lately she'd rarely had moments alone with her godfather. "Are you okay? Eating well? Getting enough rest?"

Tobias smiled. "I'm fine, my dear. When this is over, perhaps you'd like to invite this old man over for dinner sometime."

"I'd love that." Bäcklund knew the admiral wasn't okay. He looked tired and drawn. But he thrived on his work, and in here that's all that mattered. She inhaled deeply and decided this was the moment she had to get something off her chest that had been bothering her for months. "Sir, I find it hard to work with Tanner. He's so . . . young, full of crap, says whatever he likes, and . . ."

"Has aspirations way above his station."

"I was going to say something like that, yes."

The admiral nodded. "I keep him on a leash."

"Are you sure? Because sometimes it doesn't look that way." She immediately regretted saying that. "I'm sorry. It's just that half the time I don't know what Tanner's doing."

"The key thing is that *all* of the time, I do."

Bäcklund frowned.

"Is something else the matter, Mae?"

She lowered her head. "I wonder if I'm worthy of my job."

"Because you're thoughtful and don't run around shooting off whatever thoughts enter your mind?"

Bäcklund nodded.

Mason leaned back in his chair. "I've always made a point of choosing the people around me with care. General Montgomery did precisely that in the Second World War—handpicked the brightest and the best young officers to work alongside him and make him look good. Montgomery's press was overrated. He was fallible and vain. But the people around him were world class. It worked for him and it works for me." Bäcklund was about to interrupt, but the admiral held up his hand. "Your maturity and restraint act as a useful counterweight to the impetuosity of youthful Tanner. Don't doubt yourself."

"Based on what you've just said, I could say the same about you."

Mason laughed. "Indeed you could!"

"What will become of you if you fail?"

"I'll move on to other things."

"Captain . . ." She gritted her teeth; the name she'd used was her most affectionate for Tobias because it had been Mason's rank when he'd stood by her father's grave, held her hand, and whispered to her that he'd make sure she was okay.

Mason could tell she was attempting to control her feelings. "My dear" was all he said, his tone compassionate.

Bäcklund composed herself. "What did you think of Cochrane?"

"My first impressions were good; but so were my first impressions of Gibraltar until I stepped onto its dry land."

Bäcklund laughed, grateful for the admiral's quip. "Will you be going to Capitol Hill today?"

"We've all been summoned to a meeting this afternoon. We're getting a briefing on Israel's military preparations near its northern border. Word is, Israel's not ready for an invasion yet, but it's making darn sure it will be very soon."

Part of Bäcklund wished the admiral didn't have to go there. She knew he hated being thrust into such political environments, and she preferred to recall the pleasure she saw on his face whenever she cooked for him or his armed Secret Service escorts would allow him to take a stroll with her somewhere private. She felt this way because she was protective of him and knew who he truly was. "Do you think Cochrane will find out what happened in Paris and Beirut?"

"I'm not optimistic."

"So why are you pinning your hopes on him?"

Many times, Mason had asked himself the same thing. "I want to do the right thing."

"Even if it produces shit?"

"Language, Miss Bäcklund!" Mason smiled, the expression in his eyes mischievous. "We must keep our decorum."

Bäcklund nodded, pretending to look serious. "Indeed we must, sir."

Mason's gaze drifted away from her until it settled on the window. "I'm in a win-win-lose situation."

Bäcklund tried to decipher what he meant. "You've made it clear that you're very uncomfortable with Israel going to war, with or without evidence that Hamas killed the Israeli ambassador. First win is Cochrane finds evidence it wasn't Hamas who conducted the assassination—that's going to force our president to tell Israel to back down."

"Correct."

"Second win is Cochrane comes back empty-handed—that still puts the White House in a difficult position, because it's going to have to decide whether to support Israel or not."

Mason nodded.

"But the lose scenario for you is that Cochrane gets proof that Hamas deserves to be obliterated."

"And that produces an unpredictable military escalation in the Middle East, plus sucks the U.S. into the"—Mason smiled, though he looked sad—"cluster fuck."

"Whatever happens won't be your fault."

"Fault and blame don't factor. What counts is out-come." Mason rose just as the quaint carriage clock on his desk chimed.

Bäcklund looked at the timepiece that had once belonged to her father. "Why did you want to see me and Tanner?"

Mason stared directly at her. "Cochrane will relay what he finds to Patrick in the CIA and me. He trusts us, and in turn that means there are three messengers who will tell it like it is. We speak the truth, however unpalatable. But when the message is passed on, who knows what will happen? Chinese whispers that will subtly corrupt the veracity of the message? Worse, an out-and-out distortion of the message as it makes its way to the top."

Bäcklund shook her head. "You *are* the top; or at least one step removed. There is no chain. You tell the truth to those who matter."

"Providing I'm in a position to do so."

Bäcklund felt her stomach wrench. "You're not saying what I think you're saying?"

Mason placed a hand on her shoulder. "Some people might want men like me and Patrick dead before we can open our mouths. If they're successful, I want you and Tanner to speak on my behalf. Become my mes-sengers. And make sure my bodyguards become your bodyguards while you do so."

Twenty-Four

This evening, my dear Safa, we are gentlemen about town." Monsieur de Guise gestured for the boy to sit at the restaurant table, not opposite him, but instead in a seat immediately to the professor's right. "You are dressed in fine silks that make you look like a young Arab emir. They give you refinement. They are a signal to others that you have wealth, a calm and cool head, and can deport yourself in style despite your surroundings more often than not being inhospitable." De Guisetook his seat and grabbed a napkin. "I am wearing clothes befitting my status, albeit self-appointed, of seigneur. I wear a cravat because I wish people to know that I have some degree of formality when on an outing, but eschew the less flamboyant attire of a standard tie. My suit and waistcoat are heavy and handcrafted; they are chosen with care to convey to others that I have self-respect and dignity, yet lack vanity. And I carry my cane as a sign of respect to the French soil I tread. My stick is a solid thing, and shows my compatriots that it is not just my shoes that I want to connect to our beloved land."

Safa had no idea what the monsieur was talking about. Nor did he know that his guardian was English. As far as he was aware, he was a Frenchman held in high regard by the people of Rennes, and had retired from the United Nations to pursue academia in one of the local universities. Not that he cared to understand Monsieur de Guise right now. He was too excited. He'd seen restaurants since he'd been in France, but this was the first time the professor had allowed him to go to one in person.

The restaurant was in Fougères, a town approximately twenty miles northeast of Rennes. A chauffeur had brought them here—Monsieur de Guise never drove—and the car and driver were waiting outside to take them home when they'd finished dining. It seemed to Safa that he *was* an emir. Even when he was a dreamer in Gaza, he could never have anticipated that one day he'd have an evening out like this.

"You take your napkin, quick—like this, two fingers only per hand, and place it on your lap."

Safa grinned as he followed the professor's instructions.

"We are now ready to peruse the menu." He placed a finger on Safa's leather-bound menu. "I will permit myself a glass of wine. You will have a carafe of water. But aside from those rules, you may eat what you wish. One dish from the starter menu, one from the main. Dig deep into your French sensibilities and choose wisely."

Never mind learning English; more often than not, Safa struggled to comprehend what Monsieur de Guise said in French. Still, he was hungry and got the gist of his guardian's instructions. "May I have mussels to start and duck for the main course?"

"You may indeed. Such a fine choice, so I, too, will have the same dishes." He caught the attention of a waiter and gave the man the order. "Safa, how would you like your duck cooked?"

Safa was confused. "I'd like it cooked."

"Of course. But rare, medium, or well done?"

The waiter interjected. "Monsieur. We only serve the dish pink at most; our chef prefers to present it red."

Safa squirmed. "Red? Does he mean with blood?"

De Guise looked at the waiter. "We'll have it well done."

"But Monsieur, that is not possible! Our chef refuses . . ."

The professor placed his hand on his cane. "Your chef will do what he's told."

The waiter huffed. "Then you don't know our chef."

De Guise pointed at Safa. "He comes from a part of the world where to eat meat that is anything less than well done would be imprudent. A hot sun breeds deadly bacteria that lie dormant in raw flesh and can only be killed by an oven or stove that cooks the meat through. This young man has survived by taking heed of his culture's caution when handling and treating carcasses. Are you telling me that you insist my charge changes his attitude about what he can and can't eat, just because your chef tells him to?"

The waiter looked unsure how to respond.

"Your chef is not the proprietor of this establishment. Correct?"

The waiter nodded.

"Then tell your proprietor that Monsieur de Guise dines at his restaurant this evening, and his guest would like duck that is served well done."

Two minutes later the waiter returned, his face flushed red. "Monsieur de Guise, if I'd known who you were, I'd—"

"I will have a glass of Muscadet Prestige de l'Hermitage 2009."

"We only sell it by the bottle, but . . . yes, yes, a glass."

"And the boy will have water."

They ate their meal in silence because the professor wanted Safa to appreciate every mouthful of his food. When they finished, de Guise ordered a calvados for himself and a sorbet for Safa. "I will administer your medication when we are home, but tonight we work without the aid of their properties. Tell me what you see."

Safa looked around. "I see a restaurant that is full. People. Men and women."

"Numbers, dear boy. Give me detail. How many tables? Ratio of men to women?"

Safa took a moment to count. "Twelve tables. Sixteen women. Fifteen men. Two men and one woman are dining alone. Five of the tables contain more than two people."

"Excellent. You've given me more detail than I asked for. That means you are thinking ahead and with an inquiring mind. Tell me about the woman who dines alone."

"You know her?"

"I've no idea who she is, nor have I ever seen her before. But let's see if we can establish some information about her."

Safa spooned mouthfuls of the sorbet into his mouth while staring at the woman. Her face was in profile and she had no idea she was being watched. "Maybe forty years old, it's hard to tell. She looks rich. Her hair is nice. Expensive jewelry."

"And why does she dine alone?"

"Perhaps she's just finished work, or . . ."

"Yes?"

"Or she was supposed to eat with someone, but that didn't happen for whatever reason."

"Someone? Male or female?"

Safa tried to get his mind to work faster. "Male, I think."

"Why?"

"The clothes she's wearing—they seem designed to make her look pretty."

"Very good, Safa, though women will often also wish to look their best when meeting female friends. In any case, you are wrong on every front."

Disappointment struck the boy. He wondered if he'd have done better with his drugs inside him.

De Guise took a sip of his calvados. "She is probably nearer to fifty-five, though she hides her age well. Once she was a wealthy lady, but times have been tougher on her financially in recent years. She deliberately chose to dine alone and most likely does so in this restaurant once a year and always on this date."

"How do you know that for sure?"

"I don't know that for sure, but it is a hypothesis which we can test once we are in possession of further data. Deductive reasoning is what criminologists call the process. But I like to think of it as storytelling. We tell ourselves a plausible story about someone. Over time, that story comes to seem more real, less real, or an out-and-out falsehood. But without the initial story we have nothing."

Safa smiled. "I like that. A story. And the information you gave me about her?"

De Guise rested his glass on the table. "She has taken great pains to conceal her real age. Too much makeup and hair that is colored are two of several indicators that betray that fact. But the hair is most telling. Though it has been dyed, the gray roots of her hair on the nape of her neck are visible. Either that means she has dyed her hair herself and has missed parts; or more likely she had it done at a salon and has yet to make an appointment to have it redyed. Perhaps she does not have the money to do so. The jewelry she's wearing is old. Most of it looks inherited. A woman who is currently wealthy would wear at least one recently purchased item of jewelry. She's drinking a glass of champagne. Strange to do that on her own. And her expression—she does not register the people around her. They mean nothing to her. She is not here to soak up the vibrant ambience of the bistro. Her thoughts are elsewhere. Most likely they are in a place of memories. You might think she looks sad. I think she looks bitter. I deduce she has lost something, and she commemorates that loss by coming here once a year."

"Her husband. He used to bring her here." Safa was starting to think faster. "He has died. Left her with little money. She is sad because she remembers him sitting opposite her at the table she's now sitting at."

"You are becoming a fine scholar." De Guise wagged his finger. "But the story must make sense. Why the bitter expression and why the champagne?"

The combination of the two made no sense to Safa. Monsieur de Guise had previously told him that champagne was a drink that happy people drank to make themselves even happier.

"Think, boy."

It came to Safa. "Divorce."

De Guise smiled. "Superb. But who divorced who?"

"She divorced him. That's why the champagne's there. She's celebrating."

"Precisely. Yet, the bitter expression: What does that represent?"

Though he had no experience of being in a relationship, Safa dug deep and recalled the numerous Greek tragedies and other books that the monsieur had made him read. "It is regret. She regrets what she once had with the man she once loved. Or she never loved him and regrets that she married the wrong man."

De Guise patted Safa on the shoulder. "Bravo, young man. My own opinion is that she did once love him. Why else make the effort to dress in refined clothes and come here? Perhaps this was their wedding anniversary, or this is the place where he proposed marriage to her. For the sake of our story, I'm going to add that she divorced her husband after she discovered that he'd squandered their money on gambling, or bad investments, or other women, or all of those things."

Safa giggled. "The story may be completely wrong."

"But it is more likely to be near the truth than otherwise. And without the story, what do we have?"

"Just a woman, sitting at a table."

"That's my boy, Safa." De Guise pulled out a timepiece from the breast pocket of his waistcoat. "Sadly, our evening is nearly at a close. But we have just enough time for one final task. Imagine that one of the men in this room is a murderer. He is a general in the Israeli Defense Forces, and is personally responsible for ensuring that rivers entering Gaza from Israel are dry of water."

Safa frowned.

"His actions, and the actions of the men under his command, have killed thousands of your compatriots, including your mother, father, and sister."

Safa felt like he was in the monsieur's study, in pitch dark save for one flashlight's beam striking the fourth mirror. He was light-headed. His mind was outside of his body, and that body wanted to smash the mirror so that the light had nothing to reflect off.

"The man I've described is not in this room. But I want you to imagine he is, and identify him."

Safa scrutinized the room. Men and women were still eating and drinking; most of them were talking, some laughing. All but one man seemed very unlikely to be murderers. Their expressions were too soft, their physiques did not suggest a life of soldiering, they seemed to have no cares in the world. But the man who looked different was one of the solitary diners. He had a strong physique and a serious expression yet one that displayed no signs of regret; he ate his meal carefully, cutting his meat into exact cubes. He was the general, the man who daily committed a holocaust.

"You see him?"

Safa nodded, and beads of sweat ran down his forehead.

"When confronted with a man like this, most people with your heritage would convince themselves to do nothing. They take the coward's route, telling themselves any excuse they can think of to walk away. If I kill this man, they might think, he will be replaced by another, so what's the point? Perhaps they may take a more holistic stand for inaction. I am a mere speck of dust, just the tiniest flake of skin drifting in the air, they reason. Amid the billions of people who reside on our planet, what difference can I make?"

Safa could hear his guardian's words clearly, though he kept his eyes on the solitary diner.

"Such thoughts are those of evil people, men and women who are just as bad as the bad man they face, because inaction allows evil to spread and become pervasive. They forget that even a small flake of skin can nestle between a man's teeth, rot them, and cause poisoned blood from his gums to course into his body and eat it away."

De Guise looked at Safa's hand. It was gripping the steak knife. His eyes were intense, and his face was now covered with perspiration as he continued to stare at the man who was eating alone. This was good.

"He is not that man, but he might as well be because everyone in this room—excluding you and me—lets him live while they gorge themselves on rich food. They don't care about your suffering. They could not give a damn that your family starved to death. They are just as evil as the Israeli soldiers who patrol the Gaza border."

Safa lifted the knife a few inches off his plate.

William de Guise placed his hand over Safa's and gently pushed it back down. "Today's lesson is complete. Tomorrow we will commence your English lessons. We have little time, but you've heard me speak the language a lot and you are a fast learner. You don't need many words. Just enough for you to move through an English city. Or, more likely, an American one."

Twenty-Five

The twin boys were pushing their food around their plates, but neither of them were making an effort to eat their favorite meal of chicken, fries, and home-grown vegetables. Their faces were pink from crying, their eyes bloodshot and puffy. Katy Koenig knew their physical symptoms were due to grief and that her sons were otherwise healthy. Nevertheless, she decided she'd get them checked out by a doctor in the next day or two. If nothing else, it would give her a purpose in her otherwise dreamlike days.

Since Roger had died, her days would have been considerably worse were it not for the boys. With them in her life, she had to get out of bed in the mornings and do stuff. Because her nearest neighbors were miles away and her closest friends lived in other states, people didn't pop by to check up on her. Without her kids, she'd probably waste away in bed.

"Come on, boys," she said in a tone that she wanted to sound sympathetic, but came out weary and exasperated. "Eat your dinner."

Billy cut through a carrot, his knife banging hard against the china plate. He was angry and made no attempt to lift the bite to his mouth.

Tom had positioned his vegetables in a circle, his fork hovering around and around above them. The action looked wrong, like that of an anguished soul who repeatedly rocks back and forth while cuddling himself.

"If you can manage three mouthfuls of your food, I'll get you some ice cream."

"No, thanks," replied Billy.

Tom shook his head.

"It's your favorite, strawberry."

"Don't want it."

"Full up." Billy looked across the room toward a picture of his dad in SEAL combat gear. "Daddy should have been a farmer."

"Yes." Katy's voice trembled. "Yes, he should have."

Colonel Rowe had been studying the remote house and its surroundings through binoculars for hours.

Nestled in a valley surrounded by hills, the dwelling seemed to him to be that of a man who needed a retreat from the sometimes savage outside world and the work that the owner had to do in it.

He was perched on the branch of a tree, just as he imagined his forefathers had done while on big-game hunts in Queen Victoria's India. Though back then they'd have been dressed very differently. His shoes, two sizes too big for him, had blue plastic covers, and he wore rubber surgeons' gloves that stretched to the elbows. Over his clothes he wore a head-to-toe white disposable paper jumpsuit—the type worn by police forensics teams and scientists entering contaminated zones. The house was about two hundred yards away and was quiet. But he knew it was occupied, because he'd seen the owner arrive home two hours ago. Then, it had been dusk. Now, the only source of light was a sickle moon.

It was Thales's idea for Rowe to be here. No doubt de Guise knew exactly what he was doing, though Rowe took no pleasure from the task in hand. Nor did he dislike it. He was ambivalent. Having Cochrane actually in his sights would be a wholly different experience.

Katy told her boys to get out of their bath, and helped them get dry and into their pajamas. Normally, bath time was a raucous and chaotic affair, with her kids splashing each other, giggles of delight, water on the bathroom floor, bubbles brimming over the bath's edge, and Roger or Katy trying not to break their necks as they skidded on the floor and yelled at their boys to clean up. But tonight, like this week's preceding nights, the twins had bathed in silence, the bathwater was as flat as a tranquil lake, and the waterproof toys in the adjacent box were untouched. Bath time was no longer fun for them. Tonight, Katy wondered if her children even knew they'd been in a bath.

"You want me to tell you a story?" she asked them after she tucked them into their beds. She looked at the shelves containing their favorite novels and tried to establish which of the tales didn't contain scenes of death. How odd, she realized, that in children's books at least one person always seemed to die.

She was relieved when her sons shook their heads. She kissed them good night and stared at them for a moment, recalling how she would normally cherish these moments before returning downstairs to drink a cup of coffee or glass of wine with her husband. Everything was different now.

Rowe decided it was time to get this over with, and jumped down from the branch. Walking to the house, he withdrew a knife with a long, razor-sharp blade. It was designed to fillet huge sport fish such as tuna and marlin—strong and sharp enough to slice through big swaths of flesh, yet nimble enough to circumvent bones and ensure every ounce of meat was separated from the skeleton. He had respect for the blade, but in general had distaste for knives. Though he had used them many times, he preferred his beloved hand-crafted rifles. In the right hands, they were so clean, so precise. But today de Guise had wanted a point to be made, so here Rowe was, gripping the weapon of Thales's choice.

Katy cleared away the dishes from the dining room table, scraping uneaten food into the trash. Perhaps they should get a dog, she thought. The dog could eat the leftover scraps. There'd be no waste to make Katy feel guilty. Maybe a dog would also be a welcome distraction for Billy and Tom. She knew she was kidding herself. Dogs, other pets, anything similar, would simply be a Band-Aid stuck over a gaping wound. She and her boys had no choice other than to walk the path of grief, a hellish journey that no one could help them with and with nothing that could alleviate their misery. Her boys had youth on their side. They'd reach the other side. She didn't know if she would. A lifetime of grief probably awaited her. Like widows of days gone by, she'd figuratively wear black until she was placed in a coffin.

As Rowe drew nearer to the house, he could hear a human voice. Perhaps it belonged to the owner who was speaking to someone on the phone, or maybe it was coming from a TV. He trod carefully as he reached the graveled driveway. A station wagon was parked here, the same one the homeowner had used two hours ago. He stuck the knife into each of the tires—it was as easy as piercing butter—and heard them rapidly deflate while he watched the house.

He walked around the house, ducking low whenever he reached windows, and carefully tried opening each door. Most of them were locked. One of them was not. That was a bonus, though he'd brought tools to force entry in case of need.

Very slowly, he turned the door handle and eased the door open inch by inch. He entered the house, paused to listen, and walked slowly down a carpeted hallway, making no sound. There was no human voice to be heard now, only the sound of running water and dishes banging against each other coming from a room at the end of the hallway. As he passed two other doorways, he glanced in them, saw no one, and continued.

———

Katy's whole body felt like lead as she washed the dishes. The symptoms were real, and yet she knew they were a result of her brain going into meltdown. Why did the mind fail in times like these? It seemed to serve no purpose other than to tell the body that it might as well curl into a ball and die. She lowered her head, weeping over the hopelessness of her circumstances; the tips of her hair dipped into the frothy sink water.

She thrust her hands angrily into the water and shook the stack of dishes. These feelings had to stop. Grief was one thing; allowing her mind and body to give in to it and let her children down was another thing altogether. She had to be strong for them. They needed that. Tomorrow would be a new beginning. She'd cook them a hearty breakfast, and no one would leave the table until the plates were empty. Then she'd take them for a hike in the countryside. She'd talk openly to Tom and Billy about their father, tell them good stories about him, make Roger become real again, no longer let his memory be one of pain.

Roger had to be remembered for who he was—not as a form who'd transformed into a void but as a loving father and husband who could still guide his family through life.

Yes. That's how it would be. For the first time since she'd learned of Roger's death, she smiled, though a tear trickled down her cheek. Utter sorrow and renewed purpose would be symbiotic companions for a while, she decided. That was fine. But at least now her body no longer felt like a dead weight. She'd sleep well tonight. In the morning, Mrs. Koenig and her sons would hold hands and walk.

Rowe moved into the living room, adjacent to the small kitchen. From one of the armchairs, he grabbed a small cushion and walked fast into the kitchen.

Where he found a woman by the sink.

She had her back to him.

Her name was Katy Koenig.

Rowe thrust the cushion onto her mouth, pulled her back to him so she was unable to escape, pressed harder on the cushion to suppress her muffled cries, and thrust his knife into her lower back. Her body immediately went limp. Rowe held her upright and stabbed her in her belly before slicing her windpipe.

He let the dead body slump to the ground, stood motionless, listening in case there were any other noises in the house. He couldn't hear anything, save a gentle wind rustling trees. After wiping the knife clean with the same towel Katy had been using to clean her dishes, he exited the kitchen and walked upstairs. All of the rooms were empty except for one that contained two sleeping boys.

He stood between the beds, looking at each boy. They were twins, perhaps seven or eight years old. Thales hadn't told Rowe that his victim was a mother. That didn't matter. The colonel had anticipated the possibility, given Katy Koenig's age. What did matter was what he did next. He was deep in thought for a while, then decided that he would leave the boys unharmed. Thales had told him to kill the mother. Rowe had done that. He was perfectly within his rights not to deviate from that instruction.

After walking downstairs and stepping out of the door he'd used to enter the house, Rowe hesitated. He didn't know how close the nearest neighbors were, though in his drive here he hadn't seen another house for miles around. The boys would probably sleep for another seven or eight hours. And when they came down for breakfast, they'd find their mother. Fully competent adults can freeze in such moments. Boys of the twins' age would fall apart. They could die out here. He decided to make an anonymous 911 call when he was sufficiently far away, telling emergency services that he knew two boys who had been abandoned by an irresponsible mother.

Twenty-Six

I was on the verge of throwing my rental car's GPS out of the window, because the woman's voice kept telling me she was recalculating. Her complete and utter uselessness had come at the worst possible time, because I was inside West Virginia's vast George Washington National Forest. Road signs were few and far between, and even though I'm a proficient map reader, a study of my map wasn't helping because whoever had made it had omitted certain useful data such as road names and numbers and topographical features. Had I a proper hiking or military map with grid references, I would have stood a good chance of pinpointing where I was.

I decided to pull over on the side of a deserted road and turn the GPS off to give the confused thing a rest. Forests and hills were all around me. I opened my cell phone and withdrew the SIM card that was in my false name, Richard Oaks. From the concealed lining under my pants' waistband, I extracted the sim card that was registered in my real name and inserted it into the phone. After a few seconds, the cell started beeping with SMS's welcoming me to Virginia's roaming services, plus other crap. But there was one voice message from my neighbor David. His voice sounded wobbly as he asked me to give him a call. I checked my watch. It was evening London time, so hopefully he'd be home from work unless his mortuary had called him back out because fresh bodies had arrived.

He answered on the third ring. "Will, thanks for calling."

"Everything okay? The major all right?"

David's words were rushed as he answered, "Yes, yes. He's fine. We're feeding him. It's . . ."

My heart sank. "Phoebe? What about Phoebe?"

"We're all okay. No accidents. Nothing like that. It's just, Phoebe . . ."

"Yes?" I could feel myself getting anxious, but tried not to sound that way for fear of upsetting Phoebe's boyfriend.

"She's lost her job, Will. The art gallery wasn't making enough money. She went to work this morning, and that's when they told her the news. She's in my apartment, in tears. I'm speaking to you from the stairwell so she can't hear me. She's devastated. Money. She doesn't know what to do because she's got no savings."

"Shit!"

"I wanted to speak to you, because I don't know what to do either. I'm desperate to help her, but I'm on a mortician's salary. It's peanuts, just enough to pay my rent and not much left over. I did think about offering her to move in with me, but . . . thing is, we've only recently started seeing each other. It would be forced. We're not ready for that commitment yet."

I agreed. "Have you told Dickie?"

"You think I should ask the major for some financial help? I know he's got money tucked away. I'm sure he'd be happy to at least help Phoebe out with her rent."

"No." I thought about the last time I saw Dickie and he offered me cash because he thought I might be broke and would need to move. I turned him down for the same reason I was about to tell David not to ask. "Dickie needs all the money he has. He's at an age where big medical bills might come his way, if his health fails and he can't get treatment quick enough on the NHS."

"Yes, yes." David sounded panicky. "You're absolutely right. But, what should I do? I just feel so terrible that I can't help Phoebe. I *should* be the one to help her. Jesus!"

I knew Phoebe had no family to turn to because nine years ago her hippie mother had divorced Phoebe's tabloid journalist dad, gone to Morocco, and shacked up with a man who claimed that he was a prince; since then Phoebe had rarely heard from her again. At the same time, Phoebe's father had been lured into a relationship with a woman half his age who told him she was an aspiring actress when in truth she was a burglar who one day ran off with his most valuable possessions. He'd turned to drink, though that ended late on a rainy evening when a number 15 red double-decker bus hit and killed him as he was exiting Ye Olde Cheshire Cheese pub on Fleet Street.

And Phoebe's arty friends used most of their money to buy coke to shove up their noses. They wouldn't give her a dime.

Phoebe had no one reliable to help her aside from David, the major, and me.

I had an idea. "Do you have any notion how much her monthly fixed costs are—rent, utility bills, council tax?"

"I can ask her, but all of our places in West Square are the same size. My monthly bills come to around two thousand quid. Same for you?"

"Sounds about right." It seemed surreal to be having this conversation as I was imagining the Edwardian surroundings of my home while sitting in such a wholly different environment. "Do me three favors."

"Sure."

"First: give Phoebe a cuddle, buy her Chinese take-out for dinner, and tell her she's loved. Second: tell her to dust off her résumé and send it to every art gallery north and south of the Thames."

"I'll do that."

"Third: SMS me your bank details."

"My bank details?"

"Yes."

"Why would I—?"

"Because today I'm going to do an electronic transfer of two thousand pounds to your account, and I'll keep it up until she gets a job."

"I didn't call you to ask for your money." David sounded emotional.

"Tell her it's your money you're giving her."

"Will, I can't."

"You can, because I'm sending the money to *you*, not Phoebe. What you do with it is your business."

"I'm going to repay you."

"It's a gift, so don't insult me."

David was momentarily silent. "I don't know what to say. I'm between a rock and a hard place."

"One day I might be there too. Maybe I'll come to you then."

"Please . . . please do. I'll send you my bank details in one minute. Where are you?"

"Angola. The work's boring but it pays well." We said our good-byes, and after we ended the call I stared out of the window. I didn't know what I was doing. At the moment I had money, but soon I could be broke. Forethought was always anathema to me when it came to cash. Maybe I was stupid.

But I couldn't help it. Phoebe was down on her luck.

After receiving David's bank details, I swapped SIM cards again and started up my GPS. The break seemed to have done the GPS's female robot some good. With authority, she told me I had to keep driving for one mile, where I'd reach my destination. I had no reason to trust her but did as she instructed. I drove the car off the road, felt it shudder as I put it in low gear over rough ground between trees, and brought it to a halt when I was satisfied it could not be seen from the road.

"You have arrived at your destination," said the automaton.

I got out of the car, moved through woods, and crouched on the crest of a hill. I was wearing the same suit I'd worn when visiting Mrs. Koenig. But a suit wasn't going to make a difference today.

I was hoping to meet a man whose family I'd killed.

Suits don't sway the outcome of such encounters.

In the valley below was a glistening lake, adjacent to which was a large home and three outhouses. They were the only buildings to be seen. Swallows flew above the lake, alternating between diving for bugs and swooping on a bat whose daytime sleep must have been unsettled. A stream fed into the lake from the tree-covered mountainside behind it. It was the kind of place me and Johnny would have fished as kids. I wished I could turn back the clock, put my arm around him, and tell him not to accept my challenge to crawl along the tree's branch. Life was different then.

I withdrew a pair of binoculars and scrutinized the place. A Russian man was limping with a stick between an outhouse and his home. He was middle aged, wore a beard and glasses to hide the disfigurement on one side of his face, but had vigor and purpose despite the fact that my bomb had damaged him and blown his wife and daughter to smithereens. That had happened four years ago in Moscow. The man I was watching had been driving, but stopped his car when his cell rang and he was warned about the bomb by one of his assets. He'd gotten out of the vehicle to rescue his family, but was too late and was thrown across the street as my bomb exploded. He'd tried to rescue his wife and daughter, but the flames in the car made it impossible.

If I'd known his family was in the car, I would have willingly swapped places with him. Ever since, I've wished I was the one who was disfigured and had a weak limb. Or even wished I was the one in the car who was blown to pieces.

The man approached a thirteen-year-old girl called Crystal, who had been born after his premarriage dalliance with an American diplomat. Until a year ago, he hadn't known she existed. When the girl's nonbiological American father was killed by her mother, who was given life imprisonment as a result, I'd put the girl's real Russian father and Crystal in touch with each other in return for the Russian agreeing to work as my agent, to betray his motherland and relocate to the States. No doubt he hated me.

He hugged the girl, pointed at a chicken coop, said something, and smiled as she ran to the chickens with a bucket in her hand. He entered his home; I walked down the escarpment. I wasn't armed and didn't want to be, because it seemed wrong to carry a weapon into the house of a man whose life I'd torn apart.

But I had to be careful of him. As well as being the victim of my assassination attempt, he was a former

Russian spymaster, one of the smartest adversaries I'd ever faced. His code name was Antaeus.

During my last mission for the CIA–MI6 task force, I had identified and caught the mole Antaeus was running in the CIA. That would have made him doubly pissed with me.

I knocked on his door, my heart pumping fast. I was more than a little anxious. His acute mind worried me. Also, though he knew what I looked like, we'd never met in person before. This was all unpredictable.

The door opened.

He was standing before me.

I felt sick looking at the scars on his face, the droopy eye, and the skin on his hand, stretched and unnatural. I'd done all of that, plus much more that wasn't visible. "Hello" was all I could say.

I wondered if he'd swing the stick he was holding at my head. Maybe I would let him.

He didn't. Just stared at me.

"May I come in? I mean you no harm or trouble."

He said nothing.

"May I come in?" I repeated.

He shook his head. "My home is a safe place for my daughter." His English was perfect and had only a trace of an accent. His eyes were intense. "It is no place for murderers, Mr. Cochrane."

I held my ground. "You are a murderer."

He placed his walking stick in front of him. "I am an amateur historian, a museum curator. I produce counterintuitive theses on prehistoric settlements to the Archaeological Institute of America in order to unsettle their received wisdom, and I am a good father. Your definition of me no longer applies. But it does to you."

"I wish that were untrue."

"Do you?"

"Yes. I've left the service, but . . ."

"You are still associated with your former employer." Antaeus glanced in the direction of his daughter. "I will gut you if you cause us any problems."

"I expected you'd say something like that."

He returned his attention to me. "You have guilt?"

I nodded.

"Why?"

"I blew up your family."

"You didn't know they were in my car."

"A bomb is still a bomb. I put it there."

Antaeus withdrew a cheroot from a 1940s-era tobacco tin. "Yes, you did." He opened his mouth for the cigar, and I could see half of his teeth were his own. "Now that Crystal is with me, I have a rule not to smoke in the house. I'm going to have some tobacco and take a walk along the lake." He lit his cigar and hobbled past me.

I watched him. He was tall, dressed in clothes from another era. He looked like an early-twentieth-century Arctic explorer. Recently I'd made him a father, and it looked like he was a good one. But that was only one layer of his personality and abilities. I reminded myself that this Machiavellian genius was once the most powerful and invisible man in the East.

I moved to his side. "Are there trout in your lake?"

Antaeus blew smoke. Though I've never been tempted to be a smoker, its aromatic smell was nice. "Yes. Rainbow."

"Do you fish for them?"

"I take a rowboat and use a sinking line with a nymph and two droppers."

"How do the fish fight?"

Antaeus stopped and turned toward the lake. "Like I've attacked them in their home. They fight angry."

I looked at the beautiful surroundings and thought, I'd like to live somewhere like this. It seemed so peaceful and quiet. "I'm truly sorry."

"You didn't come here to apologize, and that means you're insincere."

"I'm still allowed to apologize."

Antaeus momentarily looked at me, his expression one of contempt. "Women like diamonds, but only if presented to them correctly. You present your regret as if you've stolen it off the back of a truck."

I wished he hadn't said that.

Antaeus resumed walking along the shoreline.

As I kept pace, I felt effeminate in my attire, like Patrick and Alistair had looked when they'd visited me in Scotland. My polished shoes were soon waterlogged, as were the bottoms of my suit trousers. By contrast, Antaeus had galoshes and waterproof oilskin trousers. I said, "I gave you Crystal."

Antaeus flicked the stub of his cheroot into the lake. It sizzled, then sank. "You gave me what belonged to me. What do you have in your life?"

"Nothing."

"Is that correct?"

"It's what you want to hear."

"I don't want anything from you." Antaeus increased the pace.

He looked older than his years, his body in pain because of me. His mind and Crystal were all that were left, though I admired his efforts to keep his physique strong.

The Russian pointed his stick at Crystal. She was in the distance, near the house, rubbing her dirty hands on her clean white dress, feeding the chickens and talking to them. "Why did you make the effort to give me Crystal?"

"Like you said, I merely brought you what was yours."

"A thief who finds a wallet on the street rarely returns it to its owner."

I wondered if I should put my hand on Antaeus's arm, but imagined that if I did so his reaction might knock me off my feet. "I brought her to you to give you something I couldn't have."

"Peace?"

"Yes, peace. But also purpose."

Antaeus lit another cheroot. "You and I served someone else's purpose. We spied for our countries."

"You did bad things. So did I. Even if by accident."

"As you say, a bomb is still a bomb, and it seems you have primed many of them during your life."

I grabbed his sinewy arm, not caring about the implications. "I was different then."

"Really?" Antaeus glanced at my hand on his forearm. "Your actions say otherwise." He shook my hand free. "Don't try to build bridges."

"Why not?"

Antaeus did not respond.

Crystal was laughing and talking to the chickens, oblivious to me. "Thanks to you, she's safe and happy. A couple of days ago, I cooked for two eight-year-old boys. I can't think of anything you and I've done in our professional lives that can equal those achievements."

Antaeus stopped and turned toward me. "You think that is our bridge?"

"I don't know" was my honest answer. "There comes a time when doing becomes more important than thinking."

"And I am doing. Yes?"

"Yes."

A large rainbow trout jumped nearby. It put a smile on Antaeus's face, similar to the one I'd seen on Rory's face in the Scottish glens. His tone was different when he said, "The CIA has wrung me dry. I've no more secrets to tell. What you see now is me."

"Your archaeology. Your home. Your daughter."

Antaeus smiled as he continued to look at the ripples caused by the trout. It was a natural smile, contented. "I'm free of the secret world. Here, I've everything I need. I pity you."

"I'm glad."

"Why?"

"Because I need to know there is more to life than the shit we've been through."

Antaeus sat on a rock and kept his eyes on the lake. "You are lonely?"

"Regretful."

The spymaster shook his head. "Lonely." He picked up a flat stone and skimmed it across the placid water. It bounced seven times. "Maybe both, I concede."

I sat next to him. He probably didn't like that, but I didn't care because the view of the lake was too good to resist, plus, somehow I needed Antaeus to no longer see me as his enemy, given that I was trying to get help from him and he had once thought he was smarter than me. For years, he'd been the Moscow puppeteer who'd frequently attempted to thwart my efforts in the field. We were opponents. I was fed up with that. I liked that he'd put Crystal in a pretty white dress this morning and allowed her to get her hands, and the dress, dirty by feeding chickens and healthy outdoor playing.

"I *am* sorry," I said.

"You are," he replied. He was silent for a while, and looked to be deep in thought. In a quiet tone, he said, "The CIA doesn't have all my secrets."

"That's why I'm here."

"Of course." He picked up another stone. While rubbing mud off it, he said, "Spies crave secrets. You are a spy. A scavenger."

"A murderer, a thief, and a scavenger. Do you have any more labels for me?"

Antaeus kept his eyes on the lake. "Observations, not labels, Mr. Cochrane."

I stood and turned to him, my back to the lake. "Have you ever heard of a man who uses the code name Thales?"

Antaeus kept his eyes fixed on the vista as he asked, "How does it benefit me to respond to your question?"

"You'd be helping me."

"And why would I want to do that?"

I didn't know, but I wanted him to know how I felt. "Since you've been here, have any of your former colleagues in the SVR knocked on your door with a bottle of vodka in hand and wanted to get drunk with you and relive the good old days? Have your CIA interrogators ever patted you on the shoulder and said you were the best Russian source they'd ever run? When you go to your local town to buy groceries, do people come up to you and ask to shake your hand in recognition of your incredible service to America?"

Antaeus said nothing, and his eyes were still averted.

"Soldiers returning from the battlefield may carry their own demons, but they are visible and people publicly applaud their heroism. Nobody knows who we are, and nobody cares, not even our former employers. Maybe you'd help me simply because I'm just like you and have no one else to turn to."

Antaeus looked at me, his expression no longer angry. "Still trying to build bridges?"

"Has it worked?"

"No." He smiled. "But it was a nice try."

I had nothing left to say, and was desperate not to show my disappointment.

Evidently my efforts to hide my emotions had failed, because Antaeus said, "Don't be hard on yourself. You and I have too much history to find common ground." Again, he was silent for a while. Then he said, "Thales of Miletus was a pre-Socratic Greek philosopher and mathematician. He rejected mythology in favor of fact. In that regard, he was a pioneer of his time."

I knew this, but kept my mouth shut.

"I don't know the identity of the man who uses Thales as a code name."

Now I made no effort to hide my frustration. Of all the spies I knew, Antaeus was the one person who I'd hoped knew who Thales was. His vast intellect was enhanced by a photographic memory and a mind-set to make it his business to know everything he could about the secret world, even if it didn't benefit his immediate work.

Antaeus got to his feet and stared at Crystal. To my surprise, he said, "Maybe you are right about bridge building." He turned to me. "I will tell you two things. First, I strongly suspect the man you seek is similar to Thales of Miletus. He calculates. He's a mathematician. You might do well to assume that is his vocation. Second, a few years ago I ran an operation in Prague. It was logistically complex, involved numerous assets, and took me a year to set up. I thought it was my finest work. But it failed abysmally, and to this day I don't know why. I'd covered every angle, anticipated all possible outcomes, and had set in place counterinitiatives should anything go wrong. But somehow I missed something." He paused, and when he next spoke it sounded like he was talking to himself. "Or I missed nothing but was completely outsmarted." He stood before me and held out his hand.

I gripped it.

"I'm glad we had the chance to speak, Mr. Cochrane. There's been some meaning in what you've said." He began walking back to his house, and I walked with him. "Do you have far to travel?"

"A two-hour drive back to my hotel in D.C." This was true. And once in my room, I had to transform my appearance before my last appointment in the States.

Antaeus nodded. "I wish you luck. I can't be of any more help to you beyond telling you one thing. Two days after my Prague operation was ruined by a person or persons unknown, I received a handwritten note. All it said was, 'You were superb but I was better.' It was signed, Thales."

Twenty-Seven

It was early evening and Admiral Mason had been in his tiny apartment in Washington for exactly forty-three minutes. It had been enough time for him to debone a chicken breast, sauté it alongside shallots and garlic, add tomato sauce, and let it simmer while cooking wild rice and asparagus. He served the meal on a plate, making sure its presentation looked precise, placed the plate on a tray, and took his meal into the living room. He turned on his TV, using one hand to flick through channels while eating his meal with the other. He settled on CNN.

The report was on Israel's mobilization of military units near the country's northern border. A male British reporter, in open-neck shirt and slacks, was alternating between speaking to the camera and pointing at tanks behind him. He said that while there had been no official statement from Israel as to the reason for the military maneuvers, there was plausible speculation that they were linked to the assassination of Israel's ambassador to France. And given the positioning of Israel's army, if the speculation was correct, that meant Israel was blaming Lebanon or elements within Lebanon for the murder of its diplomat. The key issue, the reporter concluded with solemnity, was whether Israel was in defensive or offensive mode toward its neighbor.

That wasn't the key issue, thought Mason as he turned off his television. Everyone could tell that the sheer scale of Israel's military mobilization wasn't a defensive tactic. In his mind, the crucial question was whether Israel was doing the right thing.

He placed his tray of food to the side, no longer feeling hungry despite having eaten only a few mouthfuls. Cochrane's task was all that mattered to him. The former MI6 officer had struck him as highly capable and confident. But Mason had also spotted what he thought looked like a hint of doubt in the man's eyes. Did he think the task to find out what happened in Gray Site was beyond him? And even if he did succeed in that task, did he believe that it would be impossible to use that information to ascertain whether Hamas did kill the ambassador?

Mason wouldn't blame Cochrane if he did have such doubts. The odds of getting to the truth were beyond ridiculous. But there was another issue that was equally troubling for the admiral. What happened if Cochrane *did* get to the truth?

Twenty-Eight

The well-groomed Caucasian gentleman and Arab boy walked along cobbled streets in Rennes, shops and seventeenth-century houses on either side of them. A midmorning mist hung motionless at street level in the small city; a chill was in the air. But the weather hadn't deterred shop owners, street vendors, and shoppers from doing business. Lots of people were on the streets, wrapped up warm in coats and scarves, smiling, moving fast, talking, laughing. It was Saturday, a time to rest and enjoy life. People were communicating with strangers about their lunch and supper plans, the food they loved, and recommendations of fine wines. The banter and gossip made the city of universities thrive with purpose and unity. Many times, Monsieur de Guise had been amazed at the hardiness of the northern French. Most of them were small in stature; some of the elderly among them had physiques that were beyond repair due to childhood malnourishment; others, young and old, were beautiful and elegant, and though they all reflected the full spectrum of any society—dumb, clever, rich, poor, loyal, duplicitous, vain, self-effacing—they all shared a trait that intrigued de Guise. They could drink and eat all the things that doctors say people should not consume, yet most of them would die at exactly the same age as everyone else and with smiles on their faces.

Safa was carrying bags of newly purchased thick, expensive clothes. They were stylish and rich in color, chosen with care by de Guise, and when the boy had tried them on in front of the shop mirrors, de Guise had thought the young teenager had transformed himself into an aristocrat. Earlier, the boy's jet-black hair had been cut in Rennes's finest men's salon. His body, though willowy and not yet fully fit, wore the clothes with panache. His eyes gleamed and his newly polished and reconstructed teeth shone white when he smiled at passersby and showed off his cute dimples.

But Safa was still a boy, and the hours of being beautified had ultimately bored him. De Guise was attuned to that and needed to reward the child. "Galettes saucisses!" he exclaimed upon sighting a regular vendor of street food. "We must partake or cry hunger!"

"Galettes?"

"Grilled pork sausages wrapped in a cold crepe. Mustard is optional though preferable."

"Pork?"

"Pig."

"I know what pork is. My religion says . . ."

De Guise patted Safa on the shoulder. "A train of thought that is suited to the climate it emerged from. Pork is susceptible to go bad when it is placed near the equator. But here"—de Guise banged his cane on the street, his tone of voice proud and caring for his boy— "we eat nose to tail. Is that not right, Alfred?"

The seller of galettes saucisses, named Alfred, grinned. "Nose to tail, Monsieur de Guise. Always." He started preparing Safa's food. "You are the professor's child, yes?"

"Quoi, monsieur?"

"The new boy."

"I am not *new* to myself."

The seller—an amateur artist who'd made more money by selling fake reproductions of the greats than his own work—grinned. "You are not." He served up the street dish. "With my compliments, young man. No charge."

Monsieur de Guise objected. "You must be paid. Chantelle needs your money. She has a household to run."

Alfred disagreed. Looking at Safa, he said, "Today's lesson is gratis but not without benefit to me. As the astute professor notes, we eat an animal from nose to tail. Nothing goes to waste. You owe an animal that." He handed Safa the wrap. "My sausages are from parts of the animals you don't want to think about, but they taste delicious. Next time you walk through Rennes and are hungry, bring some cash and only come to me." He held out his hand to de Guise. "Do we have a deal, sir?"

"We do indeed." The professor shook the vendor's hand and walked onward with his boy. "Before we get home, we must buy some provisions from the market, and if you can withstand that final burden I will buy you a dessert of fresh fruit. How do you feel?"

Safa munched on his delicious food. "I feel different."

"That is as I hoped."

Twenty-Nine

Though Admiral Mason had wanted all resources to be made available to me, even he couldn't overcome the bureaucracy that plagues secret agencies. The CIA had told him categorically that a civilian, as I now was, could not have access to any of its files or personnel. Patrick had allied with Mason and argued that it was crucial I be given whatever information I needed. But the bureaucrats in the Agency had held their ground, waved bits of paper in front of Mason, and told him to go fuck himself.

That meant that what I was about to do now was technically illegal and could land me in jail for a long time. Possibly, I could be sharing a cell with Patrick, because he'd broken rules, too, in order to give me the suburban D.C. address I was now standing outside.

To minimize my chances of imprisonment in a high-security American facility, this afternoon I'd raided one of my dead-letter boxes in D.C. and taken some of its contents to my hotel room. There, I'd carefully applied a black wig that had been cut and shaped to my size by an MI6 hairdresser asset in a safe house in London's Pimlico. I'd also rubbed my face with fake tan cream, put on glasses, and strapped padding around my gut to make me look fat.

Though it was dark, the long street was lined with houses and streetlamps. Most of the houses were illuminated. People were at home. I was conspicuous. The house before me also had lights on inside. Moments ago, from farther down the street, I'd watched the home-owner drive into his driveway and go inside. I'd thought about knocking on his front door and barging my way in, but it was risky. Officers trained in espionage tradecraft never open their doors to anyone without checking who's on the other side. And though the man in the house wasn't a frontline field operative, tradecraft techniques are known to many. They pick up such techniques by overhearing conversations in staff canteens, by being briefed by operational and security officers, and by witnessing how field operatives go about their work.

I couldn't take the chance of knocking on the door, him asking who I was, and then calling the cops when

I didn't respond. So instead, I'd brought along a set of specialist tools.

I walked fast around the house until I was in the backyard. It was more private here, but still there was a threat that I could be seen by neighbors if they happened to look out of their rear windows. The back kitchen door was locked. I worked fast. On my knees, I used a lockpick set to pin back the inner workings of the lock and rotate its chambers. The lock opened. I waited, listening for any signs that the man in the house had heard the sound. Nothing. Carefully, I pushed the door and eased it open inch by inch. After glancing around to ensure I wasn't being watched by a neighbor with a cell phone to her ear, I moved inside.

I could hear cheers and whistles coming from his TV. Moving into the living room, I saw he had his back to me while sitting in an armchair. He was oblivious to me as he watched a football game, the vibrant colors of the match affording no reflection on the screen of my presence in the dark corner of the room. He was totally vulnerable. Even covert operatives, unarmed combat experts, and specialist law enforcement officers are very vulnerable in similar positions. It takes their brain longer to react to an attack than if they were confronting it head-on. And even then, their training becomes subservient to shock, which in many instances doesn't allow them to fight but at best instinctively forces them to flee or freeze and accept a beating or death. This man lacked any expertise in defending himself. I could snap his neck before he realized what was happening.

I hoped he didn't have a weak heart as I tapped him on the shoulder.

He spun around fast and fell onto his back when he saw me, his mouth open and an expression of horror on his face. "No! What the . . . ?"

In a French accent, I said, "I'm not here to rob you or hurt you. Correction: I won't hurt you providing the conversation I wish to have with you goes well." I patted my overcoat pocket. There was nothing in there, but the man before me didn't know I wasn't packing a pistol.

He looked terrified, as he stuttered, "What . . . what . . . what do you want?"

I squatted in front of him. He tried to get up but I pushed him back down. "You were part of the CIA technical team that established the communications systems and security for Gray Site in Beirut. You were also part of the team sent to breach the site after it went silent. I want you to tell me what you found when you forced entry."

The technician used his elbows to move a few inches away from me. "Who are you?"

"An interested party."

"DGSE?"

This was good. I'd hoped that he'd assume I worked for the French intelligence service, given my accent and the fact that one of Gray Site's officers was DGSE. I smiled. "Draw your own conclusions." My smile vanished. "I won't kill you. My employers have told me that would be crossing a line. But they've allowed me to use my discretion on whether to inflict pain on you, depending upon how cooperative you are. We want answers, and we're not getting them from anyone else. That's why you and I are in a room together."

"You can't expect me to talk to a foreign intelligence officer. My job—"

"Your job is the least of your concerns right now. In any case, neither I nor anyone I represent will say a word to your colleagues about our discussion."

"It's still treason to talk to a foreign agency without clearance!"

"Only if you're betraying secrets."

The man frowned.

"We've read the CIA reports about the construction of Gray Site and the breach. After all, they were formally submitted to us by the Agency, because we had a right to know as much as you do."

"So, you are DGSE!"

"We know as much, actually as little, about what happened in the complex as your bosses do." I patted his stomach. "So, unless you've deliberately withheld information from your colleagues—and I've no reason to suspect that to be the case—then you've nothing to fear. All I want to know is whether there is a detail that's been missed. Perhaps something that didn't seem important to you and the rest of the team who forced entry."

When he spoke, the technician's voice sounded stronger and his expression looked defiant. "Why didn't you seek clearance to interview me? The CIA would probably have granted you that. They've no reason not to."

I shrugged. "I couldn't take that chance. Anyway, this is a much more *private* encounter." I sat in the chair the man had been in minutes ago. "You can sit on the floor, but don't get to your feet."

The officer did as he was told.

"Our interests in Gray Site align precisely with those of the United States. I would prefer that you didn't, but by all means tell your employer that you were threatened in your home tonight and forced to speak. That is your right. And it is also right to tell them that at no point did I ask you to betray your country. I merely wanted an off-the-record discussion with you."

"Off the record?" the man huffed. "You must be crazy."

I leaned forward. "You must use your fingers a lot in your line of work. I'm sure you'd hate to see them smashed to the point where they will never function again."

It was a threat I'd never follow through with, but it was sufficient to make the officer's face pale.

I leaned back and crossed my legs; the padding under my shirt squeezed uncomfortably against me as I did so. "Are you prepared to talk, or not?"

He was silent.

So was I as I kept my eyes locked on his.

Finally he asked, "How do I know you're from an ally service? You could be posing as that. Maybe you're working for people my agency doesn't like."

"Make a judgment."

"I'm not qualified to do so."

He wasn't. "Then ask me questions about Gray Site—questions that only the States, Britain, France, and Israel would know the answers to."

The officer rubbed sweat off his face. "Name of the CIA officer in the site?"

"Koenig."

"The number of officers who manned the station?"

"Four."

"Myself included, number of men who breached the complex?"

"Six. Three technicians, three paramilitary officers. All Americans.

"The station's remit?"

"To eavesdrop on Hamas. Purpose being to ascertain whether Hamas was responsible for the assassination of Israel's ambassador in Paris."

"The station's layout?"

"I was hoping you were going to help me out a bit more on that." That was true, and it was one of the key reasons I was here. "But I know it was an old basement wine cellar beneath a large derelict house in the outskirts of Beirut. It was accessed by steps inside the house. You put a bombproof steel door at its entrance at the base of the stairs. In the site was a corridor leading to four small rooms. The walls, ceiling, and floor were thick stone. Aside from the steel front door, there was no other way in or out of the station."

The man nodded. "Nobody except the CIA, MI6, DGSE, and Mossad knows that information. And even within those organizations, the information is tightly restricted."

"Good. So now you know who you're dealing with. Time to make a decision."

The officer lowered his head. "What do you want to know?"

"Are you certain the door was secure from the inside when you breached it?"

"Yes. And its inner locks hadn't been tampered with. It would have been impossible to do so."

"Why?"

"We tested them ourselves." He tried to smile. "Part of what we do is pick locks." He nodded toward his kitchen. "And I'm betting we're a darn sight better at it than what you're familiar with. We made the locks impossible to crack. But on top of that we decided we couldn't be complacent. So we made the inner locks inaccessible from the outside."

"The walls, floor, and ceiling of Gray Site—how can you be certain entry wasn't forced through one of them and then covered up?"

"We checked every inch of—"

"A professional could put a fake facade over a tunnel and get the coloring and texture to exactly match its stone surroundings."

The man looked up. "I know. That's why we X-rayed every inch of stone. Top to side to bottom. No concealed tunnels. No nothing."

"Tell me about the breach."

"You must have read about it in the reports."

"Tell me!"

"We used blowtorches to get through the door. Took us a while. Finally, we got the door down. Sparks from our torches ignited a sofa in the corridor, but that didn't matter because one of the paramilitary guys stood guard at the entrance while putting out the fire. Rest of us went into the complex. We reached the rooms and—"

I said, "Stop," and held up a hand. "Backtrack. What did you see when you were about to step through the entrance?"

"At first, not much because of the fire and smoke."

"Yes, yes, but once you got clear of that?"

"Wide corridor. Same metal cabinets we'd installed, lining the corridor. They were there for the Gray Site officers to store files. And nothing else."

"Ceiling?"

"Nothing."

"Lighting?"

"It was working. Plus we had flashlights."

"The rooms? I'm most interested in the rooms."

The technician looked upset. "I'd never seen anything like it before. Never want to again. The paramilitary guys moved very fast, checking each room, their weapons out. Me and my two tech pals kept pace with them because we were under orders to retrieve data.

Then we went into the fourth room. I wish I hadn't."
The officer started rocking. "Four dead guys. I didn't
know gunshots looked that bad in real life."

"They always do." I felt sorry for the guy, but
couldn't show that. "Take a deep breath and continue."

"I knew who the dead men were because they'd been
around when we were finishing off installing Gray Site.
The Israeli was on the floor, one bullet wound in his
arm, another in his stomach. The French officer was
slumped in the corner of the room, blood all over the
floor in front of him. The paramilitary guys said he'd
bled out. He was shot in the chest."

"And the British man?"

"Head down on the desk. We checked him. There
was an exit wound in his lower back."

I didn't want to ask my next question, but had to.
"The American?" My friend Roger.

The technician's body shook. "That was the worst
bit. I can still see it now. Hate it. Half of his face was
shot off. Bits of his jawbone were jutting out like . . .
like I don't know. Bone. Jagged bone."

I clenched my teeth, desperate to remember the last
time Roger and I had a drink together rather than visu-
alize the image I'd just been presented with. I failed.
But I was a DGSE officer, I told myself, not a grieving
friend. I wanted to rip off my padding and just walk

out of here. But if I did that I'd never get out without being arrested for interrogating a CIA officer, because revealing my disguise to the technical officer would quickly lead others in the Agency to deduce that it had been me in his home tonight. "What happened next?"

"We examined the site for hours. The paramilitaries got the bodies into our van. Then we sanitized the place—removed all equipment and bloodstains, bleached, scrubbed, all of us in head-to-toe disposable coveralls, even the shooters who kept guard while we did what needed doing. The X-rays I spoke about, we did after Gray Site was completely empty. And we didn't stop there. We swept the place three times in case we'd missed anything. It was backbreaking. I've never done anything as intense before. But we had to be thorough. We only just managed to get on the road before daybreak."

My mind racing, I asked, "What do you think happened in there?"

The technician wrapped his arms tight around his chest and continued rocking. "I'm just a—"

"You saw the result of what happened! I didn't. You don't need to be an operative to have an opinion."

The CIA technical officer stopped moving and looked at me imploringly. "You swear you won't say anything about this conversation?"

I nodded. "You choose whether you want to declare it or not. But I've no interest in causing you trouble." I stood, ready to leave. "Your opinion?"

He didn't reply at first and seemed to be finding the right words. Finally, he said, "I've installed covert intelligence stations in places you wouldn't believe—castles, churches, disused prisons, and on one occasion a former brothel in Mogadishu. They were fun, if that makes sense. Gray Site wasn't. It had the smell of death in there when we moved in. I reckon people died in the house above when it was shelled by the Israelis in '82." He looked at me, his eyes bloodshot. "I think being in that place day and night drove Roger Koenig mad."

PART III

Thirty

Monsieur de Guise watched his university students filing into the Rennes University lecture hall. He was standing at the podium at the front of the classroom, a table by his side, behind the table a free-standing chalkboard. The students were chatting to each other, laughing, and all of them were carrying bags stuffed with academic books and electronic devices that de Guise didn't care to understand.

This morning he was giving his students a lecture on the unsolved, highly complex abc conjecture. Most of them wouldn't understand a word that came out of his mouth. So, as he was often inclined to do, he'd decided to start the lecture with something that would engage their young minds.

Magic.

His tricks pulled in students to his classroom, which would otherwise be near empty. Full classrooms kept the university administrators off his back and allowed him to maintain his cover as a professor. He was pleased to note that when the students sat down, the hall was at capacity. As a reward to them, he was going to show his pupils something special. It wouldn't be easy, for it required dexterity and, as with most tricks, misdirection.

On the table were eight figures of men and a large metal box with no bottom. The professor looked across the room and counted the figures aloud, tapping the head of each as he did so. "Eight in total," he said in French. "Does anyone disagree?" De Guise stared at his students, deliberately silent for a while to instill more anticipation. Some of his students shook their heads. "Very well. We all agree there are eight men on the table." He turned and wrote the number eight on the chalkboard. With his back once again to the board, he lifted the metal box. "This is their prison. They have no food, no water. There are no guards to let them out for exercise. They will die in here. But maybe one of the men is stronger than the others. He will outlive them and survive for a while by eating the dead prisoners' flesh and by gnawing on their bones until there is nothing left to consume. When that moment arrives, there will be no trace of the seven dead men."

De Guise placed the box over the eight figures and his hands behind his back. "We now speed up time. Days pass. A week. Then the man who is still alive can no longer bear the agony of his starvation and thirst, so he becomes a consumer of rotting flesh and a drinker of congealed blood."

Some of the students were squirming, others nudging each other while lapping up the grotesque mental image.

"Let's assume he swallows the very last morsel and fragment of bone available to him in one month's time. That moment is now." De Guise lifted the box. There was only one figurine on the table. He was still standing. The students clapped and laughed. Monsieur de Guise raised a finger to hush them. "One man is left. Agree?" The pupils nodded eagerly. He turned and moved out of the way of the chalkboard behind him. "One," he repeated as he pointed at the board. The students gasped when they saw that the number eight previously written on the board had somehow transformed itself to the number one. The students cheered, but de Guise gestured them to be quiet again, his expression stern. "Alas, this is magic with pathos. Eventually, the survivor collapses and dies." He tapped the figure over so it was prone on the table. "One becomes zero." As he moved to his podium, the students were astonished to see that the number one on the chalkboard had been replaced by the number zero.

He gave a slight bow as his pupils stood and applauded, most of them whooping with delight.

Later that afternoon, the music of Chopin's Revolutionary Étude in Monsieur de Guise's Rennes home was accompanied by the sounds of raindrops hitting the cobbled street outside. De Guise was sitting in his leather armchair adjacent to the fireplace, which he'd lit because the early fall day had turned unseasonably chilly. His eyes were closed and his fingertips pressed together as he toyed with the idea that the music he was listening to could be used as a code—each note carrying a numerical value that in turn would define a specific letter. Such a code would be of use only to a skilled musician, but some of Thales's assets had such skills and one day the code could be of help to them.

Thales's empire was growing, thanks to the increased freelance work that had recently come his way. From the four corners of the world, businessmen, politicians, military chiefs, and even intelligence officers used his services. Almost entirely, his services were engaged via a series of intermediaries. Very few employers had direct contact with him. Most of them didn't even know he existed.

His tasking on the Paris assassination and the subsequent need to stop Cochrane dead in his tracks was different. His employer for these jobs had direct contact with him via phone. In this case there was no need for communications to take place through intermediaries, given that Thales had recruited his employer a year ago to spy on some extremely sensitive secrets. The spy had now turned employer, and after the job was done the employer would return to being Thales's employee. That was fine, because this momentary switch of roles came with a lucrative revenue stream.

But as a former high-ranking MI6 officer, Thales knew that a growing network of assets and other resources, together with a swelling bank balance, came with increased responsibilities and risks. With every new person he hired, the chances of treachery within his organization rose. The more cash he accrued, the more devious he had to be with his money-laundering structures. But all of this was easily within his capabilities and gave him no concern. Plus, few knew Thales's false name of de Guise and nobody in his employ knew his real English one.

After the music finished and the only sounds were the weather and the crackling flames, de Guise decided that he wanted to take a walk through the old quarter of Rennes. Today wasn't market day, which was good because he was keen to be alone. He was momentarily irritated when his phone rang, though that irritability vanished when he saw that the asset calling was the woman he'd tasked to track Richard Oaks's passport and credit card.

He picked up the phone, listened for thirty seconds, then ended the call.

Colonel Rowe's long, stiff legs strode over heathland on his family's estate in Norfolk, one of England's most easterly counties. The windswept and rugged surroundings were made all the more harsh by a fine rain that had persisted all day. Rowe didn't care. If anything, the wind and humidity would further test the capabilities of the hunting rifle he was carrying, handcrafted by him in former stables that he'd converted into a workshop adjacent to the estate's main house.

Seven generations of his family had lived in the vast grounds, many miles away from the nearest neighboring houses. Being an only child, Rowe had inherited the estate when his parents died years ago. They'd also left him their remaining savings, though the money wasn't enough to maintain the significant upkeep of a west and east wing that contained fifteen bedrooms apiece, 115 windows that frequently leaked and let in drafts due to their age, and a roof that was sorely in need of replacing. In many ways, the estate was an unwanted burden. Rowe had frequently toyed with the idea of selling it. He had no emotional attachment to it, no wife and kids to take advantage of the property's potential and big open spaces, and considered his parents to be cash-poor snobs who'd lived beyond their means and thought they were still in the Edwardian age.

But he couldn't bring himself to sell the estate for two reasons. First, the place needed millions spent on it and he doubted a potential buyer would want to take on that investment. Second, the expanse and privacy of the grounds allowed him to shoot.

And shooting was his passion. Especially if he had a man or woman in his crosshairs.

He wasn't a psychopath. Nor did he consider himself a killer. Instead, he believed he was a dispassionate professional who was gifted with the talent to take a man's head off from one mile away and in return receive some money for doing so.

It was all he had left in his life.

His former army regiment, the Royal Dragoon Guards, had banned him from attending its annual reunions. He had no aunts, uncles, nephews, or nieces;

no friends; and no aspirations whatsoever beyond pulling the trigger and watching his bullet strike its target in precisely the right place.

But that's not to say he was a shallow man. Given the chance to do so, he could be charming in company. He could entertain people with numerous anecdotes including the time the British monarch inspected Rowe's troops and she shouted at him because he winked at her, and for at least three months each year he'd travel across Mongolia on horseback while staying with local tribesmen.

By his own admission, he was a man who didn't belong in this era. His roguish and eccentric behavior, propensity to cheat fellow gamblers out of their bets, and complete disinterest whether big-game hunting was driving certain wild cats to extinction, would have been better tolerated if he'd been in the senior ranks of Queen Victoria's colonial army. But here he was, in the twenty-first century. And he was determined to carve out a living the best way he could, uncaring that his contemporaries were more likely to be found in investment banks and law firms.

He stopped in a wooded area of the grounds, used the sleeve of his jacket to wipe rain off his sodden face, lowered himself to a prone position and gripped his rifle. "Let's see what yer made of," he muttered while taking aim. Over a thousand yards away was a range target, hammered into a tree. He went still, allowing his body to relax so that he felt as if he were merging with the heath and soil beneath him, part of the land. That way there were no unnecessary movements, zero human frailties that would ruin his aim. Now, he was oblivious to any distractions—no sounds of the nearby sea and seagulls flying over it, or the wind racing across Norfolk's flat land and through leaning trees; no discomfort to be had from the cold rain striking the naked skin between his collar and hairline; and the rich country smells he usually adored no longer registering.

All that mattered to him were his aim, the gun, and the target.

He focused on the center of the target. It was a circle, surrounded by increasingly larger circles. When he was ready, he pulled back the trigger. His bullet hit the exact spot he anticipated it would strike—seven inches wide of the mark.

After making adjustments to the weapon's sight, he took aim again. Not at the center of the target but four inches away and at the ten o'clock position. Now, he was compensating for the wind and rain. He fired. The bullet struck dead center.

"Okay, my beauty, one more test." He attached a large silencer to the tip of the barrel. The device upset the perfect weight and balance of his weapon and required even greater skill for him to make an accurate shot. He stayed prone for five minutes, his eyes closed, just feeling the weapon in his hands, letting it become him. Then he opened his eyes, readied himself, inhaled, half exhaled, and held his breath.

The sound of the bullet exiting the gun was barely audible. The high-powered bullet struck the target in the center.

Colonel Rowe fired six more successful shots to be sure of his weapon's accuracy, then walked back to the estate's crumbling buildings. Soon the sun would be setting and he'd have to turn on the grounds' exterior lights. Only a third of them worked, but he still needed them on because without them the grounds would be in pitch darkness. And with his home's interior lights on, that would allow any ne'er-do-wells to easily get right up to the house without being seen by him. Rowe could be many things, but one thing he insisted on was never being a target.

After placing his gun alongside many others in wall-mounted racks in his workshop, and securing the building, he entered the ridiculously oversized main house. He only used three of the rooms: an oak-paneled living room with sumptuous nineteenth-century furniture, whose walls were adorned with the stuffed heads of exotic animals Rowe and his forefathers had shot; a former maid's bedroom that had a single bed, toilet, sink, bathtub, and a rail for his clothes to hang on; and the kitchen that was once used by dozens of service staff to prepare banquets for the visiting wealthy and powerful in his forebears' heyday. The rest of the house could fall down for all he cared.

He lit a fire, just a few bits of wood and coal in a fireplace that had capacity to burn half an oak tree, and poured himself a brandy from a crystal decanter. He leaned against the mantelpiece above the fire, just the way his great-grandfather was depicted in one of the room's paintings, albeit his ancestor was in fine Hussars' uniform and Rowe was in a hessian sweater and tweeds that were steaming as they dried out in the heat. On a side table he saw his cell phone flashing. Cursing, because only Thales had his number, he picked up the phone and checked its screen. It showed a missed call but there was no voice message. Thales never allowed his voice to be recorded.

He called his boss, who answered without a word on the third ring. "Sorry, sir. I was practicing."

"You did well to do so. Are you satisfied with your results?"

Rowe's back was straight as he responded, "Always."

"Excellent. Listen carefully. Mr. C has purchased a British Airways flight to London. Delays considered, he will be arriving at Heathrow tomorrow."

Rowe knew Thales wouldn't tell him which arrival time and terminal. To do so would tell anyone potentially intercepting the call which country Cochrane was traveling from, plus it would narrow down who they were referring to as Mr. C.

Thales said, "If I were you, I'd be there to greet him. It might mean an all-day wait, considering the uncertainty of timings."

"You don't need to say any more."

Thales didn't. Rowe would ensure he was in the correct arrivals hall for every British Airways flight that landed from America tomorrow. When Cochrane arrived, he'd follow him. And if for any reason Cochrane slipped through the net, it didn't matter. The next time Cochrane used his Richard Oaks credit card, Rowe would be all over him. All that mattered was that Cochrane was coming to London.

"Leave it to me." The line went dead. Rowe threw his brandy into the fire, its flames momentarily roaring as a result, and left the room to make preparations.

Years as a Mossad assassin had taught Michael Stein that less was more. His one-bedroom apartment in

Tel Aviv was stripped of all but essential items, so that he could travel at a moment's notice with no cares about any possessions he left behind. He had two sets of summer clothes and two for winter—both durable and easily washed in any hotel room sink, and a hemp satchel that was a mere fourteen inches in diameter and was all he carried when he traveled.

The satchel had belonged to an English soldier in World War II who'd carried it through Dieppe, D-Day, the backstreets of French provincial towns, the Ardennes forest, the liberation of Bergen-Belsen concentration camp, and the final push to Berlin. After the war, the soldier had stayed on in the army and had put Jewish survivors of the Holocaust into detention camps while they awaited transportation to Palestine. The soldier was an honorable man and hated what he did after the war. That's why he gave his food-stuffed satchel to Michael's great-grandfather, who was one of the detainees and took the bag from the soldier's hand through barbed-wire fencing. Michael believed the satchel was good luck.

His minimalist existence was offset by one indulgence—a mongrel dog with shaggy hair and a perpetually wagging tail, who adored his master. Michael and his pet were in the apartment playing the dog's favorite game. Michael was standing, holding out a large stone.

The dog launched himself at the stone, only for Michael to snatch it away just before the canine's jaws attempted to connect with the rock. It seemed like teasing, but it wasn't. The dog took joy knowing that his master was faster than him. He could keep this up all day. And it did him good. During the dog's last checkup, the vet had commented on the great health of the ten-year-old dog and said that he had a remarkably low pulse rate for his age.

Michael's cell phone rang, causing him to be momentarily distracted and for his dog's mouth to connect not only with the rock but also his hand. The dog looked confused as he saw his tooth marks and Michael's blood. Michael ruffled his fur, said, "This time you won, my boy," and laughed when the dog wagged his tail. Michael held the phone to his ear, blood dripping onto the floor. "Yes?"

It was the Mossad official who'd been assigned to track Will Cochrane's use of his false passport and credit card.

"London?" Michael moved to his kitchenette to fetch antiseptic for his wound. His dog licked his blood off the floor. "He must be in transit, en route to Lebanon." He ended the call and called someone else. "Got to go. Can you look after Mr. Peres?"

A man responded, "I always do."

Thirty minutes later, that man knocked on the door. Michael let him in.

"What happened to your hand?" Michael's father asked.

"Mr. Peres got the better of me." He patted his dog. "It might have done him some good to know that I'm not infallible."

"No. It'll just make him worry more when you're gone. Where to this time?"

"Britain to start with. Maybe it will end there."

"What will end?"

Michael hesitated before answering, "Clearing Ben's name."

Ben, his brother, who was killed in Gray Site.

His father stared at him. "What is there to clear? Your mother and I were told he was killed in the line of duty."

"The Americans are pursuing a line of inquiry which could suggest that they think Ben tried to cover something up."

"What?"

"Dad, I can't . . ."

"What?!"

"We're on the verge of war."

"It doesn't take a rocket scientist to work that out!" His father was pacing.

"But maybe we shouldn't be. Maybe Ben realized we're going after the wrong guys. Perhaps he buried the chance for us to find out if we're doing the right thing."

His father's face was livid. "I told you and your brother. I said, go into academia. You were both gifted enough. Not all this army nonsense. This spying. Why didn't you listen to me?"

"Put it down to youthful rebellion against parental advice." Michael couldn't stop himself from adding, "You'd have done better to have told us to join Special Forces and Mossad. Perhaps that way we both *would* now be in academia."

His father came right up to him. "Instead of my boy being dead?"

"Yes."

"Yes."

They were still, facing each other, their anger in truth a symptom of their grief. Finally, Michael's father took Michael's hand in both of his. In a gentler voice, he said, "I don't understand you or what you do. But I *am* proud of you. I was proud of you *and* Ben."

"I know, Dad."

"Can you clear Ben's name?"

"I'm going to try."

"Who's going to try to stop you?"

"A man."

"Is he capable?"

"Since he's been assigned the job, I must assume he's *very* capable."

Michael's father took a leash and attached it to Mr. Peres. Speaking to the dog, he said, "We're going to break your dad's rules and give you some doggy treats when we get home." He looked at Michael. "Whoever you're facing, just remember Ben idolized you. Let that thought stay with you."

Michael picked up his satchel. "It will. You have my word on that."

Thirty-One

In less than one week, Israel would be ready to go to war. If it did so, the outcome of its invasion of Gaza, the West Bank, and Lebanon was unpredictable because much depended upon how far Israel would go to finally obliterate Hamas. Personally, I believed Israel wouldn't stop until it was convinced it had killed every terrorist who threatened the state, plus anyone who aided and abetted the terrorists. This wouldn't be a surgical Israeli incursion; it would be the deployment of mechanized armor, artillery strikes, ground forces, and fighter planes. And that meant unbridled escalation, sucking in other states. Shiites would turn on Sunnis and vice versa. Secular states would choose allegiances. The Middle East would become a chaotic battleground, inevitably forcing military involvement from Iran, Turkey, Saudi Arabia, Jordan, other Middle Eastern states, and ultimately the West. And throughout the early days of war, Russia would be watching, trying to decide if it wanted to join the party and, if so, on whose side.

I'd be going to the Middle East on the next available flight tomorrow morning. London was merely a transit point on my route, but it afforded me the opportunity to make two stops in the capital, one of which was related to the question that had been plaguing me throughout my flight from D.C.'s Dulles airport to Heathrow—how could a man like Roger turn on his colleagues?

As I walked into the arrivals section of the airport, the thought remained at the forefront of my mind. It made no sense that Roger could have attacked his fellow Gray Site intelligence officers for no reason, and yet no one was disputing what happened. I didn't buy that he'd gone stir crazy in the underground bunker, though I didn't know what my state of mind would be like if I'd been holed up for six weeks under a city where people would kill me given the chance. Roger was an extremely resilient operator, and had countless times proven to me his ability to go the extra mile, but even the best of us reach a wall. Often it comes with age; more frequently among special operators it happens when their nerves finally say enough is enough.

Perhaps that's what happened. Roger could no longer stand the strain of covert work, particularly work that required him to descend daily into an airless hole. And he lashed out at everything around him that represented the secret world he could no longer tolerate— everything including machinery and fellow spies.

I didn't want to remember him that way. The Roger I knew had helped me track down an Iranian general who was planning genocide, engaged in a fearsome gunfight in central Moscow and withstood torture after he was captured, crept up on an SVR officer who'd pointed his gun at me and got the man to lower his weapon by placing his pistol against the Russian's head, and had a slight smile on his face as I told my bosses that I wasn't paying any attention to their mission briefings.

Roger could have rested on his laurels and retired from special operations when he left SEAL Team 6. He'd have had enough yarns from his navy days to captivate his children and others while sipping his beloved bourbon on his porch. But he wanted to push himself harder and into even more dangerous territories. So he'd joined the CIA, where typically he was deployed with only a sidearm at best, and more often with nothing to protect his life. No doubt, Katy Koenig wished he hadn't signed up for a life of espionage. I didn't blame her. She wanted her husband back.

But Roger was always a stubborn bastard. He adored his family, yet couldn't sit still. The prospect of retirement petrified him. I imagined he was near me now, doing what he'd done countless times: watching me arrive in the airport while sipping a strong black coffee in a nearby café, cash for the purchase on the table so he could move in an instant if the need arose; checking out everyone and deducing which persons could be potential assailants; covering my back.

But he wasn't here.

He was dead.

Michael Stein was in a spot that Roger Koenig would have approved of if he'd been observing Cochrane. Sipping his coffee at a table outside Costa Coffee, the Mossad assassin spotted a tall man amid hundreds of other travelers who were walking across the airport concourse. Michael had memorized Cochrane's face from a website he'd seen—the same image that had been shown across the world's media a year ago when Cochrane had been forced to go on the run because he'd disobeyed orders. There was no doubt in Michael's mind that the man in the photo was the same man he was looking at now.

Cochrane was wearing a stylish overcoat and suit, and was pulling a trolley bag. He looked athletic, moving at a fast, confident pace, yet Michael could tell Cochrane was subtly checking his surroundings.

Casually, Michael turned to the next page in the London travel guide he'd earlier purchased from one of Heathrow's bookstores. When Cochrane had his back to him, Michael followed him down an escalator toward the Heathrow Express train platform.

Colonel Rowe had no idea what Michael Stein looked like, but he categorized the blond man a few yards ahead of him as one of nine men in the airport who could possibly be tailing Will Cochrane. The man was wearing a waterproof jacket and jeans, and had a satchel over his shoulder. What drew Rowe's attention was that he was walking at the same pace as Cochrane, was traveling light and alone, and had the age and physique of a man who might kill people for a living.

There was no way yet for Rowe to be certain if one of the men around him was Stein, or even if the Mossad officer was in London. But Cochrane would inevitably be using multiple methods to reach whatever destination he was headed to in London. If someone stayed close to him for at least three stages of his route, there was a strong possibility that man was Stein.

Rowe was wearing a Harris tweed sports jacket, sweater, brown cords, and brogues, looking every bit like a gentleman embarking on a pheasant shoot on his country estate. The look was apt, because in the canvas bag he was carrying the stripped-down, silenced rifle he'd tested at his home the day before. He reached the bottom of the escalator, purchased a ticket to Paddington Station, and followed Cochrane onto the busy platform. The former MI6 officer moved to the end of the platform, the blond man took up position in the center, and Rowe stood at the other end. There was no need to get close to Cochrane so he could jump into the same car as him, for Paddington Station was the only stop on the route.

They waited for seven minutes before the train pulled up. Cochrane entered the car in front of him, and everyone else apart from Rowe got on the train, including the blond man and a few other possible tails. Rowe waited a moment in case Cochrane jumped off just before the doors closed. He did not. Rowe got on the train at the last moment.

Fifteen minutes later, they arrived at Paddington's large and bustling overland and underground train hub. Now Rowe had to be very careful, because it would be easy to lose sight of Cochrane or, if he got too close to him, arouse the Englishman's suspicion that he might be under surveillance. He kept a distance of twenty yards between himself and Cochrane; the blond man was walking in the same direction.

Rowe dearly hoped Cochrane wasn't heading toward the taxi rank, because then he would escape into the frantic traffic of London. If that happened, the colonel would have to wait for Cochrane to flag his location when he used his credit card again. Thankfully, it appeared he was opting for a cheaper and more expedient mode of transport: he was heading downstairs to the tube station.

Cochrane clearly knew the station layout, because he walked fast to the platform for the southbound Circle and District lines. The blond man also wanted to take that route; so did Rowe.

I gripped the handrail above my head, standing because there was no seat available in the packed tube. People of different skin colors were around me, some of them zoned out, meaning they were very familiar with this journey and were residents of London, others wide eyed and alert, staring at maps of the subway system, meaning they were visitors to the multicultural capital.

Nobody engaged in eye contact. It is an unwritten rule that strangers don't talk to each other in London.

Quite why has eluded me to this day. Perhaps British people and visitors to the capital sense danger. London is on a knife edge, they think; if I talk to someone, they might turn out to be crazy and attack me. Something like that. Despite the greater dangers prevalent in New York City, Washington, Mumbai, Mexico City, and Brasília, people in those cities will talk to anyone. Not so London. It has a brooding atmosphere. Order is required. And if someone talks to just one person, the city will lapse into anarchic chaos.

I got out of the tube at Charing Cross station and walked to the River Thames, then over the Lambeth Bridge toward my home in Southwark. It was raining heavily, and other pedestrians were walking fast to seek shelter, their faces screwed up as if in pain. The smell of wet tarmac was mixed with that of vehicle exhaust fumes. Below me, the sickly brown Thames was swollen and flowing fast; I couldn't imagine any form of life could be sustained beneath its surface.

Michael Stein weaved his way between tourists caught out by the downpour and savvy Londoners holding umbrellas over their heads. Though Britain's domestic security service, MI5, doesn't allow Mossad officers to operate on British soil because it doesn't trust the Israeli service, Michael had been to London many times. Once he retired, he thought he'd like the city. But as an assassin he loathed the place—too many CCTV cameras covering every inch of the inner capital, everyone watchful as if nothing had changed since the days of London being struck by German bomber aircraft and being riddled with Fifth Columnist Nazi spies, second-to-none armed police response units ready to pounce on anyone who looked like they might be preparing to blow something up, and once majestic government buildings transformed into blastproof fortresses. London was an experienced survivor—wars, Irish terrorism, Islamic terrorism, lone wolf white supremacist lunatics: the British city had been hurt by them all, but was never defeated and always got stronger as a result. Its occupants bickered among themselves—like any city dwellers—but they had unwavering loyalty to the heart of this great old country. They kept it going, no matter at what cost. Londoners were the enemy of Michael and others like him.

He followed Cochrane, his jacket collar pulled up high and his head bowed low.

Colonel Rowe was sure that the blond man in front of him was Michael Stein. Heathrow Airport, the express to Paddington, standing in the same subway car to central London, and now on foot behind

Cochrane—even a reckless gambler would shy away from the possibility that this was mere coincidence. And though he had a passion for gambling, Rowe was anything but reckless. The expert Israeli assassin who Thales had cleverly activated was following a very dangerous man. Behind both of them was someone even more ruthless.

I shut the communal front door to my apartment building and was glad of the immediate quiet. Noisy, unsociable London was outside—this was my oasis. It was 1 P.M.; David's apartment was not reverberating with his beloved Dixieland blues, because no doubt he was at work; so, too, was Dickie's apartment quiet of daytime TV or military marching tunes. Probably he was on one of his early afternoon strolls, during which he would stand to attention in front of one of the horse-mounted guardsmen in Whitehall and give the bemused and stoic man a dressing-down for not turning out in immaculate attire. But in Phoebe's home I could hear the thud of electronic dance music. I went up one flight of stairs and knocked on her door.

"Darling," she said when she opened her front door. She was wearing a sexy black dress, her heavy makeup was streaked with tears, and she was holding a glass of champagne.

I smiled. "Bit early to be celebrating, isn't it?"

"I'm drowning my sorrows. It's never too early to do that. Come in."

I followed her down her hallway, its walls strewn with weird art from her gallery. "How are you?"

"Unemployed and bored." She turned off the music. "Want a drink?"

"No, thanks." I was worried about Phoebe. Her apartment was immaculate—that was a good sign—but she clearly wasn't looking after herself. "I can't stay long. Just wanted to check in to see you were okay."

Phoebe sat in an armchair and took a sip of her champagne. "How was Angola?"

"Hot and humid, but it paid me well. Are you coping financially?"

Phoebe frowned. "David's helping me out. Don't know how he can afford to do so."

I didn't sit. "He must have savings. That's very kind of him."

She looked directly at me. "Savings?"

Astute Phoebe may well have suspected there was more to David's generosity than met the eye. I said, "David cares about you. Maybe he got his money from inheritance, careful financial planning, investments. Who cares? All that matters is that he's doing a good thing by you."

"Or maybe he got his money from a benefactor. Someone who goes places that pay well." Phoebe gulped the rest of her drink and poured herself another.

I sounded older and more draconian than my years when I said, "You can't go to job interviews smelling of alcohol."

She looked bitter when she replied, "In my industry it's de rigueur to be nonconformist."

"Your industry sacked you!" I pointed at her glass. "You need to be better than everyone else. You *are* better than everyone else."

She shrugged. "Maybe, but that's no use, because I have no interviews to go to."

"Yes, you do. I made a few calls. Pretended to be a hotshot art buyer from the States. Bigged you up. Said you were the best dealer I'd done business with. Tomorrow you've got a full day. National Gallery, Saatchi, Barbican, Tate Modern, Royal Academy of Arts, and the London Art Gallery—they all want to meet with you tomorrow."

"Meet you. Not meet *with* you. You're becoming more American by the day." She smiled, and a healthy color returned to her face. "You sure you went to Angola? Not someplace further west?"

"When I landed, the airport had a sign welcoming me to Angola."

Phoebe giggled, then turned serious. "They really want to interview me?"

"Really. And it's set up on merit. David sent me your résumé . . ."

"Curriculum vitae."

"I forwarded it to the galleries you're seeing tomorrow. They loved what they saw on paper. Now they want to see you in the flesh. Prestigious institutions, Phoebe. You've got to look your best and . . ."

"Not smell of stale bubbles." She pushed her drink to one side and stood. "Come here, Will." She held out her arms.

While she sobbed, I hugged her and whispered, "I've got to go away again. When I'm back, I'll cook for you and David and the major. We can get drunk. Make it a Saturday evening, so it doesn't interfere with your new job. David, Dickie, and I love you very much."

"You have that much certainty that I'll get a job?"

"I do."

Phoebe looked at me, her face now radiant, tears running down her cheeks. "I'd like you to try Internet dating. Nothing else has worked for you."

I smoothed my hand over the bridge of her nose. "That's the Phoebe I know. You're back in business."

She held me for a while, silent as she stared at me with her gorgeous eyes. "There'll be some idiot out there who'll fall for you."

I smiled. "Ever the romantic. *You* have that much certainty?"

She nodded.

I decided to walk to North London's Highgate Cemetery, even though it was over three miles away from Southwark and the heavens were now throwing every bit of rain they could. Despite my overcoat, I was saturated, and that was a good thing because I wanted all of my senses to remember this moment. Cold, wet, uncomfortable, eyes adjusting to the light as car headlights were turned on to compensate for the dark clouds, the sounds of drills pounding roads and vehicles' horns, throngs of unsmiling people dashing from one place to another, and the scent of a musky city that was receiving an overdue but unwanted shower— everything around me crystallized this moment.

Michael Stein and Colonel Rowe followed Cochrane, both men staying close to him, though at the same time occasionally crossing the street to ensure their pursuit wasn't obvious. Stein was armed with a hunting knife. Rowe knew he could assemble his rifle in seconds.

Last admission to the cemetery was 4:30 P.M.; I made it with only a few minutes to spare. That was intentional, because I wanted as few people around me as possible during my visit to the Victorian graveyard. I'd been here many times—first when I returned to England after serving in the Legion, and more recently to bury the wife of a dear old friend. The place was so familiar to me that I didn't need to concentrate as I walked along narrow twisting paths, my surroundings a Gothic mix of gnarled trees, moss-covered tunnels, and gravestones wrapped in vines. Elsewhere in the large cemetery were the Egyptian Avenue, the Circle of Lebanon, and the grave of Karl Marx. But I was heading to a less salubrious section—a place where soldiers, obscure writers, impoverished academics, and my mom were buried.

I reached her headstone and felt myself welling up. Not because I was in the presence of Mom—those tears had long ago faded with time. Instead, it was the fresh headstone next to hers that made me choke and feel faint. Its inscription was simple.

JAMES COCHRANE.

A HERO, A HUSBAND, A FATHER.

FINALLY YOU ARE HOME.

My dad. A man who'd performed exemplary service in the CIA. The officer who'd surrendered to

Iranian revolutionaries in '79 in order that his colleagues Alistair and Patrick could escape their ambush. A person who was taken away from me when I was five years old, and years later butchered in Tehran's Evin Prison. A human being who deserved far better than to be dumped in an unmarked grave.

I'd spent years trying to find that grave. I'd failed.

Roger Koenig hadn't. Unknown to me, he too had spent years trying to track down my father's whereabouts. Two months ago, he and some of his Iranian assets had received a lead and secretly excavated a small area of wasteland outside Shiraz. Roger hadn't wanted to get my hopes up, so didn't tell me what he was doing in Iran. After he got the coffin to Dubai, it was flown to the States, where its contents underwent DNA analysis. Even when the results conclusively proved the skeleton was my father, Roger still didn't say anything to me. He had one last thing to do, and he knew it was the right thing because I'd often told him what I would do if I ever found my father. I'd place him in a grave next to my mother.

Roger had chosen the headstone and the words on it. Only when my father was properly laid to rest did he tell me what he'd done. I'd broken down, not knowing whether I was feeling overwhelming grief, sorrow, or joy, or all of those things.

I felt that way now as I knelt and touched the stone. "Hello, Dad. I haven't got freckles and a permanent grin anymore." I don't know why those words came out, but they made tears run down my face as I remembered sitting on our home's lawn and him ruffling my hair before heading off to work. "You're back where you belong. We're all close to you."

Michael was one hundred yards away from Cochrane, hiding within a cluster of trees. He had no idea why he was in the cemetery, but he could tell that the man was emotional. Part of him wondered whether it was wrong to attack the spy here. Clearly, Cochrane had a deep attachment to the grave in front of him. He was paying his respects, perhaps grieving, and his presence in Highgate was a personal matter rather than professional business. It seemed inappropriate to intrude on that. Michael had recently buried his brother. He too had stood over a grave and wept. At times like that, one has no thoughts about service to one's country, duty to one's employer, or anything other than utter sorrow. When Michael had walked away from his brother's grave, all he could think about was their playing together as kids. At that moment, Michael had wanted to turn the clock back, be a kid again, and subsequently make different life choices.

He wondered if Cochrane had similar thoughts right now.

As conflicted as he was, Michael had a job to do. He wasn't going to kill Cochrane. Rather, he was going to hurt him so badly that Cochrane would be lying in a hospital bed for weeks—long enough for him to be taken out of the equation, for no damage to be done to the Stein family name, and for Israel to make its own decisions without meddling interference from the West.

Michael pulled out a knife. He'd make sure its blade would miss vital organs when he plunged it into Cochrane's gut.

I stood motionless for five minutes as I recalled the mere handful of memories I had of my father, together with imagining him in the tales that Alistair and Patrick had recounted. They'd told me he was a very good man, a devoted husband and father, utterly dedicated, brave, professional, sometimes mischievous, and that he had an acute intelligence masked by a laid-back demeanor. According to them, I was like him in some ways and wholly unlike him in others.

Part of me had wanted to delay coming here until I'd finished investigating Gray Site, so that I could spend time grieving or channeling whatever other emotions might come up after I'd visited my father's grave. But

I just couldn't delay seeing him. There was another reason I'd come here today. I had to understand how it felt standing above my father, knowing it wouldn't have been possible to do so without Roger Koenig. In turn, I had to let that feeling determine once and for all my thoughts on what Roger did in Gray Site. I was sure Roger didn't go crazy in the Beirut station. Nor did he kill his colleagues for nefarious reasons. A man who risks his life to bring another man's father home is not that type of guy. Roger shot his fellow workers because he had urgent, legitimate, and honorable reasons for doing so. And my conclusion added significant weight to the theory that Roger targeted the Mossad officer in Gray Site because the Israeli was trying to disrupt coverage of the Hamas meeting.

Colonel Rowe was calm as he unzipped his bag, removed his rifle's components, and assembled it. Before attaching the scope to the weapon, he looked through it. Stein was under trees, about a hundred yards from his target—a good spot, yet his proximity to Cochrane indicated that he intended to assault Cochrane with a close-quarter weapon such as a pistol or knife. Cochrane was by a gravestone, not moving, seemingly deep in thought. When the silencer was attached to the rifle's barrel, Rowe's weapon was ready. He was three hundred yards away from Cochrane, on one knee between two headstones. This would be the easiest kill he'd ever made.

I didn't want to leave, but knew the cemetery would soon be closing. The last thing I wanted was to be ushered away from my father by a Highgate official. My departure had to be on my terms. I said, "Bye, Dad. I'll see you soon. Mum's by your side. She'll take care of you."

Out of the corner of my eye, I caught a rush of movement. A man. Blond. Racing toward me. He was nearly on me as I quickly stepped back. A knife was in his hand, and he slashed it through the air toward my abdomen. I leapt to one side, the knife narrowly missing me, and as I did so I heard a dull thud followed by something striking stone. Small flecks of debris hit my face and the face of my assailant. We both glanced at my father's headstone. A projectile had hit it and chipped its corner. No doubt a bullet. The blond man seemed equally surprised and he followed my gaze in the direction the shot had likely come from.

"Down!" shouted the blond man, in an accented voice, as he launched himself at me and we collapsed to the ground behind my dad's headstone. Another shot was fired, causing more bits of stone to spray past us.

I wondered what the hell was going on, considering that the blond man had just tried to attack me and then got me out of the way of the shooter. He was pinning me down; our only cover from the sniper was Roger's recently erected dedication to my father. The blond man was exceptionally strong. And it seemed he hadn't finished his business, because he raised his knife in an attempt to strike my gut. I pulled one arm free and punched him hard in the throat, causing him to fall away, gasping for air. I got to my feet, staying low behind the stone. Another shot struck it; the sniper had clearly pinned us down. The blond man lashed out with his leg, trying to strike my ankle and topple me. I stamped on his leg before it made contact and said, "Stop! We're both dead if we keep this up."

Still on his back, the knife-wielding man kicked hard with his free leg, hitting me in my stomach and causing me to wince in agony. None of this made any sense. I had to get out of here. I ran, staying low and taking a route that kept my dad's headstone directly between me and the sniper.

The blond assailant pursued me as I raced between trees, zigzagging because more bullets were striking the ground and timber very close to me. I reached a clearing, convinced the sniper could no longer see me for a few moments until he repositioned, and spun around. As I did so, the blond man's fist punched me so hard on the chest that I was lifted off my feet and toppled onto my back. He came for me again, this time with his knife ready, a look of utter focus on his face. There was no hint of fear in his expression. No doubt, I was facing a professional. I rolled to one side as he tried to step on my face, grabbed his foot as he kicked, twisted and yanked his leg to throw him off balance, and kicked into his crotch.

This time, he was incapacitated.

After getting to my feet, I sprinted away as fast as I could. No way could I stay and fight these men. Were it only the blond man I was up against, I might stand a chance, though his strength and focus were formidable. But that man combined with an invisible sniper would surely leave me dead if I tried to take them both on. I was sure the blond man wanted to hurt me very badly but drew a line at seeing me killed; the sniper had other intentions. They weren't working together, that was clear, and that didn't matter because together or alone they could prevent me from investigating Gray Site. And that investigation was infinitely more important than making a stand against my assailants.

Thirty-Two

G od damn you, Cochrane!" Patrick slammed his phone handset back onto its cradle. He was in his office in the CIA headquarters in Langley. It was the thirteenth time today he'd tried to reach Will, but every time he'd called it went straight to voice mail. He'd left messages and sent him SMS's. No response to any of them. He understood that Cochrane was busy; maybe he was on a long flight. But Patrick had been calling all night over a twelve-hour time frame. And the protocol was that if Cochrane anticipated being uncontactable for such a length of time, he was to notify Patrick in advance.

Patrick had been in his office all night, because he couldn't bring himself to leave after hearing about Katy Koenig's brutal murder. He rubbed his weary face, called Admiral Mason, and told him that he couldn't get hold of Cochrane.

Then he called Will's former MI6 controller, Alistair, who was in London. "We've got a problem." He told him about his failed calls. "And it's not the only one. You need to get over here ASAP. Arrive no later than this evening. And I need you to bring something rather special."

Phoebe got out of a taxi and walked briskly to the front door of the apartment building. The cab ride home had been an indulgent treat, but this evening all thoughts of being miserable and penniless were out of the window. She could see Dickie sitting in his living room, watching TV. She'd check up on him later, but first she had to see David. She caught glimpses of her boyfriend in his second-floor apartment, moving back and forth in his kitchen. She entered the building, a huge smile on her face, and walked up the two flights as fast as her high platforms would let her. She knocked on David's door, struck a sexy pose, and held up a bottle of champagne.

When David opened the door, Phoebe said in a sultry tone, "Darling, tonight you and I have some big-time celebrating to do."

David's face beamed. "You got a job offer?"

"Not just one, but three!" Phoebe's full day of job interviews at numerous London art galleries and museums had far exceeded her expectations.

David gave her a big hug, spinning her around so she was in his apartment. "We'd better get the bubbly on ice. And we might need to order some more in, by the sound of things. Come through to the kitchen." He was speaking fast, he was so excited to hear Phoebe's news. "I'm cooking Szechuan chicken and noodles, one of your faves. Sound good?"

"Sounds divine." She watched David tossing meat and vegetables in a wok and adding chilies, crushed garlic, soy sauce, and a spoonful of honey. He seemed so happy, always was when in his beloved kitchen and cooking, but more than usual: right now he seemed in heaven. She knew he cared for her deeply and that it had pained him to see her so down in the dumps after she'd lost her job. He hadn't really known how to console her, because her world was so alien to him. But he had cooked for her, held her when she needed to be cared for, and was always willing to devote as much time to her as his other commitments would allow. They'd never spoken about love before; their relationship was still relatively young, plus David always got a bit flustered and embarrassed when confronted with big emotions. As she watched him now, she wondered if something inside her was changing. Specifically, she wondered if she was falling in love with David.

She'd been surprised David had been prepared to give her such generous financial support. She hadn't asked for it, didn't anticipate it, and wondered how he could afford to cover her rent. She suspected the money came from Will Cochrane. That didn't change anything, apart from reinforcing to her that she was surrounded by a family of sorts, a small group of people who cared for each other and stepped in when one of them was in trouble. David would have hated taking Will's money because he would have wanted to use his own money to help her. But far more important than his pride, no way would he have been able to live with himself if Phoebe was forced to vacate her home due to lack of money. The fact that he was able to swallow his pride for the sake of Phoebe's well-being made him all the more endearing.

"Right, my dear. Let's crack open the champers and get this"—he dipped a finger in his food and licked it—"*beauty* served up."

Phoebe went to her boyfriend, caressed his face, and kissed him delicately on the cheek. "Thank you," she whispered.

David shrugged. "Don't thank me yet. You haven't tasted this. It might not match up to the Szechuan chicken dishes you get from your favorite takeaway, though in my opinion it's an A-plus."

"You know what I mean."

David smiled. "When do you start your new job?"

"All three galleries have given me the weekend to think about their offers. And they all want me to start as soon as possible. I've got some tough decision making to do, because the jobs are all great." She remembered Will telling her she was back in business, after she had cheekily told him she wanted him to try Internet dating. He'd been trying to lift her spirits. Now was different. She really was back in business. She was also at peace. "There's nowhere else I want to be right now. I hope you know that."

David looked at his girlfriend and, as he'd done so many times, wondered why the beautiful woman was so contented to be with a guy whose idea of a perfect evening was making a mess in the kitchen and listening to Dixieland jazz. Sharing his evening with Phoebe was nothing short of a miracle. "I've not heard from Will for a while. Guess he's still sweating it out in Angola."

"*If* he's in Angola."

"Doesn't matter if he's not, really, does it?"

"No. As long as he gets home safe."

David grinned. "Then we can sit him in front of Major Mountjoy and watch what happens."

Phoebe laughed and planted a big kiss on David's lips. "I love you."

Phoebe and David had no idea they were being watched from outside. The sky was now dark; as usual, emergency vehicle sirens and the whoosh of homebound vehicles' tires on wet streets provided the city's end-of-day soundtrack.

Cochrane's apartment was in darkness.

So was the woman's.

She was in the third neighbor's home.

The fourth neighbor—the elderly gentleman—was alone in the bottom apartment, shouting inaudible words at what looked to be a political debate program on his television. The man reminded Michael Stein of his grandfather—old enough to tell the world that enough was enough and everyone had lost their minds.

Stein stayed in the darkness, close to the apartment block, in a location where he could not only observe the building but also the entrance to the Edwardian square across the street. He doubted Cochrane would come back here. The former MI6 officer would probably dismiss the possibility that Stein and the sniper had been watching Cochrane's home for some time, waiting for him to turn up so they could follow him. More likely, he would have realized that his alias passport and credit card were being tracked by them. His pursuers had been onto him, Cochrane would have concluded, from the moment he booked his flight from the States to Heathrow, and they'd stayed on him ever since. Until now.

Stein could have killed Cochrane at Highgate. And Cochrane could have killed Stein. It seemed that neither wanted to do that.

Stein was in the square in case the sniper might also come to Cochrane's home in Southwark and attempt to kill him here. Stein wanted Cochrane incapacitated, but not dead.

The sniper was there because of Thales. Stein was in no doubt about that. In his letter to the Israeli, Thales had told him that he'd deploy his own gunman. That man had followed Cochrane to Highgate, just as Stein had. The sniper was accurate and ruthless. Had Michael not rushed to Cochrane to stab him, Cochrane's head would have been taken off its shoulders. Stein didn't want that. Having recently stood over his brother's grave near Jerusalem, he felt empathy for the former MI6 officer also mourning in front of a headstone.

Stein still had utter resolution. He had to stop Cochrane. Yet he was here because he didn't want Thales's sniper to kill Cochrane. If the sniper came here, Stein would kill him.

To be ready to do so on behalf of a man who Stein did not know still confused the Israeli assassin. He was absorbing facts, making assessments that bent with the wind like trees in a hurricane. The pretty woman in the kitchen was smiling, drinking champagne, leading her partner and the plates he was holding to a different part of the apartment. Cochrane only had three neighbors. They didn't seem to be scared. These were their homes. How could they live near Will Cochrane if that man was bad?

Stein stayed for a couple of hours before using his cell phone to call Mossad headquarters in Tel Aviv. "I've lost Mr. C. Find him for me again when his documents trigger a trace. The other man hasn't come here. That is good and bad. I anticipate the need to head east, to a place close to you. I want you to confirm or deny that possibility the moment you have new data."

Michael turned away from the Southwark residences and walked. He reached the Thames and the golden lamps that aligned its banks. The river was a dark, lifeless sludge in the day, turned into something majestic and meandering at night by the clever positioning of some electric bulbs. It was supposed to be the lifeline of the city. If so, the city was being intravenously fed crap. That's what made the place rotten. Neon lights, rain, and noise struck Michael as he walked to the center of the capital while he was searching for a cab to take him to an airport and away from here.

He *did* like London. But at night it seemed angry, brooding, dark, and lonely. In the day, it seemed to be watching him, like a wife who knows her husband's cheated on her. Michael had to get out of here. Almost certainly, Cochrane was heading to Beirut. That was a metropolis far less intimidating to Michael than London. He knew every inch of the Lebanese city. It was his hunting ground of choice.

Thirty-Three

Based upon Rob Tanner's experience, being successful at Texas Hold'em poker was 20 percent luck, 30 percent holding one's nerve, and 50 percent knowing when to quit a hand. But this afternoon, the ratio seemed off, because Tanner was having quite a good deal of luck. He was competing against five other men, all former college buddies who were in jobs that earned them a darn sight more money than he took home, yet tonight were giving a heap of their hard-earned cash to Tanner because he was outsmarting them and was more often than not dealt killer hands.

They were in a home basement in D.C., the table covered with green felt, two cards faceup in the center, each man holding two cards close to his chest. Two of his friends were puffing on big cigars; their smoke hung motionless above the table, illuminated by a single ceiling lightbulb. All of them had tumblers of bourbon. A seventh man was at the head of the table. He'd lost all of his chips in early hands, and as a result was nominated dealer. He laid the third card faceup on the table.

The men examined the three visible cards and their own hidden cards.

Tanner said, "Raise." He pushed forty dollars' worth of chips in front of him.

The others responded with their decisions.

"Fold." The man to Tanner's left tossed his cards onto the table, facedown.

"Fold," said the man next to him.

"Call." This player met Tanner's bet.

"Fold."

"Fold."

Together with the initial bets of twenty dollars per player, the pot was now $240.

The dealer said, "The flop," as he laid the fourth card on the table.

Tanner examined his cards. He had an ace and a jack. On the table were two aces and two kings. His hand, then, was three aces and two kings, the best possible full house. But it was only good providing his one remaining opponent wasn't holding two kings, giving him four of a kind. If he was, Tanner's hand would mean shit.

Tanner said, "Check," meaning he wanted to stay in the hand but wasn't willing to increase the bet. He looked at his opponent.

The man was silent, his eyes flickering between his two cards that were hidden from view from Tanner and the exposed cards on the table.

He had to check. Surely he wasn't going to raise the bet?

"Raise," said Tanner's opponent. He pushed fifteen hundred dollars' worth of chips a few inches in front of him.

Tanner tried to display no emotion, but inside he was a mess. The man could easily be bluffing—the odds against him holding two kings, when two were also faceup on the table, were significant. But Tanner had seen hands like that before. It happened in poker. Was this a bluff, or was his opponent holding a deadly four-of-a-kind hand?

There was only one way to find out. Tanner pushed all of his remaining chips across the table. Not only had he met his opponent's bet, he'd raised it by another five hundred dollars.

His opponent didn't hesitate, and met the bet.

Shit!

Tanner laid his two cards faceup on the table. Would his full house win? He watched his opponent.

The man smiled and laid down his two cards for all to see. Two kings.

Tanner felt his stomach wrench. The rules of the game meant that the dealer had to lay one more card on the table. Only if it was an ace, thereby giving Tanner four aces, could Tanner win. Anything less would mean Tanner's night of poker was at an end.

The dealer said, "The river," as he laid the last card.

"God damn it!" exclaimed Tanner's opponent. He must have been distraught.

Because the card was an ace.

Tanner smiled. "Shit happens." He pulled the entire pot of chips to his side of the table, and as he did so his cell phone rang. Mason. He listened to the admiral for a few seconds before interrupting him. "What? Now? But it's a Saturday afternoon." He grimaced and moved the cell a few inches away from his ear as Mason started shouting. He could still hear Mason saying something about how ships don't stop sailing just because it's a weekend.

"Got to go, boys." Tanner cashed in his chips.

One hour later, Tanner entered Mason's office in the Pentagon. The normally composed admiral was pacing the room and looked furious. Standing and looking out of a window was the CIA officer Patrick Bolte. In the center of the room was Mae Bäcklund, wearing a summer dress she ordinarily wouldn't be seen dead wearing at work. And sitting in an armchair at the far end of the room was an immaculately dressed middle-aged man who Tanner didn't know.

Tanner winked at Bäcklund. "Didn't have you down as a dress-up kinda girl. Makes you look hot. And makes me feel weird thinking that."

Bäcklund responded, "Don't worry, because the feeling's not mutual. You stink of booze and cigars."

Tanner grinned. "Boys' day."

Mason barked, "Enough!" He looked at Patrick. "Please tell them what you've told me."

Patrick turned to face them. "I can't get hold of Cochrane."

Bäcklund frowned. "Has he lost his nerve?"

"I can't get hold of him," Patrick repeated with deliberation.

Tanner rubbed his hands. "Has he gone dark? Off the radar? I've heard those terms in movies. Do you spooks use them in real life? I really hope you do."

"Shut up." Mason locked his eyes on Patrick's. "I put my trust in Cochrane, and that trust included being kept regularly apprised of his progress."

Patrick knew he had to tread carefully with the admiral. "More often than not, he works alone. He doesn't recognize chains of command. Look, I know it's frustrating, but—"

"Frustrating?!" Mason stood. "The only thing that's stopping Capitol Hill from blundering into wrong decisions, and Israel from storming over its borders, is my ability to calm everyone's nerves. And to do that I need to look them in the eye and convince them that our man is on the case and that I'm reassured by his progress. How can I do that if I've no idea where he is or what he's doing?"

"Lie."

"What?"

"Lie." Patrick held Mason's gaze. "We have to put our trust in Cochrane, regardless of whether he's keeping us in the picture."

"No. We. Don't."

"You of all people can keep the bureaucrats off our backs."

"If I have conviction to do so, yes." Mason turned to his subordinates. "We've got minimal time left. But, based on your research, is there anyone else who can take over from Cochrane? A CIA officer? Special Forces? Maybe even FBI?"

Bäcklund and Tanner were silent.

"Admiral Mason," said the man who Tanner didn't know. Whoever he was, he was a very well-spoken

Englishman. "I flew from the United Kingdom to the United States because operatives previously under the command of Patrick and me will now no doubt be in a state of shock, having heard the dreadful news about Mrs. Koenig. I wish to offer them my condolences. But that could have waited for a few days. The reason Patrick quite rightly told me this morning that I needed to get on the next available jet to Washington is because he astutely predicted Cochrane's silence would prompt you to lose faith in our former colleague. He knew that mere words wouldn't win you over, only hard facts. The issue you've faced thus far is that hard facts have been barred to you and indeed most others within the inner circle of Western intelligence. I'm hoping to make your life easier."

Tanner asked Mason, "Who is this guy?"

The admiral locked his penetrating gaze on his subordinate. "This *guy* is one of the highest-ranking officers in MI6. His name's Alistair McCulloch." He returned his attention to Alistair. "I'm listening."

Alistair nodded at Patrick, who handed each of the three Pentagon staffers a single sheet of paper.

Alistair did the same, stating, "They are security clearance forms. Three of them have legal status in America; the other three are legally binding in the

U.K. Please read their contents carefully. Sign them if you wish. Leave the room if you do not."

Mason and his staff signed the forms and handed them back to the intelligence officers.

"Excellent." Alistair opened his briefcase and withdrew three files, all identical in content. On the covers were a series of letters and numbers. They were a code that referred to Task Force S and specifically the work of its prime field agent, Will Cochrane. "I had to bring those in a diplomatic bag. They can't leave my sight. I'll be taking them back to London when you've finished reading them." He handed the files to Mason and his staff. "This is Will Cochrane. The files detail what he's done for us for fourteen years in MI6 and the Agency. The clearance letters you've just signed mean that if you breathe one word of what you're about to read to anyone, you'll live out the rest of your lives in solitary confinement within a maximum-security prison." Alistair crossed his legs, placed his fingertips together, and closed his eyes. "Let me know when you're ready for a further chat."

Bäcklund and Tanner were the first to finish reading the files. But Mason was still reading an hour after he'd opened the file, because he was taking great pains to absorb every single detail about Cochrane and his work, while his mind worked fast and on multiple levels.

The admiral closed the file when he was finished. His expression and tone were softer when he asked Alistair, "This is all fact?"

"Indeed, all fact."

Patrick added, "Some of it I witnessed in person."

Mason was silent for a minute. "His capabilities shine through, but . . ."

"Yeah, there's a 'but.'" Patrick sat next to Alistair, opposite the admiral. "As his former managers, we'd have preferred someone half as capable and twice as obedient to run in the field. Thing is, though, that would've helped us, but wouldn't have helped getting the jobs done."

"Why did you let someone like this leave MI6?" This was to Alistair.

Many times, Alistair had asked himself the same question. "The joint task force was shut down."

"You could have easily redeployed him."

"We could have." Alistair pointed at the file in Mason's hands. "But in there he was surrounded by orders and protocols."

"Which he constantly disobeyed and ignored."

"Admittedly. But now he's out of the service, he can do what he likes and how he likes, without any repercussions."

Mason's cold expression returned. "Including not keeping us apprised of his progress."

"He doesn't work for you. Or for me. That's the deal, and we have to remember that. I'm asking you to consider keeping your faith in Cochrane. He'll have gone silent for a reason. But that doesn't mean he's not still hard at work. Please—he's done this before and I've pulled my hair out in the process. I know how it feels to sit where you're sitting now. However, he's always delivered."

Mason was deep in thought. "You two, Cochrane, Roger Koenig, Laith Dia, and Suzy Parks. That was the task force?"

"Yes. We had others come and go, but only on a temporary basis. The core full-time team was the individuals you've just mentioned."

"Koenig's dead. Cochrane's allegedly working for us, though is nowhere to be found." He darted a look at Patrick. "You seem to have no clearly defined role in the Agency. And you, Alistair?"

"I'm just like Patrick—director without portfolio. Nobody on either side of the pond knows what to do with us. So they leave us alone. And that's fine as far as we're concerned."

"The others?"

It was Patrick who answered. "Laith Dia and Suzy Parks have left the CIA. I think they thought a career in the Agency outside of the task force wasn't ever going to give them what they needed."

"Where are they now?"

"Suzy and her husband and child live in Virginia. So does Laith, though he's divorced and lives in an RV."

Mason asked Alistair, "When do you fly back?"

Alistair replied, "Tomorrow evening. I need to visit Laith and Suzy at their homes in the day. We never really had a proper chance to say good-bye."

"And where are you staying this evening?"

"Why do you ask?"

Mason interlocked his fingers. "To give myself peace of mind that I know the exact whereabouts of a senior MI6 officer who's on my patch. In my experience, MI6 officers always need to be watched. Their own country doesn't trust them, so how can we be expected to do different?" He smiled. "Actually, I ask because I'd be delighted if you'd join me for dinner. I'd dearly like to gain your insight on Britain's latest stance on support for Israel. No doubt you'd like to freshen up in your room first." He checked his watch. "May I send a chauffeur to collect you from your hotel in, say, two hours?"

"That would be splendid. But first . . ." The senior MI6 officer held out his hand. The files were returned to him and he placed them back in his case.

Mason said to his employees, "Go back to your weekend. I needed you here in case we had to get a plan B in place tonight."

When Tanner and Bäcklund were out of the room, the admiral added, "I'm prepared not to set in place a plan B."

Patrick and Alistair were mightily relieved. "Thank you."

"Don't thank me yet. In five minutes, if presented with new data, I may make a different decision."

"After he met you, Cochrane liked you," said Alistair.

The comment took Mason by surprise.

"He called me after your face-to-face in this room."

Mason said nothing.

"I can count the number of people who Cochrane likes on one hand. Most of them are dead."

"I suspect your number is too low."

"It is. Cochrane's at a point in his life where he feels brave enough to trust certain people. Friendship has come from that huge leap of faith, most notably from the three neighbors who share his London apartment building with him. Cochrane wants me to think he's his old self—untrusting of everyone, being that way because of who he is and what he does. I can see through it. He respects you and likes you. It was necessary to show you the Task Force S files, but they aren't the whole story. His telephone call to me after being in this room *is*."

Mason felt like the weight of the world was on his shoulders. "Can he succeed, Alistair?"

Alistair put his overcoat on and grabbed his case. "He can fail." He pointed at the window. "Just like everyone else out there."

Thirty-Four

I'd spent a day and most of the evening moving from one place in London to another, mostly whiling away my time in cafés and restaurants while trying to ascertain if the two men who attacked me in the cemetery were once again on my tail. Anti-surveillance is something I excel at; countless times it's saved my life. But even for someone with my training and experience, it's never an exact science, particularly in big cities where there are too many variables.

However, by the end of the day, I was sure I wasn't being followed by my assailants. That thought was merely a temporary reprieve, because there was a bigger question that weighed heavily on me—how did the men get on my tail in the first place? One option was that they knew where I lived and followed me from my home to Highgate. If that was the case, they'd either had to have been watching my home for weeks, maybe months, waiting for me to show up—and I thought that was logistically unlikely—or someone had told them I was going to be at that location at a specific day and time. And yet I'd told no one about my intended movements. This left one uncomfortable probability: my alias passport and credit card were blown, details of which had been supplied to the blond man and the sniper, both of whom had the resources and capabilities to track me via their usage. Only intelligence officers, specialist cops, and customs officials have such capabilities. Were the men who tried to kill me such professionals? Or were they being fed the tracking data from corrupt members of those professions? Either way, if I was right, every time I used my documentation in any part of the world, I might as well be calling them and telling them my exact location.

I had no other ID I could use, but calling people was one thing I had control over. My cell in the name of Richard Oaks was switched off, its battery removed so that the device couldn't be remotely attacked and used as a microphone receiver. No doubt Patrick and Mason were fretting because they hadn't heard from me. That was tough on them but necessary for me. I had no idea who I could trust.

I finished my fifth black coffee of the day, walked fast out of the café, and hailed a cab. I had to get out of Britain and examine Gray Site. But the moment I bought an air ticket for Beirut, my pursuers would know I was en route to that location.

Standing outside room 32 in D.C.'s Savoy Suites Hotel, Rob Tanner checked his watch and waited for the minute hand to tell him that it was precisely 6 P.M. He knocked five times on the door, counted three seconds, knocked twice again, counted two seconds, and gave one last knock. The door opened. Tanner's contact was standing in the entrance. The middle-aged man was wearing suit pants, a shirt, and a tie. He ushered Tanner into the room, closing the door behind him and fixing its security bolt in place.

The room looked similar to the other hotel rooms Tanner had visited during the last few days—small, clean, neither flashy nor tawdry. Its occupant always chose rooms like this because they suited his cover as a traveling salesman who only needed a place to sleep and wash before departing for work. The hotels' other occupants were like him. They kept themselves to themselves and were usually too dog-tired to care about other guests.

Tanner grabbed a bottle of beer from the minibar and sat in a chair. His contact sat opposite him, only empty floor space between them.

"What do you have?" the man asked.

Tanner took a glug of the beer straight from the bottle. "Things have moved up to a whole new level."

"I'm all ears."

Tanner tapped a finger against the bottle. "I was made to sign a document that says I'll be poleaxed if I speak to someone like you."

"Good thing people like me and you don't care about that."

Tanner ran his hand through his designer haircut. "How much longer do I have to keep doing this?"

"As long as it takes. You got a problem with that?"

"Nope."

"Good. Anyway, I reckon Mason's days in the Pentagon are numbered. I'll move you onto new things sooner than you think. What have you got?"

Tanner told him about the meeting in Mason's office earlier today—Alistair's files, Task Force S, Cochrane's background, and the task force personnel. "I don't know whether Alistair persuaded Mason that Cochrane's silence shouldn't change anything. Mason told Bäcklund and me to leave his office so he could speak privately with Patrick and Alistair."

"Your hunch?"

"Is that Alistair and Patrick convinced Mason to keep the faith with the good Samaritan."

"I agree." The man smiled with a look of sarcasm. "Three honorable men agreeing to do the gentlemanly thing." His expression turned serious. "I'll pass this on. Keep doing what you're doing. No suspicions?"

Tanner swallowed the rest of the beer. "No. I'm a pain in the ass. It distracts Mason and Bäcklund from the truth."

"Excellent."

Monsieur de Guise cleared away the dinner plates, washed the pots and pans he'd earlier used to cook tonight's dinner of partridge in a red wine jus, and brought Safa a mug of hot chocolate. The Palestinian boy was still sitting at the dinner table. Part of his mind had clarity, yet the rest was befuddled. His guardian had spoken to him near continuously throughout their meal. His words gave Safa certainty but also a sense of dislocation from who he once was.

De Guise entered his study and returned a few moments later holding a few items. "And now we must indulge in some fun, must we not?"

"Yes, sir."

"Your medicine first, though."

Safa looked at the medical kit with trepidation. "When will I be better? Soon, I hope."

De Guise injected him three times. "The human body is a miracle. It can survive most things. But you, my poor Safa, have a body that had been pushed too far. When I first met you, I knew it could no longer cope. As all bodies do at that stage, it was eating itself." De Guise removed the tourniquet from the boy's biceps. "I intervened and reversed that process. Every night, you are administered proteins, vitamins, and blockers that trick some of your neurons into believing your body is strong again and needs a fully functioning nervous system. It is a temporary trick, but we hope that by the time your neurons realize they've been duped, your body will be genuinely stronger, at which point your neurons will be your friends again." De Guise omitted to tell Safa that his needles also contained barbiturates, opiates, and lysergic acid diethylamide, which—combined with de Guise's words—produced a perception of inevitable vulnerability and desperate desire for one last chance at retribution before one's body and mind drifted away forever. He smiled. "Doctors think of themselves as gods."

He applied Band-Aids to Safa's arm, which the boy rubbed. "That can only work if gods are doctors."

"An apt observation." De Guise had a twinkle in his eye. "Gods also kill. Doctors do not."

Safa shook his head. "They do when all is lost."

De Guise had hoped Safa would say something like this. "Tell me when such situations present themselves."

Safa took a swig of his drink. It was piping hot, but the pain from the liquid's heat seemed to belong to someone else. The flavor was sweet and syrupy to his taste buds, yet acrid to his mind. It seemed an indulgent drink. One for pigs.

"They extinguish the lives of the irreparable, the suffering who've no hope."

"Your French vocabulary is improving."

"I've you to thank for that, sir."

"But your manners remain poor. You still wear your shoes in our home."

Safa was embarrassed. "I forgot to take them off, sir."

"But you won't tomorrow. Let us switch to English and see how we get on." De Guise smoothed his hands over a rectangular piece of cardboard. "We shall create people." He drew the silhouettes of six men, handed Safa a pair of nail scissors, and said, "Cut out the shapes."

Safa frowned, not understanding.

De Guise used his fingers to mimic a cutting action. "Do it carefully."

The Palestinian boy set to work. Within ten minutes, he'd cut out the shapes.

His guardian lit a candle inside a lantern and discarded the shapes. The rectangular card with the empty shapes of people was what he needed. He wrapped it around the glass cover of the lantern and fixed it in place with tape. After extinguishing all other candles in the room, so that the lantern was the sole source of light, he switched back to French and said, "Sit on the floor, in the center of the room."

When Safa had done so, the professor joined him and squatted by his side. He held the lantern at arm's length above his head and used both hands to slowly spin it around. The lamp's light cast the images of men onto the dining room walls. They were moving, yet seemed to be watching Safa. "Now we return to English. Pretend you are in the United States and wish to buy a train ticket to Washington, D.C. I am the ticket agent. In English, what would you say to me?"

Safa stared at the images on the wall, entranced, not sure what he thought about them. "Please, sir, I don't speak or understand much English, but I would like to buy a train ticket to Washington, D.C. Can you help?"

"Perfect." De Guise rotated the lantern a fraction faster. "You move amid crowds of pedestrians. How do you deport yourself?"

"Deport?"

"The way you move, the angle of your head, even your expression. Essentially, how do you wish people to see you?"

"I wish not to be noticed."

"And how do you achieve that?"

"I make myself small; I don't look at people."

"Most people would think the same, but that is not how to be invisible. To disappear in a crowd, one must be normal. Engage in brief eye contact, then break it; hold your head up as if you are taking in the sights; move with purpose, sometimes fast, other times at ambling pace; unashamedly, be a dumb tourist who doesn't care whether anyone's looking at him or not. That way, you'll disappear."

Safa grinned, though he felt tingles across his face and his skin felt stretched. It was an uncomfortable feeling. "Dumb tourist."

De Guise moved the lantern fast enough to make the human shapes become a slight blur. "You are in the center of a large crowd. No one notices you. No one cares about you. They are your enemies. More than that, they are enemies of everything you've ever held dear."

The shapes were moving so fast now that Safa's vision was blurred, his mind was confused, and his stomach was nauseous.

"What must you do to correct their imperfections?" His guardian switched back to French. "Their imperfections, Safa: What must be done about them?"

The Palestinian boy started sweating. "Please, stop!"

"Only you can make this stop."

"You hold the lantern."

"I do."

"Please stop turning it. *Please*."

"Turning it? Safa, it is motionless." De Guise twisted it faster. "It is interesting that you think the shapes are moving."

"Moving too fast!"

"Ah, I see what is happening. Your mind is projecting meaning onto the characters on the wall. It thinks they're moving. It is telling you that their speed means they can never be stopped and held to account."

"I want them to stop!"

"Then you must find a means to do so and use something to make that happen; use something that is quicker than the fastest human being."

A sharp pain stabbed behind Safa's eyes, yet he couldn't stop looking at the images. "My enemies?"

"Yes, and they wish to cause you further pain. They don't care about anything beyond mocking your weakness. If only they knew the truth. Because you are not weak, are you?"

"Don't want to be." Safa's face was screwed up, his skin now saturated with sweat.

"Perhaps you carry something that could make this end? Something fast?"

Safa nodded. "Yes."

"Something that will give meaning to everything?"

"My meaning."

"Your meaning, indeed." De Guise moved the lantern as quick as his nimble fingers could maneuver the object. He knew his charge would be in a lot of pain now, his mind disoriented yet trying to grapple onto some semblance of meaning, his body craving sleep and an end to this. "The lantern, Safa. It must stop. Has to stop. Only you can make it stop. Punish. Tell it why. Finalize all matters."

Safa sat as if frozen.

"Safa!" The professor's tone was commanding. "Only you can make it stop. It must be you. I am not your parents, but I speak with their blessing and on their behalf. Your mind and body must be strong. I have a responsibility to ensure that. Make the bad things stop!"

No longer able to bear any of this, Safa leapt to his feet, grabbed the lantern, and smashed it on the floor. "You . . . murderers!" He repeatedly stamped on the broken glass. Speaking to the lantern, he shouted, "You did nothing while you watched the crazy men kill everyone. You are fat! You only love your power. No more. No more!"

Monsieur de Guise withdrew a vinyl record and placed it on the turntable. He sat in one of his leather living room armchairs, next to a fire in the fireplace, and sipped his calvados. Safa was sleeping in his bed, exhausted from shock, confusion, and drugs that were fighting each other in his brain and were trying to take his cognitive process in conflicting directions. The professor had ensured that his charge was warm and was sleeping in a position that minimized the chances of him swallowing his tongue.

The music on the record player was Sergei Rachmaninoff's *The Isle of the Dead*, a symphonic poem that depicts Charon, the ferryman of Hades, rowing on the River Styx. De Guise closed his eyes and imagined that he was the boatman, taking young Safa to the land of the dead, the boy nervous yet beguiled by the wonder of their adventure. The man who called himself Thales jettisoned the image because it was one that belonged to romance and had no place in a calculating mind whose bedrock was the Enlightenment and reason.

But sometimes the professor couldn't resist gently testing his devotion to precision and logic; he did so to tease his mind. Occasionally the test would see his stoic thought process crumple in favor of more emotive imagery, much in the way that a highly intelligent man or woman can go wobbly at the knees at the sight of a beautiful person.

He told himself this was why he liked magic. It was his secret piece of art. A thing of beauty that was unenlightened and unabashedly ethereal. The truth was different. Like everything else about de Guise, his magic was precise trickery. It was science.

His cell phone rang. He accepted the call from Colonel Rowe but didn't speak; instead, he closed his eyes again and imagined Safa dipping his hand in the Styx, watching the black water drip off his fingers, thinking the fluid calmed the tremors in his limbs and heart.

"Sir. He got away. It appears your Israeli wishes to hurt but not extinguish. He confused my line of sight."

De Guise let Rachmaninoff's orchestral notes wash over him. "He is not *my* Israeli. And I employ you because your sight has thus far always been true. Where is the Englishman?"

"Gone. Heading to an airport, I suspect. I know where he lives, but he probably won't go there to collect his things."

"Of course. I want you to go to an airport right now."

"Sir, I don't know which airport the Englishman—"

"Of course you don't. Thirty minutes ago I received a telephone call from someone in my trust who was able to deliver far better and more instructive words than it appears you are capable of today." De Guise spoke for a further five minutes. "You've noted down the details I've just given you?"

"I have."

"Memorize and burn them."

"They may give the Englishman even greater purpose."

"Perhaps. Or maybe they will make him impotent with grief. Either way, his judgment will be clouded with emotion. Whether your action stops him in his tracks or puts fire in his heart, his mind will no longer be clear. The Holy Land will remain a mystery to him. That is all that matters." De Guise opened his eyes and watched the flames lick the wood, like serpents caressing the kindling before consuming it. "Get on the next available flight."

Thirty-Five

Being a divorced father of two teenage girls was tough for Laith Dia. He had very little cash, was a man, lived alone in an RV amid a rolling, forested landscape with no close neighbors, and was desperate for his girls to come and visit. But that was Laith's situation, and he wasn't grumbling, though he was deeply sad that he was forced to spend so much time apart from his darlings. The former Delta Force and paramilitary CIA officer did what he always did when confronted by desperate situations—one foot in front of the other; get on with it; don't fall; let the body do the hard graft even if the mind is baying for mercy.

He was busy at one end of the RV, painting over scratches on the bodywork. His home smelled of fried bacon, yet the place was clean and tidy and contained only a few mementos, including a photo of Laith free-falling from the edge of space, two photos of his daughters in pretty dresses, and a wall-mounted dagger that had been given to him by a World War II French Canadian commando. He was trying to adapt his small living quarters to hold his thirteen-and fifteen-year-old children who'd no doubt be partly repulsed by the idea but also excited by the prospect. These were the same girls who once would have followed their dad anywhere; they still would, but they were growing so fast and were evolving into women. Plus their bitch mom was filling their heads with crap about him. Thankfully, his girls took after him. They were independent thinkers and looked at life differently. Their mom hated that, and her reaction warmed Laith's heart. Still, his kids had needs for privacy.

His ex-wife had told him yesterday that if he got his place in order, his girls could come visit this weekend. When the girls were under ten, they loved the adventure of being here. But now? He didn't know. They hadn't been allowed to visit for years, and in fairness to their mom, Laith had been traveling for work almost nonstop until recently. Everything had changed since he'd left the Agency.

He heard the sound of a vehicle driving over stones he'd long ago deliberately scattered around the perimeter of his lot. He'd been expecting the noise. It belonged to a car that carried a man who would ordinarily ensure he was a million miles away from anywhere like this.

Laith felt apprehensive. Not because the man intimidated him; rather, because their personalities were so different.

He washed his hands clean of paint and opened the RV's door.

A tall, slender, blond Englishman in his mid-fifties got out of a Chevrolet rental car. "Mr. Dia," the man called out. He wore a pin-striped suit and perfectly polished shoes. "I'm a tad early."

"You're never early or late for anything." Laith muttered the words and stared with evident suspicion. "Did you drive here on the correct side of the road?"

"Ha!" The man clapped his hands once and looked around. "You live amid the bosom of a tamed beauty."

Laith asked, "You sayin' Virginia's all tits and ass?"

"With nothing to differentiate itself under its blouse from others of its kind." The Englishman smiled.

"A home's a home, dumb ass."

"Still—you are most certainly surrounded by beauty, and that says much about you." Alistair grinned, his expression boyish and cold. "Your ambience instructs your character, does it not?"

"Actually, I live here because my permit to pitch my RV says I can."

"Of course." Alistair shut his car door. "I'm parched. Would you make me a cup of tea?"

Laith's huge frame filled the entrance to his dwelling. "Coffee, Coke, beer—you choose."

"Oh dear." Alistair's smile was gone as he strode toward Laith's mobile home. "American hospitality . . ."

"*My* hospitality. Take it or leave it." Laith moved out of the way as Alistair walked briskly into his RV. "Thanks for coming."

"You've sold your car. What choice did I have?"

"I've got me a cabdriver. Well, at least a guy who has a pickup. He runs me around just fine when I call him."

"But not today." Alistair sat on a thin strip of seat along the inside edge of the RV. "I will have a coffee with a dash of milk and half a spoon of sugar."

Laith made him the drink and handed it to him. "Try not to spill it. Got my girls visiting in a couple of days. Don't want the place to be a mess."

"What age are they?"

"Thought you knew everything about me?"

"I do."

"Then you'll know they're teenagers." Laith swept an arm around. "I'm trying to work out how to get this right."

Alistair put down his coffee, his expression earnest as he said, "Most people think men like us are defined by our jobs. They forget we have other attributes."

"Meaning?"

"Meaning, you have an attribute pertaining to parenthood."

"So do you. Your two girls. Where are they now?"

"Both at Oxford University."

Laith shook his head. "Why doesn't that surprise me?"

Alistair replied, "It doesn't surprise me, either." He crossed his legs, somehow looking as much at home here as he did in London's St. James's Club. "The issue is one of expectations. They expect me to want them to be there, whereas the truth is that I expect them to be the same girls who sat on my back while I was in my suit and shuffling along the floor pretending to be a donkey."

"After a hard day being grilled by the Joint Intelligence Committee."

"Something like that." Alistair took another sip of his coffee. It tasted foul, but he showed no indication of displeasure. "They've always displayed a flair for the theatrical. I'd rather they'd gone to drama school." He looked around. "Pursued their own dreams. Not their false notion of mine."

His comment surprised Laith. "You mean that? Or is this one of your MI6 mind games?"

"Sir, you are no longer of use to me. Why would I deploy mind games on someone like that?"

"Fair point."

Alistair stood, took off his jacket and tie, and rolled up his sleeves. "Do you have a tent?"

"What?"

"And tarpaulin?"

"I got outdoors stuff. Yeah."

"Your rear window opens, I note."

Alistair was right. The window took up the entire back end of the RV.

Laith said, "You're thinking, make this bigger?"

"And better, more nuanced, with adventurous private places—yet at the same time feminine. You must make sure you have a divider between you and them, but also a divider between the girls. Privacy and personal space are important at their age. As, too, is close proximity to the people they love. Let's make this the best weekend they can remember." Alistair rubbed his hands, a smile now back on his face, his tone of voice commanding. "Mr. Dia. Lay your outdoors items on the ground beyond the entrance to your home."

Laith did so.

"Excellent." Alistair looked at the surrounding forest. "We have much at hand, though we are still missing some items. Several sturdy poles would be helpful—your height, carved from trees. Some of the flora on the outskirts of the wood line can be carefully uprooted and replanted here." He tapped his shoe on the ground close to the RV's rear window. "They will be pretty, will they not?" Before Laith could reply, Alistair continued, "Window leads to a tarpaulin construction of waterproof and windproof ceiling and walls. It is a secret corridor, of sorts. And it is immaculately aligned and leads to your tent, where one or both girls can sleep, at the other end of which is another tarpaulin corridor where you can position your bathtub. And just beyond it, the replanted flora will be visible. There are other touches I will suggest, but that is the construction outline."

One hour later, Laith had the grin of a man in heaven as he stood outside his RV and looked at the passageway he and Alistair had constructed and secured with twine and other supports. "I'll be damned."

"On the contrary, a king has constructed a palace for his princesses." Alistair winked. "You will never be damned. Not now. Your girls will be proud of their father."

"Didn't expect this from you, of all people." Laith felt emotional. He'd never had anything in common with Alistair. The Englishman seemed to have come from another planet. When he'd arrived here, Laith had expected the MI6 commander to ridicule his personal circumstances.

Alistair gently punched a fist against Laith's huge chest. "We place one foot in front of the other. Yes?"

Laith wondered how Alistair knew his personal mantra. "Yeah, though that's getting harder."

"It is." Alistair studied his former colleague. "As invigorating as it's been to help you prepare for your weekend with your children, you know that's not why I came here."

"I know." Laith looked southwest, at hills and forests that seemed to stretch on forever. Twenty-seven miles away, in the direction he was looking, was Roger and Katy Koenig's home. "Are Katy's boys still staying with their aunt?"

Alistair nodded. "Most likely she'll keep them indefinitely. She's adamant they must stay with family."

Laith was glad, though at the same time felt the same burning anger and grief that had been plaguing him since he'd learned of Katy's murder. "Are the police making any progress with their investigation into her death?"

"None whatsoever. Whoever killed her left no trace."

"A professional?"

"Yes."

"I'm thinking, someone linked to Roger's past."

Alistair followed Laith's gaze. "As am I, though there are so many variables. Roger made a lot of nasty enemies in the course of his work. There's a long queue of people who'd like to take revenge on him by murdering his loved ones."

"One of those variables might be Gray Site."

Alistair put his hand on Laith's arm. "Roger killed his colleagues. You must let go of any other possibilities that might be running through your mind, because there are none that square with the facts. Katy's death was nothing to do with what happened in Beirut. It was a tragedy that—"

"Tragedy?!" Laith stepped away from Alistair, his big frame shaking with fury. "A tragedy is when something real sad happens. Katy was butchered. It wasn't a *tragedy*. It was a killing."

Alistair was silent as he watched his former colleague move back and forth as if his body didn't know what to do with the emotions coursing through it. The MI6 officer fully understood how Laith felt, because he shared the same feelings. He'd been horrified to learn about Katy's death. And he was here because he needed to check that Laith was bearing up. He knew that the former Delta Force operative would be consumed with the desire to track down the murderer and rip his head off. The fact that he had no way of identifying the killer would be eating away at him.

Laith was still fuming as he pointed at Alistair. "Maybe it was payback for what Roger did in Beirut. The French, or Israelis, or maybe you Brit guys did it. Killed her. Revenge."

"My dear, dear chap," said Alistair softly as he walked up to Laith, uncaring if the former CIA officer might punch him off his feet. It pained him to see the normally composed and jovial operative like this. "You know that's not what happened."

The anger in Laith was swept away by sorrow. His body was shaking as he said, "It shouldn't have ended this way—the section closed down, Will out, Roger killed, his wife murdered, you and Patrick sidelined in the agencies, me playing soldier in the Guard, and"—he tried to chuckle, but the noise came out all wrong— "Suzy learning to bake."

Alistair patted his back. "We had a good run, my boy. And never forget that we made a difference."

Laith pulled away, wiped his eyes, breathed in deeply, and regained his composure. Now, he looked every bit the former Special Forces and paramilitary officer who'd conducted some of the West's most highly classified and risky missions. "Damn right. We did."

"We did." Alistair's smile was one of complete warmth. He held his hand out. "It has been my privilege to have served alongside you, Mr. Dia."

Laith shook Alistair's hand. "And you, crazy Englishman."

They stood in silence, looking out at the beautiful vista. Laith imagined his daughters arriving here and at first being repulsed by the prospect of being at one with the wilderness, but soon capitulating to the child within them and running around barefoot, shrieking with laughter as they played, explored their surroundings, got muddy, smelled their supper cooking on the barbeque, and realized that freedom didn't get any better than this. Laith would watch them while turning meat on the grill and sipping a beer. And when the food was ready, he'd belly laugh and tell them that to hell with getting cleaned up before dinner—they could sit on the ground next to him and eat their meal with their hands. Maybe he'd make a fire if the evenings got chilly, and they could sit close to it, under a starlit night sky, telling stories and cracking jokes. He imagined them saying their city-based mom would *never* let them do anything like this. He'd make no comment. They loved their mom. So had he, back in the day. Doing was all that mattered. Putting one foot in front of the other. Bitching about life and everyone in it never achieved anything.

Alistair wondered how his daughters would fare staying here. He'd meant what he said when he'd told

Laith that their natural inclinations were toward art and drama and that he'd hoped they would pursue a path that enhanced those attributes. He wished he could turn the clock back and ensure he was there on the day they made decisions about their future. They'd chosen to go to Oxford University when he was debriefing a Russian agent in Vienna. He only discovered their choices when it was too late to reverse them. "May I visit you with my girls?"

"What?"

"They, and I, would like that."

Laith laughed. "You really *are* crazy."

"Why?"

"Because you're a posh Englishman who owns half of Scotland. You don't hang out with your overachieving girls at some American's RV in the country."

Alistair smiled while keeping his eyes on the horizon. "I am a spy. I seek the unusual."

"Unusual?"

"The real things a gentleman like me isn't expected to seek." Alistair glanced at Laith, his expression warm and earnest, his tone of voice the most truthful he'd heard come out of his mouth in years. "I'd help you extend your shelter. My girls would adore the adventure. And it would do them a world of good."

"You're forgetting something."

"What, may I inquire?"

Laith shook his head, though it was clear he looked happy. "If my girls are here as well, that would mean we'd have to survive our vacation looking after four adolescent girls."

Alistair smiled. "It would be fine. My daughters are still young enough to reappraise their life choices." He breathed in deeply through his nostrils. "This place would help them. Do you hunt?"

"Used to. Don't seem to have the stomach for it these days."

"I can see why, though one still needs to put food on the table." The MI6 controller pointed at a cluster of trees five hundred yards away. "I have expert ghillies at my disposal in my Scottish estate. Some of them have been in my family's employ since I was a boy. Over the years, they've taught me things about hunting deer, grouse, pheasant, and other game. If your stomach repairs, and you have a twelve-gauge, you could sit in that cluster without being seen. Beyond it is a nice area of marshland. Duck, geese, and wild turkey might congregate there. It would be easy for a man with your skills to supply our girls with a brace or two of good meat."

"Yeah, I guess it would." Laith added, "You're welcome to visit anytime."

"My sincere gratitude." Alistair glanced at Laith. "You'll be all right, won't you, Mr. Dia?"

"I'll be okay. And you?"

Quietly, Alistair answered, "I'll be all right too. Nothing better. Nothing worse."

"You and me both."

Throughout their career of working together, neither man had spoken as many words to each other as they'd just done. On the surface, they were wholly dissimilar. Yet they were spies and parents. That made them more alike than most on the planet. Laith wanted Alistair and his daughters to come here. And when the men were reunited, they could look at each other with the unspoken knowledge that they'd spent a lifetime combating horrors that their daughters would never know about, let alone see.

"I have to go now, Laith. Remember what I said about that cluster of trees. It's an excellent place for a huntsman to hide with a rifle."

Laith placed his hand on Alistair's shoulder. "I just don't like being the huntsman anymore."

"Nor me."

The first sniper bullet hit Laith in the forehead; the second hit Alistair in the gut, dropping him to his knees; a third struck Alistair in the head.

More rounds were fired into the prone bodies.

In the distance, a tall man emerged from the cluster of trees and walked across the large area of scrubland toward Laith's RV and the two bodies outside the vehicle. In one hand he carried a silenced sniper rifle.

When Colonel Rowe reached the bodies, he examined them for signs of life. There were none. Laith Dia and Alistair McCulloch were dead.

It was Suzy Parks's favorite part of the day—6 P.M., a time when the countryside around her home seemed to become calm and peaceful, and sunshine would wane into a homey glow. Six P.M. was also the time that her toddler went to bed. She adored her little boy, but, as all parents with young kids know, there are times when it's crucial to get adult time while the cherished little one is safe, warm, well fed, and asleep.

Her husband, Andrew, had returned home from work five minutes ago. Shortly, he'd start preparing dinner. But, as ever at this time of day, he'd spend thirty minutes with his wife. At this time of year, he could do so while they both sat outside on their porch—sometimes with a mug of coffee, more frequently in the last year, since Suzy had weaned her boy off breast-feeding, a drink that contained something stronger.

He sat next to her on a wide chair suspended by ropes that gently rocked.

"How was work?" she asked her rocket scientist partner.

"Do you really want to know?"

Suzy laughed. "No."

"Thought not." It always amused him that he and Suzy could never talk about their jobs; his was so complex and specialized that one would need to be another rocket scientist to understand anything he said, and when she was with the Agency she wasn't allowed to tell him what she did. He reckoned it was one of the reasons their marriage was so strong. They had to find other things to talk about. Plus, they were bonded by their love of their unexpected child and a passion for ballroom dancing. "I've got a recipe for Mexican chili con carne that I want to try out this evening. Okay with you?"

Suzy rubbed her hand over her husband's. "That sounds good." Since she'd left the Agency and become a full-time mom, Andrew had done everything he could to help out when he got home. He knew motherhood was tougher at age forty. Among many reasons, Suzy loved him for that. He was also a fine cook.

"The recipe says not to use ground beef. Instead, you use big chunks of braising steak. Then, at the end of cooking, you use two forks to shred the meat. You good with five chilies in the pot?"

"Why not?" She bowed her head. "Alistair was supposed to come here this afternoon. He never showed up. I baked him some cupcakes."

"Did you tell him in advance that you'd baked for him?"

"No. Why do you ask?"

Her husband grinned. "If you had, that might have explained his decision not to visit."

Normally, that type of comment would have made Suzy laugh. Not today.

"It would have been nice to see him, to say good-bye."

Andrew frowned. "You okay?"

Suzy looked at the vista around their lovely Virginia home. "I heard some bad news this morning. Roger Koenig's wife's been murdered."

"What?" Andrew didn't know the Koenigs well, because they'd never been acquainted socially. Nevertheless, he'd accompanied Suzy to Roger's funeral and had met Katy. "Do the police know why?"

"It doesn't seem so. They're pulling out the stops, plus the feds are all over the case because of Roger's background. But at the moment, the killing looks random."

"Jeez." Andrew gripped his wife's hand. "Sorry to hear that, hon."

"Me too." Suzy smiled, though she felt forlorn. "They were my boys—Patrick, Alistair, Will, Laith, and Roger. So many times, they pissed me off. But they always did the right thing by me. Honorable men."

"You getting all mother hen on me?" Andrew hoped the comment would perk up his wife's spirits.

It didn't. "Probably." She sighed. "You remember when I had to go overseas when I was pregnant?"

"With clarity. You caused me sleepless nights and never told me where you were. I still don't know where you were."

"It was Berlin. The boys and I shared a big apartment while they were doing their stuff in the field and I was telling them where to go." She stroked Andrew's hair. "I couldn't tell you where I was because I wasn't allowed to, plus I didn't want you to get jealous that I was cohabiting with men." Quickly, she added, "We had separate rooms."

Andrew planted a kiss on his wife's cheek. "I don't doubt that for one second."

"Thing is, Will Cochrane bought me a book he'd picked up at the airport. It was some self-help thing about juggling work and parenting. He gave it to me. I threw it at Laith, because I thought I was being patronized. I was wrong. At least, wrong in interpreting the boys' intentions. They were in Berlin to spend days watching a hotel that contained a Russian hit squad. They took turns watching. Those that were off duty slept in their rooms; those that were on duty sat in the hotel lobby and elsewhere. When they were working, they took the book with them. All of them read it cover to cover and wrote notes in the margins about tips for my pregnancy. It was only when I got back to the States that I read the book and saw their handwritten notes." She glanced back at the house. "Still got it somewhere."

"Why are you telling me this?"

"Because it was endearing. They were like teenagers asking a girl out on a date for the first time." Suzy cocked her head. "No, that analogy's not right. More like big brothers who are helping their little sis buy tampons in the local store."

"Men can get awkward about these things, but the good ones push through that feeling."

Suzy looked back at the countryside around them.

Andrew continued holding her hand as he followed her gaze. "Going to rain tonight. We need it, though. Wash away this humidity."

"Puts me in the mood for a drink. Want one?"

"Sure."

Suzy entered her kitchen. Next to the stove, the cakes she'd baked for Alistair were resting on a wire rack. They were black in parts, the icing she'd dolloped on top had cracked, and the cherries she'd placed on their crowns had burned. She picked one up and tapped it against the work surface. It was rock hard. Suzy smiled, thinking that Alistair had done himself a service by not coming here and saying good-bye. She grabbed two tumblers, tossed in some ice cubes, went into the living room, and fixed gin and tonics. She took the drinks back onto the porch and sat next to her husband. She raised her glass. "To new beginnings."

Andrew was about to join her in the toast, but hesitated. "What was it like? The CIA? We never really spoke about it."

Suzy smiled while recalling Laith and Roger hiding out in countryside similar to this, assault rifles in their hands, listening to Suzy's instructions on their earpieces as they waited to take down an enemy combatant in Prague. "Mostly it was just paperwork."

"Really?" Andrew knew she was lying.

"It's all in the past now."

"I guess it is." He raised his glass and followed her gaze toward the forested countryside. "New beginnings indeed. I love you."

"I love you, too." Suzy squeezed his hand.

Andrew squeezed back while continuing to look at the scenery. He felt utter contentment. This was everything he needed. Suzy, their child, their home, peace. His thoughts returned to what he needed to do to cook his wife a well-deserved meal. He picked up his glass and said, "Got to get my apron on, hon. Are you stay-ing out here?"

He dropped his glass and screamed as he looked at Suzy and saw she had a bullet entry point in her head. She was lifeless, her mouth wide open and an expres-sion of surprise on her face.

She'd involuntarily squeezed her husband's hand as a bullet had entered her brain.

Patrick's home, in D.C., was beyond the budget of a government employee, senior or otherwise. The large 1950s five-bedroom house had four thousand square feet, three bathrooms, walls of glass, vaulted ceilings, a slate terrace, a garden that contained seasonal plantings and two koi ponds, a two-car garage, and a workshop cum wine cellar. His wife had designed the interior and exterior after they'd bought the house a few years ago. It wasn't particularly to his taste, but it didn't bother him. In any case, he'd taken the view that he knew shit about home stuff and therefore his wife was perfectly entitled to make the place look the way she wanted. Plus, she was a highly regarded interior designer who'd made a lot of money in the last two decades and had paid for the lion's share of the home anyway.

There were, however, two things he really enjoyed about the location. First, the garden had steps to the trails of Rock Creek Park, where he'd often take early morning walks. Second, the other luxury homes in the street were spread apart sufficiently that none of the neighbors bothered him. When he and his wife had first viewed the property, his wife had asked him in the garden if they should buy the place. He'd picked up a stone, stood with his back against the house, and hurled the stone as far as he could to try to hit the next house on the street. After the stone had fallen short of its target, he'd turned to his wife and said, "Yep. The place has my vote." Patrick liked his privacy.

His sons were now grown and had left home a few years ago. And this week his wife was in Ottawa, attending a conference for designers. That meant tonight he could eat and drink what he liked. Outside, it was dark and raining heavily. He decided he couldn't be bothered to jump in his car and buy ready-made food from the local convenience store. Nor did he want to go through the effort of cooking something from scratch at home. Standing in the kitchen, the tall, wiry, silver-haired CIA director ordered pizza, poured himself a Scotch, discarded his suit jacket and loosened his tie, and went into the wine cellar and workshop. It was the one area of the house that his wife had told him was his to do whatever he wanted with. That suited him perfectly, because the vast basement had no windows, and he hated the amount of glass in the rooms above—the windows and glass walls made him feel that whenever he was home he was a fish in a tank, available for all to see.

Though the many tools and a large rack of Bordeaux in the cellar reinforced the two main purposes of the room, Patrick had turned one end of his man-space into a comfortable place to relax. There was a wide-screen TV, a stack of DVDs, Oriental rugs, armchairs and coffee tables, and lamps.

He sat in a chair, took a sip of his whiskey, and tried calling Cochrane from his cell again. It went straight to voice mail. Exasperated, he flicked on the TV and began scrolling through local news channels to see if there were any further developments in the investigation of Katy Koenig's murder. There was nothing. The police had probably imposed a news blackout on the story, given the sensitivities surrounding her husband's work.

Forty-five minutes later, he checked his watch. The pizza place he'd ordered from was always reliable and prompt. It was unlike them to be this late. He decided he'd call the pizzeria again, using the kitchen landline.

Colonel Rowe moved through Patrick's kitchen, wearing a disposable white paper jumpsuit identical to the one he'd worn when he'd murdered Katy Koenig. He was gripping a suppressed SIG Sauer pistol. It had been his intention to use the handgun to shoot the CIA director through one of the many expanses of glass, but he'd only caught a brief glimpse of Patrick before the man had disappeared to a part of the house that had no windows. Probably that was the attic or basement. So he'd forced entry into the house to conduct the assassination at closer range.

He froze as he heard footsteps. They were very close. He readied his gun, but then the doorbell rang. He dashed to hide behind the breakfast bar in the center of the room, ducking out of sight just as Patrick appeared.

Patrick partially opened the front door until its security chain lock was at full stretch, saw the pizza guy, and opened the door.

The pizza man looked apologetic. "My moped broke down a few hundred yards from work. I had to freewheel it back and get a replacement."

Patrick laughed while taking his pizza and then paid the guy. "There's an extra five dollars for your trouble. Ordinarily, I'd suggest you get another job, but the trouble is, I rely on you for my dinner when my wife's away." He locked the door, returned to the basement, threw the pizza box onto a work surface, and grabbed a Remington pump-action shotgun from a cabinet drawer. After quickly loading the weapon's extended magazine and placing spare cartridges in his shirt pocket, he used his cell to dial 911, then walked slowly back up the stairs.

Moments ago, when he'd come upstairs, he thought he'd seen movement out of the corner of his eye. Couldn't be sure. But as he'd stood talking to the delivery guy, he had his wife to thank for being certain that there was an intruder in his kitchen. When it was dark outside and the lights were on, all the glass windows and walls reflected everything inside. That's how he saw the man crouching behind the breakfast bar.

Katy's murder, and now this. Coincidence? Patrick wasn't buying that. And that meant he assumed the man in the house wasn't some incompetent crackhead punk who'd broken into Patrick's home to steal some valuables. Rightly or wrongly, he concluded that the man he was going to confront was highly trained and was Katy's murderer.

He reached the top of the stairs, the butt of his gun planted firmly against his shoulder. He hadn't fired the gun for a while, though he regularly cleaned its barrel and working parts; just in case he needed the weapon for a moment like this.

He thought about calling out to the intruder, warning him that he was armed. He decided, screw that. A man had broken into Patrick's private property. And in all likelihood, he was an armed killer.

He entered the kitchen, scrutinizing its glass walls for telltale signs of the man. The intruder was no longer behind the breakfast bar or anywhere else in the room. Patrick walked into his spacious living room, moving his gun to cover the entire room. The entire outer walls of this room were glass; there was nowhere for anyone to hide. He wasn't here. At ground level, that left a big area of the house that had once been three rooms, but had since been converted under his wife's instructions into a single unit that she used when she worked from home. It had desks, tables containing albums of her design portfolio, sketches of house interiors on large sheets of paper attached to easels, cabinets crammed with books, photographic equipment including a camera on a tripod, and a large stereo system, which his wife used to play what she called her happy music while she was being creative.

There were archway entrances at either end of the room. Patrick came down a corridor and used one of them to enter the room.

At the far end of the hall, the intruder—head to toe in a white jumpsuit—broke cover and dashed across the workroom. Patrick fired his shotgun, the noise of the shot an immense boom, its pellets smashing through his wife's camera stand, knocking over easels, and causing one section of the glass wall to shatter. But none of the shot hit the intruder.

Patrick fired at the area where he thought the man was taking cover—a large wooden writing desk. Shards of wood were ripped off the desk, and the spraying pellets destroyed his wife's happy-music machine. Patrick pumped another cartridge into the gun's breech and fired again, walking toward the desk, fearless, anger coursing through him.

The desk was five yards away.

Patrick pulled back on the pump action.

In that moment, the intruder briefly emerged from behind the desk and fired a single shot from his pistol before diving for cover again.

The bullet struck Patrick in the shoulder.

Patrick staggered back, but managed to stay on his feet. "God damn you," he muttered between gritted teeth, his shoulder in agony.

He moved left to get a better angle on his target and blasted more of the desk to stop the intruder from firing another shot, the further pain caused by the recoil of the shot making him grimace. He wondered whether soon he'd become light-headed from the trauma. He couldn't let that happen. Not until this was finished.

One way or the other.

He walked fast to get a clear shot of the man behind the desk.

The intruder wasn't there.

He must have escaped through the archway leading back into the hallway.

Patrick spun around.

The killer was at the other end of the room. He'd used the outside hallway to double back and use the entrance Patrick had come through. The man in white was stock still, his handgun pointing at Patrick. The CIA officer fired his shotgun. But he was too late; the killer's silenced round hit him in the chest, causing Patrick to fall backward and his shotgun's discharge to hit a glass chandelier, which smashed to the floor.

Patrick breathed fast, sweat pouring over his face as he lay on his back and desperately tried to reload his magazine. The killer walked toward him. There was only time for Patrick to put one shell into the magazine and slam it back into place. His arms shook from excruciating agony as he tried to raise his shotgun and point it at the murderer. "Fuck you!" he shouted as he placed his finger on the trigger.

The killer smiled and shot Patrick in the head.

Thirty-Six

I'd arrived in Beirut. It was a city of memories for
me. A woman I thought I loved had tried to sever
my head in a house here, in which I'd discovered several
decaying corpses just before her attack. Butterflies had
blossomed out of chrysalises in her murdered father's
chest and had fluttered through a window into an azure
Lebanese sky. I'd followed them after killing the woman
I loved, but the insects were a mere glimpse of beauty
and were soon gone. A Muslim cleric had stopped me
on the street and asked me if I needed guidance. I was
glad to be in his presence. He was selfless.

That was years ago now.

I'd like to think I'd moved on since then. In some
ways I had. A killer, assassin, spy—call me what you
will—is not always that person. It is a convenient label.

Sometimes even the worst and best of us need simple pleasures, and I'd thought I'd reached a stage in my life where I wanted more of them.

I didn't feel that way now, though. My friend Roger was dead, and I'd been assaulted by two men who were a lot like me. They'd know I was here because I'd flown into the country on my Richard Oaks passport. Perhaps they were watching me now.

I entered the Four Seasons Hotel and decided not to take the elevator, instead using the fire stairs to reach the second, third, and fourth floors, which I walked along in search of a hotel cleaner. When I found three of them exiting a room and placing sheets into a trolley, I asked them for directions to my room and resumed walking, once again using the stairs to reach the fifth floor.

The room was plush, but it was just another hotel room. During my years in MI6, I'd stayed in hundreds that were similar. I suppose I was privileged to have done so, but after a short while I became immune to the pleasures of such splendor. Without a partner, they are lonely places. I'd gained infinitely more joy from staying in the homes of impoverished families in Mumbai, Dar es Salaam, and Tripoli, among many other other cities. Most of them had belonged to my foreign assets. Their partners and children gave me food, sang to me in the evening, asked me about the world, lit fires to keep me warm, and placed mattresses on soil floors so that I could sleep in comfort though they did not. Ordering room service, scrolling through crap TV channels, and hitting the minibar while lounging on an immaculate hotel room bed does not compare to eating marinated lamb cooked in a clay pot in a one-room shack and served by friends. I find five-star luxury extravagant and wasteful. Amid poor families, one never finds waste, only carefully planned generosity that must always be accepted unless one wants to offend.

I grabbed a bottle of mineral water, threw my bag onto the bed, and slumped into a chair.

Ten minutes later, the door opened. A man walked in, saw me, and exclaimed, "What the hell are you doing in my room?"

I sipped my water, straight from the bottle. "Hello, Harry."

The man was of medium height, mid-sixties, part Albanian and part Norwegian; had been schooled at Winchester College, giving him excellent English; and was a millionaire and one of the most duplicitous and treacherous bastards I'd ever met. Somehow, I liked him, even though the scoundrel had nearly killed me four years ago.

I'd not seen him since. "I note you still like to wear good clothes."

Harry's hair was thinner and grayer than when I'd last seen him, but the businessman who sometimes dabbled in arms deals and turned a blind eye to business transactions that broke numerous international laws still looked like a wealthy playboy. He grinned, his teeth immaculate and sparkling white. "You like my room so much you decided to visit, Mr. Cochrane?"

I nodded.

"How did you get in?"

"A cleaner gave me a universal key to all of the hotel's rooms. She didn't know she did. Probably right now she's reporting it lost, so that hotel security can change the key codes and supply her with a new one."

"So, you are a thief."

"Did I ever pretend to you I was anything different?"

I'd first met Harry in Sarajevo. Back then, he carried the MI6 code name Lace. He'd been introduced to me in a fish restaurant by my agency's Head of Sarajevo Station. Without me knowing who'd pulled the trigger, after the meal Harry had shot our station chief dead. He then pretended to help me track down and neutralize an Iranian general who was planning a devastating attack against New York. Harry was clever, and very careful. So much so that I never suspected he was working for the general all along. It was only after I'd killed my target that I discovered Harry's true role. But somewhere inside I suspect Harry is a good man. Halfway during our collaboration he'd had a change of heart and wanted to confess his duplicity to me. He never had the chance to do so because the general discovered his intentions and tried to kill him, forcing Harry into hiding. When I finally caught Harry, I put a gun to his head. He was convinced I was going to kill him. He told me at that moment that he wouldn't blame me for doing so. I let him live.

However, I still didn't trust him one bit.

"How did you know I'd be here?" he asked.

I shrugged. "It's been a personal hobby of mine to keep track of you. You've been here for the last five months. Business in the region must keep you here, I guess." I had taken the liberty of calling the hotel's front desk earlier, pretending to be Harry and asking them if there was any mail for me. They said there was none, but if any arrived they'd make sure it was sent straight to my room. So I knew he was here.

"I see." Harry took a seat. "What do you want?"

"Your help."

Harry laughed. "Are you serious? You want help from me, of all people?"

"Yes. The way I figure it, you know you're a dead man if you cross me ever again. If I use someone else to help me, that agreement isn't necessarily valid." I smiled. "And you have tremendous motivation to help me to the full extent of your abilities."

Harry's eyes narrowed. "And what if I can't help you, through no fault of mine?"

I pointed at him. "You've been in Lebanon a long time. It's not a wealthy country. So I'm wondering what could be here that would interest a man who usually chases the big bucks in more affluent parts of the world. Of course, there is one industry here that would pay out big time to someone with your connections and supply lines—the illicit arms industry."

Harry lit a cigarette, was silent.

"But you know you're playing a dangerous game. There are people out here who'd slit your throat if a deal went wrong; or they'd do that because they work for your competition and don't want you here. You're cognizant of that. This is your life. And that means you'll have protection around you, maybe local guys or perhaps imported; either way, people who'll watch your back. Some of them will be visible deterrents to would-be attackers; others will be invisible, watching you and your surroundings from the shadows, communicating to others on their team and to your protection detail. I'm interested in the invisibles."

Harry blew out smoke. "You want me to lend you some of my people?"

"The ones who can't be seen."

This didn't please Harry. "While they're working for you, they're not watching me."

"I only need them for a few hours. During that time, you can stay in your room and keep your bodyguards in here with you, or at least very close by."

Harry drummed his fingers on a side table, seemingly trying to weigh his response. "If I agree to this, are we square? You have no further hold over me?"

I couldn't help laughing. "Harry. The last time I had the *pleasure* of working with you, not only was I very nearly killed, but also four thousand child musicians—alongside the wives of the heads of state of America, Britain, Iran, the Emirates, Syria, and Egypt—were nearly blown to pieces inside the Metropolitan Opera House. No. Borrowing a few of your men most certainly *doesn't* make us square."

Harry smiled. "When you put it like that, I see your point." His expression changed. "Nevertheless, I didn't plant the bombs in the opera house. Nor did I know the full extent of what was being planned. In any case, you stopped the massacre."

"This is not a negotiation. It is a transaction that's already been agreed. I need at least four, better still, six of your best men and women. You don't tell them my name or anything about me. As far as they're concerned, I'm a highly valued associate of yours. We'll need communications equipment so that they can contact me if anything goes wrong. And make sure they're armed."

"Why don't you use people from your agency?"

It was an obvious question. "Because they're not at my disposal anymore."

There was a twinkle in Harry's eye. "You've finally been booted out of the service?"

"I'm not complaining. It gives me greater . . . latitude. Anyway, I wasn't exactly sacked. It was by mutual arrangement."

Harry's expression was mischievous. "You met a lovely lady and she decided it was time for you to be domesticated? No more running around, saving the world?"

"No."

"You're still single?"

"Yes."

"No one will have you?"

"You'd have to take a rather big census to get an answer to that."

"Poor, troubled Mr. Cochrane. Always alone."

I leaned forward, placed my hand on his, and put on my most insincere voice. "That's not true, Harry. I've got good friends like you." I released his hand and reclined back into my seat. "I need your team this afternoon."

"And what if I refuse?"

I didn't reply. Just stared at him.

Rob Tanner dashed out of his office as he heard keys in the lock of Admiral Mason's adjacent office. Mason was in the corridor. "Sir, I've been calling your cell."

"I was driving." Mason entered his office. "And I have no time for those wireless earpiece things. They make people look like they're talking to themselves." He slung his coat over a chair. "Gives the impression they're crazy."

"Admiral!" Tanner was breathing fast, his face flushed. "Please listen! The CIA called me this morning. It's . . ."

Mason was stock still. "Spit it out."

"It's . . . Task Force S. Most of them, anyway. They're dead. Murdered."

Mason stared at his employee. "Names."

"Alistair McCulloch, Patrick Bolte, Laith Dia, and Suzy Parks."

Mason was motionless, his expression stunned. "Details."

"McCulloch and Dia were shot outside Dia's home. Parks was killed while sitting on her porch. Bolte was gunned down inside his home."

Mason sat behind his desk. "The killer or killers?"

"No trace. The feds think it's the work of one man."

"Security?"

Tanner didn't understand.

Mason elaborated. "Has any of this reached the press?"

"No. And it never will. The Agency has made sure of that. What should we do?"

"We do nothing."

Tanner frowned. "Nothing?"

"There's nothing for us to do. The Bureau will do its job, with assistance from the Agency. We have no role to play."

"Shouldn't we warn Cochrane?"

"You know we can't get hold of him. In any case"— Mason gazed out of the window, his mind racing—"it is probably for the best that he doesn't know about this yet. I fear what it might do to him."

Compared to Harry's hotel, the sixty-four-room Cavalier Hotel, on northern Beirut's Abdel Baki Street, was more modest in size, though a perfectly present-able place to stay. Since Alistair had told me that I had to repay him anything I spent on my alias credit card, it also suited my budget. I handed the receptionist my Richard Oaks card and watched her swipe it through her bill payment machine. I imagined this was the first time she'd triggered a guest's location to two as-sassins by doing so.

I could have paid in cash. But that wasn't part of my plan.

"You wanted a room on the fifth floor, overlooking the street?"

"That's correct." It's what I'd asked for when I'd called and made the booking. And I'd also been ada-mant that it had to be one of only three specific rooms on that floor.

The Lebanese woman beamed. "Mr. Oaks. I'm delighted to say that we can upgrade you for no extra charge to one of our suites on the eighth floor. They're double the size of your room. We had a last-minute cancellation."

"Does the suite overlook Abdel Baki Street?"

"No, sir. It will be a much quieter room for you."

"Then I'll pass." I smiled. "I'm on my own. I don't need a big suite. Plus the street's important to me. Hearing Beirut—day and night—makes me happy."

The receptionist looked puzzled, but said, "Oh, okay."

I went to my room. Ceiling-to-floor curtains covered the one set of windows that overlooked Abdel Baki. Soon, it would be very dangerous to open them. But for now I assessed that it was safe to briefly do so.

Below me was a nondescript thoroughfare; on either side of the street, the majority of the buildings were midrise apartment blocks. I knew for a fact that in the building on the opposite side of the street, directly overlooking my room in the hotel, were five apartments that were empty and available to rent. Yesterday, I'd seen them advertised on the Internet and had called the realtors. After giving them a false name, I'd told them I was interested in renting one of the apartments. This morning I'd called them again, saying I was in town and would like to arrange viewings, providing the properties were still available. All of them were. I had no intention of renting any of them, but if I did, I'd have a perfect view of the spot where I was currently standing.

I closed the curtains, took a shower, shaved, and dressed in jeans, a shirt, and hiking boots.

In one hour, I was hoping to see the exact spot where Roger Koenig was killed.

Thirty-Seven

I stood at one end of the street where Gray Site was located and wished Admiral Mason had never concocted the idea to establish the intelligence complex. Something awful had happened there. It had made Roger turn on his colleagues. They reacted. All of them died in a place that might as well have been a locked-down prison.

It was midafternoon, and the street was bustling with pedestrians and traffic. Harry's team were somewhere ahead of me. Perhaps one of them was hiding in one of the many tenement blocks on either side of the street; others might have been on foot in the souk that ran for two hundred yards along the side of the road; maybe a couple of them were in a stationary vehicle, ready to drive fast or disembark on foot if the need arose. I didn't know and didn't need to. Their job was to watch me and my surroundings from whichever location made most sense. But I hated not knowing the identities and capabilities of the people I was entrusting my safety to. And though they were probably good at what they did, they weren't full-time agency operators. They were freelancers.

Then again, these days so was I.

I heard a woman's voice in my earpiece. "So far we've got nothing unusual. Proceed."

I started walking. The derelict house above Gray Site was approximately three hundred yards away on the right side of the road. Patrick had given me the grid reference of its location after he'd visited me in Scotland. I'd studied maps of Beirut and had decided the only way I could get in and out of the site unnoticed was to do so at night. But that left me exposed. If one or both of the men who'd assaulted me in London were watching the site through thermal imagery, they could knock me off my feet before I could do anything about it. So I'd concluded that I had to visit the site during the day, and to do that I needed help.

I turned up the volume of my communications kit, because the noise around me was getting louder as I walked onward. People were talking fast. Men and women in the souk were calling out to passersby, telling them about the fine silks and spices that were on offer today. And people driving in the crawling traffic seemed to be permanently leaning on their horns.

As I reached the souk, I heard one of Harry's male surveillance specialists say, "Too many people here."

The woman who'd told me to proceed said, "Just watch for oddballs."

Oddballs? It was difficult to comprehend to whom she was referring. Perhaps two Caucasian men carrying guns.

"Stop," ordered the woman.

I did so.

"Just want to check movement." Movement that might include one or more persons close to me also stopping. "Nothing unusual," she added after ten seconds. "Carry on."

I reached the end of the souk. My destination was fifty yards away. I could see it now—a house that looked incongruous amid the rather ugly apartment blocks. No doubt once it had been regal and would have been the family home of a local dignitary, a high-ranking professional, or a wealthy businessman. Artillery shells had changed all that. It was so badly damaged that it was beyond repair, and nobody had bothered to do anything with the place. I was surprised it hadn't been pulled down to make room for more tenements.

Perhaps it was left here as a reminder to local residents that they were all in range of Israel's heavy weapons.

"Keep walking," the female observer said in a calm voice. "I'm close to you."

I did as she said, while wondering whether she suspected there was a direct threat to my life. I hadn't told Harry about the sniper and the blond man who'd tried to stick a knife in me. I hoped she hadn't concluded this was merely a precautionary exercise.

"Team: anything?" the woman asked. Clearly, she was their leader.

Five men in turn replied that they'd seen nothing to arouse their suspicions.

She said to me, "You're good to go. We'll be static outside, spread apart along the street. Two of my men will be close to the house. Let me know when you're about to leave."

I walked into the first floor of the large house. The floor was as big as a medium-sized warehouse. The ceiling was intact, but most of the outer walls had big holes in them. Clearly, the area had once been partitioned into separate rooms—visible were raggedy edges of inner walls, but those walls had crumbled when the shells struck the building. The floor was just dust and earth; either it had been destroyed or, more likely, it had been expensive marble and locals had ripped it up to sell. The walls were covered with grafitti, and empty Coke and beer cans surrounded the remnants of small fires. No doubt it was a hangout for kids. I looked through the large holes in the outer walls toward the street. I could see cars passing and people walking by, but no one seemed to be looking into the building. Even if they did, they wouldn't care if they saw me in this place.

There were two sets of stairs: one would have previously allowed the homeowners to access the second floor. That floor was now inaccessible to all but the most adventurous and reckless, because most of the steps had been blown apart, leaving a treacherous drop if one got one's footing wrong. Another set of steps led down a narrow corridor. They were made of solid stone and were intact. It was the way down to Gray Site.

Since I'd been tasked on this investigation, I'd frequently anticipated this moment. It looked how I imagined it to look—exciting to a child who wanted to explore creepy places, dull and ugly to an adult. But what was at the base of the stairs would grip the attention of anyone who knew what it had once been and what had happened here. I walked down the steps.

At the bottom was a single doorway. Everything beyond it was in complete darkness. I switched on a flashlight to see ahead. Part of the bombproof steel door that had been installed by the CIA techie I'd interrogated was still attached to hinges and locks; the majority of it was lying on the corridor floor beyond, burned away from its surrounds by blowtorches. Its steel was at least three inches thick, and would take four strong men to lift it; somebody had used a spray can to inscribe Arabic words on its visible side: *A nasnās lives here. Be very careful.*

In Arabic mythology, a nasnās was half human, half creature, incredibly strong, could kill someone just by touching them, and was believed to be the offspring of a demon.

No doubt, whoever had written it was a teenager who was daring his friends and others like him to enter, and that they'd done, because there was more graffiti inside the doorway, food wrappings and other litter on its stone floor, plus even less pleasant evidence that humans had spent time here.

I stood at the threshold and looked inside. There were tall metal cabinets to my left, flush against the corridor's wall. That was where Roger and his colleagues had stored their files containing data on their Hamas targets. The files were now safely secured in the archives of the agencies that had worked in this establishment. Immediately to my right were the burned remains of the sofa that had caught fire from the sparks produced by the CIA officers' blowtorches. And at the end of the corridor were four rooms. I couldn't see them, but I knew they were there. In one of them, the gunfight had happened. I didn't want to go in that room, but I had to.

Even though I knew the CIA team who'd breached the complex had examined every inch of the corridor's walls, floor, and ceiling, I reexamined them, desperate to find something they'd missed, hoping to find evidence that someone had forced their way into the site and killed Roger and his men. I wasn't surprised that my search was in vain, but nevertheless felt tremendous disappointment. Unless there was something to be found in the rooms ahead, what I was seeing was proof positive that Roger had killed his colleagues.

Using the flashlight to guide my way, I proceeded to the rooms. The first belonged to the MI6 officer. It had cheap furniture inside, but was otherwise bare of all the equipment that would have been housed here. I spent thirty minutes examining the thick stone walls. Nothing. Ditto the second and third rooms, which had been used by the DGSE officer and Roger, respectively. They were all identical in size—tiny, no windows. After examining Roger's room, I stood for a moment, imagining how he must have felt working day and night shifts in this claustrophobic cell. I knew how

I felt just being in here for a few minutes. I wanted to get out.

I entered the last room. It had belonged to the Mossad officer. It was where everyone had died.

I shone my flashlight over the walls. More graffiti, some of it obscene, written on places where blood might have splattered. Like everywhere else in the complex, it smelled musty and rank in here. That was to be expected in a place that received no ventilation except through its single entry door. The kids who dared each other to come in here probably didn't mind; it added to the scary ambience. But as I stood in this room, I thought I smelled human death and decay. It made me want to vomit, because one of the men who'd died in here was my dear friend.

I spent nearly an hour in the room, occasionally hearing my surveillance team relay updates to each other while I examined everything. The CIA team had done an excellent job sanitizing the place. There was no evidence that a gunfight had taken place in the room or that four men had died here. I imagined what it must have looked like in the site before and after the fight had taken place.

Roger working the night shift, sending Langley the telegram about the Hamas meeting the following day, being in the complex alone, waiting for his colleagues

to arrive the next day, shooting them, and them returning fire before they died.

That's what everyone believed.

I recalled what the CIA technician had told me.

*I think being in that place day and night sent Roger
Koenig mad.*

I reentered the corridor and stood motionless, staring
at the broken entrance at the other end. I pictured the
DGSE, MI6, and Mossad officers turning up for work
and walking down the hall. No doubt they had security
protocols in place wherein they had to arrive separately
and at slightly different times. When the last of them
arrived and reengaged the door's seven bolts, it would
have been standard practice for the night-duty officer
to brief his day-shift colleagues on any highlights from
the night before. Maybe their coffee machine was in
the Mossad officer's room, they had all convened there,
and Roger had pulled his gun. Or maybe Roger had
attacked the Mossad officer while he was alone in his
office, and the others came to the Israeli's rescue. It
was impossible to be sure.

I was certain that third parties hadn't forced open
the door and shot the men. They'd have left too many
obvious traces. And the CIA techie I'd spoken to was
adamant that the locks hadn't been picked because
they were impossible to reach from the outside, let

alone unlock. I walked to the entrance and shone my torch around the edges of the steel door that were still in place around the doorframe. They were hermetically sealed. The technician was right.

I turned to look at Gray Site one last time. I had to accept that *what* had happened in here wasn't a mystery. Roger was a murderer. What remained a mystery was *why* he'd killed his colleagues.

I asked myself, What if everyone was wrong about Roger and he didn't kill his colleagues? It was probably a foolish question.

I moved my flashlight around. I turned the light off so I was in pitch darkness, my mind working fast.

"May have something." The voice in my earpiece was a male in the surveillance team. "Guy I spotted earlier in the souk and farther down the street. He's back, near the house."

I remained where I stood, desperate to gather my thoughts.

"Time for you to leave," the female team leader said to me.

"Not yet," I muttered into my throat mic.

"Description?" she asked her colleague.

"Tall, athletic build, I'd say in his late twenties or early thirties, slacks and shirt. And he's blond and has a small satchel over his shoulder."

Shit! Like the man who attacked me in Highgate. "I need more time!" I said.

"Where is he now?" the team leader asked.

"Right by the house. He's looking around."

The team leader sounded like she was running. "I'm not close enough."

"He's going into the house."

"Kamal, Mansur: both of you get in there and put him on the ground!"

I opened my eyes and turned the flashlight back on, shining it over everything in front of me.

"Kamal, Mansur: Do you have him?"

There was no response.

"Do you have him?" The team leader's tone was urgent. "I can see him! He's running out of the house! On the street, heading north. All of you: get after him."

It was time for me to go. I ran up the stairs. Two men were lying on the ground in the center of the first floor, both writhing in pain.

A woman rushed into the building from the street and crouched by the men. "Mansur, Kamal. What happened?"

One of them answered, "He . . . he dropped us."

"With a weapon?"

"With his hands and legs."

"Are you going to be okay?"

They both nodded.

The woman looked at me with a venomous expression. "Did you know about this threat?"

"I thought it possible."

She gestured to the men. "These are my brothers. They're both black belts in karate. Not that it's helped them today."

I pulled the men to their feet and said to them, "Get checked out in case you've got fractures."

They nodded.

The team leader paced back and forth as she spoke into her throat mic. "Update."

One of her men pursuing the blond man was almost breathless as he replied, "We lost him. He vanished."

The woman kicked soil off the ground, her frustration evident. She walked up to me. "The man who took down my brothers was coming for you. You're in significant danger. Harry only released us to you for this afternoon. We can't watch your back any longer. If I were you, I'd get on the next available flight out of Beirut."

I returned to the Cavalier Hotel, with no intention of departing Beirut just yet. I remained in Lebanon for two reasons: one of them would likely see me dead very shortly; the other was because of an idea I had that could potentially make the impossible possible.

I was cautious as I approached the hotel, fully aware that the blond man might be back on my tail and the other assassin watching me from a hidden location. But there was no point in me conducting countersurveillance. There were thousands of nearby places a professional could hide. I didn't stand a chance in hell of spotting anyone.

The receptionist called to me as I walked past.

She was smiling. "Mr. Oaks. You have a letter." She handed it to me.

All that was written on the envelope was my fake name. There was no stamp, no address. "Hand delivered?"

She nodded.

"One of your regular local couriers?"

"Oh, no. He was an Englishman."

I had a sinking feeling. "Short man, gray hair, a bit fat?"

"No. Tall, brown hair, with . . ." She rubbed the side of her face, her expression quizzical. "What do you call these things in English? Not a beard."

"Sideburns."

"Burns?" Her smile broadened. "That's appropriate, good name, because his were red."

"Thank you. If you see him around here again, can you let me know? Discreetly?"

Her smile vanished. "Is he trouble? I can inform hotel security if we have a problem."

I tried to make my expression reassuring. "It's nothing like that. Most likely he works for one of my Lebanese business associates." I waved the envelope and grinned. "This is probably an invitation to one of his tedious cocktail parties."

In my hotel room, I examined the envelope. It was too light to contain explosive that would detonate when the parcel was opened. But its contents might have been saturated with poison or a hallucinogenic that, when contact was made with my skin, could be sufficiently powerful to incapacitate me, thereby enabling a man to come into my room and easily finish me off. I placed a pair of socks over my hands and opened the envelope. Inside was a single sheet of paper. Written on it were words that made me involuntarily drop to my knees.

Mr. Richard Oaks

You would do well to know that your former colleagues Alistair, Patrick, Laith, and Suzy are dead. So too is Mrs. Koenig. I have erased all links to your professional past. Others will die if you persist in your investigation in Lebanon. You live in West Square, London. I believe your neighbors

are dear to you. You must weigh that value and
compare it to the value of your work.

I forced myself to my feet, my hands shaking as I
dropped the paper, ripped the socks off my hands,
withdrew my cell phone from my bag, and inserted its
battery. Moments after it powered up, I was deluged by
voice mail alerts. I ignored them and called Admiral
Mason.

He replied on the third ring. "Where the hell have
you been?"

I felt like my heart was going to burst through my
chest, it was beating so fast. "Is it true?"

"Is what true?"

"I've just received a letter. Anonymous. It says . . .
it says . . ."

Mason's tone was sympathetic when he asked, "Does
it tell you about death?"

"Yes. Lots of it. My colleagues. My friends."

With deliberation, Mason said, "Whoever sent you
that letter is a coldhearted bastard. He or she is taunt-
ing you. Probably trying to get you to stop."

"Is it true?!"

Mason was silent for what felt like an age. "Son, it's
true. Your former team is dead."

I felt like my soul had been ripped from my body.
Images raced through my distraught brain. Alistair

and Patrick, both young, driving with my father in Iran in 1979, all of them anxious because the country was in a state of revolution, but my father telling his more junior colleagues that everything was going to be all right. My father surrendering himself at a checkpoint so Patrick and Alistair could escape. Laith sitting on a sidewalk near a snowy Saranac Lake, clutching his gut because he'd been stabbed, and telling me he knew exactly what to do. Suzy using her vast intellect to identify a Russian spy catcher. Roger calmly calling in his instructions in the world's most hostile locations. And his wife asking me, "Why does everyone assume Roger shot the English, French, and Israeli guys?"

"How did it happen?"

Mason gave me details and then said, "I'm sorry. I didn't want you to know until you'd finished. That wasn't right."

I didn't blame the admiral for attempting to withhold the information. I'd have probably done the same thing in his shoes, because so much was riding on this investigation into Gray Site before Israel went to war. Time was running out. Israel would mobilize in less than four days.

The admiral asked, "What are you going to do?"

"Do you have a high-ranking contact in the U.K. Special Forces?"

"No, but I know men who do."

"I need a team of SF men to ensure no one goes near my neighbors." I gave him Dickie, Phoebe, and David's identities and addresses. "Can you do that for me?"

"Sure. I guess that means you're not coming home."

"Soon, I will be. First, I've two things I have to do."

I ended the call and sat on my bed. Nothing felt real. My head was giddy, my body shaking. Shock was kicking in; I rushed to the minibar and grabbed a can of Coke, quickly opening it and swallowing the liquid fast to get sugar inside me. Then I had to run to the bathroom, where I vomited in the toilet. I ran a sink of water, silently telling myself to hold it together, at least for just a few more days. After washing my face, I looked in the mirror and saw grief written across my face.

That had to go.

I owed it to my friends.

Mason had told me that the press had no inkling about the deaths of my former colleagues. That meant that whoever sent me the letter was their killer, or a close associate of the murderer. Perhaps it was the blond man who'd fought me in the cemetery and today had got very close to me. More likely it was the man who'd delivered the letter—a tall individual with facial hair that the hotel receptionist thought resembled burns. I wondered if he was the sniper who'd blasted chunks off Roger's headstone.

Clearly, the letter was designed to throw me into a state of panic.

The author underestimated me.

Gradually I was getting out from under my grief, getting focused, and getting ready to make someone suffer very badly.

Thirty-Eight

The White House Situation Room was at full capacity. Middle-aged men and women sat at the rectangular table, smiling insincerely and exchanging pleasantries with people they hated. Wall-mounted TV screens showed images of technicians testing the quality of the audio and visual links before moving out of the way to allow the premiers of Britain, France, and Israel to take seats in front of cameras. The American president and his chief of staff walked into the room. The chief of staff remained standing; the president sat at the head of the table, a camera pointing at his head so he could be seen by the foreign heads of state.

Admiral Mason was sitting at the opposite end of the room, quietly observing. The diminutive naval officer loathed being surrounded by the egos and agendas of politicians, though he empathized with the president's desire to have his most insightful aide present. Mason was neutral, and he looked at the world in a different way from most. The president relied on Mason's left-field thinking. And though he was high ranking, Mason was a military man, which meant he was acutely aware that there was always someone more senior than him. That reality came with the demand that he do his duty and follow orders.

But he had never been very good at following orders.

By chance or providence, this mind-set had benefited his career, rather than leading to a court-martial for disobedience.

The chief of staff called for order in the room and asked the Israeli premier to provide an update on Israel's intentions.

The Israeli prime minister spoke for fifteen minutes, saying that Israel was going to war in three days and that its military would occupy Lebanon, Gaza, and the West Bank until such time as every Hamas member was incarcerated or dead. A heated debate ensued, some arguing that Israel's actions were likely to fuel fundamentalist terrorism and broader regional conflict, others saying that Israel had a right to protect its citizens and borders. The Israeli premier was silent throughout the debate, though when the room was silent he said that Israel's intended course of action was necessary, justified, and proportionate to the threats it faced. He added that America of all countries knew that the war against terror could not be avoided.

The hawks in the room took his side; the doves urged restraint.

Mason watched the president, trying to discern what he was thinking. The man looked troubled and uncertain as he listened attentively to everyone's point of view. Mason didn't blame him. There were no easy choices to be made.

The president looked directly at Mason. When he spoke, he chose his words carefully, because only a handful of individuals knew the admiral had tasked Will Cochrane to try to find evidence as to whether Hamas had killed the Israeli ambassador. All of those individuals were U.S. nationals. "Do you have anything to add, Admiral?"

Mason shook his head, indicating to the president that no progress had been made.

The room was silent as the president turned his attention to the Israeli premier. "In the absence of any evidence casting doubt on whether Hamas killed your diplomat in Paris, my decision is that the United States of America will back your war."

Thirty-Nine

Monsieur de Guise cleared away empty dishes that he'd used to serve a breakfast of fresh croissants and pain au chocolat, purchased from one of the nearby patisseries in Rennes, then followed Safa into the living room. "Safa, I must administer your medication earlier than usual today." He smiled. "The good news is, they will be your last pills and injections. Your mind and body are fully recovered."

Safa rolled up his sleeve. "When will I see the bad people you spoke of?"

De Guise thrust a needle into Safa's vein. "In two days' time. Before then you have quite a journey to make. I have friends who will assist you with your travel and other matters."

"Where am I going?"

"The United States."

Safa grinned. "America?"

De Guise injected Safa and placed an antiseptic swab on the needle hole. "You like America?" he said while preparing the next shot.

Of course, Safa had never been to the States. But he'd read comics that had featured New York skyscrapers, gangsters, superheroes, corrupt cops, crazy villains, and mountains of readily available food. It seemed to him that America was an anarchic place, yet one that was bountiful and rich. He didn't know if he liked America, but he was certainly in its thrall.

He rubbed his arm after the third and final injection was made. He now felt as if he were floating in a warm bath; he thought he could hear singing, maybe angels celebrating Safa's recovery. The monsieur was bent over adding wood to the fire; his back appeared to grow a hump, and the sight of it made Safa laugh.

"What's so funny?" asked de Guise in a jovial tone.

"You have grown a hump, sir."

De Guise spun around and gave a theatrical flourish of his hand. "Like the Hunchback of Notre-Dame?"

"Who's that?"

"A man who's ugly on the outside but has a good soul." De Guise guided Safa to the center of the room. "Stand here and close your eyes."

Safa swayed as he did so, wondering if he might lose balance and collapse.

"Now, Safa. I'm going to place something on you. It is a jacket, though it is heavier than most. It might feel uncomfortable at first, but don't be concerned, because you'll only need to wear it for a short period of time."

The jacket was placed on him and it was indeed heavy. His guardian strapped it tightly around his chest and tummy, so tightly that Safa had to exert himself to breathe.

"What do you see?"

"Nothing. My eyes are shut, as you told me they had to be."

"Ah, but then you are not using your imagination. Pretend you are in a large crowd. Men, women, maybe even children, are around you. They speak with American accents. You can smell candy, nuts being roasted, burgers and hot dogs. People are shouting slogans. No war, they chant in unison. There are white, black, and Asian skins in the crowd. The people appear peaceful, are united by one purpose, and are walking slowly in the same direction. You join their ranks and walk with them, copying their slogans."

"Yes . . . yes, I can see them."

"Good. Do you like what you smell?"

Safa frowned. "I like burgers and candy."

"That's not what I asked." De Guise was speaking very close to Safa's ear. "Do you like what you smell?"

Safa shook his head. "It smells bad. Why does it smell bad?"

"Because the sugars and fats from the foods are intermingled with the stench of human self-loathing. You smell greasy rot and fear. It comes from the bad people. Everyone around you is bad."

"Bad because they do nothing to stop bad things happening?"

"These people are worse. They are doing *something*, but it is the wrong something. Make them go away."

"How do I do that?"

De Guise placed an object into Safa's hand. It was a pen. "To make the bad people go away, you must do two things. First, step a few paces away from the crowd and shout as loud as you can, 'Death to Israel!' Second, press the end of the object in your hand."

Safa did so.

"You are now moving faster than everyone around you. They cannot escape you. All of them will suffer."

Safa smiled. "I am a superhero?"

"You are. Open your eyes."

Safa did so and looked at the garment the monsieur had placed on him. It was an army vest, with numerous pockets that contained heavy objects.

De Guise undid the jacket's straps. "This jacket, or at least one very much like it in appearance and weight, will protect you. It will allow you to walk amid evil and remain invincible. When you are in America, my friends will place the jacket on you and guide you to the location where the bad people live. My friends will tell you what to do."

"Will I be hurt?"

"No. You will have no pain."

"Why is the jacket so heavy?"

"It carries special metals. They make the jacket like armor."

"And what happens when I press"—Safa looked at his hand—"the pen?"

De Guise patted his shoulder. "You've heard the expression, the pen is mightier than the sword?"

Safa nodded. "You once explained it to me. Knowledge and insight are more powerful than strength."

"Correct. When you are in America, the pen will be attached to a cord. The cord will be attached to your vest. That way, you can't drop the pen by accident. When you are standing in the crowd and press the pen, you will be imparting divine wisdom."

"Will the bad people thank me for making them not bad?"

"Yes, they will. But remember—what do you say before you educate them?"

" 'Death to Israel.' Why do I say that?"

De Guise glanced at a side table. On it was today's copy of *Le Monde* newspaper. Its lead article was about the U.S. president's decision to back Israel when it went to war. Much of the content highlighted the divisions within his administration, some supporting the president, others critical of his stance. De Guise needed unequivocal backing for the president's position, and most important a renewed and unwavering desire from all U.S. policy makers to support the nation of Israel. Safa's role was to give life to Israel, not death. Americans would think he was a Hamas terrorist. The assassination of Israel's ambassador to Paris had set de Guise's objective in motion. Safa would bring it to a successful conclusion by the simple act of detonating a bomb vest and massacring hundreds of peaceful American protesters. Politicians and influential members of the public who previously were against support of Israel's imminent action, or were sitting on the fence, would be horrified by Hamas's atrocity and the fact that it had been committed by a boy Hamas had brainwashed. The U.S. president's decision would receive unanimous support from people who had previously been skeptical of his position. It would be a return to the glory days of a protective uncle putting his arms around a child who's been attacked from all sides in the school playground.

De Guise didn't care one way or the other as to whether that was a good or bad thing. He was paid to manipulate state intentions and policies. What mattered to him was winning the game.

De Guise removed the jacket. "You tell everyone that Israel must die, because it is not just the act that counts, but also the motivation and mobilization of others who can follow your path. News crews will be watching the crowd. Maybe there will be CCTV cameras. Perhaps pedestrians will be filming the crowds with their cell phones. You will have an audience. Some bad people will survive your education and tell others what happened. It will be a moment in history that will dazzle the world. Before you use the pen, your words will capture the minds of good people and change things forever. It will be a wonderful thing to behold, will it not?"

Safa smiled. "It will. Your hump has gone."

The monsieur wagged his finger. "I don't mind, so long as you are not implying that I'm now the reverse of the hunchback."

Safa didn't understand. "When do I leave?"

"My friends will take you in one hour. First, you must pack."

"I have no passport."

"You didn't need one to come to France."

"Does that mean you have to put me in a box again?"

"Yes, but like before you'll be given sleeping tablets and comfortable blankets. The journey will seem quick."

Safa placed a hand on Monsieur de Guise's arm. "Will I see you again?"

De Guise looked at Safa's hand and for a moment didn't know how to respond. He'd enjoyed educating and cooking for the boy. He hadn't expected that. "I won't see you again, my dear Safa. Not in this life. But I've given you the tools to be a fine young man. There's nothing else I can do for you." De Guise brushed the back of his fingers against Safa's cheek. "For a snapshot of time, you have been a son and a pupil. But there comes a time when all parents and teachers must let go. Godspeed, young man. My final piece of advice to you: America is a harpy. It is beguiling yet corrupt and savage. Don't look at it, smell it, or taste it. Strike the beautiful beast. Make it hurt."

Forty

Mason entered his tiny home in D.C. and poured himself a glass of grog—rum, in layman's terminology; fuel to pacify deckhands and build empires, in the admiral's mind. He rarely drank liquor, but today had been particularly stressful. The normally unflustered naval officer felt that the failure of his plans had forced the president into making an uninformed decision to back Israel. Perhaps the president had made the right decision, but unless Cochrane could perform a miracle in the next two days, no one would know.

He entered his living room and turned on the TV news. A reporter was providing the latest news about America's support for Israel. With solemnity, he added that this new development had been greeted with anger from Hamas. A spokesman for the organization had issued a statement saying that America's stance was highly regrettable; an Israeli attack on its territories would result in Hamas targeting not only Israel in reprisal, but also America.

Mason turned off the TV and called Will Cochrane. He avoided pleasantries and went straight into the reason for the call. "We only have two days left. Our country has decided to back Israel. Is there any hope?"

The former MI6 officer was silent for a few seconds before responding. "I'm pursuing a long shot, but don't pin your hopes on me succeeding. All I ask is that you do everything you can to ensure that Israel doesn't act in less than two days."

"It won't. Now it has my country's support, the timetable is fixed in stone. There'll be no rash actions before the deadline." Mason hesitated before asking, "How are you holding up, given—"

"Don't ask me. Don't make me think about it. Not yet."

"There'll come a time when you'll have no choice but to think about what happened to your friends."

"I know. And I'm hoping that time is when I'm standing in front of the man who killed them." Cochrane ended the call.

Mason drank the remainder of his rum, deep in thought. The doorbell rang.

Mae Bäcklund was in the entrance, wearing jeans and a sweater, and holding a plastic container. "I brought you your dinner. Home-cooked chicken chasseur."

"Are you taking pity on me?"

"You don't need to be in a bad way to eat."

"Fair point." Mason gestured for her to enter his tiny home. "You needn't have made the effort. I'm fine."

"Are you, Captain?" Mae smiled as she stood in the kitchenette and emptied the contents of the container into a saucepan. "Just some rice or potatoes and this'll do you just fine."

Mason poured two glasses of rum and handed Mae a drink. For the most part she hated hard liquor, but rum was different. It reminded her of when she was a teenager—Tobias standing alongside her father in their country home's big study, huge windows overlooking white-blossom-laden trees and grass-covered grounds that ran on forever and contained ponies and deer, and both men with grog in hand and discussing matters of strategic importance. Sometimes they'd let her listen to them, perhaps so she could learn, and to this day she could recall the scent of birch crackling in the fire, the smell of wood polish that her father used daily on his oak paneling, and the sweet and intoxicating aroma of rum.

She took a sip of the drink and was instantly taken back in time to a moment when Mason was handsome and her father wasn't riddled with stage-four cancer.

"To your dad," said Mason as he raised his glass. "No quarter given."

"No quarter given," repeated Mae quietly. Her father had told her it was an old naval saying meaning "no surrender." She took a seat in the living room. "I have plans this evening. A man. His name's Anthony."

"Good for you, my dear."

"I haven't met him before. He'll probably turn out to be a jerk."

"But maybe he won't." Mason wondered whether Mae should have fixed an appointment at the hair salon this afternoon, and he dearly hoped she wasn't going on her date dressed like that. But his paternal role had limitations. It would be imprudent of him to comment on her appearance. Only a mother, sister, or close girlfriend could have done so, and even they would have risked fireworks. He decided to try another tack. He withdrew a wooden box from his cabinet, opened it, and took out a necklace. "Would you do me the honor of wearing this tonight? It was my wife's good-luck charm." He laughed. "Or at least

I told her it was when I gave it to her on the day we married."

At first, Mae was lost for words. The jewelry was antique, contained emeralds and sapphires embedded in white gold, and was sentimentally priceless. "Oh my. I . . . well, I'll need to get changed and . . ."

Mason placed the necklace in her hand and folded her fingers over it. "On matters of correct female presentation, you take this old dinosaur out of his area of expertise."

Mae's mind raced as she thought about dress designs, colors, and hairstyles. None of it was for Anthony. It was for the necklace and Mason's trust in her to wear the item. "Will you get some time to relax this evening?"

The admiral shook his head. "Alas, I must work."

Momentarily, Mae wondered whether she should cancel her date, stay with Tobias, and make him drink more rum so that he could forget his work and worries.

Mason seemed to have read her mind. "When I was a lieutenant commander, the frigate I was stationed on berthed in Lisbon. Most deckhands, me included, were given a twelve-hour run ashore to unwind before we sailed for Asia. The majority of men headed straight to the bars, but I hadn't been to Portugal before and wanted to explore Lisbon's streets. After a few hours, I sat in an alfresco café and drank a coffee. That's where I saw her."

"Who?"

"The woman who one day would wear the necklace you're holding." Mason sat next to Mae. "We started speaking to each other from our respective tables. Her English wasn't so good, and my Portuguese was merely a bunch of words and phrases I'd picked up from the Hispanic sailors on our ship. But we muddled by. I invited her to my table. We spoke some more until we'd exhausted every word we had in common. We took a walk, and kept walking. Side alleys, back streets, markets, a vineyard, parks, and at one stage a donkey-and-trap ride. Time ran away from us. I overstayed my leave to the extent that my captain sent a search party. Eventually I was found. The captain was sympathetic but said he was governed by navy law and had no choice other than to have me court-martialed. I asked him to consider not doing so, in return for me using my navigational skills to get his frigate to Brunei exactly on time and for him to be my best man if I could swing it to marry the woman who'd made me lose my senses. The captain was—"

"Yes." Mae didn't want the tear to roll down her cheek, but she let it anyway. "You and Dad were always the biggest rule breakers. Goodness knows how the navy tolerated you both."

"We were tolerated precisely *because* we were rule breakers." Mason placed his hand on Mae's. "Were the captain not your father, I'd still not regret disobeying clear orders. After all, if I'd followed strict protocols, I wouldn't have found my wife and we wouldn't have had two lovely daughters. You go out this evening and enjoy yourself with the young Anthony. Give him a chance and forgive him if his nerves make him come across as awkward and foolish. Walk away if he talks and moves like a movie star."

"Tonight . . ."

"I'm not your boss." Mason adopted a faux stern expression. "But your father entrusted your well-being to my care and counsel, so do as this old sea dog instructs."

Mae planted a kiss on Tobias's cheek. "Bless you, Captain." She rose to leave, but hesitated. "Tanner's been absent all afternoon. He left the office at lunchtime and I haven't heard from him since. Tried calling, but . . ."

"Mr. Tanner's use to me is coming to an end."

"What do you mean?"

Mason didn't answer. Instead, he said, "Cochrane isn't giving up."

"Great to hear."

"But he's not optimistic."

Mae was silent.

"My Beirut initiative failed; deployment of Cochrane looks unlikely to deliver, and in the process, his team has been wiped out. My dear Mae, I owe it to you to speak the truth. Be in no doubt that in forty-eight hours it is probable that I will have to resign."

Forty-One

I t was early evening as I walked into Beirut's northern coastal district of Centre Ville, an area that had been inhabited for thousands of years and had been tastefully rebuilt after most of the district had been destroyed in the Lebanese Civil War. In keeping with its tradition, Centre Ville was a center for politics, finance, business, and culture. Most of its buildings were modern in style, though there were some that had survived the war and were hundreds of years old. I was searching for one such building.

I walked through the Garden of Forgiveness, a commemoration of the tragedy of war, with exposed ruins from over fifteen civilizations including columns and other ruins belonging to the Roman city of Berytus. The presence of many people around me gave me some comfort; it was unlikely I would be attacked in such a public place by the blond man or the sniper. But I wasn't complacent, and remained vigilant as I moved away from the garden and into a pedestrian street that mostly comprised antique shops and jewelry stores. One of the shops was different. It was closed, though inside there were lights on. I rang the shop's doorbell.

A small, elderly Arab man answered. He was wearing slacks and a collarless shirt that had small scorch marks on its rolled-up sleeves.

"Mr. Wehbi? My name is Peter Sandcroft. We spoke earlier on the phone."

"Ah, yes. Come in, come in."

I entered the shop and was immediately struck by the clutter. Shelves covered all the walls, and on them were boxes, books, and stuffed animals. Sheets of different-colored silk hung from the ceiling, some of them long enough to touch the floor. On a table were burning incense sticks and an electric globe that cast images of stars onto everything in the room. A cord stretched from one end of the room to the other; on it a toy bat was suspended and moved back and forth, emitting a screech. Man-height mirrors were leaning against the walls, reflecting distorted and grotesque images of me as I stood before them. Live white doves fluttered their wings in metal birdcages suspended midair. And a ten-foot-long brass pendulum swung back and forth, fixed in the ceiling's center, at its bottom an ominous-looking scythe that was scraping a groove in the wooden floor.

The proprietor ushered me into another room at the back of the shop. It contained a wooden table, a couple of chairs, and a tiny kitchenette and sink. The man made two mugs of black tea and added five spoons of sugar into each, without asking me if I wanted my drink sweetened. He handed me a mug and beckoned me to sit at the table.

He sat opposite me and withdrew a notebook and fountain pen from his shirt pocket. "How did you become aware of my establishment?"

"The Internet."

"I don't have a website."

I shrugged. "Your shop was mentioned in a review of the old city by a tourist who'd come here. The tourist thought your shop was quaint."

"Quaint?" The old man took a sip of his tea and grinned, showing decayed teeth, no doubt a result of the amount of sugar passing across them. "The word 'quaint' suggests my shop is harmless and has some degree of charm. I'd have preferred it if the tourist had used the description 'unique,' because that is what it most certainly is. At least, in Beirut. There's no other like it."

"I thought as much." I pointed toward the front room. "You don't just sell? You actually *understand* the items you sell?"

The man nodded. "My shop has been in my family for generations. Many of the things I sell have been manufactured by me. I wouldn't sell anything unless I knew its precise qualities and workings." He opened his notebook. "You told me on the phone that you had a theory, but needed to understand whether it was possible."

"That's why I'm here. Maybe you can help."

"If I can, what do I get in return?"

I wondered how he'd react if I told him that his help might ensure that his country wasn't turned into a war zone. "I can pay you for your time."

"And what value would you put on that time?" He drummed his fingers on the table. "No, no. Money's no good. But I tell you what: write a review of my shop. And make sure it includes the word 'unique.'"

I smiled. "We have a deal."

I spoke to him for thirty minutes—the shop owner writing notes as I did so—before concluding, "My theory may be completely wrong. I just need to know if it's possible."

The man was silent, deep in thought. Then, he asked, "And this room—does it exist?"

I lied. "No. Its reality is confined to my imagination."

He looked at his notes. "Your solution is possible. Come with me." He led me back into his shop and pulled open cabinet drawers while muttering, "Where are you, where are you?" Then he exclaimed, "Got you." He handed me a roll of thin paper. "You may have this for free." He told me what to do with the paper and ripped out a sheet from his notepad. He folded the paper and tucked it into my jacket pocket. "That contains a list of the items required to produce the desired effect." He grinned. "The type of mystery you describe has fascinated men like me ever since the inception of our profession. Maybe I can steal your solution and one day use it."

I shook his hand. "Just give me a few days before you do that." I thanked him for his time and insight and headed back to my hotel.

In an empty apartment overlooking Abdel Baki Street, Colonel Rowe was in near pitch darkness, on one knee while using binoculars to scrutinize Will Cochrane's hotel room on the other side of the street. He'd been watching the hotel for fifteen hours. By his side was a suppressed-sound sniper rifle. It had no scope, but that didn't matter. Cochrane's room was no more than forty yards away. At that distance, Rowe would easily be able to put a round in Cochrane's head when he showed himself in his window.

The problem was that the room's curtains had been closed since the colonel had been watching the place. He was hoping that would soon change, because even with the room's light on and a man's silhouette visible behind the curtain, Rowe couldn't risk shooting at the shape. He had to be sure the person in the room was Cochrane. If the silhouette belonged to a cleaner or other hotel staff, and Rowe shot that person, Cochrane would go to ground; Rowe would have to wait until the former MI6 officer used his alias credit card or passport again to find his new location. He couldn't afford to wait for that to happen. Time was running out. He put down his binoculars and lifted his rifle, holding it at eye level, ready to fire.

The receptionist in my hotel smiled when she saw me approach her desk. "Your last evening with us, Mr. Oaks. You should make the most of this evening. Maybe dine out somewhere nice."

"Dining alone isn't a great way to enjoy my last day in Beirut."

Her smile broadened. "Then, don't dine alone."

"Perhaps you'd like to join me when your shift finishes?"

"My shift doesn't finish until six A.M., plus I'm happily married."

"Ah." I glanced at the entrance to the lobby. "Anything for me? Letters? Visitors?"

The receptionist began tapping on her computer keyboard. "Nothing."

"You sure? I was expecting a couple of my associates to come over. One of them is the guy who came here before—with red sideburns. The other is blond, about ten years younger."

"No. They've not been here."

"That's a pity, because I was hoping to invite them out for a beer."

"If they come, I'll be sure to let you know."

"Thanks." I took the elevator to my floor. As it was every evening, the lighting in the corridor was dimmed. I could only assume this was done to imbue a sense of relaxation. I saw no signs of other guests on the floor. The hotel was quiet; all that could be heard was the noise of vehicles in the adjacent street. I reached my room's door, looked up and down the corridor, and placed my ear against the entrance. It was a futile action because the external sounds of the city were too loud. Plus, what was I expecting to hear? I swiped my key card through the slot.

I entered my hotel room, but didn't yet turn on its lights, because I wanted to check that the curtains were closed. They were. I turned back to the room's door and the main set of light switches. As I did so, I saw the slightest flash of metal, illuminated by the tiny LED light in the ceiling smoke alarm. Instinctively, I jumped back, feeling a searing pain in my stomach as something sharp sliced across my shirt and skin.

A knife.

I saw the blade move fast again, dodged its trajectory, and moved quickly forward, trying to grab the arm of the man with the knife. I connected with his wrist. I gripped tight and ran backward, twisting his arm with all of my might and trying to drag him to the ground. He kicked me hard in the groin and spun around, but I maintained my hold and dragged him to the door, where I lunged at the light switch and lit up the room.

I was holding the blond assassin. Sweat shone on his face as he tried to yank his knife-holding hand free of my grip and slice through my palms and fingers in the process. He placed a boot on my chest and used it to kick me back and free himself.

We stood feet apart, both of us breathing fast though otherwise silent.

He moved the knife back and forth in front of his waist, waiting for the right moment to attack again. I had to let him make a move first, as I wouldn't stand a chance of preempting an attack. He stepped forward, raising his knife to head height to thrust the blade down toward my chest. I crossed my wrists and threw my arms above my head, blocking his stroke, and kicked with all of my strength into his gut. He fell back, winded. I dove onto him, locking one arm around his arm, the other around his neck, and rolling him onto his side, using my strength and body weight to pin him down. From this position, I could choke him to death.

"Drop your knife!" I squeezed harder on his throat. "You know what will happen if you don't."

He tried to move his knife closer to my body.

But I arched back, pulling his neck and head with me. "Drop the knife."

"You'll kill me anyway." He wheezed; his accent was foreign. I couldn't yet place his nationality.

"No, I won't. And I don't believe you want to kill me—not here, not in London. But you want to hurt me badly." I squeezed again, causing my captive to gasp. "I can't take any chances. If you keep hold of the knife, I'll have no choice other than to finish this."

He dropped the knife.

I kicked it away. "I'll be on my feet quicker than

you. If you try anything now, I'll have the knife in my hand and in your body before you even get to your knees. Understood?"

He hesitated, then said, "Yes."

I released my grip, sprang to my feet, and grabbed the knife.

My assailant got up, rubbing his neck and looking at me with suspicion.

From across the street, Colonel Rowe frowned. He'd seen quick movement behind the curtains in Cochrane's room once the lights were turned on; perhaps two people, though he couldn't be sure. Maids cleaning the room? Most likely. Though it was equally possible Michael Stein had entered the room and attacked Cochrane. "Open the curtains," he said between gritted teeth, while keeping his rifle pointing at the window and his finger on the trigger.

"Who are you?" I asked the blond man.

He didn't answer, just stared at me. He was a handsome man, tall and athletic.

"Why are you doing this?"

He took a step toward me.

I raised the knife so that it was perpendicular to him and at chest height, the palm of my free hand flat against the back of its hilt. If he came closer, I'd slam it forward. The action wouldn't necessarily save my life, but it would ensure the blade got him.

He looked at the knife, then me. "You want to destroy my brother's name."

"Your brother?" My mind raced. Brother? This man's accent? I thought I knew what was happening. "You're Israeli?"

He didn't reply.

"Special Forces? Mossad? Shin Bet?"

He returned his attention to the knife.

I raised it so that its tip was at the level of his eyes. "Do you know what Gray Site is?"

He nodded.

"Have you been there?"

"I visited the site before you did, earlier today."

"What did you see?"

"Nothing."

"But your brother died there?"

His eyes held venom as he responded, "Yes."

"And you think I'm here to besmirch your brother's name. To—"

"His name's Ben."

"To tarnish Ben's name? Blame him? Exonerate the CIA officer in the station?"

"You believe Ben wanted to tamper with coverage of the Hamas meeting. You suspect the CIA officer who shot him discovered Ben's intentions. You want the CIA officer to be seen in a pleasing light. The CIA man did what he should have done. He was a good guy. Ben was bad. That's what you're hoping to prove."

"What's your name?"

"Michael."

"Your family name is Stein."

"Yes."

I lowered the knife. "I think you work for Mossad, though you've had military experience."

He was motionless.

I had no idea of his intentions.

Though I was sure that Michael was a killer.

He was too calm.

"I've no interest in ruining your family name. *Please,*" I raised my hands in a gesture of peace. "Who is Thales?"

Michael didn't move. "I don't know."

"But you know of him?"

Michael nodded.

"Your assessment?"

"A manipulator with a hidden agenda."

"A person who got you to go out on a limb?"

Michael looked momentarily annoyed. "I put myself out on a limb."

"No, you didn't." I pointed at the curtains. "There's

someone out there. A man who works for Thales and who's a proficient shot. He attacked me at the same time as you attacked me in London. But I don't think you work together. How did Thales manipulate you?"

"I didn't say he manipulated me."

"How?" I repeated.

Michael looked at the curtains. "Thales sent me a letter. I've no idea how he got my home address or my identity."

"I do."

"What do you mean?"

I thrust the knife into a side table, hoping my release of the weapon would show my willingness to trust him. The knife's tip was embedded in wood, the weapon upright. "Someone is feeding Thales information about me, you, and everything else that's happened and is happening."

"A paymaster?"

I nodded. "A traitor."

Michael moved to my side, putting himself between me and the knife. His hand brushed against its blade. "I'm here because I want my brother to be free. You're meddling in Gray Site because most likely someone's financing you to do so."

"I'm here because the CIA officer in Gray Site

was a dear friend of mine and an honorable man. Subsequently his wife has been murdered; so too have my former bosses and two of my peers. Almost certainly, it was all done by Thales."

"They're all dead?"

I nodded.

"My God." Michael moved his hand away from the knife. "Thales wrote to me. He said he'd deploy a man to hunt you."

I glanced at the curtains again. "I think that man killed my friends. He tried to warn me not to continue. You've been tracking me via my passport and credit card. Correct?"

Michael nodded. "Richard Oaks. Details of your passport and card were given to me by Thales."

I walked closer to the window. "Your brother Ben and my friend Roger didn't do anything wrong in Gray Site. I need you to listen to me. And when I've finished, I want you to help me get even."

Colonel Rowe saw the silhouette of a large person behind the curtains in Cochrane's room. He aimed his gun at the center of the man's head, willing him to open the curtains and expose himself. The shadow vanished. Rowe adjusted his stance, putting one foot against the baseboard below the window in the apartment and his other farther back on the floor. He was ready to shoot the moment Cochrane showed himself. Then, Rowe's job would be at an end and the path would be clear for Thales. Rowe muttered, "Come on. Show yourself, Cochrane."

I unrolled the thin roll of paper given to me by the Lebanese shop proprietor, using tape to fix one end of it to the ceiling and the other end to the floor. Michael was with me. I lit the paper near the ceiling. It burned rapidly to the floor, the paper disappearing and leaving no trace of ash. "Flash paper."

Michael nodded.

I punched a wall mirror, causing it to fragment into large shards, and checked my watch. "It's time to leave. Good luck."

Rowe saw the flash of light in Cochrane's hotel room and had no idea where it had come from. It had traveled diagonally from ceiling to floor, and its illumination only lasted a second. He called Thales and told him what he'd seen.

Monsieur de Guise sounded uncharacteristically perturbed when he responded, "Kill Cochrane on sight."

The lights in Cochrane's room were extinguished.

The curtains were opened, though Rowe couldn't see anyone standing behind them. He waited.

Michael kept his body low as he moved along Cochrane's room, then stopped below the window and carefully raised a small fragment that he'd taken from the smashed mirror. In its reflection, he saw a man in the room across the street. The man was holding a rifle, stock still and waiting. The sniper. Thales's hit man.

Michael sent Cochrane an SMS.

Fifth floor. Directly opposite your room.

Cochrane immediately responded from across the street, but Michael ignored his SMS, dropped the mirror, stood, and dashed left just before a silenced rifle bullet was discharged. The bullet struck him in the shoulder and slammed him sideways.

In the apartment building across the street, I rushed into the room as the sniper tried to load another bullet into the chamber of his weapon. In my hotel room, Michael was down. He'd been in that room, using a piece of glass to try to spot the sniper in one of the empty apartments on Abdel Baki Street, then sacrificing his safety by briefly exposing himself to the shooter so that he could buy me two seconds of time.

It was tremendously brave and might have cost Michael his life.

The sniper heard my fast footsteps and swiveled to face me, desperately trying to load and fire his weapon at me. His expression was one of panic and surprise. I slashed the knife across one of the sniper's arms, then the other, leaving deep cuts that made his limbs go limp. I struck with the knife again, this time into his leg. He collapsed to the floor, wincing, his weapon discarded and useless.

I ripped off my belt and used it as a tourniquet above the wound in his leg. "Don't move!" I used my cell to call Michael. No answer. I called again.

This time he answered on the fifth ring. "I'm . . . I'm okay. The bullet sliced across my shoulder, but the wound's not deep."

"Are you able to get over here?"

He was breathing fast. "Just patching myself up. I brought along a medical kit in case you . . . got the better of me." He laughed, though his voice was strained. "Didn't expect to get hurt this way. Give me a few minutes."

Within that time, Michael was at my side in the bare apartment. The sniper was by my feet, partly in darkness, his face lit by moonlight and the streetlights.

I crouched by the sniper. His appearance matched

the description of the man who'd handed the letter to the hotel receptionist. I looked at Michael, didn't say anything, but tried to gauge his support for what I needed to do. Michael was silent as he held my gaze and gave the briefest of nods.

I hate torture. So often, it's pointless, barbaric, and says more about the man inflicting the pain than it does about the victim. But there are rare moments when lack of time, unusual circumstances, desperation, and the failure of other options can force one's hand. I brought the blade of the knife to his leg wound, firmly but carefully.

While the sniper tried to stop himself from screaming I asked, "What is your name?"

"Fuck you!" He was English, with a deep voice.

I looked at the wound in his leg, then undid my belt buckle and loosened it by one notch. A small amount of blood oozed out of the cut. If I undid the belt completely I could walk out of here knowing full well that in a few hours the sniper would be a corpse, or incarcerated in jail because he'd had to call for help. "Who are you?" I repeated.

The sniper tried to move his arms but winced from his injuries. He remained slumped on the floor.

"Unless you answer my questions, you'll die. It's up to you. Do you want to die?"

The sniper glared at me, his expression defiant. "You do what you want."

"Okay." I yanked off the shoe on his injured leg, causing his back to arch from the pain, and removed his sock, which I screwed up into a ball and thrust into his mouth. Now, noises from his mouth were muffled. I kicked one of his injured arms and said calmly, "I think you're the man who killed my former colleagues in the States. Maybe I'm wrong. Perhaps the killer is someone you work with. Someone *better* than you."

I pulled out the sock.

He spat, "I work alone. For a reason. No one's better than me."

I put the gag back in his mouth and moved the knife in the wound before loosening the belt by another notch. His blood was flowing freely, though it was still restricted by the makeshift tourniquet. "If you're not my friends' murderer, then you're of no use to me. You're simply a man who tried to kill me in my hotel. And if that's the case, I might as well leave you to die in here." I leaned in closer toward his face. "But if you're directly or indirectly involved in the deaths of my colleagues, know anything about the assassination of Israel's ambassador to France, have insight into what happened inside an underground intelligence station in this city, and most of all"—I pressed hard on the wound on his right arm—"can tell me all you know about a man called Thales, then you have significant value to me. If you cooperate, I'll let you live."

He shook his head violently.

I pulled the knife from his leg, watching him writhe on the floor as his blood coursed strongly from the wound. I glanced at Michael. "An hour or two?"

"At best. I'm thinking thirty minutes."

"Let's be sure of that." I fully undid my belt and tossed it across the room. "There." I patted the sniper on his head. "Death is now a certainty." I pulled out the sock and held it in front of his face. "There's no need for this now, is there? I don't have to do anything to you—just watch you fade away."

The sniper looked desperate but still retained some defiance in his expression. "I can't trust you!"

"Then who or what can you trust?" I pointed at his leg. "One thing's for sure, you can certainly trust that to do its job unless you get medical attention. There's a Lebanese doctor I know. He's only a few blocks away from here. All I need to do is call him and he'll be here in minutes. And he's very good at what he does. He'll have you patched up, without a soul knowing anything about it." I smiled. "He owes me a few favors."

"Why would you do that for me?"

"Information. I'm not after you. I want to know the truth behind the Paris assassination and what happened in this city. Give me your name!"

The sniper lowered his head. "I have your word, as a fellow Englishman?"

I nodded. "Providing you cooperate in full."

He looked uncertain.

"Time is running out for you. Make a decision!"

"I . . ."

"Yes?"

"I was ordered to kill the Israeli ambassador and your friends."

"By whom?"

"Thales."

"And who is Thales?"

The sniper shook his head. "I can't . . . I'll be a dead man if I tell you."

"The alternative is no better. Your name?"

A degree of resignation settled on the man's face. "Rowe, formerly a colonel in Her Majesty's Royal Dragoon Guards."

"The weapon you used to kill the ambassador—do you still have it?"

"Of course not. I buried it on the outskirts of Paris. When my work on this project was done, and I thought it was safe to go back there, I intended to retrieve the gun and completely destroy it."

"Where is it?"

Rowe said nothing.

"Where is it, Rowe? This is your only chance."

He sighed and gave me a grid reference.

Urgently, I looked at Michael. "Is there anyone in your organization you can call right now? Someone powerful enough to immediately put a call into the French intelligence or security services and persuade them to deploy police? We need that gun retrieved, examined, and its ballistics compared to the bullet found in the ambassador's chest. The results need to be sent to Israel ASAP."

Michael nodded. "My boss has that sway." He pulled out his cell and moved to the other side of the room.

"When I get the doctor to repair your injuries, I'm going to stay by your side. If I get a call from my friend"—I pointed at Michael—"in the next few hours saying you've just spun me a pack of lies, I'll cut your legs off."

"It's the truth."

I held the bloody knife under his chin. "You sure?"

"Yes." Rowe lowered his head again. "I'll have to disappear. Go on the run." He looked at his bloody leg and smiled at the irony of his observation. The smile vanished. "Thales will use everything at his disposal to track me down and kill me."

"That's your problem, not mine." I put the tip of

the blade against his skin. "Have you been to Gray Site?"

Silence.

"Did you help on the day it happened?"

Rowe laughed, and blood trickled from his mouth, its color matching that of his sideburns. "I did more than *help*."

"Of course you did." I told him what I thought had happened on that day. "I suspect there would have needed to have been at least twice as many men with you as there were Gray Site operatives to get it done. Eight men?"

Rowe frowned. "Thales said no one would know how we did it."

"Well, *I* know. Was it you who stayed behind? Or was it Thales himself?"

"Thales insisted only he had the skills to pull it off."

"Why is he manipulating Israel to go to war?"

"He's paid to do so."

"By whom?"

"I don't know. Do you?"

"I have my suspicions." I reattached my belt as a tourniquet to Rowe's thigh. I could see the assassin was getting weak. "You must tell me who Thales is."

"You promised me you'd call the doctor."

"I will. Two things need to happen first: you telling me Thales's name; and my Israeli friend receiving confirmation the sniper rifle you used in Paris has been found."

"I could be dead by the time—"

"Let's hope both happen quickly."

Rowe used his elbows to force himself to a sitting position on the floor, his back against the wall beneath the window, his face wracked in pain from the exertion. "His name's Monsieur de Guise."

"He lives in France?"

"I don't know exactly where, though I suspect it's somewhere in the north of the country, since that's where we usually meet."

"Vocation?"

"I've no idea."

"A Frenchman?"

Rowe coughed violently. "He plays the part exceptionally well. But he's English."

"Anything about his previous life?"

"I don't know. None of us do. He pays us. That's all that matters."

I sat next to Rowe, my back leaning against the same wall. "We must wait."

"My life . . ."

"Depends on your rifle being found and its chamber matching the gun that killed a senior Israeli diplomat." I looked at Michael. He was staring at his cell phone.

Twenty minutes later, it rang. Michael listened. He snapped shut the phone. "Local French police have found a weapon—high-powered, military-grade sniper rifle. It's being rushed to a DGSE facility in Paris. DGSE is in constant communications with my country, the CIA, and the Pentagon. The French are confident they can get a ballistics analysis to Mossad within an hour. Sounds impossible, but they will try. And Mossad's confident it can prove one way or the other whether the weapon was used by Rowe to kill the Israeli ambassador." Michael pointed at his phone. "Without a match, this means nothing."

Rowe croaked, "It'll be a match. Rest assured. And you can match the weapon to me. I always wear gloves, but I didn't wear a mask. They seem so crude. I like to be at one with my rifles when I fire them. Traces of my DNA will inevitably have transferred from my cheeks and mouth to the weapon."

Michael said, "We'll take a sample from you. But, how do we know you were acting on orders from Thales rather than Hamas? We only have your word."

Rowe looked proud as he told the Mossad officer, "I only take orders from Thales. No one else. Who he chooses to take orders from is his business."

Michael beamed at me. "If that's true, you did it. You've got the evidence needed to stop war."

"He's got evidence and has established what

happened in Gray Site," Rowe said, his voice distant, "but it's not enough to stop war."

I turned to him and frowned. "What do you mean?"

"This has been a sideshow. State allegiances are created by shared fear. Thales didn't care about such things, though he used them to earn his keep. An Arab boy of Gaza goes to America. Boom, boom. He scorches the earth. The world won't care any longer about what I tried to do. Or you, for that matter."

"A sideshow?"

"Followed by a reaction to something else. Unstoppable. Too late. Too last minute. The world looks at carnage. Israel moves forward again. America must support the country. So, too, many others. Unstoppable."

"Who is the boy?" I asked with urgency. "Where is he going? What's his target?"

Rowe answered, "I helped Thales get him out of Gaza, but I don't know his name or anything else about him. That was kept from me." He was growing faint. "There's no reason for me to lie. I don't win from this. Only Thales wins. I don't know specifics, but I do know the boy's target is someplace in America. Nothing overly dramatic. An Archduke Ferdinand spark—enough to create hell."

I nodded. "Colonel Rowe?"

"Yes." His voice now sounded slurred.

"The man standing in front of you is called Michael Stein."

"I know."

"My name is Will Cochrane."

"Of course."

"The Israeli man in Gray Site was Ben Stein. The American man, Roger Koenig. One was a brother, the other a friend. You butchered Roger's wife and left her two sons without parents. You shot my father's closest friends, as well as a brave man and woman."

"It was nothing personal." Rowe was seemingly growing distant from the room and our situation; life was ebbing away from him. "I just did what Thales told me to do. You'd have done the same. When are you calling the doctor?"

"There never was a doctor." I thrust the knife into Rowe's chest.

Forty-Two

Via Paris's Charles de Gaulle airport, I flew overnight to Washington, D.C. The journey seemed endless. I poured black coffee down my throat and wished the flight attendants would stop trying to feed me congealed scrambled eggs and other crap while I watched the news on the back of the chair in front of me. Today officially became tomorrow, and reports said that Israel was ready to go to war in twenty-four hours but had decided to postpone that action based on new evidence about the assassination of its ambassador.

Before I'd departed Beirut, Michael Stein had told me the ballistics analysis was in no doubt that Rowe's rifle had killed the man. Though it was guilty of numerous other atrocities, Hamas wasn't guilty of this particular crime.

But the ballistics evidence wasn't enough. According to what Rowe had told me, we were all about to be sucker punched. A boy would do that.

And remobilize Israel's military machine.

Before I'd set off for the U.S., I'd called Mason plus some contacts I had in Homeland Security, warning them about an imminent attack and asking them to start investigating what targets the Arab boy might be focusing on. I'd also called my neighbor Phoebe. She was fine, as were David and Dickie. She had started her new job at the Tate Modern, and was oblivious to the fact that armed plainclothes SBS men were discreetly protecting her apartment building.

It was dark outside the craft. In the dim cabin light, I could see most people were asleep; some were reading; others were talking to each other while standing in the aisles; a few were pinging a summons to flight attendants to service their needs. Even if Israel did go to war, in the short term U.S. citizens were right to be unconcerned. Anything that happened wouldn't immediately affect America or its nearby cousins, but in the medium to long term, what Thales would achieve would unleash devastation of the kind that creeps up behind the unwitting and rips their guts out.

Lone wolf terrorists, ill equipped to fight their cause on battlefields, would draw strength from their

indignation at Israel's war and strike the state's sup-
porters in more nefarious ways.

When the plane landed, I was like one of those travelers I normally loathe—staring at the seat belt light,
poised to jump to my feet and grab the bag I'd stowed
in the overhead bin, ready to barge my way up the aisle
even though it would barely buy me any extra time
when we hit the gridlock of passport control and bag-
gage collection.

I was desperate to get out of Dulles airport.

There was nothing I could do to help catch the Arab
boy. But it was within my power to expose a traitor. I
wished Patrick, Alistair, Roger, Suzy, and Laith were
in the States, ready to help me. They were people I
trusted wholeheartedly and who'd consistently given
me their unconditional support.

I walked through the arrivals hall of the airport and
made a decision to call someone who'd tried to appre-
hend and kill me a year ago. Her name was Marsha
Gage. She was a senior agent in the FBI, and I respected
her tenacity and honesty. I didn't have her cell number,
so had to try to reach her via the switchboard of the
Bureau's J. Edgar Hoover Building headquarters. It
was only eight thirty in the morning, so I didn't know
whether she'd be at work.

She was, answering her office phone almost immediately. "Agent Gage."

I exited the airport and spotted a line of yellow cabs. "Mrs. Gage, this is—"

"Will Cochrane." Marsha sounded pissed. "Are you back on my turf, causing problems?"

"Yes and no."

"Tell me about the yes part."

I told her what I needed. "Can you get me clearance to the building?"

"Of course. Where are you?"

"Just leaving Dulles. I'll be there in less than an hour."

"You don't go in there without me and my men." Her voice was stern. "And if this turns out to be a false accusation, you might as well kill yourself." She gave me details of where we should meet and hung up.

I felt weary in the back of the cab, traveling east toward the heart of D.C. Being under constant threat had put my body in a state of hypertension; it was now starting to relax and craved sleep. But my mind wouldn't let it rest because so much was at stake. I'd achieved what I'd set out to do, and more, and yet my accomplishments now seemed irrelevant.

The cabdriver was an amiable young Indian man who spoke nonstop during the journey about the England cricket team and its current tour in his home country. It seemed surreal to be receiving an education on Britain's national sport from a non-American in the States. I didn't have the heart to tell him that just because I was English didn't mean I knew a thing about cricket.

"Do you work here?" he asked as he brought his cab to a halt outside the Pentagon.

"No. I'm unemployable," I added without thinking. I gave him a tip and walked fast across the huge parking lot, a suitcase in my hand, probably looking like a government official who was returning to work after an overseas trip.

Agent Gage and four of her men were outside the building, watching me as I approached. Marsha Gage was wearing a black pantsuit and white blouse, her long hair pinned up. She said, "A year ago, I told you never to come back to the States again."

"Actually, you told me never to come back here and cause trouble."

"And what does this look like?"

I smiled and held out my hand. "It's good to see you, Agent Gage."

The last time I'd seen the Bureau's best agent, I was in an orange jumpsuit and shackles in a maximum-security penitentiary.

She hesitated, then shook my hand. "Do you have any evidence?"

"It's circumstantial, yet logical."

THE SPY HOUSE · 451

Marsha laughed. "We have federal jurisdiction to enter this building. But I'm not carrying a warrant, and I can't stand in a court and swear an oath that I've conducted an investigation that gave me the right to interrogate a person here." Her demeanor got colder. "I'm warning you, if this turns out to be a heap of crap, then I'll have no hesitation in arresting you."

Her men, all burly and wearing matching dark suits and sidearms, stared at me, hostility and suspicion on their faces.

Marsha lowered her head, seemingly trying to make a decision. She looked at me, clapped her hands once, and said in an authoritarian tone, "On your head be it. Let's go!"

There were of course problems with guns and dodgy Englishmen being allowed past the security gates of the Pentagon, but Marsha handled the affronts of the building's security guards with an equal measure of aplomb and bullshit. She showed them her ID, cited national security and the authority of the attorney general, phoned the Bureau's director and got him to call the Pentagon's head of security, and paced back and forth while ranting that today was a good day because she could put away a lot of people for obstructing justice.

I called Admiral Mason and told him I was here with associates and would dearly like it if he could authorize us to enter the building and see him. The result was like a pin thrust into a balloon. With apologies from Pentagon staff, we were ushered through the security gates and guided to Mason's office.

I thought about Admiral Thomas Cochrane, the tenth earl of Dundonald, as I entered Mason's oak-paneled, nautical-themed office. I'd liked the fact that in our only face-to-face encounter, Mason had mentioned him, but honestly, it enhanced my sadness to be back here.

Mason was standing in the center of the room. The diminutive gray-haired commander was wearing a pin-striped suit whose jacket was buttoned, a navy blue tie, and black shoes that were gleaming with polish. He seemed like a general standing on a battlefield surveying the aftermath of a war that had gone wrong.

By comparison, the twenty-something man who was also in the room looked nonchalant and exuded contempt, as far as I could tell. Like Mason, he was well dressed in a suit, though he wore it like a spoiled rich kid. The thirty-something woman by his side was different. She repeatedly glanced at me, my associates, and the admiral, her expression alternating between worry and deference to Mason. No doubt she was loyal because he was her boss. Maybe there was a stronger bond in place.

Mason looked at me, rather than the FBI officials. There seemed to be a hint of disappointment in his eyes, yet also the stoicism common to most leaders. His back was ramrod straight; his intelligence was palpable. "A problem?"

"To be corrected."

"By you?"

I gestured to Marsha and her men. "By people better than me."

"You feel uncomfortable being here?"

"I do."

"Why?"

"Because I'd hoped for something else."

Mason gestured to his two colleagues. "Rob Tanner and Mae Bäcklund. They work for me, and are security cleared to the highest level. You did well to find the rifle."

I responded, "French police found it, not me."

"You directed them where to look. But you told me on the phone it isn't enough."

"No. Another strategy is in play. It's beyond my control."

The admiral placed his hands behind his back, looking every inch the quiet and calm officer. "Thales composed and conducted a symphony, but he was paid to do so. You think I tasked him?"

Marsha Gage stepped forward. "Sir, we have no proof of that."

"Then why are you here?"

"Because Cochrane doesn't get things wrong."

"Doesn't he?" A slight smile emerged on Mason's face as he kept his eyes locked on mine. "What haven't you got wrong?"

I answered, "Alistair and Patrick knew I was going to be traveling under my Richard Oaks identity. They would have kept that secret. But the first time I came here to meet you, I was carrying my Oaks ID. I had to hand my passport and credit card to security, ready for me to collect it when I left the building."

Mason's smile vanished. "And you think I arranged to have your identity details copied while you were meeting me?"

I was silent as I stared at a man who I liked and respected.

Rob Tanner exclaimed, "You can't just barge in here and accuse our boss of something this ludicrous!"

Mason gestured for him to be silent. He walked right up to me and quietly said, "If Thales is operating under instruction, then there will be a precise agenda behind that instruction. Israel goes to war. It makes enemies, but then it's always going to have them. That isn't the agenda. Renewing friendships and winning new friends is. I'm assuming you have the same thought?"

"I do."

"And you think I've enacted a strategy to build new support for Israel by forcing its hand into war, and to hell with the consequences of how many Israeli and Arab soldiers and civilians die in the process?"

I was silent.

Mason walked to his desk and opened a diary. "I have the exact time and date that you came here."

"I hoped you would."

"Then you'll support what I'm going to do next?"

I gestured toward his telephone. "Yes."

Mason dialed an internal number, spoke for a minute, and concluded, "I want a name." He waited, then said, "Nobody leaves the building without my permission to do so. Put the Pentagon in lockdown." He replaced the handset in its cradle. No one spoke as he walked back to the center of the room and stood, deep in thought.

"Ordinarily, somebody from my office approaching the front security desk and checking the ID details of one of my visitors would be routine. But under these circumstances it is treason."

Mae Bäcklund pointed at Tanner. "You! That would explain all your absences from work. Your behavior.

Your . . . you accessed and copied Cochrane's fake ID and relayed the data to Thales!"

Mason stood before her and Tanner. "Rob Tanner's an employee of the CIA, planted here to keep an eye on me."

Tanner's face flushed. "Sir, that's—"

"The truth, and I suspected it the moment your résumé landed on my desk. Recently, Patrick was able to confirm my suspicions. He found out about you and your handler. You've been telling your CIA handler everything that's been going on in my office—meetings in hotel rooms with him, parks, phone calls from your car in the Pentagon parking lot. Did you honestly think you'd fool me? But that's the worst of it. The Agency simply wanted to ensure that I was doing my job, so it put you in here deep cover." Mason's expression was cold as he added, "Get out of my sight, and when the building's no longer in lockdown I want you to leave here and never come back."

The ordinarily cocky young man looked bereft as he left the room. He was right to suspect that not only were his days in the Pentagon over, but soon he would be forced to leave the CIA as well.

Mason's eyes moistened as he looked at Bäcklund. "But I *have* been a fool. My one blind spot. My goddaughter."

Bäcklund looked incredulous. "You can't be serious!"

"You copied Cochrane's Oaks passport and credit card, and relayed their details to Thales. You are Thales's employer."

Bäcklund tried to object.

"The security desk has just confirmed to me that it was you who requested Cochrane's ID!"

"I was just checking up on him. That was all. *Please*, my captain. This is a big mistake."

"I'm no longer *your* captain! One of the reasons I hired you was because you had sufficient independent wealth not to worry about the pittance I paid you. If only I'd known that decision would turn out to be catastrophic." Mason shook his head. "The other reason was because I thought I could trust you, of all people."

Marsha Gage said, "We'll take her away for questioning. But we'll need a confession or more evidence. None of this is proof positive of guilt."

Mason pointed at me while keeping his eyes on Bäcklund. "This man's friends and colleagues are dead, leaving behind children who no doubt are distraught and afraid. Because of you, Mr. Cochrane was attacked and nearly killed. I urge you to make a confession. It's the least you can do."

Bäcklund looked venomous. "You're making a mistake!"

"No. The mistake is all yours." He glanced at Gage. "Miss Bäcklund is gifted and capable, but I suspect she's never dabbled in crime before, nor has she received expert training to cover her tracks as a criminal or spy. If you do a forensic analysis of her life during the last few weeks, what is your estimate of finding further evidence to prove her guilt?"

Agent Gage shrugged. "I'd say eighty—no, ninety percent likely."

"Ninety percent." Mason stared at Bäcklund. "Ninety percent. Agent Gage, do I have authority to offer a plea bargain?"

Gage took a moment to consider his question. "Providing you can swing authority from the attorney general and your bargain is reasonable in the eyes of the law, then yes, I don't see why not."

The admiral nodded. He said to me, "Such a plea would offer a choice between the devil and the deep blue sea. But, in this case one might be slightly more preferable to the other. You understand?"

"Yes."

"Mr. Cochrane, you've suffered more than most. I won't offer the plea if you understandably decide that Mae Bäcklund must face the devil."

I looked at her and for some reason felt numb. "Offer her the plea."

Mason asked, "Why?"

"Because it's what I want and because it's what my dead friends would have wanted."

Mason stared at Bäcklund. "And therein is a reason why your duplicity and treachery should cause you endless shame. Mae—confess and you'll get life imprisonment; maybe there'll be the hope of parole in your later years. Keep your mouth shut, let the FBI unpick your life and find just one link to what's happened, and it will be the death penalty."

Bäcklund's eyes widened. "You wouldn't do that to me!"

Mason placed his hand on her arm. "If I don't intervene, you'll certainly get the needle. But I promised your father I'd look after you. *Please.* A life in prison is better than no life at all."

"And that is how you look after me, is it?!"

"At this stage, it's all that I'm able to do."

Bäcklund lowered her head while brushing Mason's hand away. "I don't want to die."

"But you were very willing to allow others to die."

"Not by my hand!"

"No. Your hand simply paid for their murders."

"I . . . I didn't know it was going to be like that. Not at first. It was all his idea. He did it."

"He?"

"Thales."

Mason's voice was commanding when he said, "You must speak plainly and truthfully now. My offer to commute your death penalty will not stand if we have to force the truth out of you. If in five minutes I'm still standing here asking you not to lie, then there'll be no phone call to the attorney general requesting clemency."

Tears welled up in Bäcklund's eyes. "I'm so sorry, Tobias."

"So am I. Why did you do it?"

Bäcklund hesitated. Then emotion and fear consumed her mind and body. Her legs buckled and she would have collapsed had Mason not grabbed her and held her upright.

"Why?"

Her lips trembled. "Me playing politics. Getting a taste of how it might feel if I make it big time one day in Capitol Hill. Giving Israel the friends it deserves."

"And you did all of that knowing it could ruin the career of *your captain*?"

She shook her head. "I didn't know you'd set up Gray Site and would investigate what happened in there when things went wrong. I didn't know you'd get involved, full stop."

"And yet you kept going when I became involved. Far worse, you didn't tell Thales to back down when people started dying."

Bäcklund burst into tears. "It was escalating beyond my control. I couldn't stop him."

"He's hired help! You could have told him to stop!" Mason felt incredulous that his goddaughter could have done this. "You were in direct communication with Thales?"

Bäcklund nodded.

"His name?"

"Monsieur de Guise was the only name I knew him by. And before you ask, I don't know anything else about him. He approached me about a year ago"—she darted a guilty look at Mason—"to spy on you and what was going on in the Pentagon. I did precisely that. Then one day I asked Thales if he'd temporarily work for *me*."

"Because you had the grand idea to play God and get Israel sitting at the top table." Mason shook his head. "I employ two associates and both of them turn out to be spies. Thing is, though, one of them was just doing his job." He nodded at Agent Gage, who told her men to put Bäcklund in cuffs and take her to the Bureau's headquarters for in-depth questioning.

"Just one moment," I said, and addressed Bäcklund, "Do you know what happened in Gray Site?"

She didn't answer.

I stepped closer to her. "I'll tell you what I think happened in Gray Site."

I recited my theory to the room. On the day that the site's personnel were killed, Thales and approximately seven of his men tailed one of the intelligence officers to work, knowing that the officer's three colleagues were already in the station complex. The officer reached the locked steel door and sent his colleagues the correct security code for the day via text message, which told them that it was safe for them to unlock the door from the inside. They opened the door, whereupon Thales and his men stormed the complex, overpowered the four intelligence officers, and killed them with their own weapons. With the bodies carefully arranged, the scene was set to look as though the officers had turned on each other.

Thales ordered his men to leave. He locked the door behind them, knowing that Western intelligence agencies would send a search party to the site as soon as possible. He also knew that the only way they could force entry through the thick steel door was by using blowtorches. He ran a strip of flash paper from the inside of the door to a nearby sofa. He ran a second strip to a smoke incendiary device; perhaps one that comprised materials listed for me by the magic shop owner in Beirut—ingredients that included potassium nitrate, sugar, and baking soda. Both sofa and smoke bomb were only three feet from the door. He doused the sofa with flammable liquid and secreted himself in a cabinet in the corridor, opposite the sofa. The next day, the CIA rescue team torched the door. The heat ignited the flash papers, which burned to the sofa and smoke bomb, igniting both. Flash paper was used because it leaves no trace after it's burned. Ordinarily, Thales knew at least one of the men in the rescue team would stand guard at the door. He had to move him farther into the complex; the fire achieved this, getting the guard away from the door and facing the burning sofa, with Thales's cabinet behind him. Thales exited the cabinet, hidden from view by the smoke, and escaped.

The rescue team didn't believe the smoke was suspicious because they thought it was from the sofa. In part they were right because cheap sofas, as this one was, can give off a very black smoke when on fire. They put out the fire and began sanitizing the station and making preparations to remove their dead colleagues to a safe extraction point for return home.

"Did I get anything wrong?" I asked Bäcklund.

Bäcklund now had a look of resignation on her face. "Thales was accompanied by nine men, not seven. But otherwise that's exactly what happened. It was Thales's idea when I told him about the telegram sent by Gray Site's CIA officer. Thales had already warned a senior contact in Hamas that the organization needed to be careful because we might be listening in to their conversations. Damn idiot Hamas guy mentioned Thales's code name during the site's intercept of his call to a colleague."

"There's an Arab boy. He's in the States. Where is he? What's his target?"

"I don't know."

"Lie! Where is he?"

Bäcklund was imploring as she said, "Truly, I don't know. This was Thales's fail-safe. I knew about it in principle but agreed with him when he said it was best I didn't know details, in case"—Bäcklund swept an arm through the air—"something like this happened."

Agent Gage stepped up to her. "You can forget the plea bargain if you can't tell us where the boy is."

Bäcklund had tears running down her face.

Gage said, "You've got a chance to live."

Bäcklund was silent, a look of anguish on her face.

"She's telling the truth. She doesn't know where the boy is." I looked at Mason, who nodded his agreement with my assessment.

Agent Gage and her men took Bäcklund out of the room.

"Admiral Mason, I want to apologize for thinking it was you behind all this."

"No need to apologize, Mr. Cochrane." Mason sighed. "You were right to suspect me. And, hopefully, glad to be wrong."

"I am. But are you glad?"

Mason stared in the direction in which Bäcklund had been led away. "No, I'm not glad," he replied in a near whisper.

"You can't blame yourself for what she's done."

"I can. I gave her father my word I'd look after her. I failed him and I failed his daughter."

"Admiral . . ."

"It's a fact and one I must live with for the rest of my life." Mason's expression and demeanor returned to that of a quiet professional. "There's no denying you did a superb job investigating Gray Site. I must admit I didn't think you'd pull it off, you had so little to go on."

"It's irrelevant now. Are there any leads on possible targets for the Arab boy?"

"The Bureau, Homeland Security, NSA, CIA, and every police force in the country are cooperating on this," Mason responded. "It's a needle in a haystack. There are *so* many possible targets. We've put extra security around forthcoming public events, VIP addresses, rallies, government buildings including embassies, everything we can. But it's not enough."

"There must be something I can do."

"Like what? Run around America, trying to find an Arab kid before he does something bad in the next twenty-four hours? Your job's done. And technically you're once again unemployed. So here's what I'm thinking: Would you be interested in consulting for me, only me, same deal as you had with Alistair and Patrick?"

"Off the books, deniable?"

"Hard, complex work on issues that could damage Western interests and security." The admiral held out his hand.

I gripped it and answered, "Yes."

I was about to leave when Mason said, "The Agency and its allies will do everything they can to find Monsieur de Guise. Do you have any ideas about where they might start looking?"

I could have told him that my starting point would be northern France. And given Antaeus's suspicion that de Guise had some connection to mathematics due to his Thales code name, I could have added that I'd look at the staff list of every French university and school. Instead, I answered, "One thing you'll learn about working with me is that there are some things you're better off not asking."

I smiled and left the room.

Forty-Three

Police estimated that at least five thousand Orthodox Jews were in the parade. They were men, women, and children of all ages, the men wearing skullcaps or black hats, the women tichel scarves or sheitel wigs. Dotted alongside them at various positions in the procession were cops on horses, and at the front and rear of the demonstration were squad cars with flashing emergency lights. Many of the people were holding banners or placards with slogans such as JEWS AGAINST WAR. Intermingled in the crowd were people of other ethnicities and creeds, including Palestinian Americans who were holding hands with their Jewish friends and walking with them in solidarity. The demonstration had been planned weeks earlier, when it looked like Israel was going to unleash hell against its terrorist neighbors.

Because Israel had delayed its decision to go to war due to new evidence that suggested Hamas wasn't behind the attack on its ambassador, the mood in the procession was considerably more jovial than it might otherwise have been. Slogans were chanted, but they were coming from people with smiles and looks of relief on their faces. People were singing, and some of the kids were spinning around and dancing. New Yorkers who were not part of the demonstration for peace stood and watched the procession, some calling out their support from the sidewalk and cheering them on. It was afternoon, and the sun was shining. There was a palpable sense of optimism.

As the procession turned onto Fifth Avenue, Safa moved into the ranks of the parade and walked alongside a Jewish man who was marching with his wife and kids. "Sir, I'm from Gaza. May I hold your hand?"

The man smiled. "Today we are all brothers." He gripped Safa's hand and held it aloft. "A new beginning," he shouted.

Safa's jacket felt tight and very heavy. The men who'd brought him to New York had made him drink odd-tasting water that made his head feel weird; the effect was identical to how he'd felt after Monsieur de Guise had administered his medication. The sounds of people around him seemed to ebb and flow in volume, like the noise of seawater advancing and retreating on a beach. His vision was blurred, and the movement of people seemed erratic, as if they were moving fast and then not moving at all. The horses ridden by the police officers looked as big as elephants, their tails slashing the air like whips. And de Guise had been right about the smell here; it was as rotten as decaying corpses in the Jabalia refugee camp.

He was surrounded by people his guardian had warned him about. Safa didn't understand what was wrong with their desire for peace, and they didn't look bad. But de Guise was always right, so Safa told himself to stop thinking and keep walking.

His free hand was inside his jacket pocket, clutching a cylindrical metal object the size of a tiny flashlight. At its end was a button. The men who'd fitted the jacket on him had told him not to press the button until he was several blocks down Fifth Avenue. When he did, he'd move faster than all the bad people. That was the truth, de Guise had told him, though what it meant was beyond Safa's confused and heavily drugged brain.

His legs were stiff; they'd been so cramped when he was traveling in a box to the States. He felt a sharp pain behind his eyes, and the noise in his ears now resembled that of a buzz saw. Under his jacket, his torso was covered in sweat, though he didn't know why because he wasn't particularly hot. Nobody took any notice of him. He guessed he looked normal; maybe people thought he was the Jewish man's son.

A small part of his mind assumed he was carrying a bomb and that when he pressed the button he'd die along with everyone close to him. But he couldn't process that thought, and the rest of his brain was telling him that nothing was real. It was like he was in two dreams at the same time, one of them bad, the other good.

His part of the procession drew close to a shop on the avenue. According to the monsieur's associates, this shop was his goal.

A few more paces and he'd be there.

He moved his thumb closer to the button in his pocket.

He tried to think clearly, but even his memories of the monsieur's French home were now distant and intangible. Though he could remember Monsieur de Guise's observation.

When you are standing in the crowd and press the pen, you will be imparting divine wisdom.

What was it that Safa had to say before he did that? Oh, yes: Death to Israel.

He was so close now and felt a pang of fear. He didn't know why he suddenly felt scared, but the emotion brought back the memory of his father dying on his bed in Gaza. Did his father feel fear at the end? Was that why this memory had come to him? He frowned, sweat from his forehead entering his eyes and causing them to screw up in discomfort. His father had passed to heaven with no drama, no complaints, and no evident pain. Despite everything that had happened to him, he'd left this world with dignity.

Safa was alongside the shop.

His father's dying words suddenly entered the boy's mind.

Evil lurks on both sides of the border, but it isn't and cannot be pervasive.

Safa had a moment of clarity, as if someone had thrown a bucket of ice-cold water over his face, or tossed him into a fire and told him to burn.

Panic overwhelmed him. He released the Jewish man's hand and shouted in the little English he had, "Bomb! I have a bomb!"

At first, no one heard him. There was too much noise from the crowds, too many people singing and chanting. Safa shouted again, and this time people near him took notice. Horrified, they relayed what they heard, turning to others and shouting the word, "bomb." People screamed, ran while telling others why they were doing so, parents grabbed their kids, some people dove for cover or just threw themselves to the ground by their feet, others ran over them. Police horses were unsteady on their feet as officers tried to guide them toward Safa through the people along the avenue.

Safa pulled out the metal object, attached to which was a cable. "I don't want to die!" He held the object up. "I don't want you to die!"

Cops on foot were walking slowly to the boy, their sidearms unholstered and pointing at Safa's head, the nearest to him yelling, "Drop it, now!"

Safa started crying uncontrollably. In Arabic he asked, "What is this? What has happened to me?" He remained the only person standing amid a mass of bodies that stretched for hundreds of yards along the avenue.

The approaching cops had looks of urgency on their faces, each step toward the boy taking them closer to the possibility of their own deaths. "Let it go!" said one of them.

Safa's body was shaking, and tears flooded down his smooth face.

A hand touched his shoulder. It belonged to the Jewish man he'd walked next to.

"Get away from him," barked a cop.

But the man stayed still, nodding at Safa, making no attempt to grab the device from his hand.

Safa knew with all of his heart that the man was wholly good. De Guise had lied. Everything had been a lie. Safa fell to his knees, let go of the device, and grabbed the Jewish man's lower legs, hugging them. He was a boy who wanted his mommy and daddy back. Why was he here? His cries of anguish were so loud they echoed off the buildings.

The police rushed to him, grabbed his arms, and put them behind his back, where they were cuffed. One of the cops radioed for bomb disposal units. Other officers grabbed people onto their feet and led them away from Safa.

The officers with Safa were in a state of near panic, yet managed to prioritize professionalism and bravery. One of them asked in English, "Will it detonate if we remove the jacket?"

Safa didn't understand his words.

Another officer tried to get the Jewish man away from the scene.

But instead the man crouched before the boy, and said, "I know a bit of Arabic. They're asking if the bomb will blow up if they take the jacket off you."

Safa started crying again. "He made my mind go strange."

"What is your name?"

The boy stuttered, "Safa, Safa."

The Orthodox man smiled. "A good name. It means innocent, does it not?"

Safa nodded.

"Did you put the jacket on?"

"No. Men . . . men put it on me."

Officers in bomb-disposal suits arrived on the scene. The regular cops withdrew, pulling the Jewish man with them.

But the man kept eye contact with Safa as he was walked quickly backward. "God saved you, little man. And that means He loves you. And in the end, you were strong enough to save us."

The experts analyzed and safely removed the jacket and placed the garment and its contents into a bomb-proof container. Police helicopters with marksmen hovered overhead as sirens wailed in all directions. As far as the eye could see, all civilians had been evacuated out of the area; only emergency services personnel and their vehicles remained on the scene.

"We need to get the boy down to the station," said one of the bomb-disposal officers.

Another disagreed. "He needs medical attention. Look at his eyes. He's been drugged."

For now, Safa's future was uncertain. But in time, it grew to be one of redemption and joy. His identity was withheld from the media, and the authorities rejected the option of putting him in a juvenile detention center in favor of giving him quality medical rehabilitation, a state education, and a visa to stay in the States. Safa never knew that a powerful admiral named Tobias Mason had ensured the Palestinian boy's new path. Nor did he know that Mason had handpicked the foster parents who cared for him until he graduated from college. Within a few years he became a professor at his alma mater.

One day, a Jewish man came to visit Safa after a classroom lecture. After much petitioning with the police to establish Safa's identity, the man's inquiries had come to the attention of Mason. The admiral made an exception to the rule of Safa's anonymity, and told the man Safa's whereabouts. When Safa saw him at the back of the lecture hall, he noted that the man's hair was grayer than when he'd held his hand on Fifth Avenue all those years ago. But his smile was just the same—good. They became friends, and remained friends thereafter.

Forty-Four

Monsieur de Guise was, as ever, elegantly dressed as he walked along the cobbled streets of Rennes, though today he was wearing a thick woolen overcoat, scarf, and wide-brimmed hat over his expensive clothes, for it was early winter and there was a bite in the air. With each step, he jabbed the tip of his maplewood cane against the road, a slight smile on his face, placing his fingers at the tip of his hat as he passed women walking in the opposite direction. Some of them smiled, probably thinking he was like an old-fashioned Victorian gentleman who was inspired by the civility, academic culture, and regal architecture of the city's old quarter.

He took his usual route toward the Thabor district, walking past restaurants and cafés that were making preparations for their evening service.

For weeks, Thales hadn't thought about his failure to successfully conduct the Israeli project. That was in the past; he had other projects planned. And in any case, Bäcklund had paid him up front and handsomely for his attempts to get Israel to go to war. She wouldn't be asking for a refund, given that she was in solitary confinement and had more pressing concerns. The fact that Safa had failed to detonate his bomb vest and remobilize Israel's military machine was no longer of consequence to him. If Israel was prepared to risk leaving its dangerous neighbors unchecked, that was its decision, not his. And Safa had simply been a pawn. Thales had no further need for him, nor would punishing the boy's failure in any way benefit Thales.

De Guise turned off a main thoroughfare into a cobbled side street containing more eighteenth-century half-timbered houses. He was pleased to be alone on the street, heading home to a warm fire where he'd listen to Chopin or Mozart while preparing his evening meal of filet de boeuf grillé, purée d'épinards, and poêlée de champignons. He wanted to cook a good meal because it would be his last in Rennes for some time. Tomorrow, he would advise his students that he was taking a sabbatical and departing for other shores for an undisclosed period. He hoped they'd miss the magic tricks he performed for them, though no doubt they wouldn't miss his subsequent explorations of obscure mathematical theorems. That was their loss, not his.

He turned into another narrow and empty side street.

He'd been here before with Safa, swinging his cane, educating the boy about the city's history and adding that in this very street a witch had once been dragged from her home and taken to the city outskirts where crowds watched her be consumed by fire. De Guise missed the time he'd had with Safa. No doubt, what he'd done to the boy was awful, but in other ways he believed he'd saved the boy from a less noble death in Gaza. And along the way he'd given him schooling, dignity, and health, in what were to be his final days. That was a good and unusual thing. Practitioners of death rarely get the chance to better their victims' lives before obliterating them.

It was time to move on. He put all thoughts of Safa out of his mind and smiled because Thales had outwitted everyone. He continued walking.

That's when the sniper round hit him in the gut. He gasped and staggered on the cobblestones, fruitlessly trying to use his cane to stay on his feet. After collapsing to the ground, he lay in the middle of the street, blood dripping out of one corner of his mouth, a look of utter surprise on his face.

At the end of the street, Michael Stein smiled as he collapsed his rifle and left the empty building. His work was done.

A big man walked fast out of an alley and stood over de Guise. He was wearing a suit and overcoat and pointing a pistol at de Guise's head, his expression cold and focused. "It took me a while, but I found you."

"Who . . . ?"

"I've lost dear friends because of you. Did you think your actions would go unpunished? That wasn't ever going to happen, *Thales*."

De Guise wheezed and said, "My name—"

"Is William de Guise, lately a mathematics professor in one of this city's universities. It took me a while to track you down and establish with certainty that you weren't who you claimed to be."

"William de Guise," he rasped, his life ebbing away. "Thales."

"Thales."

"I played those parts well, I believe. Even so, my employer was clear about the risks I was taking."

"It seems you didn't heed Mae Bäcklund's advice."

"Bäcklund?" De Guise laughed, then coughed blood out of his mouth and onto his chin. "Bäcklund."

"You should have been more prudent."

480 · MATTHEW DUNN

"I . . ." De Guise winced as he gripped his cane. " . . . was simply told what to do. To . . ."

"Murder."

"Maybe. Yes, I suppose I was involved in that. Who are you?"

"You should know who I am."

De Guise nodded. "Of course. You are Will Cochrane."

"Correct." The man shot de Guise in the head.

In the distance, a man watched the former MI6 officer walk fast away from the dead body and disappear into the labyrinth of streets. He lowered his binoculars and smiled. Poor Monsieur de Guise. He'd done what he'd been paid to do with verve and creativity. And he had carried off the observer's sleight of hand with poise, a sleight of hand that included pretending to be Thales.

The mastermind called Thales turned and walked away.

Acknowledgments

With thanks to Judith; my two brilliant mentors, David Highfill and Luigi Bonomi, and their second-to-none teams at William Morrow/ HarperCollins Publishers and LBA Literary Agency respectively; and Sam Reynolds of www.samreynolds. co.uk.